THE CURSE

A NOVEL

MICHAEL TODD BARRETT

Pleasant Word
A Division of WINEPRESS PUBLISHING

Pleasant Word (a division of WinePress Publishing, PO Box 428, Enumclaw, WA 98022) functions only as book publisher. As such, the ultimate design, content, editorial accuracy, and views expressed or implied in this work are those of the author.

ISBN 13: 978-1-4141-1206-0
ISBN 10: 1-4141-1206-8
Library of Congress Catalog Card Number: 2008901609

“She held out to me cool water
in the desert of my loneliness.
Birds sang;
flowers bloomed;
hope returned as she took my hand....”

Thank you, Sharon

PROLOGUE

May 1851

AN EVIL PRESENCE, filled with a lust for vengeance and death, lurked along the backwaters of the Louisiana bayou, hovering over the water, surveying its morbid handiwork. A flat-bottomed houseboat, tethered to an old, dead snag near the shore, listed to one side as it slowly took on water. Aboard the boat, two bloated corpses lay at opposite ends of the small cabin, each still clutching a single-shot dueling pistol, though neither pistol had been fired. Blood at the back of each man's skull had dripped from their matted hair onto the cabin floor to form small pools, long since dried. Both men had been shot from behind and then expertly disemboweled. The perpetrators were long gone. The presence, gleeful at its accomplishment, brooded, at the same time remorseful that nothing remained on which to wreak its hateful vengeance. It lingered only for a short time, savoring the victory, and then moved on, following the perpetrators in search of a new hunting ground.

A short distance away, invisible to mortals and unnoticed by the hateful evil as it passed by, a Centurion—a minor warrior in the service of the Most High—kept a watchful eye as he rested a gentle hand on his sword. His mission remained true and his resolve unshaken. His eyes narrowed with sure purpose as he watched the presence slither away. He didn't need to follow. His direction was clear.

CHAPTER ONE

NATHAN WALKER'S PRAIRIE schooner creaked as it rocked back and forth on its wooden joints along the dusty Applegate Trail. Dust rose from under the hooves of the two plow horses harnessed to the wagon. Nathan shifted his weight to relieve the ache in his lower back and buttocks. Twelve months on a hard, wooden seat had done what years behind a plow couldn't. Or maybe it was age.

Journey's end—Oregon Territory—was in sight on the crude map he clutched in his beefy hand even though he could not see it on the horizon. He swept the wide-brimmed leather hat from his balding head and wiped the sweat from his brow with his shirtsleeve.

In the wagon, fifteen-year-old Katie sat cross-legged with her back against a feather pillow reading the Bible she cradled in her lap. Her mother, Ruth, sat in front next to her husband. She stuck her head into the wagon.

"Katherine? Have you finished your lessons?"

Katie looked up into her mother's gray eyes. They seemed tired. Though not yet forty, her mother seemed old to Katie. Ruth's hair, once the color of honey, was mostly gray now. Her once flawless skin now showed the signs of hard work and age. Even so, beauty lingered. Most folks who had known Ruth when she was young thought Katherine favored her.

"No, Mama, but I'm nearly done."

"See that you read every one."

"I will, Mama."

"No slackin', Katie!" Nathan said cheerfully as he flicked the reins he held loosely in his big, rough hands to keep the team moving at a steady pace.

"I know, Papa." It was a lesson learned from as far back as she could remember. "You gotta read!" he would say. "You can't know the Lord's will if you can't read His Word!" Her earliest memories were of her mother and father sitting in front of the fire in the cool of the evening at their Missouri farmhouse. Ruth would sit in her rocking chair reading from the Scriptures. Nathan, in clean overalls after a hard day's work would listen, sometimes sitting on the hearth with his back to the fire, sometimes standing in the open doorway gazing out at the fields of corn, or at other times, sitting in his favorite chair with Katie in his lap.

"Read that part again, will you, Mother?" he sometimes would say as he leaned back in his chair.

Katie picked up her Bible and continued her lesson.

"For we wrestle not against flesh and blood, but against principalities, against powers, against the rulers of the darkness of this world, against spiritual wickedness in high places."

Katie sighed. They were pious words—high sounding—but what good were they out here in this wilderness? She had been fourteen when the wagons first rolled out of Independence. That was almost a year ago. She felt as though her whole life had been spent in desolate solitude, away from friends and all she knew that could give her a sense of belonging. Her wrestling, it seemed to her, was against the untamed wilderness her father had brought them to.

"They still with us, Katie?" Nathan called back.

Katie peered out of the back of the wagon where Ben Elam and his wife followed in their own wagon. Behind it on foot, Ben's three boys prodded twenty head of cattle, breeder stock for the new herds Ben and Nathan intended to build in the new land. Dust drifted from their hooves into the afternoon sky.

Sixteen wagons left Independence together in the summer of 1851, but bad weather stopped them for the winter before they could cross the Rockies. Four wagons turned back. The rest waited at Fort Bridger until spring before continuing on. One wagon lost an axle on an obscure mountain pass and had to be left behind. Of the remaining eleven, nine unhitched their teams for the last time two weeks ago to settle in the Applegate Valley of the Oregon Territory. But Nathan was determined to press on.

"Yes, Papa. They're still there."

She leaned back against the side of the wagon, her Bible in her lap. It had been an uneventful trip, at least compared to some of the stories she had heard. The wagon was heavy. Nathan insisted on bringing Ruth's most cherished possessions—her mother's cherry wood chest of drawers, the rocking chair Nathan bought after her parents' wedding, and her mother's good china, even though Ruth had objected strenuously. Nathan was not one to change his mind once it was made up. The extra weight took its toll on the team and Katie had to walk most of the way while Nathan and Ruth took turns, one walking while the other drove the wagon. Now, near their destination, provisions were low and that made the load a little lighter. Nathan had decided it wouldn't hurt for them all to ride for a few miles. Katie was grateful for the rest.

She crawled to the front of the wagon and peered out. "How much farther, Papa?"

Nathan shrugged. "We'll see what's up ahead a ways."

An hour later, Nathan slowed the team to a stop beneath a giant fir tree on a ridge overlooking a green valley cut in two by a lazy, green river. Sounds of churning water echoed through enchanted timber.

Katie watched as he dropped the reins and climbed down off the wagon seat. The trail followed the ridge. Nathan stood near the edge and looked down the steep embankment. The noon sun beat down on his face as he pulled off his hat and wiped his brow with his forearm. Out ahead, the mountains seemed to separate to reveal an open valley. Tall grass rustled in the breeze. The river cut across the middle of the valley, lazily snaking its way toward the Pacific Ocean, still a hundred miles away.

At the far end of the valley, a modest village of a half-dozen log buildings with freshly split cedar shake roofs hugged the river. Thin wisps of smoke wormed their way skyward from several of the chimneys of the small smokehouses behind the cabins. Here and there, herds of cattle and a few oxen and horses grazed along the hillsides around the outskirts of the settlement. Beyond, in the distance, another mountain reached up and kissed a resplendent blue sky. Katie and her mother joined Nathan, and they all stood in silent awe.

Ruth reached out to take her husband's cracked and calloused hand. "Oh, Nathan! It's beautiful!"

"It ain't Missouri," he said.

Katie could hardly contain herself. "Is this it, Papa? Is this the place?"

Nathan studied the panoramic view for another moment and then nodded. "Yep. This is it. Somewhere down there is home!" Ruth squeezed her husband's hand. Nathan sighed, "This is what I've been looking for."

Ben Elam, a short, thin man of forty-five with a slight limp—the result of a wagon accident many years before—hobbled up behind them. "Wheeew—ie!" Ben said. "That's somethin' awright!" He looked up at Nathan. "This it, Nathan?"

Nathan nodded. "Let's get those teams moving. I want to be home by sundown."

"Home?" Ben asked.

"Yep. Home. It's down there—somewhere. I'll know it when I see it."

"I ain't never met a man who knew more'n Nathan what he wanted," Ben said to no one in particular. Then he leaned forward and spit onto the dusty trail. "Beg your pardon, ma'am," he said to Ruth.

Ruth ignored him as she turned to walk back to the wagon.

Ben pulled a chaw of tobacco from his shirt pocket. "Wheeew-ie! Purdy place!" he said again as he bit off a hunk of the brown wad and stuffed it into his cheek. "Looks like your religion paid off after all!"

"God has guided us," Nathan said quietly.

Ben stuffed the plug of tobacco into his shirt pocket. "Whatever you say, Nathan," he said, and then hobbled back to his wagon.

Katie watched as her father stood for another moment, his eyes fixed on the green valley. He'd said it often enough ever since they crossed the Rockies. This wasn't the wide-open spaces and gentle rolling hillsides of

Missouri. And even though some found it difficult to make the transition from life on the plains to the mountainous regions of the Northwest, Papa said he had been looking for this place all his life.

Nathan turned slowly and walked back to the wagon. Katherine and Ruth were waiting for him on the wagon seat. He climbed up next to them, took the reins in his big hands, and flicked them over the horses' backs. The wagon lurched forward as they began the descent down the slope of the mountain into the valley.

Katie climbed into the back and grabbed her mother's hairbrush. She studied her face in her mother's small mirror and gently brushed her hair back. It would have to do. She'd seen cabins in the valley, which meant people, and she had no intention of letting them see her with a year's worth of trail dust clinging to her. She took the towel that hung from a nail, now nearly a rag from a year's worth of use, and moistened it with water from a canteen. Rolling up her sleeves, she scrubbed her face and arms as best she could.

Ruth peered into the back of the wagon from her perch on the wagon seat next to her husband. It hadn't been easy dragging her family from the relative comfort of an established home and the comforts afforded by the stability of a long-standing community relationship. But when Jed Morrison had come into town that day, just back from the Oregon Territory with tales of the wide-open west with its gold strikes and the promise of land, Nathan listened. Ruth saw in his eyes that his heart tugged at him to go, and when he began to talk of making the trip out west, Ruth resigned herself to it. When he came home one spring day and said he had sold his share of the farm to his brothers, she offered none of the traditional female arguments.

Now, though, watching her daughter beat the dust of two thousand miles from her clothes, she felt those arguments surfacing. Katie, with her vivid blue eyes and her honey-colored hair could have had her pick of suitors back home. But out here…

Katie looked up at her mother and smiled. Ruth smiled back as she reached into the wagon and took her hand. "Excited?"

"Do you think there will be—people?" Katie asked.

"You saw the cabins."

"I know, but…you know what I mean."

Ruth squeezed Katie's hand. "Don't worry," she said softly. "God will provide."

Katie sat back, leaning against the side of the wagon with her diary on her lap, chewing absentmindedly on the end of the pencil for a moment before she began to write:

> Dear Diary,
>
> We saw cabins today. Papa is heading for them. Our long journey may be coming to an end. I only wish I knew for certain. It has been a strenuous trip, and I had begun to fear that I should never see another human face besides those of my family again...

By late afternoon the three wagons entered the valley, following the trail along the river. By evening they reached the first cabin of the little settlement. It was a small log building that stood a few yards from a primitive barn about a hundred yards from where the river met a large stream flowing out of the mountains.

Standing on the rustic porch of the cabin was a large, bare-armed man in dirty overalls, a flintlock at his side, and a week's worth of whiskers bristling over his round face. He nodded as the wagons passed and then stepped carefully from the porch to the ground, ducking low to avoid bumping his head on the log that served as a beam to support crude log rafters.

"Evenin'," Nathan offered.

"Evenin'," the man said. "Name's Silas. Silas McCoy. You folks come in on one o' the wagon trains?"

Nathan nodded. "Sixteen wagons when we started. We came up the Applegate. Left the others a few days back."

"Most folks stay on the main trail," said Silas.

"Hmm," Nathan grunted, and then motioned toward the well-worn wagon ruts in the road. "Looks like you been getting your share of company."

"Yep. Been a lot of folks through here in the last few months. I'm beginnin' to wonder if I ever shoulda left Kentucky. It's gettin' so's a man cain't find no place to hisself no more."

"Well," Nathan said, looking around, "it looks like there's still plenty of room."

"Yeah, maybe. But for how long?"

Nathan motioned toward the road. "What's up ahead?"

"This here trail runs clean through to Portland, if you've a mind to go that far. Most folks been settlin' along the river—some purdy good towns sproutin' up 'bout thirty, forty miles or so."

"What about there?" Nathan said, motioning toward the mountains from which the creek flowed.

"I ain't been more'n a mile upstream myself. There's some good, flat bottomland near the creek, but there's Injuns too. Folks say there's a whole tribe that lives up in them mountains."

"Do they give you any trouble?" Ruth asked.

"Nope," the man shook his head. "Least ways, not so far. I seen a couple o' bucks walkin' along that ridge a couple o' weeks ago. But they never come down, an' I didn't go up to meet 'em. Seems like a right good arrangement if you ask me."

"What do you think, Mama?" Nathan asked without looking away from the mountains.

Ruth sighed. "What about the Indians?"

Nathan studied on it for a minute. "Well, the man says they're no trouble. Maybe—"

"But no one is bothering them here. If we invade their land, it might be a different story."

Nathan thought for a moment. "The Indians around here are supposed to be peaceful enough. If we run into any trouble, we can always turn around and try somewhere else."

"But...what about Katie?"

"We'll all be fine," Nathan reassured her. "I've gotta look."

Ruth slipped her hand around Nathan's arm and locked fingers with him. "All right, Nathan," she said softly.

"It'll be fine," he whispered gently. "Trust in the Lord."

"I trust you," she said, but it had never been more difficult than at that moment.

The first morning's light found Nathan climbing up on the wagon seat next to his wife. He took the reins in his big hands. "Well, Mother," he said to Ruth, "you with me?"

Sleep had eluded Ruth for most of the night, but by morning she had found peace—the demons of doubt and fear held at bay by the assurances of her faith in God. She slipped her hand under her husband's arm. "I've trusted you since the day I married you. I'm not about to stop now."

"How about you, Katie?" he called into the back. "Everything secure?"

"Yes, Papa."

Ben Elam's three boys were kicking a can across the dusty trail in front of Silas's cabin. Ben stood with his wife on the front porch.

"I suppose your mind is made up," Nathan said to Ben.

"I reckon it's a good place for a general store," said Ben. "Seems like it'll grow. Me an' the missus reckon we'll grow with it. Don't worry about the stock. I'll have the boys look after 'em 'til you git settled."

Nathan flicked the reins and the wagon lurched forward.

Katie stuck her head out of the back of the wagon and watched with a sense of loss as the cabins disappeared behind them. It had been so long since they had seen anyone but the people of the wagon train. And when they had come to any small settlement along the way, Papa and the other men had been cautious, giving them a wide berth, or if provisions were low, camping a few miles away and sending in someone to buy food. Papa had explained about the danger of the untamed west and the need for caution, but it was difficult for her to understand why there was a need for such wariness, and she felt as though she were a prisoner of the wagon's solitude.

When they happened upon the little settlement and the cabins the night before, she had allowed herself to hope her father would settle close by. But now she felt her heart sink as the cabins disappeared around the bend in the road.

Nathan followed the creek for most of the day, slow going since the dim pathway, worn down by deer and elk or the occasional Indian who hunted the valley, was the only trail. When the sun buried itself behind the mountain, they stopped for the night.

The next morning at first light they were on the move again. At mid-morning they came to a wide spot in the trail where a long-ago fire had cleared out the pine and fir trees, leaving an open meadow of several pristine acres. Tall grass waved in the gentle breeze. The creek meandered through the little valley, and then made a sharp S-bend to the west. Nathan pulled back on the reins and the wagon slowed to a halt.

"It's a good place," Ruth said after a moment.

Nathan nodded, but said nothing.

Ruth reached around and rubbed the back of her husband's neck. "You know this would make a good place for a home."

Nathan studied the meadow. "Maybe." He sat in silence for a moment longer and then said, "We'll see," as he slapped the reins again. "Git up!"

They followed the creek for another two hours until the valley floor narrowed to a draw just wide enough to allow the wagon to pass between the creek and the mountainside. Nathan pulled back on the reins and the wagon stopped.

"Nathan," Ruth said as she surveyed the slim passage. "Don't you think we should go back? We've passed several good places. And that one by the bend in the creek this morning was already half cleared—perfect for farming."

Nathan nodded. "Maybe," he said, but then flicked the reins and the wagon lurched forward. They continued on, but the going was slow under the great canopy of trees. Running water babbled a few yards away, but dense thimbleberries and ferns hid the creek from view. The trail, once clearly defined and easy to follow, was now dim and narrow. The wagon rocked back and forth as the team struggled to find easy passage. Finally, the wagon rolled to a stop in front of a fallen log that blocked the trail. Nathan leaned back and dropped the reins in his lap.

"What are we going to do, Papa?" Katie ventured after a moment.

"We can't turn around. There isn't room," Ruth said, trying not to accuse.

"We'll have to move the log," Nathan said.

He took a deep breath and climbed down. "Help me with the team," he said to Ruth. "Katie, get a rope from the back of the wagon."

Ruth waited until Katie was out of earshot. "Nathan," she said, "can't we look for a place to turn around as soon as this is done?" She couldn't conceal the frustration in her voice.

Nathan shook his head. "Just one more hill, Mama. Just one more hill. If I don't find it by then, I promise we'll turn around and go back to your meadow."

Ruth sighed. "All right."

Nathan lashed the log with a rope and slipped the loop of the other end around the neck of the horse he'd freed from the harness, and then he slapped the horse on the rump with the loose end of the rope. The horse arched his neck as it dug its heels into the soft earth and strained against the rope. The log resisted for a moment, then slid away from the trail, leaving a path just wide enough for the wagon. Soon Nathan had the team harnessed again.

Ruth came up behind him as he stood catching his breath and put her hand on his big shoulder. "I wish I knew what it is you are looking for," she said softly.

"I wish I knew," he responded, looking out ahead at the undiscovered trail. "I'm not sure myself. I just know I've gotta keep looking. But I promise, just one more hill!"

In a few moments they were on the move again.

An hour later, the wagon rolled to a stop. Thimbleberries and dense undergrowth made further passage—without considerable effort to clear it away—impossible. To the right, a wide spot offered just enough room to turn the team around.

Nathan's big shoulders drooped. "All right, Mama. You win," he said.

Ruth took her husband's hand. "Why don't we stop and eat first?"

Nathan nodded.

Katie climbed down out of the back of the wagon and ran around to the front. "Is it all right if I go for a walk?"

Nathan looked around. "I guess it'd be all right. But don't go any farther than you can see the wagon, understand?"

"Yes, Papa, I'll be careful!"

Katie bounded off ahead. Ruth and Nathan watched as she bent down to inspect a wild flower, chased a squirrel up a tree, and danced happily along the trail.

"Come on," said Ruth, walking to the side of the wagon, "let's get something to eat."

Nathan followed her, but he was sullen. She handed him a chunk of hardtack out of the burlap bag that hung from the side of the wagon, a strip of venison jerky, and a tin cup full of water from the water barrel. "Disappointed?" she asked.

Nathan shrugged as he walked over to the edge of the trail and sat down on a cushion of pine needles. Ruth followed. She stood at his back with her hands on his broad shoulders and began to work the muscles between his shoulder blades with her thumbs.

"We've seen some pretty remarkable country," she said, trying to reassure him. "We'll not find any better."

Nathan nodded. "I know. It isn't that." He paused as he gazed out among the trees. "Ever since we left home, I've had this itch—to see what's on the other side of the next hill."

"Only since we left home?" she chided.

Nathan smiled weakly.

"I don't think you're alone," Ruth said thoughtfully. "Lots of folks are moving west."

Nathan chuckled. "I suppose so." He shoved the jerky into his mouth and tore off a piece. "I guess lots o' folks get the fever."

"Lust is a treacherous partner. It never gives what it promises."

"I know. But it isn't lust. Leastways, I don't think it is. I don't have to own the land. I just have to see it."

Ruth sat down next to her husband, slipped her hand through his arm, and held him close. "Lust is in the air, Nathan. Everybody's looking for gold or land or a way to take it away from those who already have it. But it's not for us. It isn't what He's called us to."

"Yeah," he said, "I know."

"Papa! Papa!" Katie cried from beyond where the trail disappeared. "Come quickly!"

Nathan shot to his feet, grabbed his flintlock as he dashed past the wagon, and ran in the direction he had last seen his daughter. Ruth followed him, holding her long skirt in a bunch above her feet.

"Over here, Papa! Come quick!"

Nathan raced along the trail, checking the breach of his rifle as he ran. His eyes searched the wilderness ahead, taking care to notice any movement on either side and dodging the trees that were now so dense that the trail zigzagged back and forth along the ridge. Katie's voice came from directly ahead over a small rise.

Nathan crested the rise and stopped. Katie stood only a few feet away with her back to him, but when she heard his footsteps, she turned. Nathan could hardly believe his eyes. Spread out before him, surrounded on either side by the majestic, timbered mountains, was a great meadow of tall, green grass lazily waving in the gentle summer breeze. Katie stood on the edge of the shimmering waters of a deep blue pond where cattails and patches of berry bushes randomly encroached along the shore. Beyond it, a small grove of oak trees spread over the far end of the pond like a giant canopy. A herd of five or six deer were just picking themselves up and scampering away into the cover of the great trees.

"Isn't it wonderful, Papa?" Katie beamed.

Ruth joined her husband. "Oh! It's...beautiful!" she said.

Nathan nodded, looking down into his wife's face. "It's home," he said. "I'm home!

CHAPTER TWO

KATIE STUDIED HER face in the mirror that no longer adorned the inside of the wagon, but now hung on the coarse log wall of the two-room cabin. Twenty-two months had passed since the Walkers had first discovered their little valley. Two winters were behind them and the spring rain of the last three weeks promised a rich harvest in the fall. The original meadow, roughly twenty acres of tillable land, had grown through the sweat and blood of Nathan's own two hands to nearly eighty acres.

Nathan had established an easy peace with the Indians, and occasionally some of the men from the small band that lived about twenty miles to the east brought game to trade for flour and salt. They were peaceful enough, though there had been some trouble. But Nathan figured it had more to do with the Grave Creek Massacre than it did with any real threat from the local tribes. Many whites, fearful of the Indians, wanted them removed to a reservation. Some of the more unscrupulous adventurers among the settlers exploited the fears of their neighbors by staging a massacre and claiming that the Indians had started it. Nine Indians, mostly young men, were ambushed and murdered at Grave Creek, causing a stir among the settlers who feared the Indians would retaliate. But Nathan would have none of it, and freely traded with the few meager bands that populated the surrounding region.

A small, two-room cabin a few yards from the pond had replaced the original lean-to shack Nathan had built to shield them through their first winter. Nathan planned to add to it during the coming summer. A dozen chickens clucked and scratched in the yard between the house and the pond, as well as a young, strutting tom turkey for which Nathan had bartered with Ben Elam on the last trip into town in exchange for a cord of firewood. The old lean-to shack now served as a makeshift barn until better arrangements could be made.

The fall price of beef had been good this year. Nathan had sold twenty head at the auction a few months back for top dollar. Luxuries were scarce, but he'd hired old Skeet Morris part time to do chores around the barn. For a man his age, and hobbling around the way he did, Skeet got a lot done by the end of a day. It was the only reason Nathan tolerated his cantankerousness.

"You about ready?" Ruth called out from the front porch.

"Yes, Mama!" Katie said as she primped her hair one last time.

"Let's go!" Nathan called out from the wagon seat. "I don't want to be late!"

Katie hurried out the door and hopped up onto the back of the wagon.

"We'll be back after church!" Nathan hollered across the yard to Skeet, who was busy tending a broken gate hinge. Skeet raised his hand over his head and waved without looking up.

Nathan slapped the reins and the wagon, its canvas cover removed, turned and headed out of the yard toward the well-worn trail. Katie leaned against the side of the wagon with her diary in hand and began to write:

> Dear Diary,
>
> It has been a month since we have made the trip into town. It is more than I can bear, and I think I shall die of loneliness....

The morning sun sat low on the eastern horizon and was beginning to peek through the trees along the ridge. "I talked to Ben the other day," Nathan said as the wagon rumbled along the road. "He said another family moved in on the other side of the river."

"Did he say where they were from?" Ruth asked.

Nathan shrugged. "Back east was all he knew."

Word of new families always piqued Katie's interest. "Do they have any...anyone my age?"

"Ben didn't say," Nathan said. "But he did say they'd be in church today. He said he met the father and he was a godly man."

"We could use a few more of them around here if we ever expect to tame this wilderness," said Ruth. "Although it's beyond me what Ben Elam would know about godliness."

"Now, Mother," Nathan said sternly, "Ben's a good man—and a good friend. And I expect God will deal with him in His own time."

"That may be. But I've heard the language he uses when he thinks no one is listening. Why, just last month Mrs. Wallace was in the store—she went in to see if Ben could get a spool of burgundy thread for that dress she's making for Reverend Walters' wife—and Ben had his head under one of the shelves along the back of the counter. He raised up when her boys ran after a coon that had come in through the back door. Well, when he hit his head, the things that came out of his mouth! Of course, when he saw Mrs. Wallace standing right there behind him, his face turned three shades of red. He apologized and said how he was having a bad day and that he didn't reckon anybody was in the store and how he didn't usually go in for such words."

"Now, Mother," Nathan said, "just because a man swears once in a while doesn't make him the devil's henchman."

"Well, maybe not. I just think—"

"We'll just pray for him and let the Lord tap him on the shoulder in His own good time."

The wagon rolled steadily along the road to town. The road had been cleared of logs and brush over the last two seasons and that made the trip to town easier and faster. It hardly took two hours these days. The creek babbled softly a few yards to the south. "Walker Creek," folks in town called it.

Settlers were moving in by the dozens. There were the Henrys (two miles downstream) and the Eerdmans (new arrivals who were just now clearing a place for their cabin). Katie watched each new arrival, hoping desperately to meet people her own age.

The wagon rolled along through the trees until it came to the clearing where the creek made a sharp S-bend. As they left the cover of the great trees, Nathan could see chimney smoke coming from just around a gentle curve in the road.

"Looks like we got new neighbors in your meadow, Mama," Nathan said, gesturing toward the smoke.

Near the S-bend in the creek was a crude, newly built lean-to log shack. It had solid walls of log construction on three sides and was open in the front. It was nestled in against the mountainside a few yards from the road. Deer hides covered the opening and hung to the ground. A young man in his twenties, muscular and tall with dark, curly hair, leaned against the wall. He was wearing a dirty shirt and holding an axe. As the wagon approached, another young man about the same age and build appeared around the far side of the shack. He was a little taller, with dark hair that was not as curly as his companion's. His face was covered with a three- or four-day growth. Held loosely in his hand at his side was a worn and rusted flintlock rifle.

Nathan pulled back on the reins when he was abreast of the shack. "Morning," he said. The man in the doorway nodded as someone inside the shack called out, but Nathan couldn't hear what was said. The young man turned and stuck his head inside the shack. "Looks like neighbors, Ma," he said with a leering eye toward Katie.

Katie immediately disliked him, though she felt a little guilty judging someone so quickly. He was handsome in a rugged sort of way, but something about him repulsed her. Her high-button dress revealed nothing, but Katie could not resist the sudden urge to cover her breasts with her arms. Looking away, she raised her arms instinctively and crossed them over her chest.

"Name's Nathan Walker," Nathan offered. "And this here's my wife and daughter."

Ruth nodded a polite hello. The man nodded back, his eyes still on Katie, but said nothing.

"You folks moving in?" Nathan continued.

"Looks that way, does it not?" the young man sneered in an accent that betrayed his French ancestry.

Creole, Nathan thought.

Nathan met his eyes. They were dark and threatening. "We live upstream a ways. Looks like we'll be neighbors." Nathan paused for a response, but there was only an awkward silence. "Well, if you folks need anything, you let us know."

He was about to move on when one of the deer hide flaps fluttered back and an older man stepped out into the clearing. He was wiry, stoop-shouldered, bald, and missing most of his front teeth. Behind him, a large, frumpy, dark-haired woman wearing a dirty apron stood in the opening. Nathan could make out someone standing just behind her, partially hidden in the shadows.

"Is this the way to treat company, Veré?" the man scolded in an accent thicker than the young man's. He turned to Nathan and offered a toothless grin. "The name is Andre Doucet. We arrived only a couple of weeks ago. We work to get everything ready for colder weather," he said as he motioned around him with his hand. "You must forgive my boy. He is, how you say, full of himself."

"Where you folks from?" Nathan asked.

Andre gave Veré a sly glance out of the corner of his eye, and then said to Nathan, "We have come out from the east."

There was something amiss here, and Nathan knew it, though he couldn't be sure how he knew. But there was something—something about the look in the man's eyes, hard and calculating, that didn't match the too-wide smile. Maybe it was the way his eyes seemed to always look away when he answered. Maybe it was the easy way he gave his answers without actually revealing anything of substance.

Ruth spoke up. "Did you have a pleasant trip?"

"It was...uneventful," said the old man through a devious smile.

"Where abouts back east?" Nathan asked.

"So many questions," Veré grunted as he went back into the shack.

"We're on our way to town—church meeting," Ruth said quickly. "You folks are welcome to join us."

The other young man at the far end of the shack spoke up. "We tend our own religion."

"My other son, Yves," said the old man as he gestured with a wave of his arm. "And it is true. We...we have our own religion."

"Well, welcome anyhow," Nathan offered, and then motioned toward the deerskin flaps at the front of the shack. "You folks are going to get mighty cold come winter if you don't do something more permanent. If you need help, our place is about two miles up the road. Just holler!"

"We thank you kindly, neighbor," the older man said as he nodded.

Nathan slapped the reins. "Git up!"

Katie sat down again in the rear of the wagon and watched the two men go inside the lean-to shack. *A strange family*, she thought. *And unfriendly.*

As the wagon rolled along the road away from the shack, Katie saw one of the deerskins on the lean-to flung aside. A girl of eighteen or nineteen stepped into the light of the clearing. She was tall and dark, with the blackest hair Katie had ever seen. It hung to the middle of her back, thick and untamed—wild as its owner standing barefoot in the grass. Her golden skin flowed out of a thin blouse and skirt that revealed her flawless form. Almond eyes, vivid and cat-like, yet hard and calculating—piercing, as if they could discover innermost thoughts if they so chose—gazed down the road following the wagon. Katie could feel them searching her out.

Their eyes met. Katie stared for a moment, and then she looked away as those eyes—those dark eyes—seemed to probe into her very soul. It was a warm, spring day and the morning sun was high over the eastern ridge, but Katie rubbed her hands on her shoulders and hugged herself against a sudden, dank chill from within as the wagon rolled slowly away from the clearing.

Andre Doucet was a poor man. Besides his two sons, his wife, and his daughter, Kyra, he had only a few chickens, a pair of sheep he hoped to build into a full-fledged flock, and a broken-down old milk cow that had wandered into camp the first week of their arrival. But something else shared the dusty lean-to shack by the S-bend in Walker Creek—a presence, evil and brooding, filled with a hateful lust for vengeance…and death. It slogged from the far side of the shack, unseen but casting a pall as it slinked along, watching as the buckboard disappeared around the bend. Hate and vengeance were its evil purpose, but an un-breachable barrier protected the three occupants of the wagon. A golden sword flashed next to the wagon, as if to warn away any attempt to harm.

Patience. Time was on its side. Walls had been broken before. If not now, another time…perhaps.

A small crowd of ten or twelve mulled around the churchyard, talking and laughing, as Nathan's wagon rolled to a stop at the hitching post. Ben Elam was there in the yard talking to Jack Wallace. The preacher was there too in his black robe and wide-brimmed hat, holding his Bible and talking to Mrs. Elam and a woman Katie had never seen. A half-dozen children were playing on the grass at the side of the church building—a log structure big enough to hold fifty people at one time. The church had a crude, bell-less steeple at the front and hand-split cedar shingles that still had the look of fresh wood. The reverend's wife, a young, handsome woman with neat, brown hair greeted folks as they entered the church.

Nathan climbed down from the wagon and walked over to join Ben and Jack. Katie followed her mother to where the preacher was standing with his back to them.

He turned. "Oh, good morning, Mrs. Walker!"

"Morning, Reverend Walters," Ruth responded as she nodded an acknowledgment to the well-groomed woman standing with him. She was tall and confident-looking.

"It's been some time since we've seen you and yours!"

"Yes, it has," said Ruth. "Nathan's been working on clearing another five acres, so we've done our worship at home for the last three weeks. But I don't mind telling you, it's good to be here!"

"And this only my second month in the pulpit. Why, I was beginning to think you didn't like my sermons!" he chuckled and then turned to the woman standing next to him. "I don't believe you've met, have you?"

"No, I don't believe so," Ruth said at the same time the reverend said, "Mrs. Walker. This is Mrs. Jakes."

"How do you do?" both women said at the same time.

"And you know Mrs. Elam?"

"Yes, of course. We were on the wagon train together. How are you, dear?"

"I'm very fine, thank you."

"And how is Ben this morning?"

Mrs. Elam nodded toward the circle of men at the far side of the churchyard. "He's worse than a treed bobcat when it comes to church. I finally got him to come, but he's none too happy about it."

They all laughed.

Ruth turned to face Mrs. Jakes, who appeared to be in her mid-forties. She wore her hair in a tight, perfect bun. She was lean and fit, her long, slender fingers and narrow hands calloused from hard work.

"The Jakes have just moved here all the way from Pittsburgh," the reverend continued. "They came in with one of the wagon trains along the Applegate, same as you folks, if I'm not mistaken. They're clearing a place up river a couple of miles."

"Welcome to our valley," Ruth said. "I'm sure you'll love it here as much as we do."

"So good you could make it this Sunday!" the reverend said, turning back to Ruth and Katie with obvious delight.

"It's good to be here," said Ruth. "It gets a little lonely out there after a few weeks. And poor Katie with no one her own age. It's—"

"Ah! Where is my head! I almost forgot! There is someone your age," he said to Katie. "Mrs. Jakes, where is the rest of your family?"

"I'm not sure. They were here a few minutes ago. Perhaps they've already gone inside."

The reverend motioned to a small boy playing with the others a few feet away. The boy stopped running and walked sheepishly toward the reverend as though he expected a stern scolding for some unknown offense. "You know the Jakes?" the reverend asked.

The boy nodded, looking at Mrs. Jakes.

"Good. Now you go inside and tell Mr. Jakes to bring his family and come outside for a moment. I want him to meet some folks. Do it quick, boy, and there'll be an extra piece of peppermint for you after the sermon!"

The boy's eyes widened as he dashed off and disappeared into the open doorway. He returned a few moments later, leaped off the steps to the ground below, and ran past the reverend and the three women. "They're comin'!" he said as he ran past.

Katie felt her pulse quicken. The adjustment from the civilized life in Missouri she had known to the wild and solitary life of a pioneer had been difficult, and she was lonely for companionship. There were neighbors, and most had children, but none were her age. She longed to have someone with whom she could share her secrets and desires—the desires of a young woman.

She had felt the first seeds of adolescent yearnings budding within her even before she had left Missouri. She remembered the day of another church social, so long ago it seemed, when Tommy Atkins had sat next to her under the oak tree and had tried to kiss her. She protested loudly, and poor Tommy was embarrassed beyond repair, spending the rest of the day enduring the other boys' taunting. Then only a week later she had found herself on the trail to Independence to meet with the rest of the wagon train.

Katie remembered those days fondly, though with some sadness. She felt as though she had spent her whole life on the trail, where the luxury of innocent flirtations and convivial gatherings were replaced with the struggle just to survive. While other young ladies back home were attending socials, she was skinning game from the day's hunt for an evening meal. While those other young ladies were vying for the affections of some handsome farmhand or city dandy, she was nursing the blisters on her feet, her only reward for walking twenty miles a day. While other young ladies were confiding with one another concerning secrets of love and tribulation, she had only the impervious ears of the horses that pulled the wagon.

When they finally had reached their destination she had hoped to find something of her former life in the form of new friends and community. But the struggles of the trail were replaced by the struggles of building a new farm in a new place on virgin land. As the months, and then years, passed, she began to feel as though she were doomed to a life of loneliness here in the mountains of the Northwest. At seventeen she felt old, as if the world were passing her by.

Reverend Walters grinned mischievously. "I think Katie will enjoy meeting young Mr. Jakes," he was saying. "In fact, I was hoping she'd be able to make him feel welcome here in Creek Junction."

"Oh, I'm sure she will," said Ruth. "I'm sure she'd like any excuse to get out of chores."

"Wouldn't we all!" said the reverend with a chuckle. "Wouldn't we all! Ah, here's our newest family!"

Katie turned to see a man of fifty step onto the portico of the little church. He was lean and tall—a perfect match for his wife. He was wearing a wide-brimmed beaver skin hat that sat comfortably on his head. Wisps of gray salted his temples and a neatly trimmed beard hugged his face. At his side were two small boys, about nine and ten, who looked very uncomfortable in Sunday clothes. They hurried to keep up with his great strides.

Quinlan Jakes stepped confidently off the portico to the ground and joined his wife.

"Dear," she said, "I'd like you to meet Mrs. Walker and her daughter, Katie. And I believe you have already met Mrs. Elam. Her husband is the one who operates the trading post."

"Yes, we've met," he said with a warm smile. "It's a pleasure to meet you, Mrs. Walker. And you, young lady," he said to Katie.

"And these are your children?" Ruth asked, motioning to the two young boys who were obviously not Katie's age.

"Two of them," said Mrs. Jakes. "This is Jefferson and Jeremy. Boys, say hello to Mrs. Walker and her daughter."

"Pleased to meet you, ma'am," the two boys said in unison and then scampered off.

Mrs. Jakes turned to her husband. "Quin, where is John?"

"I don't know. He was with me a moment ago," Quin said, looking around. "He must be around here someplace. Ah! Here he is," he said, motioning across the churchyard. "John! Come over here!"

Katie followed Mr. Jakes' eyes to the place across the yard. A young man walked briskly toward them. He was tall like his father with sandy-brown hair and a dimpled chin. He stood erect, proud, and confident, a trait no doubt inherited from his father as well. The muscles in his arms and shoulders tested the fabric of his freshly pressed shirt. As he came closer, Katie could see his eyes. They were the most vivid green she had ever seen. And kind, Katie could tell. He smiled broadly.

Katie blushed and looked away for a moment. Then she regained her courage. Her eyes met John's.

"This is our son, John," said Mrs. Jakes when he had joined them. "John, this is Mrs. Walker and her daughter, Katie."

"Pleased to meet you," he said to both, but he only saw Katie.

CHAPTER THREE

ON A SUMMER Sunday afternoon, Kyra Doucet stuck her feet into the crystal clear water babbling softly along Walker Creek. She sat alone on the bank a short distance from her family's lean-to shack and sang to herself as she slowly kicked her feet back and forth in the water.

Mindlessly fingering the gold medallion dangling from a gold chain around her neck, she picked it up and held it reverently to study its intricate design. The beauty of its hand-worked gold entranced her. The delicately webbed pattern had been expertly crafted from a single piece of gold the size of a silver dollar. Tiny five-point stars formed a circle around the head of a goat. The meaning of the ancient inscription that circled the outside edge had been lost for centuries.

Kyra held it up and let the sunlight stream through the webbing, illuminating the goat's head and the ring of stars. Deep in the tiny crevasses, undetectable to the human eye, traces of the blood of its previous owner lingered.

Legend had it that it had belonged to the old woman of the swamp—that old crone never seen but believed to live out among the backwaters of the Louisiana bayou in some secret hideaway where she could work her incantations undisturbed. How it came to be in the possession of her mother, Kyra didn't know.

Andre Doucet called out from the shack, "Kyra! Quit your day dreamin' and come help your mother!"

"In a minute," she said, not really caring if he heard her or not.

He stood in the opening, holding the deerskin flap in his hand for a moment, and then threw his hands in the air, muttered something, and went back inside.

Kyra lay back on the grass near the water's edge with her hands behind her head. The sun was high in the sky and the air was warm. In the distance she could hear the sound of an axe as it bit into one of the giant fir trees along the edge of the clearing. Her brothers, Veré and Yves, usually quite willing to avoid hard work, had discovered the prankish joy of watching the giant trees fall to the ground. She could hear them laughing.

The water ran deeper here at the S-bend than in the rest of the creek, slowing to little more than a drift a few yards beyond where Kyra laid on the bank. She turned on her side and watched the road. *He should be along any minute.*

Her dark eyes—intense and resolute—searched the road toward town. She was bent on her lustful purpose. In a moment, a wisp of dust drifted across the road down by the timberline. A horse and rider were coming. She knew it would be him. She slipped into the water, swam a few feet, and slipped out again, the thin fabric of her blouse clinging to her shapely form, revealing the soft, gentle curves of her torso.

The horse and rider slowed as they approached. John Jakes pulled back on the reins and stopped as Kyra walked to the edge of the road.

"Morning, Miss Kyra," he said.

"It is a nice day for a ride," she said, her dark eyes flashing.

"Yep," John said, trying to keep his eyes from wandering too far a field. There was an awkward silence. "Been swimming?" John asked, feeling stupid as soon as he said it.

"How can you tell?" she said with a wicked laugh.

John could feel his face flush.

"Are you on your way upstream?" she asked. Her eyes smiled as she cocked her head to one side.

"Yep," John said, feeling more foolish by the minute. "I reckon I'd better be going."

"What is your hurry? Come sit with me," she said as she moved closer and held the reins of his mount.

"Sorry. I haven't got time. Maybe some other time."

"Maybe," she replied. Her dark eyes beckoned.

John kicked his horse as Kyra stood to one side, reluctantly letting him pass.

From the cover of the timbered hillside, a presence watched as horse and rider trotted away. But for the moment, it was concerned only with the girl. The medallion glistened in the sunlight against her bronzed breast. Slinking along the ground, covering a great distance in only seconds, it rose and hovered over her.

Kyra clutched the medallion in her fist as she watched John Jakes ride away. The metal was warm to the touch, beyond the warmth of her body or even the sunlight on a warm day, and it felt suddenly warmer. She held it up in front of her. It glistened brightly. The circle of stars twinkled and seemed almost to move around the head of the goat, whose eyes glowed bright green. The presence settled down to the earth. Kyra sat back down on the grass beside the creek, thinking of John.

High in the mountains above Creek Junction near the source of Walker Creek, a battle raged. It was a small, insignificant skirmish by anyone's standards except for those who found themselves locked in its deadly grip—and on the losing side. A hunting party of twenty men from the tribe of the Molalla Indians to the Southeast happened upon six men of the more peaceful and ever-dwindling band of the Umpquas, and attacked them with a fierceness worthy of their reputation.

Three of the six lay dead and two were dying, mortally wounded. The lone survivor, youthful Monteneha, on his first hunting excursion as a man, ran swiftly through the woods. The broken shaft of an arrow protruded from the flesh of his lower leg. Blood ran freely from a wicked wound.

He had fought valiantly, inexperienced as he was, but his comrades, taken by surprise, fell in only a matter of seconds, leaving him to fight alone. So Monteneha ran, limping and bleeding. Soon the loss of blood would drain him of his strength. But for now, the heat of battle and the fear of death gave him the grit to continue.

Two of his arrows had found their mark. One of the twenty braves was dead; he was sure of it. Another was wounded in the thigh—not a mortal wound, but it surely would slow him enough that Monteneha would not have to deal with him. The others were all in pursuit.

As he ran, Monteneha could see out of the corner of his eye a swift runner closing in from the west. He could hear the others approaching behind him. His mind searched frantically for a way of escape as his feet pounded the earth. He ran through a thicket as branches stung his face. As he neared the high bank along the edge of a stream flowing peacefully twenty feet below him, his wounded leg gave out. He tumbled headlong down the embankment into the water. The embankment was sheer on both sides, making it impossible to climb out the way he had come. Below, an uprooted fir tree had fallen during the last big rain, pulling up its entire root system and leaving a hollowed-out cavity beneath it. A young deer that had paused for a drink a few yards away raised his head in a moment of indecision and then bounded away along the middle of the stream, disturbing the muddy bottom.

He had one chance. Monteneha's heart pounded in his chest. There was no time to think. He quickly crawled into the hollow spot beneath the roots of the great tree and burrowed in as far as he could, just as the braves leaped down into the streambed. Monteneha watched and waited with his knife at the ready for one last stand. But all eyes were on the muddy trail in the water left by the young buck. Monteneha watched as they followed the stream away from his hiding place. In a few moments they were out of sight. He would have to act fast. Soon they would discover that the prey they sought was not the one who had left the trail of mud in the water. If he was going to escape, it would have to be now.

John hurried along the trail, a stoneware pot lashed awkwardly to the back of his saddle. It was becoming a habit. The Walkers were a reliable source of milk and eggs for a half-dozen of the new settlers including the Jakes, who were busy trying to get a cabin up before winter. Lately, since that day last May in the churchyard to be exact, John had become an eager volunteer to make the weekly ride to retrieve a gallon of milk. The last four Saturday mornings, just before noon, found him on the road out to the Walker ranch.

Nathan Walker looked up from his labor on the new foundation for a third room to the cabin. He struggled to move one of four large jasper boulders. The clip-clopping of horse hooves came from down the road just out of sight. Nathan knew who it was.

"Morning, Mr. Walker!" John called out as he rode up to the house.

"Morning, John. What brings you out here?" Nathan said, as he did every Saturday.

John was never sure if he was joking, but there was always a twinkle in his eyes.

"I came for milk and eggs."

Nathan nodded, turning away to hide a smile. "So long as that's all you're after," he said.

John grinned sheepishly. "Is—ah—is Katie around?"

"In the house," he said, motioning toward the front door.

John dropped the reins of his horse, quickly untied the pottery jug from the back of his saddle, and stepped up onto the wooden porch of the cabin. The door was ajar and Ruth was inside, busily attacking the dirty floor with a broom. "Good morning, John," she said as she set the broom in the corner.

"Morning, Mrs. Walker."

"Here are your eggs," she said, handing him a small wooden slat box Nathan had split from a log. A dozen eggs fit neatly inside.

"Yes, ma'am," he said, taking the box under his arm. "Mother needs milk this morning too," he said, holding up the pottery jug.

"That'll be fine. You know where the barn is."

"Yes, ma'am. I reckon I'd better get at it."

"Help yourself," she said. "You know, it seems like your daddy would get a cow of his own—what with three growing boys at home."

"Yes, ma'am. He's going down river next month. They've got good milk cows down on the Kirby spread. He's been real busy with the cabin, but it's almost ready for winter so he says it's time to think about stock. He's going down to pick up a few head of beef cows, and Mother made him promise to bring home a milk cow. So I reckon we'll only be needing milk for a few more weeks."

"Well, that's fine. I guess you won't be needing to make that long trip out here anymore, will you?"

"Yes ma'am—well, I don't mind too much," John said as he fidgeted with the box of eggs. "I mean—well, I may still find time to come out once in a while, if that's all right with you?"

"Oh, I suppose we could always do with company." She smiled. "You'd best be getting to your milking. Milk's in the cow—cow's in the barn," she said, motioning toward the back door.

John opened his mouth to ask for a pail, but Ruth beat him to it. "In the corner by the back door."

John set the eggs on the table and started toward the back door, but then stopped as if to ask another question.

"She's out back, churning up a batch of butter."

John grinned as he headed for the back door with the pail dangling from one hand and the pottery jug tucked up under his other arm.

"Morning, Katie," he said when he was outside.

Katie looked up from her churn. "Oh! I didn't know it was this late! I must look a mess!" she said, brushing a wisp of hair from her face.

"You look fine to me," John said as he set the pail and jug on the ground.

Katie blushed as she went back to her churning, working the churn handle up and down. "Here," John said, taking the handle in his own hands, "let me do that for you."

Katie stood back. "It's almost done."

John grimaced as he gave a tug on the long pole. "Yep. Feels that way."

The two of them stood in silence until John finished. The only sound was the rasping of Nathan's handsaw, coming from the other side of the cabin, and the muted sloshing of the churn.

"There! I think that's about it," John said, taking the lid from the churn.

Katie began scooping out the butter with a wooden paddle and placing it in a large clay tureen.

"You and your folks coming to church tomorrow?" John asked.

"Yes, I think so. Papa's hurrying to finish the floor to the new room. But I think we'll be there. Papa doesn't like to miss worship."

John smiled. "Good."

Katie returned his smile. John was a handsome man, tall and rugged, but with a gentle spirit. His family loved God and took their worship to heart, and John was no exception. He was a man of quiet resolve with a good sense of who he was. Katie liked that in a man.

John took the tureen from her hands and the two walked side by side into the cabin.

"Just set it on the table," Ruth said as she cleared a place for him. "I'll need to salt it before I put it up."

"Yes, ma'am." John placed the tureen on the table and stood back as if waiting for something else to be said. "Well," he said after a moment, "I guess I'd better be getting to that old milk cow."

"I guess so," said Ruth, eyeing the two of them. "Katie, why don't you give him a hand?"

"Yes, Mama," said Katie as she and John headed for the back door.

"And children—"

John and Katie paused at the back door. Katie gave her mother a disapproving look.

"Keep the barn door open."

Katie blushed. "Yes, Mama."

Out in the yard and out of earshot of the open back door of the cabin, Katie fumed. "We're not children! I'm seventeen! And you're nearly twenty! I don't see why she—"

John took her hand and smiled. "It's all right."

Katie's temper eased. Her embarrassment at her mother's little indignity gave way to the embarrassment of knowing she had overreacted. She blushed.

Inside the barn, the milk cow stood at the manger, chomping impassively on a mouth full of hay. Four or five barn cats darted eagerly around John's feet, running between the legs of the cow and dodging her half-hearted attempts to swat them with a hind hoof. John set the jug on the shelf over the manger, took the one-legged stool that hung on a nail, and sat down with his forehead against the cow's warm flank. He reached under the cow, grabbed two teats and began kneading them with his big hands, squirting milk into the bucket.

"Did you come by the Doucets' on the way here?" Katie asked.

John thought for a moment. There was no other way to get to the Walker's from town. "Uh-huh."

Katie nodded. "Papa's building the new room for a bedroom. He says I need a room of my own, now that I'm a grown-up woman."

"Uh huh."

"How were they?"

"Who?"

"The Doucets. You must have seen them when you rode through."

"Oh, yeah. Well, I didn't see all of them. Just Kyra."

Katie felt the blood in her cheeks rising. "Oh," she said, trying not to sound obvious. "And how is she?"

"She was taking a swim, last I saw." John was eager to change the subject. "When do you think your father will have the room done?"

"Three or four weeks. He says it's got to be done before the harvest, or he won't have time to finish it." There was a long silence as John continued to milk the cow. "Do you think she's pretty?"

"Who?" John said, stalling for time.

"John Jakes! You know very well who!"

"Kyra? Oh, yeah, I reckon so."

Katie leaned against the side of the barn. "She's a bit strange, don't you think?"

"Oh, I don't know, maybe a bit." There was another pause.

"Mama says they're the unfriendliest folks she ever did see."

"Well, maybe they just need a friendly hand."

Katie's jaw tightened.

When the bucket was full to the brim, John stood. He set the bucket out of hoof-shot of the cow and hung the stool back on its nail, and then took the jug from the shelf, removed the cork, and carried it over to the bucket of milk. "Help me with this, will you?" he asked.

Katie pushed away from the wall and lifted the bucket over the jug in John's hands. She tipped it carefully toward the open spout as milk began to flow into the jug.

"That's good," he said. "Should we take the rest into the house?"

Katie shook her head. "We've still got milk from this morning. I'll give it to the cats." She poured the remaining milk into a crockery bowl sitting just outside the stall where the livestock could not reach it, and then started toward the door. The bowl disappeared in a swarm of cats.

"Katie?" John looked suddenly serious as he replaced the cork and set the jug on the shelf next to the bucket. She turned to face him, her face flushed as her eyes met his. "I'd be pleased if you'd sit with me tomorrow in church—if it's all right with your papa."

Katie could feel the color in her cheeks again. "I'd be pleased to sit with you. And I'm sure Papa won't mind."

"Oh, Quin, look at his leg!" Beth Jakes said. John and his father knelt next to her, hovering over the wounded Indian lying on the ground in front of their cabin.

"I found him just off the road about a mile from here," John said. "He was in the grass, hiding—trying to hide anyway. If I hadn't seen the grass move, I never would have seen him. I think he's out of his head."

"Dirty heathen's bleeding all over the place!" Quin grumbled.

"He's a man," Beth scolded. "Same as any white in town without the Savior."

"He's an animal! As wild as any in this wilderness!" Quinlan rubbed his chin and sighed. She was right, of course, and he knew it. "It doesn't look good. Look at the wound. And the swelling. There's poison in there that'll spread like a timber fire in August." He shook his head. "That leg'll have to come off."

"Oh, Quinlan, no! He's an Indian. He'll die!"

"He'll die if it doesn't."

Beth shook her head. "He won't survive as an Indian."

Quin nodded. "Maybe not. But it's the best chance he's got!"

"Couldn't we find a way to get him back to his own people?"

Quin was shaking his head even before she finished. "I don't know what good it'd do. Besides, his people migrate. They follow the river with the seasons looking for food. That leg needs tending. He'd never survive."

"We don't know that!"

"Maybe. But—"

"What'll we do?" she said softly, turning back to the man lying on the ground.

"We'd better get him inside. John, you go to town and get Ben. He's fairly good with this sort of thing, and if anyone can help, it would be him."

John stood to leave. "And John," Quin said, putting his hand on his son's shoulder, "don't tell him it's an Indian."

CHAPTER FOUR

NATHAN WALKER WATCHED from a distance as his daughter tossed bits of stale bread to the wild geese that swam along the edge of the pond near the cabin, gently coaxing them with soft words. The corners of his mouth curled upward as she slipped on the muddy ground and nearly fell in.

Fatherly concern would not let him hold back. "Be careful!"

"I will!" she said. Then she slipped again.

Nathan chuckled to himself as he picked up the axe and went back to work, splitting the last few cedar shingles for the roof of the new room. With a little providential favor, he hoped to be finished by nightfall—as long as the axe handle held out.

"Nathan!" Ruth called out from the front porch.

"'Round here, woman!" he called back.

In another moment, Ruth appeared at the corner of the cabin. "Which shirt do you want me to press?"

"Shirt?"

"Yes, for tomorrow."

Nathan, puzzled for a moment, started to answer, and then slapped his leg with his big hand. "The social! It clean slipped my mind!"

"We can't disappoint your daughter. She's been looking forward to this for a month. And besides—"

"I know, Mama, I know!" he said as he tossed the axe on the pile of shingle bolts that were stacked along the wall of the new room. The handle, already worn and cracked, struck the corner of the cedar log. The handle broke in two just above the head of the axe.

Nathan swore.

"Nathan!"

"Sorry, Mama, it slipped," he said, still looking at the broken handle. "Looks like I'll be making a run into town," he sighed.

Ruth slipped her arm around her husband's waist as they walked side by side toward the front door of the cabin. She spied Katie walking wistfully along the shore of the pond.

Ruth paused to watch her. "She's a young woman now," she sighed.

"Hm," Nathan almost grumbled.

"Where has the time gone?"

Nathan shrugged. "She'll probably go and get herself married one of these days."

"I think it may be sooner than we think," said Ruth.

Nathan agreed. "That young John Jakes has been hanging around like a horse fly on a hot day."

Ruth smiled. "Not everyone here thinks he's a pest."

Ruth took her husband's hand as they watched their daughter feed the geese. "Well, he's a good man," Nathan said a moment later. "There's no denying that. And he's a hard worker when he's not over here with that lost-pup look in his eye. I suppose she could do a lot worse for herself." He pulled Ruth close to his side and began gently stroking the back of her hair.

Ruth drew a deep breath and let it out slowly. Her eyes sparkled. "I've seen the look in her eyes when he comes around, or even when his name is mentioned. Look at her now." Ruth smiled. "Look at the way she glows. Yes, she's in love. And that young Mr. Jakes's interest in eggs and milk is somewhat suspect too."

Nathan grinned. "He does seem to use a goodly amount of both. Well," he said as he looked back at the room he'd been working on all summer, "I hope she has a chance to use this new room."

"Come on," Ruth said as she pulled Nathan toward the door. "Coffee's on."

Katie sat down in the tall grass at the edge of the pond. Three or four geese, heartened by the promise of food and the lack of threatening gestures, braved their way to the shore and began to creep toward their newfound friend, ever mindful of the natural order of things, and never letting familiarity or an empty stomach remove the last vestiges of fear. Katie held out a chunk of bread in her hand. "Come on," she said softly in a singsong voice.

One of the geese, a young gander, managed the courage to waddle a little closer while the others held back near the water. He inched close and craned his neck toward the piece of bread until he could snap it from Katie's hand and then waddle indignantly away, wagging his tail in triumph. The others scurried after him, hoping to steal his treasure, but they soon returned. Katie, bored with the game, tossed the remainder of the bread near the water's edge. Wings beat the water, sending a spray as the geese fought for the right of possession.

Katie lay back on the soft ground with her hands behind her head. It was a wonderful day. The sky was blue and a gentle breeze made the air feel cool and refreshing. A golden eagle screeched overhead as it made a lazy circle high above the treetops, searching for its next meal. Katie's eyes sparkled as they drank in the beauty that surrounded her.

There was a special reason for her cheerful mood, more than the simple beauty of the Oregon mountainside. The last two years had been hard for her. She had given up everything—and by no design or wish of her own. She was not consulted or questioned as to her feelings on the matter. Oh, sure, they asked if she wanted to go out west, but the decision had already been made. It was thrust upon her. And being an obedient daughter, she was forced to tear her roots from the only soil they had known and move nearly a whole continent away to a hard and heathen land.

Her life seemed so simple before. It was laid out for her, patterned after three generations of Walkers before her, and she never had questioned it. She would marry—well, she hoped—have children and live and die in the same Missouri town where her grandparents had settled, lived, and died. She never considered herself brave or adventurous, and never in her wildest dreams would she have considered the life of a pioneer. She knew her father had wanderlust, but she had lived her whole life listening to his tales of youthful exploration along the Mississippi and his dreams of one day moving west. It never occurred to her he really could mean it.

She had entered the new adventure with resignation. When they had found their new home, and she had seen how utterly alone she would be in this vast wilderness, her resignation had turned to apathy. But then a wondrous thing had happened. Out here, miles from any human contact, a beacon of hope had shown through on a Sunday morning. She had prayed—prayed hard—but she had doubted too. And if the truth were known, she had given up any hope that her prayers would be answered. But there he stood, tall and handsome, with his hand extended to shake hers. It was calloused and strong and his touch sent a chill down her spine as old hopes and dreams began to surface again. These last two months had rekindled a fire Katie knew she never should have let die. In her young life she had been taught to trust in God, but the faith she claimed was not her own; it was her parents' faith. She only clung to it as a baby would cling to its mother's bosom. As she grew toward womanhood, she began to seek her own faith. But then, on the verge of full blossom, she had given up. Too quickly, she now realized. On the peaceful banks of the pond, Katie bowed her head in silent prayer.

Dear heavenly Father, I thank thee for thy loving kindness. And thy grace, which thou hast shown me. Dear Lord, please forgive me for my want of faith! I know I have been selfish, and I want now only to serve you. I acknowledge my unworthiness, but my prayer is that you would find me your willing servant.

"Hey!" came a voice as Katie felt a hand on her shoulder.

She whirled around. "Oh!" she said. "John Jakes! You startled me!"

"I'm sorry," John said, pleased with himself. "I thought you heard me coming."

Katie looked down at the ground. Her face glowed red. "I was thinking."

John was leading his father's horse by the reins. He let them drop and the horse began to graze by the pond. John plopped himself down next to Katie and leaned back on his elbow.

"You must have been thinking pretty hard."

Katie blushed. "I was."

John picked up a small stone and threw it into the middle of the pond. "Pretty day," he said.

"Mm-hmm." There was an awkward silence for a moment as they sat watching the geese. "How's the Indian you rescued?" Katie finally asked.

"He's much better this week. Father thought he'd lose his leg for sure, but Ben tended to him and managed to save it. Ha! Ben was madder 'n a hornet when he found out we got him all the way out to the ranch for an Indian! But he calmed down some when Mother offered him some of her peach pie. Anyhow, he fixed up that leg real good. We thought the Indian would die of fever for sure the first week or so. But he's a tough one—he put up a fight. Ben says he'll limp some, but he'll live. Father says we'll make him a ranch hand—give him odd jobs around the barn and such."

"Well, at least he'll have a home," she said. "Does your papa think he can be tamed?"

"Yeah, he'll tame," John said. "He's already learned a few words. And he's grateful we saved his life."

"Is it hard? I mean, having him there—aren't you worried?"

John laughed. "To tell you the truth, he doesn't seem all that different than anyone else—once you get to know him."

"I'd be afraid to have an Indian around the house."

"No need. We're gettin' to be good friends, him and me."

There was another long silence as the two of them sat watching the geese before John spoke again. "So, what were you thinking?"

"Thinking?"

"When I first came up."

"That's none of your concern, Mr. Jakes," she said playfully, hoping he wouldn't see the flush in her cheeks.

"Then it doesn't?"

"Doesn't what?"

"Concern me."

"My thoughts are a private matter. That makes them of no concern to anyone else."

"You weren't thinking of me, then?"

Katie turned away. "And what if I was? Don't be impertinent!"

John reached out and gently turned her face toward him. "Is it impertinent to want to know your thoughts—to know if I have a place in your heart?"

Katie studied his eyes. John caressed her cheek with the back of his hand. "You have mine, you know," he said.

"And you have more than a place in mine," she said. "You have my whole heart."

John leaned close and kissed her.

"Y' know, I've been thinking a lot lately too," John said as he lay back on the grass.

"And what have you been thinking?" she whispered, putting her finger to his lips.

"Oh, about you and me, and, well, there's something I'd like to ask you."

Kyra Doucet caressed the medallion with her long, slender fingers, entranced by its beauty, as she sat cross-legged on the dirt floor of her family's lean-to shack. Across the room, her mother, father, and two brothers sat at a crude table near the fire pit that vented through an open hole in the roof. They were engaged in a lively discussion but she heard none of it. The eyes of the goat's head glowed bright green—and seemed to call to her.

"It is done!" said Maud Doucet, a frumpy woman with sad, hollow eyes, and jet-black hair with two odd streaks of gray at either temple.

Her high cheekbones hinted at former beauty, but years of hard work had robbed her of all but the memory.

Yves toyed with the knife that was always at his side or in his hand. "We should not have left!"

"Fool! There was no other way!" his mother scolded.

"No one knew," said Yves. "No one would ever know."

Andre Doucet pulled the pipe from his mouth. "They knew. And they would have come." He lowered his voice to a near whisper and leaned forward. "They may still come."

"How could they know? They—"

"You think no one would recognize your handiwork?" the old man said. "You and your brother have made a reputation for yourself. A distinction that gave us a disadvantage among…certain people."

"We are not afraid," said Veré. "They deserved to die! I would cut the throat of any man who did what they did—any man who stood in my way!"

"Cutting their throats would have made things much easier, I think," said Andre.

"It does not matter now," said Maud. "We are here, and here we will stay. What is done is done. We will make this our home. And we will forget the past."

"That will be difficult," Andre muttered, "since Kyra wears the medallion."

Monteneha pushed himself up off the cot, leaned back on his elbow, and rubbed his sore leg with his free hand. The bandage was much smaller now, barely covering the nearly healed wound, but his leg ached in the morning. The whites had been kind and he was grateful. He knew of many in his village who had died slow and pain-filled deaths from wounds less severe than his own, and he knew the medicine of the whites was strong.

He rolled over to the side of the cot next to the rustic log wall of the cabin. Pulling a small wedge of flint from his belt, he scratched another notch in the log just low enough on the wall to be out of sight. A row of forty-eight marks told him the leaves would soon fall and his people would be moving down river.

He put the flint back in the pouch on the inside of his belt and swung his feet over the edge of the bed, cradling his wounded leg in his hands for support.

The cabin door swung open, exposing the bright sunshine of a new day. Beth Jakes entered holding two headless chickens by their feet in one hand and an axe in the other. "Well! Good morning! How are we feeling today?"

Monteneha nodded. The language was strange, but he was beginning to grasp certain words and phrases. "Good. I—feel good," he said as he tried to stand.

Beth set down the chickens on the table. "Here, let me help you," she said as she took his arm and helped him to his feet. "How's that?"

Monteneha nodded again. "Good." He made a walking motion with his fingers. "I walk."

"All right," Beth said, "but don't overdo it. Just stay around the yard." She made a circle with her hand. "Don't go any farther than the barn. Barn! Understand?"

Monteneha nodded. "I stay." He wasn't sure if she was telling him not to go any farther than the barn, or to go to the barn, but it didn't matter. He was still weak, and walking any great distance was the last thing he wanted to try at the moment. But he was tired of the cabin and the sunshine would feel good on his face. The idea of a walk to the barn and back appealed to him. After that, he could worry about what it was the white man's woman was trying to tell him.

He limped slowly onto the front porch, favoring his leg but able to put most of his weight on it—something he could not do only yesterday. The apparent progress pleased him. He took his time descending the steps and then hobbled slowly across the yard. Young John Jakes, just returning from his visit with Katie, rode up. He stopped to watch for a moment, and then waved when Monteneha noticed him. Monteneha waved back. John headed for the house, where he met his mother near the front porch as the Indian hobbled across the yard.

"Looks like he's doing fine," he said as he leaned against the hitching post.

"It's a miracle of God," said his mother. "Nothing short."

John nodded. "Ben's pretty good with that sort of thing. Better than a doctor, some folks say."

"Credit Ben Elam for his cleverness, but don't discount the power of the Great Physician. It was his doing. By all rights," she said, motioning toward the Indian, "he should be dead."

John patted his mother's hand. "I know, Mother."

Beth reached down and put her other hand on his. "Live your life by it, Son."

The two of them watched as the Indian made a circuit of the yard between the barn and the cabin, pausing occasionally to study the hills around the clearing, and then hobbled over to the steps and sat down.

"Tired, my friend?" John asked.

"Tired," Monteneha responded. "But—good. I leave soon."

John's face darkened. "Not too soon, Monty," he said as he rested his hand on the Indian's shoulder. They had decided to call him "Monty." It was easier to pronounce than his Indian name, and the Indians considered it a very great honor to have a "white" name.

"I should say not," said Beth. "You're doing so well with your English. And we could use a hand around here."

Monty thought for a moment. "I have good friends here," he said. "Maybe stay and help John. Maybe."

"In the meantime, how about some fried chicken?" asked Beth.

"Fried chicken," John repeated, raising his eyebrows for emphasis.

"I like chicken. Mother Beth fix good food."

John laughed. "Father says that's why he married her!"

Beth motioned toward the horse. "You'd better put him up and brush him down."

"Can't. I've gotta make a trip into town first."

"But what about supper?"

"I'll be back. It'll only take a couple of hours. There's something I've gotta do."

"Now what is so important that you have to go to town now?"

John swung up into the saddle. "Just an errand. I'll be back soon. And when I get back, I may have some news!"

Ben Elam stood at the entrance to his trading post. Although it was little more than a log shack, it had something many of the homes in the area did not have: a real wooden plank floor, hand-hewn from the trees that once grew on the very spot. There were dried goods on the shelves along the four walls. Sacks of grain and beans down the middle formed an aisle ending in a counter of split logs that had been hand-planed smooth. A plume of smoke wafted from the smokehouse behind the store and drifted up into a sky of brilliant blue. The faint smell of smoked venison was in the air. Beyond the smokehouse, close to where the river slowed to a crawl, the black iron of a steam engine rested quietly in the middle of a clearing a few yards from the water's edge, awaiting the last few touches to make the new sawmill operational.

Ben watched as a cloud of dust rose from the trail a half-mile down the road. It was warm this afternoon. The air was still. Jack Wallace was in town and his two boys were chasing a squirrel through the churchyard across the road to the south about a stone's throw away. Ben watched them for a moment and then turned his attention back to the dust cloud that came closer. He soon recognized Nathan Walker's unmistakable silhouette against the early morning horizon as he bounced up on the wagon seat.

"Morning, Nathan!" he said as the wagon pulled to a stop.

"Morning, Ben. Have you got that new sawmill up and running yet?"

"Almost! Crew's been working sunup 'til dark. They're waiting on the blade. It's supposed to be coming in on the next mule train. Driver down on the Humboldt said he'd drop it off. What brings you to town?"

"Aw, that old axe handle finally gave out. You got a new one?"

"Yep," Ben said as the two men entered the store. "Wouldn't be much of a storekeeper if I didn't!" Ben reached into the barrel by the doorway that held several wooden handles, as well as two or three shovels and a scythe, and pulled out one of the axe handles. "Here. This one looks good," he said, eyeing it closely. "The grain runs true all the way through."

He handed it to Nathan who held it up and sighted along the length of it, squinting with one eye. "Yep, looks good to me. How much?"

"Dollar and a half," Ben said as he reached into his pocket for the tobacco pouch.

Nathan whistled.

Ben sidled around the counter. "Come all the way from Illinois. Solid oak! Come in on the last wagon train," he said apologetically.

"Well, I gotta have it." Nathan dug into his pocket, pulled out a small coin and set it on the counter. "Can I owe you the rest?"

"That'd be fine, Nathan." Ben picked up the coin and put it in his own pocket. "Nothing I can do about prices. If it's shipped in, it's gonna cost more."

"I know, Ben. It's just that money's hard to come by."

"Well, you know I'm always willing to trade. Goods or gold—don't matter to me."

"Not much gold up where I am," Nathan mused. "Of course, I don't spend much time looking for it."

Ben chuckled. "None here neither," he said, motioning toward the floor. "And I looked! It's a fool's venture if you ask me. Had a couple o' miners come through here last week. Said they left California dead broke—just the way they got there three years before. I tell ya, they looked a sight—beat-up old skins for clothes and a couple o' broken down old mules that'd turn a buzzard to repent o' meat." Ben shook his head. "Said they were going to try it up on the Snake River. I guess some folks never learn."

Nathan chuckled. "Well, I've got my hands full as it is—just trying to feed my family."

"How's that new room coming?" Ben asked as he stuffed a wad of tobacco into his cheek.

"It's almost done. I've got a few more shingles to put on the roof and it'll be ready. I was gonna have it ready tonight, but the ol' handle gave out just about half-a-day too soon. Now it'll have to wait until after this here social tomorrow."

"I'll bet Katie is beside herself," said Ben. "Young girl like that needs a place to herself."

Nathan shrugged. "She's got other things on her mind lately."

Ben grinned. "Would it be that young Mr. Jakes?"

"It would," said Nathan.

"Has he asked her yet?"

"Not that I know of. And I ain't been asked for her hand yet."

"Well, I expect he will. He's a proper young man, and besides, I doubt if his folks would let him skirt around propriety."

Nathan chuckled. "No, I reckon not!" Nathan leaned against the counter and crossed his legs. "So, you and the Missus going to the social tomorrow?"

"Seems that way," said Ben, shaking his head. "I reckon that ol' preacher is bound and determined to get me in church one way or another!"

"I reckon it won't kill you."

"Maybe not. But I aim to see that it don't! Don't get me wrong. Religion is fine for some folks. It just ain't for me."

Nathan shrugged. "Whatever you say, Ben. Whatever you say."

John Jakes bobbed up and down on the bare back of the horse as it trotted down the well-worn trail toward town. He knew Nathan would be in town today. Katie had told him her father needed a new axe handle and John was determined that today should be the day. He knew what he wanted—and Katie had said yes. Now came the tough part: Nathan Walker! But John was confident. He had all his lines well rehearsed. He would say to him, "Nathan," no, no, umm, "Mr. Walker, I love your daughter very much and she loves me. And with your permission, sir, I'd like to marry her." Yes, that was what he would say. It was perfect, short, to the point, confident, and respectful—all the things that were important in this sort of thing.

John tugged on the reins at the fork in the road and the horse, accustomed to the harness of a plow or wagon, responded slowly to the unfamiliar commands. John preferred his father's spirited stallion to the old plow horse, but his father needed his own mount for a ride to scout for strays.

John could see the trading post up ahead, and his heart began to beat a little faster. The Wallace boys stopped their play for a moment and waved as John rode by. John liked children, and he always had time to stop and talk, throw a ball, or admire a freshly caught snake. But not today. John nodded but kept going.

The boys stood in the street, watching the back of John's head as it bobbed up and down.

"What's with him?" Thad Wallace wondered aloud.

His brother shrugged, and then they went back to their play.

John slid off the horse and threw the reins over the hitching post in front of the trading post. His heart was beating fast and his palms were clammy. He rubbed them on his pant leg as he stepped up onto the boardwalk. Nathan Walker stood inside next to the counter. John took a deep breath and walked in.

"Mornin', Mr. Elam."

"Mornin', John."

"Mornin', Mr. Walker," John said, clearing his throat.

Nathan smiled wryly at Ben and then nodded at John. "Mornin', John."

John stood in the doorway for a moment, unsure of what to do with his hands. He looked at Ben, then at Nathan, then back at Ben.

"You need something, John?" Ben asked.

"Well," he said, "Mother needs a sack of cornmeal."

"Your father picked it up yesterday when he was in town," said Ben. "Don't tell me you young'uns done-in that whole sack already!"

John blushed. "No, I reckon I forgot." John looked around the store—not really at anything in particular—and scratched the back of his head as he tried to think. Nathan leaned back on the counter again and crossed his legs. There was a twinkle in his eyes.

"Well, I guess I'd best be going," John began as he turned toward the door.

"You got something on your mind, John?" Nathan asked.

"Well—uh—yes, sir—now that you mention it. Could—uh—could I have a word with you, sir?"

Nathan savored the moment. "Sure, John. What's on your mind?"

Ben turned away, rubbing his day-old beard with his hand and hiding an impish grin.

John hesitated and then motioned toward the door. "Could I have a word with you in private, sir?"

Nathan and Ben exchanged a knowing glance as Nathan pushed away from the counter. "Sure, son," he said as he followed John toward the door.

Kyra Doucet sat in the back of the rickety wagon with her bare feet dangling over the rear as it bounced along the dusty road into town. Her mother and father sat up front, talking quietly to themselves and whispering occasionally. Kyra fingered the medallion as her mind wandered. John Jakes was on her mind—he was always on her mind lately.

"Mother?" she said wistfully as she held the medallion up to the sun. "Where did you get this?"

Maud Doucet looked at her husband, as if waiting for him to answer for her. "Why do you ask, child?"

"Did you get it from the old woman?"

"What does it matter?" Maud said.

Kyra sensed emotion in her mother's voice, but it only made her more determined. "Does it have power?"

"It is a beautiful trinket. Nothing more!"

"You do not believe it has power?"

"No," Maud said as she turned away.

Kyra leaned back against the side of the wagon, her slender arm draped over the edge, studying the medallion's intricate design. She remembered the day her mother gave it to her. It was buried deep in the small wooden chest in the corner of the wagon, the very corner where she now sat. But the wagon was not on the smooth road along Walker Creek. It was in the middle of the prairie, three months out of New Orleans. She had seen it before. "I would very much like to have it," she had said as she fastened the chain around her neck. She remembered her mother's frightened face as she turned and walked away.

"Where did you get it?"

"Enough, child! It is a silly old wives' tale. That old witch had no power except fear! Now, do not bother about it any more!"

Kyra's eyes narrowed like those of a cat ready to spring on its prey. "It may have belonged to the old witch once. But that is not where you got it."

The color drained from Maud's face. She sat, stone-faced.

Reverend Walters knelt down in the flowerbed by the front steps of the new church. It was a warm day—too warm for hard work, but his usual routine of morning Bible study and preparation for a Sunday sermon had been interrupted by the tapping of a woodpecker on the fir tree just outside his study. It was not a bothersome sound, and the reverend found himself rather enjoying the symphony of God's creation. It soon became apparent that study on a beautiful day like this one would be impossible.

Sweat dripped from his brow and ran down his cheeks as he dug in the earth to plant each new pansy, provided by Mrs. Wallace from her garden.

"Mornin', Reverend."

Reverend Walters looked up from his gardening into the hardened face of Nathan Walker. "Oh, good morning, Nathan! I didn't hear you ride up."

Nathan dismounted, dropping the reins near a patch of green grass, and then sat down on the front steps of the church. "Ol' Joe is a light stepper. Makes him a good hunting horse."

"I reckon it would," the reverend said with a chuckle. "What brings you to town, Nathan?"

"Had to pick up an axe handle."

"You getting that place of yours cleared?"

"Yep. 'Bout eighty acres so far. And I hope to have another ten cleared by fall. I made a deal with one of the new buyers down river for the logs. They sent up a scout to see if they can make a go of hauling them out."

"Is Ben in on this?"

"Yep. If they can get them to the mill, wagons will haul the finished product down river."

"That's a sizable distance. Are they going to be able to do it?"

Nathan shrugged. "I don't know. It's still a long way to drag them. They're too big for wagons, and the creek ain't big enough to float them. But some of them boys are mighty tricky. And they need the logs. I suppose if they need them bad enough, they'll find a way."

Both men chuckled.

"Will you and your family be in town for the church social tomorrow?" the reverend asked.

"We'll be here, I expect. We've been looking forward to it all summer. Anyhow, I reckon the women will insist on it after I give them the news."

"Oh? And what news is that?"

"I just ran into young Mr. Jakes, who was anxious to ask for my daughter's hand," Nathan said.

"Well, Nathan!" Reverend Walters said as he jumped to his feet and began pumping Nathan's hand. "That's wonderful! And I should say it's not a great surprise! Congratulations! Oh, and I suppose I should ask, did you give your consent?"

Nathan nodded. "Quinlan Jakes raised his boys right. John's a good man, and I think he'll make a good husband for my little girl. And besides, I doubt if I could stop them even if I wanted to. But, yes, Mother and I approve."

"That's wonderful. So when's the happy day?"

"That's female territory," Nathan said, holding up his hands. "I reckon they'll be wanting to talk to you about it. And I'm sure they'll likely want to set a date tomorrow as soon as the details can be worked out."

"That'll be fine!" Reverend Walters said with a broad smile. "This'll be my first wedding here! This is wonderful! Just wonderful!"

John Jakes was giddy. All the emotion of the morning—the waiting, the not knowing, and the fear—all were gone. In their place was a feeling of triumph along with a sense of invincibility. Katie had said yes, and Nathan had given his approval! And now the whole world was his. It was a long ride home, but first he would ride out to the Walker place to tell his bride-to-be the good news!

Nathan stood in the churchyard talking to Reverend Walters as John rode past. John waved, whooping as he spurred the horse to a gallop. Nathan and the reverend waved back.

Walker Creek babbled softly along the side of the road. The waters were low this late in the season, but deep pools formed along the backwaters that were home to large communities of trout. Madrone, willow, and aspens intermingled with wild blackberries, creating thickets along the shore. A herd of elk grazed quietly along the far bank, taking only a passing notice of the young rider.

John followed the road, daydreaming about the future. His father would help. He knew that. Quinlan Jakes promised to provide a hundred and sixty acres of bottomland as a wedding present. He could apply for a claim for the section to the north. And John was sure the community would get together for a house raising. Of course, he would have to do much of the work himself, but their ranch was only a few miles upriver from town. If he could talk his father out of that little clearing along the banks south of the main house, he could cut his own timber, float it downstream to Ben's new mill, and maybe make a deal with him to mill the lumber for a new house for a fair share of the lumber. Anyway, it was worth asking—and dreaming.

The horse plodded along the familiar trail almost without guidance. Up ahead, a wagon sat in the middle of the road with one end of its rear axle on the ground at the end of a long, narrow gouge in the hard-packed dirt of the trail. The wagon wheel rested against the side of the wagon.

Andre Doucet stood next to his wife with a knit cap in his hand as he scratched the top of his bald head.

"You folks havin' problems?" John asked as he rode up.

Andre wiped the sweat from his forehead as he shrugged. "It would seem so," he said, and then turned to face the wagon. "The collar nut has worked itself from the axle. There does not appear to be any permanent damage, but I cannot lift the wagon high enough to put the wheel in its place."

John looked around. "Maybe I can help," he said as he dismounted.

"I would be forever in your debt," said the old man.

Maud Doucet moved silently around to the back of the wagon, but said nothing.

"We may need a lever of some kind—" Andre began.

"I think I can lift it," John said, backing up to the wagon and placing his hands under the carriage. "You ready?" he asked.

"It is quite heavy, young man."

"I can handle it."

Andre hurried to roll the wheel into place and nodded to John that he was ready. John took a deep breath and lifted with all his might. The wagon rose. Andre pushed the wheel onto the axle. "All right, young man, that will do it! Merci. Thank you!"

John let the wagon ease down on the wheel. From behind him, he heard Kyra's sultry voice. "My! You are so strong!"

John turned to see her walking up from the creek. Her feet and the bottom of her dress were wet. Her eyes danced, and she seemed to be mocking him. "It ain't that heavy," he said.

"Oh, but it is! My father and mother could not lift it," she said. She was smiling, but her eyes were virulent.

"And what about—"

"I do not lift wagons," she interrupted with a laugh. "Come! We will go for a walk while my father finishes what he is doing."

"Kyra!" Maud called out.

"We will not go far," Kyra called back impatiently as she reached out and took John by the hand.

"I don't think I should," John said.

"You heard me say we will not go far. My parents are here. What can happen? You will be safe with me," she said, still mocking. "I will protect you."

John knew he should leave. He felt foolish. "All right," he said. "We'll walk for a little while."

"Come," she said as she led him by the hand, "let us go down by the water."

Andre and Maud watched as their daughter disappeared into the thicket of berry vines and alder trees. "Perhaps we should not permit her to go with this young man," Andre said.

"And who could stop her?" her mother said. "You know as well as I, she does as she pleases. Just as she has always done."

"Yes," Andre said softly. "I wonder sometimes if—"

"If what?" Maud said.

"We have paid a heavy price on her behalf. And she wears a constant reminder of it."

"What do you wonder?"

Andre turned back to the wagon. "I wonder if we shall ever get this wagon back on the road."

Maud struck Andre's shoulder with the back of her hand. "Sometimes, old man, you try my patience! What do you wonder?"

"Be quiet, woman! Do you want them to hear?"

"What do you wonder?" she said again.

"Oh, I think you know as well as I," he said, nodding toward the place where Kyra and John disappeared. "I think you know. I wonder if her part in the matter was entirely as we prefer to believe."

"What we did was right!" Maud said. "And as for the reminder, it was there for the taking. It is solid gold. Someone would have taken it—if only the fish, so why not us?"

"Gold," Andre said in disgust. "It does us no good hanging from her neck! And it may one day prove to be more trouble than we bargained for."

John followed Kyra as she strolled along the banks of Walker Creek, trying not to notice the soft lines of her form. Her dark hair hung down to her waist, gently blowing in the breeze. The muscles in her thighs stood out as she climbed onto a big rock that jutted out over the water. Her bare feet made no sound.

"Come sit with me," she said as she sat down.

John obliged, reluctantly. "Your father should have that wheel fixed by now," he said as he sat down next to her. "Maybe we should go back."

"There is time." Kyra cooed. "Do not be afraid."

"I'm not afraid," John said.

"Of course you're not," she said with the same mocking tone.

John could not help staring. She was beautiful—and desirable. Her thin dress clung to her, revealing all that John could want in a woman. "That's some medallion you got there," he said, his voice quivering slightly.

"It was a gift from my mother," she said, lifting it from her breast between two fingers so John could see it. "Do you like it?"

"It's very interesting," he said as he reached out to touch it.

Kyra closed her fist and pulled away. "Do not touch it!"

"I'm sorry!" John stammered. "I didn't mean to—"

Kyra smiled, letting the medallion fall on the chain around her neck and rest on her golden skin. "It is warm to the touch. Would you like to touch it?"

John blushed.

"Go ahead. Take it in your hand. I will let you." She leaned back on her arms and tossed her head back, letting her hair fall around her shoulders.

She was pretty all right. John's heart beat only for Katie ever since that first day in the churchyard. He knew from the first moment he met her that he wanted to make her his wife. And in these last few months the idea of making a home with her was all he could think about. The land, a little clearing for the house, and a hundred other things, and now it was all set. Yet in the last few months, every time he rode out to the Walker place, there was Kyra. She always seemed to be out in the road or by the creek, but she never failed to be where she would run into

John on his way. He even tried to change the times when he would pass her place, but she always seemed to know. And that dress. Kyra filled it well. To watch her move made him wonder—wonder what it would be like. John felt his heart pound as he leaned closer.

He took the medallion between his fingers, brushing her soft skin as he lifted it and held it still attached to the chain around her neck. His hands trembled. Kyra leaned closer. "Do you like it?" she asked.

John gave a foolish grin. "Yeah, it's real pretty. You say your mother gave it to you?"

Kyra caressed the back of John's hand that held the medallion. "You have strong hands."

John could feel the blood drain from his face. "Farmin's hard work."

Kyra slipped her fingers between his and clasped his hand, clamping the medallion between their palms and pulled his hand close to her lips. She kissed the tips of his fingers.

"I like your hands," she said. "They are strong hands."

She kissed them again. "I think they are very nice."

She kissed them again. "Would you like to put them around my waist?"

He looked up from the medallion. Her almond eyes were fixed on his.

"Your hands are trembling," she said.

John tried to pull away, but she tightened her grip. "Do you like me?" she asked.

"Yeah, I like you."

"Then why don't you put your arms around my waist? I will not bite you," she said playfully.

John jerked his hand away, breaking the chain around her neck. The medallion fell to the ground, rolled a few feet, and tumbled into the water, where it came to rest on a rock a few inches from the surface. He rose quickly to his feet. "I'm sorry, but I can't—"

"My medallion!" Kyra cried as she scrambled toward the water's edge.

"I'm sorry," John said again.

Kyra thrust her hand into the water and felt around the bottom of the creek bed, her dark eyes searching for the glimmer of gold.

"Let me help," John said after a moment. He took a step closer to the creek.

"No!" Kyra cried. John stopped, startled at the sharpness in her voice. In another moment, her hand came up out of the water with the medallion. She clutched it tightly, kneeling by the water as though in prayer, not moving except for a slight rocking back and forth, holding the medallion to her cheek.

"I'd better go," John said. He hurried back to the wagon where Maud Doucet held the reins to his horse.

"Where is Kyra?" Maud asked.

"She's down by the water," John said as a crimson hue returned to his cheeks. He swung himself up into the saddle. As he did, Kyra appeared.

"Thank you for your help," said Andre.

John nodded as he spurred the horse and galloped off toward the Walker ranch.

And evil eyes, filled with hate, watched from a distance.

CHAPTER FIVE

"MY BABY!" RUTH Walker cried as she threw her arms around Katie. "Oh, this isn't possible! My little girl! Why didn't you say something? Oh, there's so much to be done!"

"I wanted to wait until Papa got home," Katie beamed.

"Have you decided when it is to be?"

Katie was radiant. "Not for certain. We haven't set the date yet, but we want to do it as soon as possible—next month, if it's all right with you and Papa."

"Oh, we can't possibly do it in a month! There's so much to be done! What about the dress? We have to—" Ruth bit down on her lip.

"I was hoping I could wear the dress you wore when you married Papa."

Ruth's eyes glistened. "Oh! I'll have to get it out. I hope it isn't reduced to dust by now! Oh, my baby! My little girl!"

Nathan stood patiently to one side. "Now, Mother," he said, "it isn't like this was totally unexpected. Why just the other day—"

"Oh, I know, but it's just that...oh!" she said, turning to Katie. "Where will you live?"

"John's father wants to give us a hundred and sixty acres along the river as a wedding present. And John figures he can stake a claim for the section to the north." Katie beamed. "It'll be good farm land once it's cleared. And we've already picked a spot for the house."

The corners of Ruth's eyes glistened as she held her hand to her face.

"Oh, Mama, don't cry."

"I can't help it!" Ruth said as she reached to hug her daughter. "Let's announce it tomorrow at the social. We can get together with the Jakes and make the arrangements. Beth will want to…oh, there's so much to do!"

"Congratulations, Son." Quinlan Jakes shook his son's hand and squeezed his shoulder with the other. "She'll make a fine wife."

Beth Jakes waited her turn beside her husband. "I'm so happy," she said softly as she slipped her arms around her son's broad shoulders and held him close. "Katie's a fine girl."

"I know, Mother."

Monty sat on his cot in the corner, trying to understand all that was being said. John's two younger brothers, Jefferson and Jeremy, stood by, listening.

"Is she gonna live with us?" Jefferson asked.

"Where's she gonna sleep?" asked Jeremy.

"They'll have their own place," Quin answered. "They'll make a home on that clearing down by the river."

"Where you shot that buck a couple weeks ago, John?" asked Jeremy.

John nodded. "Uh-huh."

"Can we come see you when we want?" Jefferson asked.

"Yep. You two can help me build a house, if you want."

"Yeah!" they said in unison. Both boys ran out the door, arguing about who could use the axe first and who would fell the first tree.

Beth turned back to her son. "Have the two of you decided when this is to be?"

"We don't want to wait," John said. "We'd like to be married as soon as we can—next month, if possible."

"I'll talk to Ruth," Beth said. "There's much to be done, but I think we can manage." Beth cupped her son's face in her hands. Tears formed in the corners of her eyes. "I'm happy for you, Son."

"Thank you, Mother."

"Well," Beth sighed. "I guess we'll have to make some plans. When do we announce the big event?"

"Katie wants to do it tomorrow night at the social," John said. "Is that all right?"

Beth looked at her husband. Quin nodded. "I think we can manage it," he said with a grin.

"Good," said Beth. "Then it's all set. We'll make the announcement tomorrow."

Ben Elam stomped the dirt from his feet as he came through the back door of the trading post and into the living quarters behind the store. His youngest son, twelve-year-old Alexander, followed at his heels. Curious Indians had congregated around the giant cylinder of the steam-driven mill and Ben was fearful they would damage it. He had gone out to chase them off.

"Are they gone?" his wife asked.

"Yeah. Least ways for now. I don't reckon they could hurt it none. But I don't want to take no chances." Ben reached into his shirt pocket for the tobacco pouch. Turning to his young son, he said, "Someone's out front. Go help 'em."

Alex scurried off through the narrow doorway that separated store and home, pausing as he remembered his mother's admonition to always close the door when customers were in the store.

"So what did you want to tell me?" Mrs. Elam asked.

"'Bout what?" Ben said as he fumbled with the tobacco pouch.

"I don't know. You said before you went out that you had news."

"Oh! I clean forgot! Nathan was in today while you were out to the Wallace place. He came in to get a new axe handle. Anyhow, young John Jakes came in an' asked to talk to him. And, well, it seems he and Nathan's daughter are gonna get hitched!"

"That's wonderful! Did you find out when the happy day will be?"

"Nope. I ain't heard yet. But I figure they'll make an announcement tomorrow night." Ben stuffed a wad of tobacco into his lower lip. "Young John don't strike me as the waitin' kind."

Andre Doucet was deep in thought as he fingered the wooden stock of the nearly new rifle that stood in the corner of Ben's trading post, with its fine crafted wood, its polished breach and barrel, and the expert engraving along the stock. He longed to own such a gun. His own antiquated weapon sat on the rickety wagon seat outside the trading post. From where he was standing, he could see it near the front door, resting against the seat, rusted and worm-eaten. It was never new—at least as far as Andre was concerned. Handed down to him from his father, it looked old even then. It held no sentimental value for him, but served only to remind him of his station in life. He was not a happy man, although he hid it well from the outside world.

"Can I help you?" young Alex Elam recited as he had been instructed. Yves and Veré stood together in the far corner of the store. Maud was busy pawing over a bolt of cloth near the rear. Kyra stood near the front door—brooding.

Andre turned to face the young boy as he came into the store. "Well, young man, are you the proprietor of this establishment?"

"No, sir. That'd be my pa. He's busy right now. Can I he'p you?"

"Well, now, that depends. Would you be interested in a barter to profit us both?"

The boy looked puzzled. "You mean tradin'?"

"Of course, young man, of course!"

"You'd have to talk to my pa about it. You want me to get him?"

Andre gave his sons a sly glance across the room. Yves nodded, but Veré was facing the wall, holding something close to his chest. Andre's eyes shifted. "Is he close by?"

"He an' Ma are in the back. I'll get 'em."

The boy hurried through the door behind the counter. In a moment it opened again and Ben Elam appeared. "How'd do."

Andre put on his best horse-trading face. "Good afternoon! You are the proprietor of this establishment?"

"If you mean, do I own it, the answer'd be yes. What can I do for you folks?"

"My sons shot a fine elk that we would like to exchange for some provisions. Is this agreeable to you?"

"Maybe," Ben said with a wary eye on the two young men at the other side of the store. "Depends on how long ago you bagged him. Is the meat fresh?"

"Last evening, along the stream two or three miles from here. I believe it is called Walker Creek."

"You the new folks Nathan was tellin' me about?"

Andre shrugged. "We have only arrived this spring."

"Ain't seen you in here before," Ben said as he kept one eye on Yves.

"We have been busy with the business of settling in. And we have very little money," Andre said as he waved his arm through the air. "We have only our labor—and this fine elk."

"I reckon I can take a look," Ben said and then turned to the open door at the back of the store. "Ma! Will you come out here?"

In a moment, Mrs. Elam entered the store. "I gotta go out front for a minute. Will you stay here an' help these fine folks?" he said, gesturing toward Yves and Veré. Ben exchanged a knowing glance with his wife as he motioned Andre toward the front door and followed him out. He nodded a polite acknowledgment to Kyra as he passed by.

"Well!" Mrs. Elam said when Ben and Andre were outside. "Can I help you find anything?

"You have some very nice things," Maud said, running dirty fingers over the bolt of cloth.

Mrs. Elam fidgeted nervously with her hands. "Would you like me to cut you a piece?"

Maud smiled through sad eyes. "Our kind can only admire from afar," she said.

Mrs. Elam looked away.

Maud's eyes shifted toward her sons and then back again. "We are poor people with poor ways. Fortune does not smile on us."

Mrs. Elam reached for the bolt of cloth, taking care not to touch Maud's hands as she took it and set it back on the shelf. They were dirty hands—unwashed, old, and bent—but not calloused. "Maybe when you folks get established," she said.

Maud's eyes flashed. Mrs. Elam clasped her hands together as she tried to think of something to say. "Will you folks be going to the social tonight?" she finally said.

Maud sneered. "I do not think so."

"I expect there'll be a wedding announcement," Mrs. Elam said nervously.

Kyra, who had been only half listening before, straightened.

"There'll be some mighty good food," Mrs. Elam continued. "And it would be a good way to meet your new neighbors."

"I do not think so," Maud said.

Kyra moved closer to them. "Where will it be?" she asked.

Both women turned to face the young girl. "Why, at the church, of course," Mrs. Elam said.

Yves had slowly made his way to where the two women were standing. Veré held back, facing the wall. "We are not—" Yves began.

"I would like to go," Kyra interrupted.

"You do not have a dress to wear," Maud said.

"Oh, that's all right," said Mrs. Elam. "Lotsa folks don't have new. It doesn't have to be new, so long as it's—" her voice trailed off.

"So long as it's what?" Maud asked.

Mrs. Elam could feel her face brighten. "Well, what I mean is, I'm sure anything she has would be fine.

John and Monty squatted next to the babbling waters of the river, surveying the clearing that would be the site for the new home John intended to build for his bride. "Why are there no trees in the lowlands?" John asked.

"My people set fires," Monty said, spreading his arm across the valley.

"Fires?" John asked, surprised. "You mean they intentionally set fire to the land?"

Monty nodded. He stood up and searched around him for a moment until he found what he was looking for. His broad face beamed. "See," he said, holding the stalk of a broad-leafed plant in his hand. Black ooze ran down the length of it.

"Tarweed," John said, "What about it?"

Monty held the round seedpod at the end of the stalk in his hand. "Good food. My people eat. Burn land," he said waving his arm again. "Pick up."

He held up the seedpod and motioned as though he were smashing it in his hand.

John raised an eyebrow. "You mean that old tarweed is good to eat?"

Monty nodded. "Make good food."

John shook his head. "Not likely," he said. "What about all that black tar?"

"Burn land," Monty said. "Tar—go away." Monty tried to remember the words.

"I reckon it must dry out the seeds," said John, scratching his head.

"Women make food," Monty said, and then playfully tossed the seedpod in his hand at John.

"Hey!" John cried as he caught it and threw it back. Monty ducked out of the way, wincing at the pain from the wound in his leg. Both men began to laugh.

The afternoon sun beat down, reflecting off the water and shimmering in the still pools that collected along the banks. Steelhead trout swam in the pools, hugging the shady banks to avoid the heat. Monty sat down on the grass and lay back with his arms behind his head, his long black hair falling askew beneath him. John sat down next to him.

"This good place," Monty said after a moment. "You make house?"

John nodded. "Yep. Right over there." He pointed to the highest point in the clearing.

Monty nodded his approval. "You make wife?"

John grinned. "Yep."

"Katie make good wife."

John's eyes danced at the sound of it. *Wife*. She would make a good wife. *Wife. Wife, wife, wife, wife, wife!* It sounded good. *Mr. and Mrs. John Jakes!*

"How does white man make wife?" Monty asked.

"We have a wedding. The man and the woman get together with a bunch of friends and family, and a preacher."

"What is preacher?"

"Preacher?" John puzzled for a moment. "Well, he's sort of a…that is…he teaches about God—you know, God? Anyhow, they all get together and say a few words. Then the man and woman are married—hitched, you know?" He clasped his hands together to make the point.

"Mmm," Monty grunted. "We have same. Preacher and wedding." He rolled over to one side and leaned on his elbow. "When, John?"

"You mean when's the wedding? I don't know. We have to decide that tomorrow night at the social."

"Mmm. Social." Monty knew of the social. It was all anyone talked about for days. "Whites make fun."

John laughed. "Yep, fun!" He pointed at Monty and then back at himself. "We'll all have fun!"

Monty laughed and pointed at John's chest. "You make fun!"

John leaned forward. "Yeah, I'll have fun. But you're coming, too!"

Monty held up his hands and shook his head. "No good place for Indian. Some whites make trouble."

"Nonsense!" John insisted. "These are good Christian people. They won't make trouble. Anyhow, if they do, we'll fight 'em together!"

Monty looked down at his leg and shook his head. "John fight alone maybe."

John put his hand on his friend's shoulder. "There won't be any fighting."

Monty shook his head. "Bad trouble between Indian and white. My people hear, before I come, some say Indian kill white. Some say white make look like Indian kill white." Monty shook his head with wide eyes. "Good I stay in house."

John shook his head. "Yeah. Grave Creek. I heard about all that. But not all whites want to make trouble for the Indian. Besides, you'll be with me." John squeezed Monty's shoulder with his hand. "You're my friend. And if my friends aren't welcome, then neither am I."

Monty fell back on the ground again, staring at the summer sky. John was a good friend. He knew he could trust this white—even with his life. He did trust him. But the others he was not so sure about. The great chief had made friends with the whites and had even helped them with many things, but Monty was never sure if it was because the chief trusted them, or if he knew it would do no good to resist the massive onslaught of the great hordes of whites. "I come if you say."

"Good," John said, "because there's something I want to ask you. It's the custom at the white man's wedding for the groom, the man, to have a friend stand with him. He's called the 'best man.'"

"Groom is man who make wife?"

"Yeah. Anyhow—"

"Why groom not best man?" Monty interrupted.

John opened his mouth to answer before it occurred to him that he had no idea. "I don't know. It's just the way it is. It's custom."

Monty laughed. "Why woman not marry best man?"

"He's just called the best man! It's custom. Why do you wear a white eagle's feather when you go to war?"

Monty shook his head. "Not same. Eagle feather give strength of eagle. Not give feather to women or small ones. Give to warrior. Why not best man, man who marry woman?"

John threw up his hands. "I don't know!" he laughed. "But I want you to be the best man. Will you do it?"

Monty nodded. "You want best man; I do for you, my friend."

John lay back on the grass next to his friend. Neither spoke for a long time as they watched a single cloud drift across the sky. John was about to doze off when Monty chuckled. "Katie not marry best man."

Maud Doucet struggled with the pail of water as she hobbled under the heavy weight of it back to the lean-to shack; she set it down near the entrance.

"Veré! Come here and bring in this pail of water," she said in her own tongue. She stood for a moment, catching her breath.

"Veré!"

There was no answer. She lifted the pail again, struggling through the door and over to the crude, stone hearth around the fire in the middle of the room where she set it down.

"Veré!"

Her bones ached. The joints of her fingers were sore and stiff and red. She worked the joints, shaking her hand to restore the flow of blood, and then bent down to pour the pail's contents into the caldron that rested on the open coals of the fire, mumbling to herself.

"Fools!" she said under her breath. Life had not been kind to Maud Doucet. All her life had been a struggle—with men mostly, it seemed, always fighting them off as a young girl in the French Quarter of New Orleans. When Andre came along, all that changed for a while. But soon she had two male children to contend with. Men had robbed her of her youth, and now her whole existence revolved around serving men. And to make matters worse, there sat Kyra in the corner on the floor with her knees against her chest, holding that cursed medallion!

"Is that all you think about, child, that medallion?"

Maud sat down in the rocking chair by the fire. "The young man by the river, he is very handsome."

Kyra held up the medallion to the light of the fire. "It may have power. But it did not help them, did it?"

"Help who?" Maud said.

Kyra met her mother's eyes. "Those men."

Maud was pale. "What men?" she almost whispered.

Kyra smiled, turned, and walked over to the fire, staring into the middle of the flame. "Of course, they did not know how to use its power."

Maud's expression was grim. "And you do?"

Kyra did not answer.

Maud was torn between her fears and her curiosity—no, not curiosity, her need to know. "What men do you speak of?"

"The men who visited the swamp."

Maud raised an eyebrow. "They were men of means. And of power."

"Their power did not help them very much, I think," Kyra taunted.

"They had their own kind of power—the kind with friends in high places, the kind that could seek us out. It is best not to speak of it."

Kyra turned her attention to the medallion. "It talks to me."

Maud leaned forward in the chair. "Nonsense! It is a piece of metal—a testament to the craftsman! Nothing more!"

"Why do you raise your voice, Mama," Kyra's eyes were piercing, "if it is nothing more?"

Maud settled back in her chair. "I am tired of hearing about it," she mumbled.

Andre, who had been tending the wagon wheel, entered the shack. "What is the arguing about?"

"Your daughter thinks the medallion has power."

Their eyes met. Andre's face fell. "What did you tell her?"

Maud waved her hand through the air. "The same thing I have always told her, that it is only a medallion."

Kyra ran her fingers around the edge of the medallion. "Are they dead?"

"You ask too many questions," Maud mumbled almost to herself as she got up from the chair, hobbled over to the fire, and began to stir the contents of the caldron.

Andre turned to leave. "It is best to leave the past behind," he said, and then ducked out through the opening and was gone.

Maud finished her stirring and hobbled over to the deerskin that hung over the opening of the shack. "Forget the medallion," she said. "It is nothing. And if it did have power, you are not the one to master it! Forget it, child."

Maud waited for an answer but Kyra ignored her, holding the medallion up to the light of the fire. Maud whirled around, threw back the deerskin in a fit of anger and disappeared, muttering to herself.

Kyra settled back against the wall thinking of John. He was desirable. His clean face and innocent smile made him something to possess, to conquer, and to bring down as a hunter brings down a prey. She had made up her mind to have him the first moment she laid eyes on him. It was in town, the first day they arrived. He was standing near the trading post admiring a string of fish that two young boys had caught. John hardly noticed her, she was sure, and it made her want him all the more. But as he began to court that Walker girl, her desire turned to lust, and her lust turned to obsession. Turning men's heads was never a challenge for Kyra. They would make fools of themselves for her. Men fought over her. Some men would kill for her. She could have any man she desired—except one, and it gnawed at her like a wolf stripping away flesh from bone.

The medallion seemed to glow.

Kyra studied it as she held it up to the light. She must find a way. She never knew the old woman. No one ever saw her. Yet Kyra was sure she was more than legend. The stories little children told among the shadows along the wharf, the whispers of their mothers and fathers, the terrified looks of those who had ventured deep into the swamp, and now this bit of metal that seemed to call to her. She could feel her heart beating faster.

She needed power—power beyond her physical endowments—and now she could feel the medallion pulling at her, drawing her. John would be hers. She could have him—for an hour, a lifetime, or cast him away at the moment of victory. It mattered little to her, only that he be hers. She was not afraid.

She stood and held the medallion high, reveling in its beauty. It seemed to offer a promise as her heart filled with the lust for power. "Medallion!" The eyes of the goat's head glowed bright green. "I call upon you! I call upon the great powers of darkness within you! Seek me out! Find in me a new mistress! I call upon you to empower me with all that you possess! Medallion! I raise you up! I call upon you to reveal your great secrets to me! Medallion! Obey me!"

The medallion seemed to glow brightly. It was suddenly warmer, and now she felt it burning in her hand. She clutched it tightly, sensing the power as it flowed through her. Beads of sweat rolled down her cheeks and locks of her hair clung to her forehead.

She held out her arms in triumph as an evil presence engulfed her, clutching her, holding her, and dragging her mind wherever it willed.

Veré and Yves sat on the ground, leaning against the stone wall of the cold storage that had been dug into the side of the hill a few yards behind the shack. They were nursing a bottle of wine stolen from the trading post. A fallen log rested a few feet away. Veré held in his hand another new treasure: a shiny new knife also stolen from the trading post. He flung it at the log, sticking the point into the soft wood, and then pulling it out and tossing it again. Andre, brooding and sullen, passed by without saying a word.

"Our saintly father is deep in prayer, it seems," Yves mocked. "Why do you not join us?"

The lines in Andre's face deepened. "Can the two of you find nothing constructive to occupy your time?"

Both men laughed. Veré bowed low in mock tribute. "What would you have us do, most noble Father?"

"You could begin by skinning and dressing that elk you brought in last night before the meat goes bad."

Veré and Yves both laughed.

"Maybe we should pay our neighbors a visit," said Veré. "I think I would like to go see the young girl. I think I like her very much. She is very pretty. She deserves better than the little boy who rides for eggs and milk, no?"

Yves laughed. "Maybe we should both go, eh?"

Andre gave his son a hard stare. "Forget her. Your sister begins to suspect," he said.

"Suspect what?" Veré said. "Was she there? I do not think so. And the only ones who were there are here," Veré motioned to his brother, "or feeding the fishes at the bottom of the swamp."

"She believes the medallion has power."

Yves jeered. "An old wives' tale!"

"Shut up!" Andre growled. "If she knows where it came from, she must know who had it when we…when we found it."

"And what of it?" Veré asked. "She has no reason to suspect what we did."

"She has every reason!" said Andre. "She knows what we would do."

"What of it?" Yves asked. "She is our own flesh and blood. Would she bite her own flesh? And what of them? Those two crocodiles—they deserved what they got!"

Veré nodded in agreement. "What they did—they forfeited their right to live!"

"And what of you?" Andre questioned. "Do you not think of the same thing with the young girl?"

"You do not think they deserved to die? She is our sister—and they violated her."

Andre shrugged. "Perhaps. But I wonder if she is the tender flower she would have us think."

"You think she lied?"

Andre shrugged.

"It makes no difference," said Yves. "It makes no difference at all!"

"Hurry, Mama!" Katie called out from the front porch of the cabin. "We don't want to be late for the social!"

CHAPTER SIX

NATHAN PULLED BACK hard on the reins. The team of two horses slowed and then stopped in front of the churchyard next to a half-a-dozen other wagons and three saddled mares. Loose hay had been scattered along the ground in front of them, and each grazed contentedly. The sun was setting low on the mountains to the west, sending rays of light through the boughs of the trees along the ridge. Iron lamp stands adorned with brightly colored bows encircled the churchyard. Kerosene lamps flickered, sending trails of black smoke into the dusk of the late afternoon sky.

Reverend Walters was busy with last minute arrangements at one of the heavy wooden tables that had been brought by one of the folks from up-river. A group of young girls in their early teens whispered and giggled in the shade of a maple tree. Ben Elam stood with a group of men at the far corner of the yard next to a lilac bush Mrs. Walters had planted only that spring. Occasionally they would all laugh. Silas McCoy, the man who first greeted the Walkers when they arrived in the valley, stood with Jack Wallace and two other men—newcomers. Folks were going in and out of the church carrying their favorite dishes, cakes, or pies, and two or three men in their Sunday best hurried about with their fiddles, trying to decide where best to set up for the dance.

Ruth waited for Nathan to come around the wagon. He reached up to meet her as she settled into his arms from the high seat. "Thank you, dear," she said. "Now, will you get the basket from the back? Katie, you take those linens over to Mrs. Wallace. She's over by that table at the end. See?"

"Yes, Mama," Katie responded as she looked around the yard for John. Her heart sank a little. Ruth reached out and squeezed Katie's arm. "They'll be along. Don't you worry."

Ruth reached into the back of the wagon for the warm bundle of freshly baked bread, neatly wrapped in her finest linen cloth. Both women carried their bundles over to the table. "Ah! Thank you, ladies!" Reverend Walters greeted them.

A group of ladies mulled around the table. "Everything looks so nice!" Ruth said to Mrs. Peters.

"It does indeed," Mrs. Peters responded. "Some of the ladies have been working on it all afternoon."

Mrs. Wallace finished arranging the pies at the end of the table and joined them. "This will be some social! I hear folks are coming all the way from Deer Creek!"

"Well," said Reverend Walters, "we'll have plenty for all of them to eat. Why, we've got enough here to feed the five thousand!"

"It should be a night to remember," said Mrs. Peters.

"It may be indeed," said Reverend Walters as he gave Katie a wink. "It may be indeed!"

Over by the lilac bush, Ben Elam kicked a pebble with the toe of his boot as he listened to Tom Henry and Hance Eerdman. "Yeah, I got me a big bull elk up by Fletcher's Peak a couple nights ago," Tom was saying. "But I was afoot. And by the time I made it back to the house, it was near dark. So I waited 'til morning, saddled up, and rode out an hour before first light. But by the time I got back up there, why do you know that ol' bull was gone! There weren't hide nor bone anywhere to be found. I tell you, I couldn't figure it. I mean, even buzzards woulda left something!"

"That's over near them new folks ain't it?" said Hance. "Up there just below Nathan's place?"

"Yep," said Tom. "Less than a mile as the crow flies."

"You don't reckon someone stole it, do you?"

"Well, that ol' bull didn't get up and walk out. That's for sure."

Hance leaned to one side and spit. "A fella'd have to be pretty low to steal another man's kill."

Tom and Ben nodded in agreement. Hance turned to Ben. "You met them new folks yet, Ben?"

Ben nodded. "Yep. They were in yesterday."

"I hear they're a strange bunch," said Hance.

"They're different," said Ben. "That's a fact. They keep pretty much to themselves, though."

"I heard some strange tales from some of them that lives close to 'em," said Tom. "And Silas McCoy over there says he's been missing some chickens."

"Me and the missus rode out to the Walker place last week to pay a call," said Hance. "And, of course, I had to ride right by that ol' shack. One of them boys was laid back against the side of the house with a bottle in one hand and a knife in the other—just sticking it in the ground and pulling it out again. If it weren't for that, there wouldn'ta been no work at all gettin' done. And right there in the middle of the day!"

"Beats me how they make a livin'," Tom said. "Ain't nobody seen 'em do a day's work. Ain't that right, Nathan?"

Nathan Walker joined them. "It's none of my affair. As long as they mind their own business, I'll mind mine."

"It might be your business if you start losin' stock," said Hance. "I said it before and I'll say it again. They're a strange bunch. Them boys of theirs is plain mean. I seen 'em throwin' rocks at a digger squirrel, an' they hit it square. But the thing didn't die right off. So they kept throwin' rocks, only not so's it'd die, just so's it'd squirm around an' try to get away. They was laughing and havin' a grand ol' time 'til that squirrel finally gave up the ghost.

"An' that girl of theirs. I heard she's always out late at night, walkin' the woods, talkin' to herself. I tell you, they're a strange bunch. What do you say, Ben?"

Ben glanced in Nathan's direction. "Aw, I reckon it ain't none of my affair."

Nathan gritted his teeth. He was not the kind of man who thought deeply about things. Most of the time he just knew how he felt; if he liked or trusted someone. He didn't like or trust any of the Doucets. And Hance was right. The boys were just plain mean. But gossip left a bitter taste in his mouth. "As I said, so long as they stay to themselves, I can abide having them as neighbors," he said.

Tom, Hance, and Ben all agreed.

The sun settled between two mountain peaks to the west, and the flames from the lanterns that surrounded the clearing flickered and danced, giving the churchyard a festive glow. The soothing sound of the river echoed through the trees. Four men stood near the entrance to the church, tuning their fiddles. Katie sat impatiently on the steps, watching the road that followed the river upstream, her hands clasped nervously in her lap.

So much had happened in the last few weeks, she could hardly believe it. In a few hours or even minutes, she supposed, the whole world would know that she and John were to be married. John was the handsomest man in the valley, and Katie figured she was the luckiest woman alive. But it was his soft eyes and gentle, yet strong, spirit that drew her to love him. He would make a good husband, and when the time came, a good father to a passel of children. They had talked. Family was important to Katie. She was pleased when John was the one to bring it up. Yes, he would make a fine father to her children.

Oh, how I wish he would get here!

She took another long look down the road before she stood to the sound of clip-clopping beyond the rise in the road. In another moment a wagon appeared behind two large geldings, trotting toward the churchyard with Beth and Quinlan Jakes seated in front and the two young boys in the back, playfully tugging at each other's bow ties. Monty leaned back against the side of the wagon, trying to get comfortable. Beside the wagon, a sleek bay stallion with a rider sitting tall in the saddle pranced against a firmly held rein.

John Jakes scanned the crowded churchyard until he spotted his bride-to-be standing on the wooden steps of the church. He spurred his mount to a gallop, passing the wagon as the two geldings shied to one side and then fought against the reins to catch up. Quinlan held them back.

At the hitching post, John was out of the saddle before his mount was completely stopped. Katie met him as he threw the reins over the post and took off his hat. They faced each other in silence, suddenly unaware of the crowd.

"Good evening, Miss Walker," he said with his hat in his hand.

"Good evening, Mr. Jakes," she responded. Her eyes sparkled.

They turned and walked side by side toward the table. John asked her if she wanted punch. She nodded. John took two glasses, lifted the ladle, filled the glasses to the brim, and then handed one to Katie.

People were beginning to stare. Katie's mother stood with a group of women near the makeshift canvas pavilion that had been set up as a dance stand. The women were smiling and looking at them. Without words, John and Katie began to move away from the crowd toward the sound of the river.

"You scared?" John asked when they were alone.

Katie nodded. "Uh-huh, a little. You?"

John nodded.

"It's not too late …"

John stopped and put his arms around her. "I said I was scared, not sorry,"

Katie studied his face. It was strong, but not hard. She reached up and stroked his chin with the back of her fingers. John held her close in his arms. "Do you want to go through with it?" she asked.

John's eyes narrowed. "'A man who looks back is not fit …'"

His answer pleased her. "I love you, John Jakes. And I'll give you strong sons!"

Katie blushed. The words were out before she knew she was going to say them. Startled by her own boldness, she looked away.

John put his hand under her chin and gently turned her to face him. His own face flushed and his knees felt like a newborn colt's. He could see in her face that Katie was already looking to him for leadership.

"Words don't come easy to me," he said. "I …" They were failing him even now. "I'll be a good husband to you. I promise you that. And if we are blessed with children," John's face brightened still more, "I'll be the best father in the whole world."

"I know you will," Katie said softly. She reached up and took his face in her hands. John leaned down, paused for a moment, and then as gently as he knew how, kissed the only girl he had ever kissed.

Veré sulked as he threw a broken-down saddle on the only horse the family owned, brooding at having to do even the slightest bit of work. When he had finished, he led the horse around to the front of the shack and called out, "Kyra!"

Kyra had been sitting impatiently inside, eager to get on with her evil purpose. At Veré's call she shot through the deerskin flap and hurried to put her bare foot into the worn stirrup.

"You should not go alone," he grumbled. "It will be dark soon."

"Does my dear brother worry about me?"

Veré shrugged. "They are not our kind. You should not go alone," he repeated.

"You are welcome to join me," she said as she swung up into the saddle.

Veré was silent.

Kyra held the horse for a moment. "I can take care of myself. I am not afraid."

"Maybe you should be," Veré sneered. "Maybe we would not have to pick up the pieces you leave behind."

Kyra reined hard to one side and dug her bare heels into the horse's flank. Veré shook his head as he watched her disappear into the night, and then he went back inside the shack.

Kyra slapped the long reins, flicking the horse low in the flank. It was unnecessary since she was already in a pleasant gait, but Kyra enjoyed confusing the animal with conflicting commands as she held the reins tightly. She felt power. The sensation had washed over her as she held the medallion high only a few hours before. Any fear or doubts she may have had disappeared at that moment, leaving her with a strange sense that she could do anything she pleased. Now she was confident. This wedding would not take place. John Jakes would be hers for whatever time she willed. After that—the devil may care!

The ride into town was several miles, which gave her time to think and plan. As she bobbed along, she held the medallion in her fist, occasionally fingering it between her forefinger and thumb, offering silent prayers to her god. Less than an hour later she rode up the rise in the road just outside of town. The horse slowed as the flicker of the lanterns lit up the evening sky. As she rode over the top of the rise, she could see the church and the circle of lanterns. People were mulling around, dancing, eating and drinking, talking in small groups, and laughing. She held the horse for a moment as she watched from a distance.

She felt suddenly strange—drained, as though something was holding her back. Something about the circle of lanterns made her uneasy. She sat for a moment, puzzled, and then kicked the horse with her heels. The horse plodded along slowly toward the church. Kyra circled around, skirting the ring of lanterns just out of sight. No one noticed her.

She reined the horse toward the hitching post and dismounted, leaving the horse at the rail. She crept over to one of the lanterns and stood with her feet just outside the boundary of the lanterns.

Something held her back—something within the circle threatened.

She looked around. There were people everywhere. The owner of the trading post was clapping to the music and stomping his feet, his wife at his side. Over near the church the mother and father of that wretched girl talked and laughed with John's parents. But there was no threat that she could see. Still, there was something.

Kyra hesitated, but then, with new determination, stepped inside the circle of the lanterns—and for the first time in a very long time she was alone.

Outside the circle, an evil presence lurked, brooding and sullen, lamenting the boundary and watching, fearful of the consequences of a fair fight as well as the sight of a golden sword that flashed in the middle of the circle.

"Excuse me!" Reverend Walters shouted over the music. "Excuse me, everyone!" He held up his hands and waited for the noise to die down.

John and Katie stood at his side, flanked by their parents and John's two brothers, who were squirming in their new suits. Monty stood back in the shadows a few feet away.

"Excuse me for interrupting all the fun," the reverend said with a warm smile. "Now I know that some folks think that is what preachers do best," he said to some chuckles in the crowd. "I have an announcement to make, and I'd be obliged if you'd give me your attention. Most all of us here tonight are new to the valley. Even you old-timers have only been here a few short years. I have been among you only for a few months. All of us have begun a new venture in a new land and we have the opportunity to make it into something grand. It's always a pleasure to be a part of something good and noble. That's why it gives me great pleasure to tell you that we here in Creek Junction are going to be blessed with our very first wedding!"

The sounds of murmuring mingled with the clapping of hands.

John and Katie responded to Reverend Walters's outstretched hand and stepped forward. The reverend held up his hand to quiet the crowd. "I know God has His hand on these two children, and I hope you will join me in a word of prayer in asking for providential blessings on their union."

At that, the crowd obediently lowered their heads. Monty, unsure of the custom of the whites, followed John's lead. In the shadows of a great fir tree, Kyra's face darkened as she felt her purpose being thwarted.

"Dear Father in heaven …" Reverend Walters began.

John gave Katie a furtive glance as they stood with heads bowed, listening. She was beautiful and he wanted her. And now that he had made up his mind this was what he wanted, he saw no reason to wait. As far as he was concerned, they could marry tomorrow.

"… I call upon Thee at this hour of great happiness …"

Katie could feel her palms growing clammy as she tried to hide her shaking hands. No one was looking, but she felt as though every eye were upon her. She felt giddy, as if her feet would leave the ground at any moment. She was happier than she could ever remember being in her life, and soon she would be Mrs. John Jakes!

"… and a time of solemn reflection as these Thy two children …"

Ruth Walker held her handkerchief to her face, sobbing quietly with tears streaming down her cheeks. This was a moment she had waited for, hoped for, and feared for seventeen years—and now it was here! Her baby was getting married, and it was all she could do to contain her joy! Yet there was a sense of loss too.

"… embark on one of life's most challenging journeys …"

Monty stood quietly behind his friend, trying to understand the words. He knew *happy*. He knew *children*. And he knew *father*. But the rest of the words of this white shaman came too fast to grasp—and yet he was strangely drawn to them, as though they had power. He listened intently, searching for any sign of familiarity.

"… I beseech Thee, Lord Jesus, to impart Thy great blessing on them—now and for all eternity. Station Thy protecting angels around them …"

Ben Elam bowed respectfully as the reverend, a man he admired for his goodness and his dedication to the people of Creek Junction, continued his prayer. It was a good thing, these two young'uns getting hitched, but all this talk of Jesus made him uneasy.

"… and hinder the adversary from his destructive purpose …"

Quinlan Jakes reached out to take his wife's hand as they stood together in silent agreement. Beth responded to the warm touch of his hand, squeezing it as she inched a little closer to him, remembering her own happy day many years ago.

"… may their household be one that seeks to serve only You.…"

Kyra stood silently with her dark eyes fixed on the reverend, seething with jealousy and rage, but fearful. Only a few hours before she had felt invincible, as though the powers of the universe were at her disposal.

Now she felt alone and helpless. The medallion felt cold and lifeless in her hand.

"Bless them and their posterity in this happy union, in Thy Son's name, amen."

Reverend Walters finished his prayer. The crowd began to stir, and soon they had gathered around John and Katie. The men shook hands while the women surrounded Katie, clucking their approval and each offering her own version of the perfect wedding day.

John held Katie's hand as they greeted their friends and neighbors and accepted words of wisdom and congratulations. "We think the last Saturday of next month," he said in answer to Mrs. Elam's question. "We want to be married as soon as possible."

"Mama says we can do it by then," said Katie. "That's still nearly six weeks away and it will give John a chance to clear the land for our house."

"Well, that sounds so exciting!" said Mrs. Elam. "Will you be building a large house?"

"John says we can build three rooms to start. But we want to build a real frame house instead of logs."

"Yep," John agreed. "I think I figured a way to get the logs down to your new mill. Maybe we'll be your first customers!"

"Well, won't that be just fine!" Mrs. Elam beamed. "And I'll tell Ben to give you two a real good deal!" She smiled at them, gave the Indian behind them a wary look, and then turned to help herself to a piece of peach pie. Monty stood stone-faced, trying to understand all that was happening, and trying even harder not to look threatening as the women pointed and whispered.

John turned as slender fingers took hold of his arm. "Evening, Miss Kyra," he said as his cheeks flushed. Katie's eyes flashed.

"So you are to be married?" Kyra asked softly.

"Yes!" Katie said, holding John closer.

Kyra cocked her head to one side. "You will still come and walk with me by the river?"

John squirmed as his face brightened. "No! That is, not unless you folks break another wagon wheel," he said quickly, watching Katie out of the corner of his eye.

Kyra's eyes danced with a wicked smile as she pulled away from John, caressing his arm with her fingers. "We will see," she said.

John watched as she walked away and sat down on the grass under a fir tree.

Katie observed him with jealous eyes. "What was that about?"

John turned away. "Oh, nothing much. I helped them fix a wagon wheel—you know, her and her folks."

"And what was that about walking by the river?"

The muscles in John's neck tightened.

"Nothing!" he said.

"It wasn't anything," he added softly after a moment.

Katie pulled her hand away. Jack Wallace was next in line to greet the happy couple. "Congratulations, you two. I know you'll be happy together."

Katie bristled.

"Thank you, sir," John said as they shook hands.

"You two let me know if there's anything I can do when you get ready to put a shoulder to that new house, you hear?"

"Yes, sir. We will."

Several more people were eager to greet them, but soon the line dwindled and John and Katie stood alone as the music played. Some folks began to dance and others lingered around the tables spread with good things to eat.

"Look," he said when they were alone. "It wasn't—"

"Excuse me," she said as she started to walk away. "I don't feel well."

John blocked her path. "Please, listen to me," he said.

"I've heard quite enough, thank you!" Katie stormed off toward the church.

John caught up with her as she started up the steps. He grabbed her by the hand. "Come on!" he said, leading her into the shadows. "You've got to listen to me!"

"Listen to what? You said yourself, it was nothing!"

"I know. But—" John tried to catch his breath. "Look. It wasn't like it sounded."

"How did it sound, Mr. Jakes? If you said it was nothing—then it was nothing!" Katie pulled away from John and stormed up the steps into the church.

John stood for a moment, unsure if he should go after her or give her time to calm down.

In the shadows at the back of the church, John heard the rustling of grass as someone stepped into the light. It was Kyra. "You have had a lover's quarrel, no?" she purred.

"Yeah. Thanks to you," John said.

Kyra moved closer until her shoulder brushed against his arm. "It is too bad," she said, "but you cannot blame me. After all, it was innocent enough—our little walk together."

John blushed as he remembered the feelings he had when Kyra held his hand the day before. "Yeah, innocent."

"After all, you could not leave us stranded with a broken wheel, could you?" Kyra cooed. "She should have listened to you—this bride of yours." She took John's hand and pulled him toward the darkened shadows at the back of the church. "Come with me. I will listen to you. We will talk."

John took a step as yesterday's feelings came rushing to the surface. Through the open window above them John could hear the sounds of happy hobnobbing as women exchanged recipes and canning tips and the men talked of plowing and harvesting. The threesome of fiddle players sawed out their tunes in the open air behind him. A multitude of sounds mingled to create a festive mood. But a still, small voice whispered in John's ear. He planted his feet firmly.

"No!" he said. "I'm afraid I can't, Miss Kyra."

"Do not be afraid," Kyra said.

"I'm not afraid," John said, "but I can't go with you."

Kyra's eyes narrowed. Her jaw clenched. "Don't be so foolish! Do you not know that I am beautiful? I belong to you! You want me. I can see it in your eyes. Come. We are alone. Let me show you happiness!"

John shook his head and pulled his hand away. As he started to leave, Kyra ran in front of him. "No man refuses me!" she blurted out.

"Pardon me, Miss Kyra," John said as he tried to walk around her.

"No man refuses me," she said again, blocking his path and putting her hands on his chest.

John's jaw was set. He could see the fire of passion in her eyes, but his own rage began to surface. "I'm sorry, Miss Kyra, but I know what I want."

"You will regret this day," Kyra said. "My brothers will not take kindly to what I will tell them."

"What can you tell them? There is nothing between us."

"There is."

"No, there isn't. And there never will be."

"That is not what I will tell my brothers."

"Tell them whatever you like! But I'm going to marry Katie Walker!"

"You fool! I am not interested in that. Marry her! But come to me!"

John was dumbfounded. He felt like he should have an answer, but none came. He shook his head in disgust and walked away.

Inside the open window a silhouette sat back in the darkened corner of the room—listening. Katie Walker had heard enough. She ran to meet John at the front door of the church.

CHAPTER SEVEN

TWO WHITETAIL DEER, startled by a horse and rider, bounded across the road and disappeared into the dense underbrush beneath the canopy of fir trees. The morning sun was high in the sky and a gentle breeze offered a cool kiss against the summer air. A small wisp of dust drifted across the road with each step of the gray gelding that pranced proudly down the middle. The rider, confident he was closing in after nearly two years of searching and eager to complete his mission, kept his mount at a quickened pace. White foam gathered around the saddle cinch and the horse's withers. The river sent out its soothing sounds from a short distance away.

The rider, Detective Noah Miller, sat tall in the saddle beneath a bowler hat, dressed in the finest eastern attire and polished black boots. His black mustache was neatly trimmed. A nearly new cap-and-ball Colt revolver rested comfortably in the holster on his hip. Hidden beneath the lapel of his coat, a "pepperbox"—a small, Derringer-sized handgun with revolving barrels instead of a cylinder—offered double security. In the scabbard lashed to his saddle, a single-shot buffalo gun hung, stock up, within easy reach of his right hand. The left-hand saddlebag held papers, identification, a badge that verified his authority as a Pinkerton man, and an arrest warrant for murder.

Miller swung a tired and sore leg over the saddle and stepped to the ground in front of the Creek Junction Trading post. He strode onto the wooden planks of the boardwalk, stopping in front of the open doorway to arch his back against the pain from a long day in the saddle. Habit forced him to survey the street once more before he entered the store.

At the far end of the room, a slight, middle-aged man leaned on his elbows behind the counter.

"Mornin'," Ben Elam said.

Miller nodded.

"You new around here?" Ben asked.

"Just rode in," Miller said as he picked up a shovel from the barrel and pretended to look it over.

"I thought so. Don't get many dudes up here—uh, meanin' no disrespect."

"None intended, none taken," Miller said indifferently. He could see the storekeeper didn't fit the description: young men in their twenties and dark-complected. "You live alone?"

"Just me and my family," Ben said. "But they're over at the church cleaning up."

"You folks have a to-do?"

"Yep. Last night. Folks came from near twenty miles away. Some of the best cooking I've had in years! Uh—but don't say nothing to the Missus."

Miller smiled, something he rarely did. "What was the occasion?"

"Oh, no special occasion. Just neighbors getting together to have a good time."

"Have you been around here long?" Miller asked.

"Yep. Me and the missus and the three boys, of course, been here about two years."

"You know most of the people around here, then?"

"I reckon so. Most of them were here last night."

Miller set the shovel down in the barrel and picked up a grubbing hoe. "Still plenty of land around?"

"Yep. Land for the takin', if you're willin' to work it. You lookin' for some land?"

Miller studied the hoe. "Where would a fella go if he wanted seclusion?"

"You looking to hermit yourself?" Ben asked to stone silence. "Well, I reckon you could go just about anyplace around here, up river a mile or so, the other side of the river, up Walker Creek. Ain't many places you can go and not be by yourself, I figure."

Miller set the hoe back in the barrel. "Any new folks lately?"

Ben shook his head. "Not many. Most folks just pass through on their way to bigger stakes. But we manage to do a fair business."

"No one has moved in recently, then?"

"None that I can think of."

"Not, say, in the last three months?"

Ben shrugged. The man's questions were beginning to annoy him. And he had asked a bushel basket full of them without answering even one of Ben's. "You lookin' for anybody in particular?"

Miller was not yet ready to reveal his purpose. "Where could a fella find a place to stay for the night?"

Ben shrugged. "You might try the church. Reverend Walters is always ready to lend a hand. And I know he gives some of the miners that pass through a place to bed down. It's on your way out of town. You can't miss it."

"I'll do that," Miller said. "And thanks."

Out in the street, Detective Miller swung up into the saddle and reined the horse around. The simple log structure of the church stood in the middle of the clearing on the other side of the road only a stone's throw away. Two men were taking down the lanterns that surrounded the churchyard. Miller rode up to the hitching post and dismounted.

Reverend Walters pulled the glove from his right hand as he made his way across the yard. "Good morning, Friend!" he said with his hand outstretched.

Miller took his hand. "Morning."

"My name is Reverend Walters. Glad to meet you, Mr.—"

"Miller."

"Well, Mr. Miller, what brings you to Creek Junction?"

"Just passing through. I was hoping you could provide a place for me to stay for a few days."

"I think I can arrange it. How long will you be staying?"

"Two, three days maybe."

"Do you have business in Creek Junction?"

"Something like that."

"Well," said Reverend Walters, "I suppose it's your own affair. Anyhow, I never turn down a man in need of a place to stay or a decent meal. Why don't you follow me and I'll show you where you can put your things? We have a cot in the back. It's not much, but it's a place to hang your hat, so to speak."

Reverend Walters led Miller through the church between the hand-built pews to a door in the back. "Right through here," he said, motioning through the door with his hand.

Miller obliged. The room was small—barely big enough for the narrow cot and a chair that sat against the wall, but a narrow window opened up to the river a few yards away. "This'll be fine," he said.

Reverend Walters turned to leave.

"Oh," said Miller, digging into his pocket, "I can pay."

The reverend smiled. "There's a collection plate near the front. If you would like to contribute, you are very welcome to do so. But there will be no charge for the room."

After the reverend left, Miller unstrapped his gun belt and threw it on the cot. The reverend would certainly know if there were new people in the area, but he didn't know whom he could trust. He would wait, check around first, scout the area, and see what he could find out.

They were here. He was sure. His sixth sense told him so and it never lied.

Kyra felt a renewed sense of power as she sat cross-legged on the mountaintop, high above the little shack where she and her family lived. The medallion dangled from the chain held loosely between her fingers. The luster had returned.

She held it up, remembering the previous night and pondering her failure. It confused her. But she knew instinctively there was something about the church or the people who were there that had robbed her of her power. And she knew she must avoid it—and them—at all costs. The trouble was, which ones should she avoid? All of them? She didn't think so. That preacher was certainly one to avoid. But what about the others? The mother and father of that wretched girl, to be sure. She had seen them as the preacher prayed, nodding their heads in silent agreement with him. It was unsettling. And John's mother and father as well. She knew they prayed. The others were of no concern to her. They were strangers who she had no reason to think she ever would see again, nor did she have any reason to think they posed any threat to her.

But there was more. There was something about the place. She didn't know what it was, but she was sure she was right. The place itself held torment and failure for her. She felt it even before she stepped inside the circle.

Yes, the circle. She remembered the feeling she had as she stepped into it. Emptiness and loneliness, as though some power greater than her own resided there.

In her hand, the medallion again seemed to glow brightly. She knew what she must do. John would be hers. No man could resist her. No man ever had. She would wait for him at a time and place of her own choosing. Then she would spring her trap and he would be hers. She held the medallion high. Her chest swelled as her heart quickened.

"Medallion! Give me power! I call upon you! Hear me! I call upon the dark power within you! Grant me the desires of my heart!"

Above her, unseen, the presence basked in the foul stench of evil passion.

"Good morning, Mr. Miller!" Reverend Walters said from behind the meager desk in the corner of the church. "You're up bright and early today!"

Miller paused. He had hoped to leave unseen, but now…well, now was as good a time as any, he figured.

"Morning, Reverend. You're up early yourself."

"I'm afraid it's a matter of routine for me. We have church in about two hours. Will you join us for services this morning?" he asked.

"'Fraid not, Reverend. I have business to attend to."

"Certainly not on the Sabbath?"

"No rest for the wicked, as they say!" Miller chuckled, and then he cleared his throat when he realized he laughed alone.

"Well," said Reverend Walters, "God be with you."

"Thank you, Reverend. And I trust you'll have a good day." Miller started toward the door and then hesitated. "Reverend?"

Reverend Walters looked up again from his studying. "Yes, Mr. Miller?"

"You wouldn't know of any new folks around, would you? Old man and his wife, couple a young bucks, and a girl? One of them wearing a gold medallion?"

"Friends of yours?"

"No, not friends."

"I see," said Reverend Walters. "Well, I'm new here myself. But I understand that there is a family up near the Walkers. Name's, uh, 'Doucet,' I believe. They came about the same time as I did, or so I understand."

Miller nodded. "Thanks," he said.

Monday morning found Katie once again sitting at the edge of the pond near the cabin, feeding the geese bits of stale bread left over from the social two nights before. Of the whole six hundred and forty acres under Nathan Walker's care, this was her favorite place.

A peaceful breeze rustled the tall grass and sent ripples across the water. She lay back with her arms behind her head, her diary beside her on the ground. Pleasant thoughts of the night of the social filled her mind. John was so handsome in his father's good shirt. All the girls thought so. She remembered the way the muscles of his arms and chest pressed against the fabric of his shirt as he stood clapping to the music. Her cheeks flushed at the thought.

A hawk circled above her, sending down lonely cries. Katie half watched as her mind turned to other things. Two children? Three? Six, maybe? She wanted children. Enough to fill a home, and more. Sons. And daughters. A daughter would be nice. At least one. John would want sons, of course, and she would do her best to give them to him.

The house would need to be big—big enough so they could raise a family in comfort. She imagined her kitchen, a place where she could feed her brood after a long day's work. They would live a happy life. She was sure of it. John loved her. And she loved him more than anything. She couldn't imagine loving anyone else. They would work hard, and build a home and a life. And nothing, not anything, could stop them. Her life seemed so perfect now. With God's help they would live and die here in Creek Junction, she and John and their children and their children's children. The thought rested comfortably in her mind as she lay back, basking in the warm sun.

She picked up the diary, opening it to her last entry, and began to write:

> Dear Diary,
>
> Saturday was the day of the church social. It was a day of surprises. Kyra caused some mischief, which at first gave me great distress, but in the end I discovered my love to be the man I have always known him to be, even before we met. I sense in Kyra something sinister. Papa says I am imagining things and that I should pray for her. I know this to be true and I do pray, albeit a prayer of obligation rather than one of sincere motives. I fear we have not seen the last of her meddling. Still, all things considered, it was the happiest day of my life! Yet I could hope, and do hope, that a greater day is yet to come.

Veré slung the meager bundle of furs onto the counter at Ben Elam's trading post.

Ben eyed them closely. "Not bad," he said. "I reckon I can trade for twenty pounds of beans. That suit you?"

Veré grunted. Ben pulled the bundle behind the counter and then slung a burlap bag full of dried beans in its place.

"You make a good living for yourself," Veré sneered. "How can we live?"

"That's the going rate for furs these days," Ben argued. "Maybe you folks should consider farming your land."

Heavy boots echoed on the boardwalk outside. In a moment, Reverend Walters' silhouette filled the doorway.

"Ah, good morning, Reverend!" Ben called out.

"Good morning, Mr. Elam! How are you this morning?"

"Fine, Reverend, fine! A bit like molasses in January with no more sleep than I got over the weekend. But fine. What can I do for you?"

Reverend Walters nodded to Veré. "Morning, Sir."

Veré shrugged.

"Well," the Reverend said to Ben, "it seems the ladies have gotten together and, well, they've decided that the flowerbeds in front of the church need the feminine touch. They sent me over, at the behest of Mrs. Elam, to fetch a hoe and a rake. Do you have them?"

"Sure do! Right over here in the barrel. Make you a special deal on them, too!"

"Well," the reverend said, clearing his throat. "your missus, that is Mrs. Elam, suggested that we borrow them."

"Oh," Ben said with less enthusiasm and wondering to himself how he could sell a rake and a hoe as new if they had been used. Ben slowly pulled them from the barrel. "I reckon you'd better just take 'em—keep 'em for the church."

"Why, thank you, Ben. That's very generous of you. And I'm sure the Lord will bless you for it."

Ben nodded, but the only blessing he could think of that he wanted was the money for the rake and hoe. Reverend Walters turned to leave.

"Oh, Reverend?"

"Yes?"

"There was a feller in here the other day. He was lookin' for a place to hang his hat for a few days. I sent him your way. I was wonderin' if he found you."

"You mean Mr. Miller? Yes, he found me. He rode out this morning, though. I think he was looking for someone." Then, turning to Veré, he said, "I think he might be headed out your way."

Veré's eyes widened. "We are strangers here. We do not know anyone who—"

"He isn't from around here," Reverend Walters interrupted. "He looked like he was from back east by the way he was dressed. Anyhow, he said he was looking for someone new to the area. I thought he might be family, so I told him he should try your place."

"That was very...kind of you," Veré said, trying to hide his rage.

"Well," said Reverend Walters, "you might watch for him."

"Oh," said Veré, "you can be sure." With that he slung the sack of beans over his shoulder and hurried out to the rickety wagon in front of the store.

Reverend Walters and Ben watched him ride off.

Ben shook his head. "Just about the unfriendliest folks I ever did meet."

"Yes," Reverend Walters said, only half listening. The lines in his forehead deepened as he watched Veré ride away. Something troubled him about the young man—the tone in his voice, something in his eyes. Reverend Walters had learned over the years to know men. A gift from the Lord, he always thought. It was a sense that told him when a man was not all he seemed. It told him now that there was more to Veré. He wondered if he had just unwittingly endangered an innocent man.

Yves watched from the doorway of the lean-to shack as Veré pulled back hard on the reins from his perch on the rickety old wagon seat. The broken-down horse skidded to a stop, reared up, and then danced and snorted as it fought the harness. Veré jumped down in a cloud of dust.

"What is wrong with you?" Yves snapped. "Are you trying to kill the only horse we have?"

Veré waited until he was close enough to speak just above a whisper. "Have you seen anyone?"

"What do you mean?"

Veré took his brother by the arm. "Someone is here."

"What do you mean?"

"I mean, someone is here!"

Yves gritted his teeth as he looked around, fingering the knife in his belt.

"I was in town. They said there is a stranger. From back east. Asking questions."

"What kind of questions?"

"He was looking for newcomers. The good reverend sent him to see us."

Yves cursed under his breath. "We must remember to thank him," he said, still fingering the knife. "This stranger—have you seen him?"

Veré shook his head. "No, but he is nearby," he said, scanning the hillside around the shack.

"We must tell the old man of it," Yves said.

Veré nodded. "After dark, then?"

Yves nodded. "We will wait."

"Who could it be?" Veré asked.

Yves shook his head. "We cannot take chances. It was a fine houseboat. And the governor is not a forgiving man. Not to mention the loss of members of his staff. He will not rest until they are avenged."

"You think this could be a Pinkerton, then?"

Yves shrugged. "Who knows? But we will not wait for introductions. Tonight it is a full moon. We will go hunting, you and I."

High above the shack, Miller sat on a rock with the buffalo gun across his lap, watching the two men in the valley below. A half-eaten can of cold beans lay on its side next to him. There would be no fire tonight. He checked the breach of his rifle to make sure the powder was still dry. There was no real need. It was summer, and he had not crossed any streams or rivers since he had loaded it. And he hadn't seen rain since west of the Rockies. But these two, if it was them, were no fools. They were cunning and dangerous—as dangerous as any Miller had ever encountered. He wasn't about to take any chances.

The sun hung low on the jagged peaks of the western horizon. In the distance, the muted hoot of a grouse echoed between the great trees. Miller gritted his teeth. He was used to all types of men. He had cleaned the scum from some of society's darkest corners, but these two were the worst.

He was in New Orleans when news arrived of the murders. He was just leaving the office of the local constabulary where he had delivered a prisoner. A young man with a frightened look burst in and insisted the constable follow him out into the swamp—a rather unpleasant prospect. And murder in the swamp was cause for only the slightest concern. But Miller's face turned grim when he learned who had been murdered—two high-ranking members of the governor's cabinet surely would pique the interest of Mr. Pinkerton. Miller decided to save himself the trouble of a trip back to Chicago only to be ordered back to New Orleans to investigate. He had offered to ride out with the constable.

What they found surprised even him. Two men, dead for maybe ten hours or more, disemboweled, but not before they had been shot in the back of the head at close range. They appeared to be in their forties, distinguished looking—even as they lay dead on the floor of the houseboat. One of them had a faint, red ring around his neck, as though someone had forcibly removed a small chain—a necklace of some kind, or maybe a medallion. Whoever had done it had also tried to sink the houseboat by shooting holes in the hull. But it only had settled on the bottom in the shallow water.

It wasn't the murders that bothered him, or that these men had been shot from behind. Murder was Miller's business and he was used to it. What bothered him was the condition of the bodies. There was no reason to mutilate them. They obviously died instantly, before their bodies hit the floor, so why cut them up like that? Miller winced at the memory of the two men with their bellies split open, the contents strewn about the cabin floor. Whoever did it enjoyed it.

Miller shifted his weight as he craned his neck to make sure the two brothers were still in sight. He rubbed his chin. It would be dark in an hour. He had no desire to try to take them in the dark. They were cunning. Taking them would be difficult enough without the hindrance of darkness. No, the best thing to do would be to wait until it was light, and then hope that the two men would leave the shack, preferably separately, and then he could take them on neutral ground. Yes, that would be the most prudent thing to do. He had waited this long. He could wait another day.

He picked up the can of beans and began to finish it. When he was through, he unsaddled his horse, pulled his bedroll from the saddle, and settled down on the soft pine needles beneath the great trees, going over in his mind the details of his simple plan, confident that the element of surprise was still in his favor.

"What are you up to?" Kyra asked as she stood at the corner of the shack, watching her two brothers arguing in the dark over their father's old flintlock.

Veré and Yves whirled around. Veré let go of the gun. Yves stood holding it. "What is it to you?" he asked.

"It is of no concern," she said, turning to leave.

It was only then that they noticed her tears.

Veré raised his hand. "What did you want?"

"It is of no concern," she said again. "I will tend to it myself."

"Tend to what?" Yves asked.

"It is nothing—the gathering at the church—but it is nothing."

Veré and Yves looked at each other. "What of it?" Veré asked.

"It is nothing. Only, you were right. I should not have gone."

"Did something happen?" asked Yves.

Kyra shrugged. "A young man. He…I should not have gone!"

Kyra turned and ran into the shack.

Veré and Yves followed.

Kyra stood facing the wall.

"What of this young man?"

"It is nothing. He only—"

"He what?"

"He thought he could…but it is nothing," she insisted.

Veré clenched his jaw. His brother fingered the knife in his belt.

"Who is this young man?" Veré asked.

"You must forget it," said Kyra. "It was nothing."

Veré pondered for a moment. "Was it the one who rides through here? The one they call John Jakes?"

Kyra pretended to sob.

"Answer us, Sister! Was it the one who is to be married?"

Kyra did not answer. There was no need. The seed had been planted.

It was a beautiful morning and John decided to go for a ride. Yesterday was a fruitful day. He had cleared much of the land where the house would be and today he would look for foundation stones. But first, a good ride to clear his mind. He leaned forward in the saddle, holding the reins with one hand and clutching his rifle with the other as the horse mounted a steep hill.

His mind was not on hunting, though. He thought of his bride-to-be and the life they would build—and more immediate problems such as how to get the lumber for the house to the river. It would take a large team to drag the logs that far and John could not afford mules. He was sure he could count on his father for the use of his six oxen. And perhaps Nathan would allow him to use his team. But the trees on the land were large, and even a team twice that size might not be enough.

The sun was not yet visible in the east, but first light was an hour behind him. Morning dew covered the soft mat of pine and fir needles that covered the ground. John loved this time of day.

The horse crested the top of the hill, pausing for a moment before John nudged him with his heel. To his right he could see all the way to the valley below where the river disappeared around the mountain several miles away. To the north, Walker Creek flowed into it, although from here John could not see it.

The hunting was good along the creek. John knew of several places where deer and elk grazed, especially in the canyon on the opposite side of the hill from the Doucet place. There was good water almost year round, except for three or four weeks before the rainy season, according to Nathan, and it was shielded on three sides by steep hills, making it difficult for predators to make an approach, and the deer knew it. He followed the ridge north.

An hour later, John rode up to a small game trail and turned west to follow it. Below him lay a fertile valley with green grass surrounded by heavy forest. Beyond the next hill was the road that followed Walker Creek. John figured he must be close to the Doucet place.

He dismounted, leading the horse a short distance along the trail, where he could get off a good shot down into the valley below. Fresh droppings, steaming in the first rays of the morning sun, told him there was at least one deer close by. He looped the reins around a small sapling, quietly moved up the trail a few yards, and knelt down, studying the scene below him.

After several minutes and no sign of game, John mounted his horse and continued up the trail through the dense foliage until he was at the top of the ridge. The undergrowth was thick, but he could hear Walker Creek babbling in the distance far below him. Through the trees, he could make out the outline of the Doucet shack below.

Up ahead, next to the trail, he could see the smoldering remains of a fire with a blackened coffee pot sitting askew on the embers. A few feet away, a gray gelding grazed peacefully. Next to the fire, a saddle rested on its horn and a man's bedroll was spread out on the ground. John caught the faint smell of coffee.

The bedroll was empty. John dismounted a few yards out. "Hello, the camp!" John studied the land, but there was no sign of life. "Hello, the camp! Anybody here?"

John led his horse as he entered the camp. Something didn't look right now that he was close-up. The bedroll was lying as though someone had thrown it aside—an odd way for a man to leave his only source of warmth on cold nights.

And beyond, near where the horse grazed, saddlebags lay on the ground, their contents emptied and strewn about. An empty bottle of whisky sat near the fire. The grass around the fire was matted. Heel marks dug into the earth.

Must be more than one, John thought.

He made a circuit of the camp. Near the edge of the clearing that overlooked the valley below, an empty can of beans rested on the grass next to a bowler hat. John picked up the hat, absentmindedly running his hand along the brim. He looked down at his fingers. There was blood on them.

In a corner of the shack, Andre Doucet's rusted flintlock stood in its place as it always did when Andre or the boys were not using it. Next to it stood a much larger gun—a buffalo gun, clean and new, a rare prize that any man would be proud to own.

Evil, unseen eyes gloated, reveling in another victory.

CHAPTER EIGHT

"I FOUND HIM up above Walker Creek," John said to Reverend Walters as he patted the gray gelding on the flank. "All the gear was scattered around and it looked like there might have been a scuffle." John handed the reverend the bowler hat. "I found this in the brush near the campfire."

Reverend Walters noticed the spot of dried blood on the brim. "It's Mr. Miller's all right. And that's his horse."

"He one of the new folks up-river?"

The reverend shook his head. "Just a stranger. He rode in two days ago and wanted a place to stay. I let him have the room in the back of the church. But he rode out yesterday morning and never came back."

John's face darkened. "I took a good look around—down the side of the mountain, up the trail as far as I could see any tracks—all the way to Fletcher's Peak. But I didn't see anyone, and I figured I'd better not leave the horse."

"You did right, Son," the reverend said.

"Maybe he got lost and couldn't find his camp."

"It doesn't seem likely with the road in plain sight just down the side of the mountain. A fella'd have to be pretty green not to be able to find his own camp so close to the road. And Miller didn't strike me as being green."

"What should I do with the horse?"

Reverend Walters motioned toward the back of the church. "Put him up in the corral. I'll have Silas McCoy tend to him later."

"What about this Mr. Miller?"

Reverend Walters rubbed his chin. "I'll have Silas ride up-river in the morning and notify the sheriff up at Mill Creek. He may want to look into it."

"Yes, sir," John said as he turned and led the horse toward the corral.

Reverend Walters looked down at the blood stained hat, remembering the look in Veré's eyes when he'd told him of Miller's questions. Was it his imagination? Or was it that sixth sense of his that told him when a man was not what he seemed. It had bothered him all night as he had tried to sleep, wondering if Miller could be in danger. He had prayed for his safety. Now, with the blood-stained hat in his hand, he longed for some comfort, something to soothe the nagging feeling in the back of his mind that told him something dreadful had happened, and that it was too late for second guessing.

John returned from the corral. "Do you want me to go get Silas?"

Reverend Walters looked up. "Huh? Oh, no, I'll take care of it, John, thanks."

John mounted his own horse, tipped his hat to the reverend, and rode off along the river toward home. It would be late afternoon by the time he got there—too late to start working on the new house. His mother would be worried. He had left early in the morning without telling anyone. There didn't seem to be any need at the time. He had planned on being gone only a few hours.

Monty was supposed to meet him at the clearing. John hoped he had not tried to do any of the heavy work by himself. That leg of his wouldn't take much abuse just yet.

Maud Doucet lifted the pot of coffee from the fire and filled a dirty tin cup. "What mischief have you gotten yourselves into now?" she asked with tired eyes.

Yves and Veré sat across from each other at the table, bolting the last of the venison roast they held in their hands. They looked at each other in silence.

"I heard you laughing last night," Maud said after a moment, and then waited for a response. "Laughing…at the moon, maybe?"

The two men looked at each other and then down at the table.

"Last night. There was a fire," Maud pressed. "I could see it on the mountain."

"What of it?" Veré asked.

Maud shrugged. "I only wondered." She shuffled over to the rocking chair near the fire and sat down. "I thought perhaps we might have had a visitor on the mountain. But then I heard you laughing."

Yves gave his brother a wicked grin. "No visitor, Ma."

Maud sipped slowly from the cup, eyeing the big gun in the corner next to the old flintlock. "You did not come home last night. I heard you early this morning. What were the two of you up to?"

"We made a fire. Up on the mountain. We slept by the fire under the stars. We were too tired to come home."

"You were too drunk maybe!" Maud said.

Veré dismissed her with a wave of his hand.

Yves pushed away from the table and stood to leave. "So much concern!" he mocked.

The two men slipped out of the shack as Maud watched them, grim-faced.

They were wild, those two sons of hers. She had always known it. As they grew, she could see cruelty in them. When they were very young she'd seen them torture small animals caught in the traps they set near the water's edge. They had also tormented those who were smaller and weaker than themselves—or worse. She wondered what it was they were planning now.

Maud tried to shake the memory of the houseboat from her mind. It wasn't the killing so much. They deserved it, those men, after what Kyra said they had done to her. It was the way her two sons had wallowed in the grisly scene, their lust for blood that went beyond revenge, if that was indeed what drove them.

When they had come west, she had hoped that, somehow, things would change—a new life in a new land. Now she realized the futility of it. Her eyes went to the big gun standing in the corner, silently accusing.

Kyra hunched down near the edge of the creek with all her attention on the small piece of flat, rough-hewn fir she held in her hand. She held a small knife in the other, digging and gouging at the wood with the tip, her whole being focused on her wicked purpose. It was crude, but it would have to do. Still, she mused, it should be pottery, or better still, lead. She had heard stories about the old woman, and her methods for working spells. She had not seen, but she had heard. These things should be done just so, but the limits of her surroundings made it impossible. The wooden plank would have to do.

She worked diligently, carving out the letters and brushing away the chips as they fell away, pausing only once to finger the medallion as she read the inscription she had chiseled:

I bind on earth the heart of John Jakes to beat only for me. Cursed is the one who stands in my way.

She took three small pieces of cord, stolen from the trading post when no one was looking, and wrapped them around the piece of wood, tying them tightly. She held out her forefinger, puncturing the flesh with the point of the knife, and let three drops of blood fall on the board beneath the inscription.

She sat back, sucking the blood from the small wound on her finger. She read the inscription over and over silently, as though repeating it could add to its power. She threw her head back and clutched the plank to her breast. John would be hers. She would will it. The powers would obey her, she felt sure. She had done everything right. Nothing could stop her.

She carried the plank to the edge of Walker Creek a few feet from where the waters entered the S-bend. She knelt down in the soft sand and began digging with her hands. When she had finished, she placed the board in the hole and covered it over, spreading the sand carefully as she repeated over and over under her breath the words she had carved into the wood. She felt power as she lay back on the beach with her hands behind her head, confident of success.

Overhead, the presence gloated, equally confident of another victory, yet carefully considering the danger posed by the ever-present enemy.

Monty sat on the front porch of the Jakes' cabin with his eyes fixed firmly on the road.

"You waiting for John?" Jeremy asked. "How come he ain't working on the house?"

Beth sat in a rocking chair at the other end of the porch. "Isn't," she corrected.

Jeremy cringed. "Aw, Mother!"

"I won't have you talking like a hillbilly! We may not be in Pittsburgh, but that's no reason to start acting like barbarians!"

"But, Mother, John says 'ain't'!"

"Not in this house, he doesn't! Now you run along, and don't forget what I said!"

"Yes, Mother," Jeremy sighed.

Monty watched as the boy trotted off toward the open field where his brother was playing. Beth could see the Indian's troubled look as he returned to watching the road, and it reminded her of her own concerns. It was not like John to leave without saying anything. Sometimes he would go hunting in the morning, but he was always back in two or three hours—in time for breakfast.

"Let me know if you see him," she said, turning to go inside.

Monty nodded silently. The world of the whites was new and unfamiliar. He wondered if they felt or thought as he did. He remembered the night of the social, and how he watched as the girl with the black hair argued with John. The words were lost; they came too fast. But the message was clear enough. The girl was angry. John was angry, too, but it was a different anger. John was determined. But the girl—there was hate in her eyes. Monty did not trust her. She was beautiful to Indian as well as white, but her eyes menaced. Now, he felt uneasy. He was sure, though he couldn't be sure why, that there was danger for his friend.

Monty stood up, stretched, and then hobbled toward the barn. It had become a ritual of sorts, his own gauntlet, a measure of his progress, to the barn and back, first once, then twice, and now as many as four times before his leg would fatigue. As he returned to the house the second time, he could see dust on the road as a rider approached. He stood and waited. It was John.

"You gone much time," he said with concern as John dismounted.

"There was trouble. C'mon, I'll tell you about it."

John walked slowly as his friend hobbled toward the house. Beth met them at the door, drying her hands on a dishtowel. "Where have you been?"

"John have trouble," Monty said.

"What kind of trouble?"

"I was up near Fletcher's Peak above Walker Creek. I found a camp, fresh tracks and hot coals in the fire, but there was nobody there. It looked like there had been a fight. Anyhow, after I looked around and couldn't find anyone, I picked up all the gear and took it to town. Reverend Walters is sending for the sheriff up at Mill Creek. He thinks maybe something happened to him."

"Who is 'him'?" Beth asked.

"A stranger is all I know. He rode in day before yesterday and took a room at the back of the church. He rode out again yesterday morning and never came back."

"How do you know he wasn't just out hunting?"

John shook his head. "His horse was still in camp. And besides, there was some blood."

"Oh, my!" Beth said as she held her fingers to her lips.

Monty remained quiet, but his jaw tightened. The world of the whites was different. Yet one thing remained the same in any world. There were good people and there were bad. And a small voice in the back of his mind told him there was danger here for his friend. He didn't understand, but he knew he would stick to John as a young fawn sticks to its mother's side.

From outside the shack, Andre Doucet could hear his wife as she questioned his two sons. He waited for them to come out and motioned for them to follow him as he shuffled around to the back of the shack. "Did you take care of the little matter?"

Veré reached inside his shirt, pulled the pepperbox from his waistband, and then shoved it back again.

"What did you find out?" Andre asked.

"Show him," Veré said to his brother. Yves reached into his rear pocket and produced a folded piece of paper. He opened it and handed it to the old man.

Andre's face fell. "So, a Pinkerton."

Yves grinned. "And that is not all. Come." He led the way to the cold storage dug into the hillside behind the shack and went inside. A moment later, he returned, holding a Colt revolver. "It is magnificent, no?"

"You fool! You cannot keep it! If they find it—"

Yves held the gun tightly in his two hands. "They will not find it! And what if they do? Who is to say that it does not belong to me? There are no markings. I will say it was a gift from a friend before we arrived!"

Andre scowled. "You are young and careless. You will send us all to the gallows with your carelessness." He shook his head and motioned toward the mountain. "What have you done with him?"

"No one will find him," Veré said. "We buried him deep."

"And what of his horse?"

"We are not fools," Veré grumbled.

Andre nodded. "Good. Then I suggest you dispose of that piece of paper. And if you value your lives, you will get rid of those guns as well."

"They are fine guns," said Yves. "I do not think I will part with this one so easily."

Veré held his hand over the bulge in his waistband. "We will be careful, Father."

"I see," Andre sighed.

"And besides," Yves nearly whispered. "We may have need of them."

Veré scowled at his brother.

"What does he mean?" Andre asked.

"He is a fool," Veré said, giving his brother a hard stare.

"And you are the fool if you think—" Yves began.

"Shut up!" Veré commanded.

"What does he mean?" Andre asked again.

"It seems there is another who would compromise our sister."

"What do you care about your sister?" Andre demanded. "You care only for yourselves!"

"Yves shrugged. "Would you have your only daughter compromised? Do you not care for her good name?"

Andre grunted. "What do you care about a good name?"

"You pick a fine time to question motives," Yves said. "Perhaps you recall another time? You were willing enough then to have us defend her name!"

Andre clenched his jaw.

Yves laughed. "Do not worry. We will do nothing to jeopardize your high standing in the community," his voice mocked. "Besides, we have other plans."

"What other plans?"

"Nothing you need trouble yourself with."

"You will do nothing to harm this young man!"

Veré laughed. "For a time. And there are many ways to harm a man. It seems my brother's thoughts have turned to love."

Andre gave them a quizzical look.

Veré and Yves laughed again. "Do you not remember what it is to want a pretty girl?"

Andre turned grim. "No!"

Andre's two sons laughed as they walked away, leaving him alone and frightened.

Katie sat at the edge of the pond with her diary in her lap, praying:

> "Dear heavenly Father, I know thy great love. I know that I'm a sinner before thee. I thank thee for thy many blessings, which I cannot number. Forgive me for my selfish and trivial doubts. Father in heaven, protect John. I love him as surely as I know that you love him. Please, dear heavenly Father, keep him from the adversary's grasp."

When she finished, she opened the diary and began to write. She felt ashamed of the distrust she had shown John, letting irrational female feelings take control, if only for a brief moment. But faced with the truth about Kyra and her evil intentions, Katie worried.

What had Kyra said? "No man refuses me!" There was a certainty in her voice when she said it; and there was more. Something else she said made the hair on the back of Katie's neck bristle. She was sure it was not an idle threat. She could hear the wicked determination in Kyra's voice as she played it back in her mind.

Kyra's voice had lowered to little more than a whisper. "You will live to regret it!" she had said. And Katie believed her.

> Dear Diary,
>
> The day quickly approaches when I shall become Mrs. John Jakes. With God's help, I know we shall be very happy. Yet, I could wish that circumstances were somewhat different. Though I have every confidence in my intended, I am sure that Kyra plans more mischief. I can only hope that it is childish mischief and nothing more. Still, I have a strange foreboding, and I fear that she may cause us some distress… .

"Katie!" Ruth called out from the house.

Katie closed her diary. "Yes, Mama!" she said as she stood and walked toward the cabin. The shadows of the trees were long as the sun nestled on the western ridge.

"What is it, Mama?"

"Your father wants to ride down to the Eerdmans' to look at their new bull calf."

Nathan appeared around the corner leading the team that was hitched to the wagon. "We won't be long."

"It'll be dark soon," Katie said.

"We should be back before then," Ruth said as she climbed into the wagon. "There are some corn muffins on the table and some fresh milk. Stay close to the house. Oh, and don't forget to feed the chickens."

Nathan slapped the reins.

"Yes, Mama," she said as the wagon lurched forward. She watched as it disappeared over the rise, wondering how many more times she would see it before she left home for good.

A rabbit scampered across the road behind the wagon. Long shadows shimmered on the waters of the pond as a gentle breeze sent ripples across the surface. The majestic mountains were still. It was a good place. Katie let it all filter through her mind as she surveyed the scene. For two years it had been home. Funny how she never really appreciated it before, but now, with the certainty of leaving, it somehow seemed closer to her heart.

She ambled toward the pond, taking in the beauty that surrounded her. The afternoon air felt cool on her cheeks as the breeze rippled through the trees. A fish broke the surface of the pond in search of an insect for supper, sending circles of rings toward the shore. Katie started to sit down, but then, remembering the chickens, hurried across the clearing past the house.

The hen house stood a few yards from Walker Creek. Beyond it was the barn her father had built their first summer. Chickens clucked and scratched around the crude, log corral, and a few were perched along the top rail of the fence. A few more scratched the ground in and around the barn.

Katie went to the wooden barrel filled with chicken feed that sat just inside the barn door. As she lifted the lid, chickens fluttered behind her. She turned. The old cow chomped quietly on the hay Papa left in the manger only a few minutes before. Old Joe, Nathan's saddle horse, was in the stall at the rear of the barn, nervously pawing at the ground.

"What's the matter, boy?"

Joe skittishly danced to one side. Katie could feel her heart beating faster. "Is someone there?"

A young barn cat sprang to the top rail of Joe's stall. Startled, Joe tossed his head.

"Oh! You silly cat!" she said with her hand over her heart. She started to turn back to the barrel when she heard chickens fluttering and clucking in the tack room next to Joe's stall.

"You cats leave those chickens alone!" she said, storming toward the doorway that led to the tack room. But as she approached, the dark figure of Veré Doucet left the shadows and stood in the open doorway. Katie froze.

Veré grinned.

"What are you doing here?" she said, trying not to sound frightened.

Veré continued to smile. Katie heard a noise behind her, but she was afraid to look.

"My brother and I decided to pay you a call," Veré said. Katie could sense someone standing behind her. She made a move toward the door. "I think you'd better leave!"

Knife in hand, Veré leaned against the doorjamb, blocking her path. "My sister does not like you very much," he said.

Katie could hear footsteps behind her. "I said, I think you'd better leave or Papa—"

Veré's grin broadened as he shook his head. "Your papa left with the wagon. We saw him. No, I think we are quite alone, the three of us."

Katie stepped back against the muscular form of Yves. He rested a firm hand on her shoulder and laughed. Veré stepped closer. "Our sister does not like you very much. She thinks you are very bad. Is that not so?"

"As you say," said Yves.

"But we do not think you are bad," Veré continued. "We think you are, how you say, very nice. And so, we thought we would come see you."

Katie's temper flared. "You came to steal chickens most likely!"

Veré laughed. "We take a few home with us maybe, no? But not for a little while, I think." He took another step closer.

Katie turned, struggling to free herself from Yves's grip, but he held both her arms from behind. She screamed.

"There is no one to hear you." Veré laughed.

Katie's heart pounded. Her mind raced. Her eyes darted from side to side as she tried desperately to think of a way out. "Dear Lord, help me!" she called.

"He cannot help you," Yves taunted. "There is only Veré and me. Come," he said as he grabbed her wrist, "we will help you."

"Yes," Veré cackled, "we will help you! We are handsome men, no? Much better, I think, than this little boy you are to marry."

"What do you intend to do with me?" she said. Her voice quivered.

The two men looked at each other and began to laugh. "Come into the hay. We will show you."

Katie frantically searched the room for a weapon—any weapon. There was a pitchfork, but it was behind Veré near the doorway. She lunged for it, but Veré held her tight. His eyes flared with lust—and rage. It was the look of an animal—preditor instinct brought to life by the helpless flutter of wings, animal passions aroused by the scent of easy prey. Katie tried to think.

Yves pushed her toward the door that led to the hay room. Veré took a step backward and tripped over the pitchfork. He stumbled and then fell backward. Katie raised her foot and brought the heel of her shoe down on the toe of Yves's moccasin. He let out a yell as he danced on one leg.

Katie pushed him, but he fell toward the door, blocking her escape. She turned and ran toward Joe's stall, throwing open the gate. It crashed against the side of the barn and swung closed behind her.

Yves followed her with Veré close behind as they threw open the gate and chased her into the stall. Joe sidestepped and reared. Katie ran behind him, but Yves grabbed Joe's halter and pushed him to one side.

Katie faced him. For a moment they stood, neither of them moving.

Veré stood in the doorway. "Go on! Take her!"

Katie was pale. She could not move her legs. She stood, trembling and frightened. The only movement was the quivering of her lips as she silently prayed, "Help me, dear Lord! Help me!"

Yves took a step closer. As he did, Katie could feel her knees buckle under her as the room went black. Yves reached out to catch her, but as he did, Joe, still skittish, whirled around, knocking Veré out of the stall, where he fell against the barn wall.

Yves turned, still holding Katie as she slumped unconscious to the floor. Joe sidestepped again, reared, and then whirled around. Yves's attention was on the girl. She was beautiful. He had known for months that he wanted her, and now she was within reach—to take, to have, if only for a short time. But the close quarters of the stall and the nervous snorting of the horse caused him to divert his attention for a split second as he spun around to face the animal. The last thing he saw was Joe's massive hoof as it smashed into his face. He fell, dead before he hit the floor.

Veré, still slumped against the side of the barn, shook his head. The impact against the wall had dazed him, but a moment later he pulled himself to his feet. In the stall, Katie lay still. He could see her chest rise and fall in steady rhythm. Next to her lay the lifeless body of his brother. But his eyes went immediately to a point beyond them both, beyond the horse that stood, still frightened and pawing the ground, in the corner. His face turned white as he ran in terror from the barn.

In the stall, invisible to all but a select few mortals, a golden shield, clear as crystal, guarded the young girl, protecting her on all sides, as a magnificent, golden sword disappeared into its sheath.

CHAPTER NINE

BEN ELAM, THE unofficial town doctor because of his experience with horses, leaned over the bed in the new room Nathan Walker had built for his daughter. "How're you feelin', young lady?"

"I'm fine, I think. Just a little weak," Katie said as she held her hand to her forehead.

"Well, you just let Ben have a look at you," Nathan said.

"How did I get here?"

"Your mother found you in the barn," Nathan said. "I carried you into the house."

"How long was I out?"

"Not long," Ruth said.

"What about Yves?"

Nathan was grim. "Don't you worry about it, Katie. You just lie back and take it easy until Ben has a look at you."

"They came into the barn," Katie said, fighting the tears. "They tried to—"

"They?" Ben asked.

"Yves and his brother. They—" Katie bit down on her lip.

"It's all right, Honey," Ruth said softly.

Ben poked and prodded. "Does that hurt?"

Katie shook her head.

"How about that?"

"Uh-uh. I feel fine. Just a little weak."

"Well, you don't have no broken bones—near as I can tell."

"Did they…did they hurt you?" Nathan asked.

Katie shook her head. "They grabbed me. I ran into Joe's stall, but then I suppose I fainted."

Ben nodded. "Yep. That's what she did awright. She just fainted, pure an' simple."

"Thank God!" said Ruth.

"I reckon I'd hang on to a horse like that," Ben said. "Looks to me like he saved your life."

Ruth drew a deep breath. "The hand of God saved her—one of his heavenly angels."

Ben chuckled. "I never figured no angel to look like no horse. But I reckon the Lord does work in strange ways."

Ruth stroked her daughter's forehead.

"You just rest easy," said Ben as he stood. "You get a good night's sleep, an' you'll be fine in the mornin'."

Nathan motioned for Ben to follow him into the other room as Ruth blew out the lamp and followed them.

"I'll get a couple of men to come back in the morning to pick up the body," Ben said, digging into his shirt pocket for the pouch of tobacco. "Looks like we'll have our first burial in Creek Junction before we have our first wedding."

"What about Veré?"

"I don't rightly know. Reverend Walters sent word for the sheriff up at Mill Creek this mornin' on account o' that other feller that lost his horse. Anyhow, we oughta let him handle it."

Nathan's eyes were dark. "I'd feel better if he wasn't running around loose."

"Well, I reckon we could get a few of the boys together. 'Cept I doubt if he'll hang around. He's probably halfway back to wherever it is he come from by now. Best let the sheriff handle it."

Nathan clenched his jaw. "I knew they were a strange bunch, but I never figured them to be dangerous." He struck the log wall with the side of his fist. "I never should have left her alone!"

"You cain't never tell about folks. I knew a feller back in Missouri. Why, he'd charm the whiskers off a bobcat. Everybody figured as how he'd end up as mayor or preacher or somethin'. Then one day he up an' shot a man over a two-dollar bet. Anyhow, I wouldn't pay it no mind, Nathan. He's likely long gone by now."

"With God's help," Nathan almost whispered.

"Yeah, well, I'd keep that old flintlock close by just the same."

Nathan watched as Ben rode away, and then went back into the house. He stuck his head in the door of Katie's room.

"Good night, Papa," she said from her bed.

"Good night," he said as he shut the door to the new room.

Nathan was a hard man, a tough man with a hard head and a habit of charging through, especially when he knew he was right. He was no stranger to fighting. He had a deep scar under his right arm, the only medal of valor issued for a skirmish with the Indians along the banks of the Ohio many years before. There was a gap between two of his back teeth where a man had knocked one of them out in a drunken brawl when he was young. He was a fighter. He was born a fighter and fully expected to die a fighter.

But something happened to him on the day Katie was born. Something unexpected, at least by him—something he was not looking for and had even resisted most of his life. There was no bright light, no peel of thunder, no sounding of trumpets—only a sense of the wonder of life and his own inadequacy to live up to the great responsibility to the little bundle in his arms.

There was something else. He knew he could not approach a holy God. He didn't know how he knew, he just knew. And suddenly it mattered. It never had before, but suddenly it mattered a great deal. Something told him there was no way to bridge the great gulf between them—he and God. He knew about Jesus, Ruth made sure of that, but he always had felt that religion was for women and children—or the weak—but not for him. But on that day somehow he could see for the first time the mighty hand of God reaching out to him. And he knew it was Jesus. From that day on, Nathan did his fighting on his knees.

Nathan Walker fell to his knees by the bed and, with his wife at his side, began to pray.

John raced down the road a short distance from the Walker place early in the morning, goading the horse for more speed. Monty followed at a distance, but the old plow horse was no match for Quinlan Jakes's spirited Morgan stallion. They had been on their way to the Walker place. John was eager to tell his bride of the progress on the new house, but as they rode through town they met Ben Elam out in front of the trading post as he opened for business early in the morning. Ben told them the news about Veré and Yves's attack the night before.

John pulled back hard on the reins as the horse skidded to a stop in front of the Walker cabin, sending a cloud of dust across the yard. John dashed onto the front porch and through the door. Ruth and Katie sat at the kitchen table sipping tea.

"Oh, John Jakes! Didn't your folks teach you to knock?" Ruth scolded. "You gave me such a start!"

"Are you all right?" John said as he knelt down next to Katie. "Did they—?"

"I'm fine."

John pulled a chair close and sat down. "Ben said one of them was killed."

"Yes," Ruth said. "Yves. Joe kicked him. It was horrible."

"What about the other one?"

Ruth shook her head. "Nathan and a few of the neighbors went down to their place this morning, but there was no sign of him. His folks weren't much help, and Kyra threatened to kill anyone who went snooping around."

"Did they look?"

"Oh, yes, over the Doucets' protest. They searched the cabin and looked around. But he wasn't there."

John's jaw tightened as he searched Katie's face. "Are you sure you're all right?"

"I'm fine," she said, caressing his face with her hand. "Thanks to Joe."

"Thank the Lord," said John. "Thank the Lord."

The planks of the front porch echoed with the sound of footsteps. Nathan ducked low through the doorframe and came in. He was solemn. "Morning, John."

Ruth's eyes were expectant. "Did you find anything?"

Nathan shook his head. "Nothing. Hance Eerdman and I combed the whole western slope. There was no sign of anyone. And all the Doucets' stock is still behind the house, such as it is. If he lit out, he did it on foot."

"Are you going to keep looking?" John asked.

Nathan shrugged. "We'll keep our eyes peeled. My guess is, he's still around, but it's a big country."

John gritted his teeth as he stood. "Well, I'm gonna do more than that."

Katie held his arm. "No, don't!"

"I'm not going to let him run around free. I don't want to keep looking over my shoulder, wondering where he is and whether or not he's carrying a grudge for his brother!"

"Don't go running off half-cocked," said Nathan. "You let the rest of us handle it. We've sent for the sheriff up at Mill Creek. And the whole town has been warned about what happened. Right now the best thing we can do is stick together and keep our eyes open. But if you go running around these woods by yourself, you could get hurt."

"I can take care of myself."

"That may be, but he's dangerous. And there's no reason to think he'd fight fair. So you just calm down. I don't want my daughter to end up a widow before she's even married."

Monty stood on the porch just outside the door. "You listen, John. Mr. Nathan say right. Is good to fight like fox, not like bear."

John was uneasy. "What if he comes back?"

"It'd be the best thing for us," Nathan assured. "We'll be ready for him. But we'd better stick together and not go running around these woods with a bur under our saddle. So you just take it easy."

John shook his head. "I still don't like it."

"You're no different than the rest of us," Nathan said, "but you gotta use your head. And right now the best thing we can do is wait."

Monty slipped away quietly. John was angry, and Monty knew men don't make good decisions when they are angry. Quinlan Jakes's horse stood near the back of the house, grazing peacefully on a clump of green grass. Monty took the reins in his hand and led the animal away. When he was a few hundred feet from the house, he loosened the cinch and dropped the saddle to the ground. He hated stealing his friend's horse, but John surely would try to do something on his own. This was the best way to stop him—or slow him down.

Monty rubbed his sore leg and then hoisted himself onto the back of the horse. This was no job for a white. It was a job for an Indian, someone born to tracking, someone who had been raised to track as a way of life, someone who knew the savage ways of the wilderness—someone who could fight on savage terms.

He prodded the animal with his heel and started up the mountain. His only weapon was the knife in his belt. He would need better. The place where his tribe had fought, the place where he was wounded, was only a few miles away—an easy ride. Perhaps his bow still lay where he dropped it. It was worth a look. Then he could deal with this man who had threatened his new friends.

John plodded along the road toward home on the back of the old plow horse, wondering how he was going to explain to his father that his prize Morgan stallion was gone—and so was the Indian.

Quin was never sold on the idea of having the Indian in the house. "He's a savage," he had said. "He'll steal us blind the first chance he gets."

John could only imagine what he would say about the horse. It was gone and so was Monty, but why? One minute he was there, and the next he was gone! John tried to remember if he had said anything—anything at all that may have made his friend angry, or feel unwelcome. But there was nothing. They were talking—just talking. The last thing Monty had said—what was it? "Fight like a fox, not a bear." Yeah, that was it.

But why would he leave, unless—

John prodded the horse with his heel as a sense of urgency entered his mind. Had Monty gone off to find Veré himself? He hoped not. Veré was a dangerous man. Everyone in town knew he was mean. Monty was right. A fox is cunning. But a fox is no match for a bear, especially one that likes to hurt living things.

Maud stood grim-faced, near the entrance to the shack as Silas McCoy and Hance Eerdman carefully lifted Yves's tarp-draped body from the wagon and carried it inside. Andre leaned against the corner, watching. Reverend Walters stood by, solemn and white. He tried to put his hand on Maud's shoulder, but she pushed him away. "Wouldn't you rather have him buried in the cemetery?"

Maud looked at him and sneered. "We tend our own," she said.

"It's up to you, of course. It's just that, well, I hate to see—"

"We have no need, nor want, of your pious words, Preacher. You and your self-righteous kind."

"Ain't no call for that, ma'am," Hance said. "It ain't the preacher that done-in your boy. Fact is, it was an accident, pure and simple."

Maud's eyes flashed. "It was no accident."

"I don't know what else you'd call it," Hance said as he shoved his big hands in his pockets. "It ain't nothin' but an accident when a man gets hisself kicked by a horse. An' anyhow, it wouldn't a happened no how if your boy wasn't up to no good."

"Hance!" Reverend Walters exclaimed, and then turned to Maud. "I'm sorry about your boy, ma'am. I truly am." He turned to leave. "C'mon, Hance. We'd better go."

Hance shuffled off toward the wagon.

Silas followed. Reverend Walters took the reins and held the team for a moment. "If you change your mind, ma'am, I'd be happy to help with the burying."

"Humph!" she said and then stormed into the shack.

Reverend Walters flicked the reins, and the wagon lurched forward. Andre leaned against the side of the shack. He looked tired, the reverend thought, but there was coldness in his eyes. It was not the coldness of grief, the kind of detachment that allows for some small comfort in times of great sadness and gives the heart time to heal. It was the coldness of hatred turned inward, a hate that burns, eating at a man until it is the only thing that is left.

Reverend Walters lifted a silent prayer heavenward. His heart did its own kind of burning. He ached for men like Andre Doucet. The answer was so simple, and yet few ever conquered the demon of bitterness once it found a foothold. He had seen it before in other men. His own father had let failure turn him from a loving and kind man into a vengeful and unhappy one. The reverend, then still a small boy, watched how his father was unable to understand and less able to do anything about it. As the reverend grew and the message of Christ's love invaded his life, he vowed to be a beacon to others as best he was able. But some men, most it seemed, would never see, clinging to their bitterness and nurturing it as though somehow in their bitterness lay their hope.

"She had no call," Hance said after a while.

Reverend Walters thought for a moment. "Grief never appeals to the mind, Mr. Eerdman, only to the heart."

The three of them, Silas, Hance, and the Reverend Walters, sat in silence the rest of the way into town.

From inside the shack, Kyra could hear every word as the two men from town delivered her brother's body. She stood in the corner, silently watching as they set him down on the cold dirt floor and then left the way they came. Neither of them seemed to notice her.

She fingered the medallion. There was no love lost at the sight of the morbid bundle in front of her on the floor. There was never anything resembling love between her and her two brothers. Yet there was a passion.

She looked down at the small bit of gold in her hands. Yes, there was a passion, a link between her and the rest of her family, a bond, though not one of love. A kinship, a common goal of survival—survival against the conventions of the outside world. And of justice. Not the justice of moral interest or duty at least, but a perversion of justice that demands not payment or restitution, but revenge. And revenge was her passion.

That Walker girl. She had done this. She was the one standing in the way. And now Katie had caused the death of Kyra's brother as surely as if Katie had struck the blow herself! Kyra held the medallion high. Her chest swelled. She could taste the lust for vengeance. Katie Walker must pay!

"She will pay! By the power of the medallion, I swear! She will pay!"

As soon as it was dark, Veré stole quietly across the clearing and into the shack. He sat down on the floor next to the fire and rubbed his sore side, where he had fallen against the side of the barn. There was at least one broken rib, he was sure, but otherwise he was fit enough to make the journey over the mountains. But he would need a horse.

"No!" Andre said firmly. "You will not take our only link to prosperity. No!"

"It is my only link to freedom!" Veré shouted. "I cannot make the journey over the mountains on foot!"

"If you had not been a fool, you would not need to make the journey at all," Maud said.

Veré clenched his jaw. Her words cut deep. About the only thing he had that he could call his own was his pride, and it had been stomped into the earth by a mere girl. Now he must leave his home and the only source of comfort and convenience he knew. Not that they could lay anything of consequence at his feet. The girl was unharmed. The only harm to anyone was to Yves. It would be easy enough to say that they intended her no harm, that it was all in fun, and that Yves's death was an unfortunate accident.

But what about the Pinkerton? Could others be far behind? He was sure there would be others. He couldn't risk the attention that this latest incident would bring. He must leave. But first, there was the matter of revenge.

"Take the Colt revolver," Andre said. "You have paid a high enough price for it. Take your brother's gun." He tossed the pepperbox across the table toward Veré. "Take as much food as you can carry. Only leave the horse and go!"

Veré's eyes went to the corner, where the old flintlock stood. "Where is the buffalo gun?"

"It is hidden," Maud said, "where it will stay!"

Veré was furious. "I want it! Give it to me!"

Maud shook her head. "Leave it! It is payment enough for the trouble you have brought down on us!"

Veré took a step forward. "I will have it!"

Andre stood between his son and his wife. "Go! You must go! There is no other way! Go now!"

Veré stood in silence, but his eyes narrowed. He took the pepperbox and stuffed it into his waistband, then picked up the sack stuffed with jerky, beans, and bread and tossed it over his shoulder. "I will go," he growled, "but first, a small matter to attend to." He turned and disappeared through the deerskin flap and was gone.

Monty kept watchful, Indian eyes on the Doucet cabin from the highest point on the ridge overlooking the peaceful valley. The only thing to break the silence of the warm summer night was the soothing sound of Walker Creek. It had been dark for more than an hour when Monty settled in next to a yew-wood tree. Now, he waited.

After he had left the Walker place, it had taken only an hour, thanks to the speed of Quinlan Jakes's stallion, to find the battlefield where he and his friends were ambushed by the enemy tribe a few months earlier. The braves who had chased him must have returned to pilfer what they could because the weapons his fellow warriors had dropped were gone.

A few scattered bones and bits of clothing were all that remained. He couldn't remember where he had dropped his own bow—somewhere between the place where his friends fell and the tree by the stream where he had hidden was all he knew for certain.

He had backtracked slowly along the path he had taken months before, hoping the braves had somehow missed it. He breathed a sigh of relief when he found the bow lying on the ground just above the bank where he had fallen into the stream.

The horse's swiftness brought him back to the ridge above the Doucet shack in less than an hour.

Below him in the clearing, all was strangely and darkly quiet. No one entered or left the cabin. Smoke drifted from the hole in the roof that provided a vent for the fire ring inside.

Suddenly, light assaulted the night as the deerskin flap that covered the cabin's doorway flew back. Veré stormed out.

Monty watched as Veré crept away from the cabin, cowered down next to the road for a moment as if weighing his options, and then sprinted across the clearing and entered the trees directly below him.

His Indian eyes searched the darkness. He wasn't sure what he should do. It was never good for an Indian to kill a white, but his mind was set about one thing: he would not let Veré harm his friends.

A game trail along the top of the ridge a few feet away from where Monty knelt granted ease of travel to hunter and hunted alike, and it was a good place to move through the valley without being seen. Monty expected Veré to climb the slope to the ridge and use the trail, no matter which way he decided to go.

The woods were still. Monty strained to hear the slightest sound. After several minutes had passed, he grew restless. Veré should have passed through here by now.

He waited a few minutes longer, listening. He began to worry. There were only a couple of directions Veré could have gone. South would have taken him toward town, a foolish venture, and Monty was sure Veré was no fool. If he planned to go north, the best route for someone with Veré's troubles would be the security and seclusion of the trail. And besides, Monty had seen him enter the trees.

Monty had a bad feeling in the pit of his stomach. Surely Veré wouldn't try something as stupid as going back to the Walker place? That prospect was his only reason for being here. Yet he had hoped Veré would exercise better judgment. After a few more minutes, he decided it was time to move. He slipped quietly onto the back of the horse and headed up the trail to the north.

The trail followed the ridge above Walker Creek for several miles before it turned east. It was only a small game trail, but it was well worn. Some of the settlers used it as a hunting trail, and his own people used it from time to time for the same reason. Monty kicked the horse in the flank with his heel.

It was a dark night with no moon and the going was slow, but early morning found him above the Walker place. He dismounted quickly, slung his quiver over his shoulder, and with his bow in hand he began working his way down the mountainside toward the clearing. At the timberline, he paused, watching Nathan Walker's cabin. It was quiet and still. Calling upon all the cunning of his ancestors, his eyes scoured the mountainside for any sign of movement along the ground. Something told him he was right; Veré was here. He crouched low under a fir tree and waited.

Several hours went by with no sign of Veré. The dim light of dawn soon pushed darkness aside in favor of the new day. There was no sign of life in the clearing, but smoke drifted skyward from the Walker chimney. The pond's water shimmered in the sun's first rays. Monty searched the clearing and the surrounding trees again. The sounds of birds chirping in the distance echoed across the clearing, and a hawk screeched out its lonely cry above the mountaintop behind him. It was peaceful. He began to hope that his fears about Veré were wrong.

At the far end of the clearing behind the house, he could hear a man's faint voice. He followed the sound. Nathan was prodding the milk cow into the barn for her morning milking. He must have left the cabin through the rear door because Monty hadn't seen him until now. Monty watched as Nathan disappeared behind the corral. He turned his attention back to the trees along the edge of the clearing.

Minutes crept by. The milk cow appeared around the barn by the corral, followed by Nathan, who carried a pail of milk.

The front door of the cabin opened. Katie appeared, her apron bundled in front of her with day-old bread. She crossed the clearing to the pond. It seemed peaceful enough. Yet Monty could not shake the feeling that Veré was here.

Veré could have gone the other way. John's ranch was down river a few miles, but Veré would have had to go through town to get there. Last night Monty was sure Veré wouldn't chance it. After all, he had no quarrel with John.

But he kept remembering John's argument with Kyra. And John told him how she had threatened him.

No, the risk would be too great. If vengeance was on his mind, Monty was sure he'd seek it here. Men like Veré were cowards. And cowards only act when they are certain that the odds are heavily in their favor. Monty began to hope that Veré had simply disappeared into the mountains, and they would never see him again.

Katie stood at the water's edge, throwing bits of bread to the geese that waddled along the shore. Monty scanned the mountains to the south. A young doe grazed peacefully along the edge of the clearing—a good sign that all was well. He turned his attention back to the trees to the north.

His heart sank. About two hundred feet down, a few feet in from the clearing under a Madrone tree and only a stone's throw from the pond, the glint of steel caught his eye. He sat forward, straining to see, and then rose to his feet. Nathan had been clearing trees near where he saw the glint. Perhaps it was a shovel or a pick resting against a tree or stump.

There it was again!

He moved swiftly down the mountainside, making no sound. It couldn't be Veré. If it was, he had passed unseen in front of where Monty was hiding. He refused to believe that a white man could manage such a feat. He silently castigated himself for letting it happen as he ran, ignoring the pain in his leg.

Every few seconds, he could see the flash. It was no shovel. It moved. He raced along the ground, dodging the heavy brush. He pulled an arrow from his quiver, placing it against the bowstring as he ran. Now he could make out the form of a man kneeling down. In his hand, he held a revolver pointed at Katie.

Monty raced. His feet pounded the earth as he searched his heart for every bit of strength and speed he could find. He saw the man pull back the gun's hammer. It was Veré.

Monty dropped to his knees and raised his bow. He drew back and fired in an instant. The arrow hissed as it cut the air. Monty held his breath as Veré turned to face him and then swung his gun hand around to fire. But the arrow caught his wrist, piercing it through. Veré screamed out in pain, dropping the gun. Monty reached for another arrow, but as he drew back, Veré disappeared into the underbrush.

Monty, his bow set, froze as he scanned for any movement. He could see the revolver lying on the ground next to the tree. Confident that Veré was unarmed, he let the bow go slack. Cautiously, on cat's feet, he moved to the spot where Veré had crouched down. He bent down, eyes on the place where Veré had disappeared, and picked up the gun, tucking it into his belt.

A trail of blood led off into the woods. Monty followed it, but it soon became apparent Veré was circling around to the right. With animal cunning, the hunter had become the hunted, and Monty knew it. But it was too late. He heard the click as Veré pulled back the hammer of Miller's pepperbox. Monty whirled recklessly, drew back his bow, and let the arrow fly. It sailed past Veré.

Monty stood facing him.

Veré grinned, aimed the pepperbox at Monty's heart, and squeezed back on the trigger. The hammer came forward.

Monty held his breath.

He could hear the sounds around him, more vivid and distinct than he had ever noticed before. The breeze as it rustled the boughs of the trees. The chickens clucking down by the barn. The sound of his own feet against the soft pine needles that covered the ground. He braced himself for the expected roar of the gun and the blow that was surely to come. The hammer came down and struck its flint against the lock of the gun. Monty heard it click. No shot!

His eyes met the frightened and confused look in Veré's eyes as they stood facing each other for a brief moment of indecision. Veré looked at the gun and then at Monty. He cocked it again, but Monty took full advantage of the reprieve and hit Veré at the waist with all his might. Both men fell to the ground. The gun bounced a few feet away.

Veré struck the Indian with his fist, knocking him down. Veré jumped to his feet and started to run, but Monty caught his foot, tripping him. Veré whirled and kicked. Monty caught a blow in the face and fell back, dazed. When he regained his senses, Veré had disappeared again. The pepperbox lay on the ground where Veré had dropped it. Monty picked it up and carried it with him.

He took his time getting back to the horse. Veré's tracks would be easy to follow. He was wounded and frightened, and Monty wanted time to collect himself and let the wound in Veré's wrist fester. Soon it would begin to throb; he would get careless. Monty took his time.

He climbed onto the horse and trotted down the trail to where he had last seen Veré's tracks. They headed east. Monty followed.

Hours later, as the sun set low, Monty crested a high ridge overlooking a small valley never seen by the white man's eyes. His eyes searched the land below. There was a clearing with scattered trees. To the right, a rocky formation jutted part way into the clearing. Monty knew from hunting trips with his father that there was a small cave at the far end of it. Veré's trail led there.

He circled around the clearing, staying well within the seclusion of the trees until he was a few hundred feet away from the rocky formation. He dismounted, looped the reins over a tree limb, and moved quietly along as he placed an arrow on his bowstring.

Monty knelt a few feet from the mouth of the cave, still not visible because of the dense undergrowth. The ground was soft. He could see where someone had stepped, leaving a shallow depression. Monty raised the bow, cautiously watching the brush near the opening. Veré was here, and he wished he knew if he was armed. He hoped he had no gun, but after his encounter this morning, he knew better than to assume it. He would prefer to take him alive. He had no desire to be the first one of his tribe to kill a white man. But if Veré did have a gun—.

His ears perked at a slight noise. Monty's mind raced to pinpoint its origin, but before he could react, he was hit from the side. He felt the blow as a sharp pain ripped through him. He sprawled to the ground.

A large, dark hand picked him up by the hair. Monty lashed out wildly with his fist, catching the man under the arm. Veré brought his knee up savagely, but Monty turned, deflecting the blow, and then swung with his full force, striking the man under the chin. Veré fell back, but was on his feet again in an instant. For a brief moment, Monty faced him. In his hand Veré held a bloody knife. Monty glanced down at his side. Blood soaked his shirt.

Veré lunged, taking full advantage of surprise and the Indian's weakened condition. Monty pulled his own knife from his belt but then dodged to one side and fell. When he struggled to his feet, Veré lunged again but Monty hit him low in the knees with his shoulder and rolled, coming to his feet, where he turned to face his opponent. Veré paused for a moment and grinned. Then he began to laugh. There was a dead snag lying on the ground next to him. He reached out and broke off a large branch, raising it over his head like a club. Monty planted his feet, glancing from side to side and looking for a way out. He was trapped between the rocky formation next to the cave and the steep cliff on the other side.

Veré took a step closer. Then another and another. Monty stepped back until his back was against the rocks of the formation. Veré's sinister grin broadened. He swung the branch, but Monty ducked. Veré brought the branch quickly around again, catching the Indian square in the chest. He fell back, dazed and disoriented, but he could see Veré's dark shadow as it came toward him, arm raised, brutal determination in his cold eyes. Monty fought to remain conscious. Veré stepped closer and lifted the branch higher. But Monty could see beyond him. There was someone there, someone he had never seen before—a warrior with a crystal shield in one hand and a golden sword in the other.

Monty felt himself rise, though he wasn't sure how. His hand thrust forward.

It was dark when Monty woke, but the moon was high and the valley glowed mysteriously. Beneath him, Veré Doucet's body lay cold. Monty struggled to his feet. His body ached, and he was so stiff he hardly could move. Remembering the wound in his side, he lifted his shirt gingerly to inspect the damage. It was deep, but the bleeding had slowed. He knelt and with his knife cut a strip of cloth from Veré's shirt and held it against the wound. He stood and looked around. He needed rest, and time. He knew he never would be able to ride a great distance. And besides, where could he go? He had killed a white man.

He limped over to where the horse was tied, led it back to where Veré lay, and then went into the cave. Veré had left a small pack with some food and a few clothes. He picked it up and carried it out, setting it near the body. Then he began to tear the clothes into strips. When he was finished, he lifted Veré onto the back of the horse, using the strips of cloth to lash the body securely to the horse.

There was no going back. The white man took a dim view of an Indian who killed one of their own—even a man such as this one. It mattered little whether the Indian had reason.

He would rest. The cave would provide shelter, and there was enough food in the pack to last a few days. By then, with luck, he could hunt his own game. In a week, maybe two, he could travel.

Monteneha removed the horse's bridle, stood back, and slapped it on the rump. He watched as it disappeared, and then went into the cave.

CHAPTER TEN

IT WAS A long, quiet ride into town. John sat in silence next to his father as the buckboard rolled along the dusty road. The only sound was the clip-clopping of the horse's hooves on the hard-packed trail. It had been a long two days. The sheriff from Mill Creek had organized a search as soon as he had arrived only an hour or so after daybreak the same day Monty had disappeared on Quin's prize stallion.

Their search had been two-fold. First, find Miller or his body, and second, find Veré Doucet and bring him in for questioning.

The horse plodded along until they were down to little more than a crawl. Quin flicked the reins. "I hope you've learned your lesson—about Indians, I mean."

John sat in silence.

"They're wild," Quin continued. "They have their own ways. They're savage. They live by their own kind of law, if you want to call it that." He waited for a response, but John said nothing. "Anyhow, I hope from now on you'll be more careful about trusting a savage. It's one thing to take one in and nurse him, but it's quite another to turn your back on him. Indians can't be trusted. Do you understand?"

"He didn't steal the horse," said John. "At least, not without good reason. He's my friend. He wouldn't do that to me."

Quin grew impatient. "I'd like to know what good reason there could be for stealing a valuable stallion? That horse was the beginning of a herd."

"I told you before," John said, raising his voice. "I think he went after Doucet."

"Don't raise your voice to me, boy!"

John settled back on the seat. "I'm sorry, Father. I mean no disrespect. But it's the only reason he would have taken the horse."

Quin shook his head. "A hundred and fifty dollars is reason enough. Except he's probably pulling a travois by now. They'll work him like a pack mule until he's no good for anything else. We'll never see him again."

John said nothing the rest of the way into town. It did no good. And besides, it was difficult to argue his case as long as the horse was gone. Quin pulled up in front of the trading post and stopped. Ben Elam met them out front.

"Any word yet?" Quin asked.

"Nope," said Ben. "Most everybody's give up by now. Sheriff's up above the river with a couple o' the boys—Silas and Hance, I think. Anyhow, they should be back any time."

"No sign of the Pinkerton man?" Quin asked.

Ben shook his head. "An' no sign of that no-account gypsy neither. If you ask me, we ain't never gonna find neither one of 'em.

"What about Monty?" John asked.

Ben gave him a curious look. "That Indian?" he said, shaking his head. "Ain't likely gonna find an Indian if he don't want to be found. You best forget about that horse, boy. He's long gone."

John could feel the heavy burden on his shoulders. "I'm going for a walk," he said to his father as he stepped down from the wagon.

"Well, don't run off. I'm going inside to pick up a few things for your mother, and then I want to head home. It doesn't look like there's much we can do around here."

"I won't be long," John said, walking away. The last few days had been hard, what with worrying about Katie, wondering if Veré was coming back, and not knowing about his friend. John knew it should be the happiest time of his life with the wedding only a few weeks away, but instead he felt the weight of the world.

He trusted Monty in spite of what his father said. A part of him wanted to ride out and look for his friend. After all, if Monty had gone after Veré, he may be in trouble. But where would he look? Half the men in the valley had been out searching for the Pinkerton, and for Veré. They found the pepperbox and assumed it belonged to the Pinkerton, although they couldn't figure out what it was doing all the way over at Nathan's place unless Veré had it and dropped it there. They found blood and a few hoof prints in the soft earth, but they lost the trail at the ridge. Did Monty find Veré? And if he did, where were they? So far, all they had were questions.

John found himself down by the river. He sat down on the bank, watching the water as it coursed slowly along. He sat for a long time, tossing sticks into the water and watching them drift downstream.

He was hardly aware of the commotion down by the trading post until someone called to him. It was Nathan.

"Over here!" he called back.

"You'd better come quick," Nathan said when he was a few feet away. "I think you'll want to see this!"

John scrambled up the bank. Nathan greeted him at the road. A few yards from the trading post, a group of men stood in front, milling around and talking.

"Come on," Nathan said to John.

"It ain't purdy," Ben was saying.

"Been dead at least a couple o' days," said Silas.

"Better get him in the ground," said Hance. "And soon!"

John pushed his way through the crowd. In the middle of the circle, Silas McCoy held Quinlan Jakes's stallion by the reins, a body draped over its back. "I found him a mile or so back, grazin' alongside the road. I know'd whose it was right off."

John stepped closer. "Who is it?"

"Looks to me like the brother of that gypsy. Kinda hard to tell after this much time in this heat, but it looks like his clothes."

"Can you tell what happened to him?" Quin asked.

"He's got a knife wound in his chest," Silas said. "An' this here's kinda funny." He pointed to Veré's wrist. "A hole—run clean through."

"What do you figure?" Hance Eerdman asked.

Silas shrugged. "No tellin'. 'Cept maybe a knife, or—"

"An arrow," Nathan offered.

Hance whistled. "That'd take some shot."

They all agreed.

"How'd he get all trussed up like that?" Ben asked.

"I don't know," said Silas. "But this here's Quin's horse. 'Bout had to be that Indian, I figure."

"So who's gonna tell his kin?" Hance asked.

"I will," came a voice from down the road. It was Reverend Walters. "I heard what happened," he said. "One of the Wallace boys just came and told me. This is something I should do."

Nathan shook his head. "I gotta go right by there on my way home, Reverend. It might as well be me."

Reverend Walters held up his hand. "Life and death are my business, Nathan. The family will need comfort. Maybe I can give them some."

"Ain't much chance of that, Reverend," said Ben.

"Maybe not, but I have a duty to try." He reached out and took the reins.

"Suit yourself," said Ben. "Only don't go gettin' your throat cut for your trouble!"

"I'll be careful," he said to Ben, and then turning to Quin, he said, "I'll have your horse back in a few hours,"

Quin nodded.

The crowd watched for several minutes as Reverend Walters led the horse down the road.

"Well," said Nathan as he swung himself up onto Joe's back, "I reckon I'd better get on home. John, you want me to tell Katie anything?"

"Just that I miss her."

Nathan nodded and then reined Joe around and galloped off, passing Reverend Walters on his way.

John and Quin walked back to the wagon in silence. Quin took the reins in his hands and held them for a moment, and then handed them to John. John took them without a word and started up the road.

Neither of them spoke until they were almost home.

"It's good to have him back," Quin finally said. John was silent. "Looks like that Indian friend of yours must have done his own tracking."

More silence.

Quin looked down at his hands. "Look, John. You know I'm not a man given to humility. It doesn't come easy, but—well, it seems I was wrong. And I'm sorry."

John nodded but did not respond. They rode on for a while before John said, "I wonder where he is?"

"Hard telling. I'll be hanged if I understand him. But if he's smart, he won't come around here. Once the word gets out, they'll be looking for him. It won't set well that an Indian has killed one of the settlers."

"Not even after what they did?"

"It won't matter. You've heard about the Grave Creek massacre. It won't make any difference to the army or to most of the settlers once the rumors get started. Especially if some of those Indian-haters from down on the Humbolt hear about it. No, the best thing he can do is make himself scarce."

John felt empty. It wasn't what he wanted to hear, but it was true, and he knew it. The thought made him sick.

Kyra was down by the creek when Reverend Walters came walking up, leading the horse by the reins. She watched as he walked past her without saying a word, stopping at the shack. The stench of death followed close behind.

Maud came out of the shack. Her face, full of defiance at first, turned quickly grim when she recognized her son's lifeless body.

"What have you done?" she shrieked. "What have you done with my boy?"

From somewhere around the shack, Andre joined her.

"We found him outside of town," Reverend Walters said.

Andre cut the strips of clothing, letting the body fall to the ground.

"Who did this?" Maud said.

"We don't know. This is the way we found him."

"Liar!" Maud said.

Andre leaned over the body to examine the wound in Veré's chest. But there were no tears. "Someone will pay," he mumbled.

"I'm sorry," Reverend Walters said. "I'm truly sorry." He wished there were more he could say.

Kyra came up from the creek and stood over her brother's body. "So, the good people of Creek Junction are rid of another stain. No doubt they are comforted."

Reverend Walters clenched his jaw. It was something he rarely did. "No, ma'am." He led the horse around to face the road. "As I said before, I'd be happy to help you with the burying if you have need."

Maud's eyes flashed. "And as I said before, we have no need of your pious words!"

The Doucets watched as Reverend Walters led the horse back the way he had come.

"They will pay," Andre said as he disappeared around the corner.

Maud nodded her agreement. "We will have our revenge!"

Above them, a presence, consummate evil, vile and grotesque, savored the moment. Things had not worked out as planned—not exactly as planned, but still it was a victory of sorts. The enemy had thwarted. But still there was the foul stench of death in the air, soothing to the nostrils. True, it was not the deaths it had planned, but they would do. Any death would do. And there was still time. From the days of antiquity, time was its ally—and its only buffer against the promise of judgment. In the meantime, there was a certain amount of freedom to feed on the sufferings of mortal men. And deception was its favorite tool. There was more to do here. Care should be taken. But with planning, and the help of the willing, there was still more to be accomplished.

It settled down, hovering just above the ground, gripping the girl and her family, holding them, dragging them, toying with them as it pleased.

Katie sat impatiently on the banks of the pond with her legs tucked under her. It was only two more days until the wedding. John should be along any minute.

She tapped the pencil absently on the open diary in her lap, trying to think of something to write. But her mind was a jumble of thoughts and emotions. She found herself, these last few days, writing the same things over and over. Every entry was about John and the house, or John and the work clearing the land, or John and his concern for Monty. With each new day, the bitter memories of the last several weeks seemed to dim a bit more. She felt sure they could be forgotten all together if it weren't for Monty's disappearance.

She had grown closer to John, shared secret thoughts and feelings. The bond between them grew strong. She loved him so much it hurt. But most important to her was the knowledge, the comforting reassurance, that he loved her.

Still, all was not right for him, and she wished more than anything that there were something she could do to help him. He had spent many hours searching for his friend and had covered many miles. He had even run across a tribe he was sure was Monty's tribe. He was impressed by their warm hospitality. They offered him food and a place to spend the night. But if they knew anything about Monty's whereabouts, they wouldn't say.

Katie tried to be a comfort, even though with John's repeated and prolonged absences there was little progress on the house.

She suddenly realized her leg had fallen asleep under her. She stood, rubbing it to restore circulation, and then walked slowly around the pond, turning every so often to watch the road.

From beyond the rise in the road she heard the clopping of horse's hooves. In a moment, John crested the rise on the back of Quin's prize stallion.

"Good news!" he said as he dismounted. He patted the horse on the flank. "The mare we bred him to is with foal!"

"That's wonderful!" Katie said as she walked alongside him to the house.

"Yep," he said as he wrapped the reins around the hitching post. "Father says he'll give us the foal for a wedding present." John stroked the horse's neck. "It'll give us good brood stock to start a herd."

"That's wonderful. But what if it's a he?"

John smiled. "You'll have to pray that it isn't."

"I will," she smiled. "When is her time?"

"Well, it'll be a few months after the wedding—early spring."

John continued to stroke the horse's neck.

Katie reached up and put her hand on his. "How is the house coming?" she asked.

John shrugged. "It'll be ready."

They both were silent.

"He's all right," she said. "You must believe that."

"Maybe. But there was a fight. There had to be. There was blood. What if he was hurt? What if Veré did as much to him as he did to Veré?"

"I don't believe that," she said. She put her arms around his neck. "We must have faith. God will provide."

"I reckon you're right. Anyhow, I have no choice."

"I'm sure he's all right. Have faith."

John was grim. "I wonder if I'll ever see him again?"

John took Katie's hand and they walked together toward the pond. "Only two more days," he said after a while.

"Mm-hmm," she said, squeezing his hand. "I can hardly wait for you to see the dress. It's so pretty. Mama has been working so hard."

"I wish it was today," John said.

"Me, too." Katie blushed.

They continued to walk, stopping occasionally to watch the geese that swam along the shore. "I'll be glad to be in our home, our own home," she said.

"Me, too."

Katie looked wistfully down the road toward town. "It's hard," she said. "I hate going past their place and seeing—"

"I know," John said. "Those grave markers right next to the road don't help. And Kyra is always out by the creek."

Katie nodded. "She makes me afraid, the way she looks at me when we ride by. She's always there. I'm afraid of her and what she might do."

"Well, it won't be much longer, and we won't have to ride by so often. Besides, what can she do?"

"I don't know. But I don't trust her. She's so hateful. I can't forget the things she's said. And her whole family has made it no secret that they hold me responsible."

"But it's ridiculous! How can they blame you, or anyone?"

"I don't know, but I'm afraid."

John stopped and held her close. "They won't hurt us. I won't let them."

Katie rested her head on his chest. She felt safe when he held her. "What can we do?"

"I know one thing we can do," John said. They walked hand in hand to the edge of the pond and knelt down. It was becoming a habit. John took her hands in his and began to pray.

CHAPTER ELEVEN

WATER SKIPPERS SKITTERED along the surface of the small pools of stagnant water along the banks of Walker Creek in these waning days of summer. Out near the middle, a small trickle made its way around the smooth rocks of the creek bottom toward the river a few miles downstream.

Inside the cabin, Katie sat nervously near the open doorway as her mother adjusted her veil. "There!" she said as she stood back to admire it. "Now take it off and put it away until we get to the church. We don't want it to get dirty before the ceremony! Oh, I wish you could wait to put on the dress at the church!"

"Yes, Mama," Katie said. "Could you help me with it?"

"Of course, dear," Ruth said. "Oh, you're so beautiful!"

Katie could hardly believe that today was her wedding day. The time had gone by quickly for her.

Everyone in the whole world was invited, or so it seemed. Folks were coming from as far away as Mill Creek for the first wedding in the valley.

Katie fidgeted nervously with her hands.

"Oh, Mama," she said as she studied her face in the mirror. "Do I look all right?"

Ruth, who was already fighting tears, felt herself losing the battle. She held a handkerchief to her face. "Oh!" she said softly.

It was warm and the air was still, except for an occasional breeze that whispered through the valley. Nathan ducked his head as he came through the front door with his hat in his hand, looking tense and out of place in his new shirt and bow tie.

"You ladies about ready? We don't want to keep the man waiting. And I expect he's watching his watch if he has one."

"He has one," said Katie. "His folks gave it to him for his birthday—solid gold."

"Well," Nathan chided, "I expect my daughter is marrying into refinement! Got a gold watch and a house—all before she's even married."

"Oh, you hush!" Ruth scolded. "This is no time to be teasing her."

Nathan held up his hands in mock surrender. "Now, Mama, I got a right to know that my little girl is gonna be taken care of. After all, we don't want her marrying a vagabond."

"You know very well that John Jakes is no vagabond." Ruth reproved. "Why, he's cleared nearly twenty acres with almost no help at all, except for his Indian friend."

Katie swelled with pride. "And floated the logs down to the mill," she added. "He's got most of the lumber for the rest of the house already, and almost one hundred dollars besides."

"You hush now," said Ruth. "You're as bad as your father. You know it isn't proper for a young woman to discuss matters of business, especially on her wedding day!"

"Well, we'd better get going," Nathan said, "or they'll have to start without us."

"Just a moment longer," Ruth said through her tears. "I just want to look at her." Light from the outside streamed across the floor through the open doorway. Katie stood in the midst of it, her honey hair reflecting the rays. A radiant smile beamed from her face and her eyes danced with joy.

Nathan couldn't find words. She was beautiful—a young woman, radiant and graceful in her white wedding dress, looking more like an angel than the little girl who fed the geese down by the pond. He felt a lump rise and stop in his throat.

"The wagon's ready," Nathan finally said as he turned away.

Ruth dabbed the corners of her eyes with her handkerchief. "We're ready," she said. She started toward the door and turned, put her arms around her only child and held her tightly. "I love you, Baby," she whispered through her sobbing. "Remember what I've said. Remember!"

"I will, Mama, I will." Katie wept softly.

"C'mon, you two," Nathan said. "We won't get there before dark at this rate."

Ruth pulled away, allowing Katie to pass, and gave the dress one more careful eye. Nathan helped his daughter up onto the wagon seat and then went to the other side to help his wife, handing her the reins to the team. He walked to the back of the wagon, took the reins of his horse, and swung up into the saddle. "All right, ladies, let's get going."

Nathan and Ruth talked as they rode along, but Katie heard little of what was said. She kept thinking of John.

Soon the wagon crested the rise in the road just before the S-bend in Walker Creek. None of them spoke as they rode past the two grave markers under a fir tree a few yards from the lean-to shack. Kyra sat at the edge of the creek. Katie and Ruth looked straight ahead but Nathan tipped his hat. Kyra glared. Katie could feel Kyra's piercing eyes and it made her uneasy.

Kyra watched as they disappeared down the road, fingering the medallion. Hate filled her mind as she stormed toward the corral behind the cabin. She hitched the tired old horse to her father's broken-down wagon, and a few minutes later she was on her way to town.

The church was simple. Logs cut from the site on which it stood formed rustic walls and a roof, and cedar shingles kept it dry on rainy winter days. Smaller logs served as a handrail along the outer edge of the front porch. Ben Elam had donated the first oak boards off the sawmill for the double doors at the entrance. Hance Eerdman put the tools of his trade from the old country to good use and fashioned them into two hand-carved, arched doors with a cross that came together in the middle when they closed.

Inside, modest pews on either side faced the pulpit at the front. Behind the pulpit, a doorway led to a small room where Reverend Walters kept his meager desk and a cot to offer to strangers passing through.

Nathan dismounted at the hitching post in front of the church. "Easy," he said as he helped Katie down from the wagon. "We don't want to get that dress dirty."

"Yes, Papa."

Reverend Walters greeted them as he hurried across the yard. "Well! Are we ready for the big day? You aren't nervous are you, young lady?"

"A little," said Katie.

"Everything will be fine," he said with a warm smile. "Just follow me. I'll show you where you can freshen up a bit. Mrs. Walters is waiting for you inside."

"Are the Jakeses here?" Ruth asked.

"Yes, everyone is here. We're ready to get started as soon as you are!"

Nathan held back. "I'll meet you inside, Mama," he said at the bottom of the steps to the church.

"All right, Dear," Ruth said.

"Where do you want me, Reverend?" Nathan asked.

"Just wait here. When the time comes, Katie will meet you here. We'll do it just like we rehearsed."

The church was full, but only a few people were sitting in the pews. Most were mulling around, talking and avoiding the white linens that had been laid down the center aisle.

Ben Elam greeted Nathan at the door. "Big day, Nathan. I expect you'll be mighty glad when it's over."

"Yeah." Nathan sighed. "I don't know who this is harder on, me or the wife."

Ben chuckled. "Well, them two young-uns is in fer a real pull. But I reckon we all carry the load best we can. Seems like they's gettin' off to the right start, though—church weddin' an' all. Me an' the missus set about our'n the same way. Don't seem like it hurt us none."

Nathan had one eye on the door. "Mm-hmm," he said.

"I figure religion's got its own place," Ben continued. "I mean, I figure it's good fer young-uns to learn about right from wrong. An' the preacher's got a right important job lettin' a feller know when he's plowin' too close to the creek. 'Course, I reckon one day a week is enough for any man."

Nathan watched the corner of the building for Katie. "I hope they worship every day," he said without thinking.

"Don't get me wrong, Nathan, I figure a man should do what he thinks is right. But I don't figure God'll hold it against a man if he don't warm a pew every Sunday."

Nathan heard Ben for the first time. He took a deep breath. "There's only one way to make God happy, Ben, and that's to do things His way. And the Savior is His way."

"Well, I figure me an' God is awright. I mean, I ain't no worse than the next man. An' I try to be a good man an' take care o' my kin. Yep, I figure me an' God is awright."

Nathan only half listened. Too much on his mind. He'd put this away for later. He would make a trip into town—maybe next week—and he and Ben could have a talk about spiritual things. Nathan found talking about his faith difficult, but God's prompting was sure. He knew he'd put it off long enough. It was time—and Ben was a good friend. Nathan knew he owed him the truth.

Reverend Walters appeared around the corner of the church followed by Katie, Mrs. Elam, and Mrs. Eerdman, who dutifully held the corners of Katie's dress to keep it from touching the ground.

"Excuse me, Ben," he said as he took his daughter's hand. His hands were trembling.

"All right," Reverend Walters said clasping his hands together, "just like we rehearsed it." With that, he disappeared around the corner.

It seemed like hours to Nathan, but soon Mrs. Walters' spinet piano began to play.

"You know what to do?" Nathan whispered to Katie as he offered his arm.

"Mm-hmm." She nodded.

Nathan looked down at his little girl. She had a tear in the corner of her eye. Nathan took an awkward step as they started down the aisle, but the slow pace the reverend made them practice made him feel clumsy. He could feel his face flush.

At the front of the church, the reverend stood, Bible in hand, with John and John's little brother, Jefferson, standing in as best man. Every head turned. In the front row, Ruth held a handkerchief to her face. Beth and Quin Jakes stood and the congregation followed their lead. The music rose. Reverend Walters nodded to Nathan.

Katie saw only John.

Kyra sat under a giant yew-wood tree, watching from the road a safe distance away, as Nathan and Katie disappeared through the front doors of the church. She clutched the medallion tightly in her hand, chanting to herself, repeating the words with ever-increasing intensity. "I bind on earth the heart of John Jakes! Cursed is the man or woman who stands in my way! I bind on earth the heart of John Jakes! Cursed is the man or woman who stands in my way!"

Her dark eyes burned as she watched, afraid to chance a closer look for fear of the circle. She repeated the curse over and over, each time becoming louder, until the whisper became almost a shout. But her cries went unheard.

She stood and began moving closer to the circle of the clearing. When she stood only a few feet away from the edge of the grass, she stopped. Fear washed over her. She could not understand, yet something told her it was not safe. She continued her chanting, now back down to a whisper, never taking her eyes from the doorway to the church. She could hear music. She crept close to the boardwalk and listened. An old piano played the "Wedding March." Soon the music stopped, and the only sound was that of her own breathing as her lips formed the words of the curse.

"Do you, John Jakes, take this woman to be your lawfully wedded wife, to love her and cherish her, in the sight of almighty God, as long as you both shall live?"

John stammered to get out the words, his voice wavering slightly. "I do."

"And do you, Katie Walker, take this man to be your lawfully wedded husband, to honor him and to obey him, in the sight of almighty God, as long as you both shall live?"

Katie turned to look at John. "I do." She extended her hand obediently, only half hearing the words that followed.

John listened, slipping the ring on her finger at the reverend's command.

"I now pronounce you man and wife. You may kiss the bride." John leaned down to meet Katie's waiting embrace, lingering for just a moment, and then turning to face the congregation. The piano began to play, and John and Katie started down the aisle. Soon the entire congregation was outside in the churchyard, congratulating them and offering words of encouragement.

Kyra watched from a few feet away, hidden behind a fir tree, muttering the curse.

A presence with an evil purpose watched as the inhabitants of the little town celebrated and laughed, mingled and danced, kissing the bride and offering words of wisdom to the groom. But its gaze was not on the people. It was fixed firmly on the unseen entity behind them, a minor warrior in the service of the Most High, yet majestic and pure with eyes that danced, radiating goodness and purity, and a benevolent purpose. He towered above the human crowd who were unaware of his arrival, and his gentle eyes flashed his vigilant resolve. In his hand he held a golden shield, clear as crystal and appearing to be separate from and yet part of him at the same time, flowing like mercury from his right hand.

The presence hissed and groaned in a blustery display, but the Centurion with the shield stood his ground, confident in the knowledge of his source of authority. He knelt close to the people in the meadow and lowered his shield to the ground in front of them, covering and surrounding them, never taking his eyes from the evil enemy that cowered at the sight of the Centurion.

Kyra fell to her knees, clutching the medallion in her hands, gripping it tightly with all her might. She was tired, but her mind would not let her rest. Her head hurt from thinking. She hated Katie with every ounce of her flesh. And she no longer wanted John. She only wanted to hurt them both. She imagined what it would be like to kill them, to make them suffer as she suffered. She let the medallion fall around her neck as she held her hands to her head, pressing against her skull as if to squeeze out the pain. The presence retreated for fear of a direct confrontation.

Kyra rose to her feet and began to walk toward home, forgetting the wagon and the team that grazed by the road. Soon, she was running. She ran as hard as she could. Her heart beat in her chest until it felt as though it would burst, and still she ran. Her bare feet were bleeding as they pounded the ground, but still she ran. Her legs were numb. She stumbled and almost fell, but still she ran.

When she reached the clearing by the S-bend in Walker Creek, she ran to the bank where she had buried the board with the curse. She fell back on the ground, gasping desperately to fill her lungs with air. She had failed. She felt sick and alone, but even now something would not let her give up. She rose heavily to her feet and took the medallion in her hand, breaking the chain from around her neck. She could feel its power.

Hate consumed her. Vengeance filled her heart. It was all she had left, all she wanted. She would have her revenge. She would will it! Instinctively, she understood that something prevented her from harming the two people she hated most. It was as if some great barrier stood between her and her victims. But she would have her vengeance. If not against them, then against the ones they loved. The medallion held power. It was a key, a door, and a link to something more powerful.

And she only needed to find a way to unlock the door and harness the power.

The presence hovered with eager anticipation.

Kyra knew she could not harm them, but what could she do? It had to be something eternal, something to inflict injury for all time. But how? A curse against the couple was useless if there was some power protecting them. A curse against their offspring? Yet the name "Jakes" must continue in order for the curse to continue.

The corners of Kyra's lips turned upward in evil delight. She would have her vengeance—and nothing, not even death, would prevent it. She held the medallion high above her head in her two hands. Her heart beat hard in her chest. Ah, yes, she would have her vengeance. John and Katie would pay.

She considered a new curse. She knew what she must do. She would not curse them with barrenness. The name "Jakes" would continue—it must! It was not enough to inflict what surely would be a fleeting injury. No. It must inflict its pain anew with every generation.

The women were the key. It was a woman who had injured her. It was a woman who stood in her way now. She knew what she must do. The women of each generation would bear the burden of the curse. She clutched the medallion tightly until blood ran down the palm of her hand.

She began to shout: "I swear by all that is unholy that so long as the waters of Walker Creek course, no woman-child born of the union between Katherine Walker and John Jakes, born with the name of Jakes, will ever bear a living child!"

She drew back her arm, hesitating for a moment, and then threw the medallion into the still waters at the S-bend in Walker Creek, where it sank to the bottom. "So long as the waters course!" she screamed. "So long as the waters course!"

PART TWO

THE PRESENT

CHAPTER TWELVE

THE MID-AFTERNOON TRAFFIC of Southern California freeways always made Rebecca Lindsay uneasy. She hated it. But today, her reason for being there made it seem worse.

She looked up at her husband as he drove, studying his ruggedly handsome features. His hair had been long when they met. Now he kept it cropped close. The earring of his younger days was gone. He wore a sports shirt and tie, loosened at the collar now because of the heat.

She saw strength in his face. Perhaps it was the quiet confidence she could see in his pale blue eyes. Or perhaps it was the way he set his jaw when he knew he was right. Or perhaps it wasn't in his face at all, but in the way he walked or the quietness of his voice. Rebecca wasn't sure why or how she knew, but his strength was the first thing she had noticed about him when they met. It was what had attracted her to him. And now, six years after they had first met and five years of marriage had confirmed her first impressions of him. He was a man of simple virtue and strength. She knew she could trust him, and she loved him for it.

Rebecca Lindsay rested her head on her husband's strong shoulder as he drove.

"Do you think they found anything?" she asked.

Brad Lindsay shrugged indifferently. "I don't know. We'll find out in a few minutes."

Rebecca reached across the console of their late model Toyota and took his hand. "I hope so," she said softly.

"I hate the city," Brad said, looking over his shoulder as he moved from the middle lane of the freeway to the slow lane.

Traffic was always bad by three in the afternoon, and he and Rebecca avoided it as much as they could—usually. But not today. Today they had no choice.

It was warm. The afternoon sun took full advantage of the car's black vinyl roof—and the fact that the air conditioning wasn't working.

"We could always move up the coast near Aunt Billie," Rebecca said.

"And what would I do? Commute?"

Rebecca shrugged off the cynical tone in his voice. "You could find something. Orange County isn't the only place that needs new houses." She hugged his arm and kissed the tips of his fingers. "Besides, I think you could do just about anything you wanted if you put your mind to it."

Brad didn't answer. It wasn't the first time the subject had come up. Rebecca always made it sound like playful banter, but deep down they both knew that if she had a choice, she'd choose to live somewhere else besides Southern California.

Brad uttered a mild profanity as the taillights in front of him served notice. The hood of the car dipped down as it came to an abrupt stop in the middle of the freeway.

"We've gotta get that air fixed," Brad said as he wiped his brow with his shirtsleeve.

"I'll take care of it tomorrow," Rebecca said. "Can you take the other car or do you want me to drive you?"

"I'll take the Plymouth," he said as he grimaced.

It was quiet for a few minutes as Brad concentrated on the traffic and Rebecca was lost in thought, then she squeezed Brad's hand. "I really do hope they found something we can deal with."

Brad patted her leg with tender care. "I'm sure they did," he said. "Don't worry."

Rebecca brushed an errant strand of long brown hair from her face as the moving car generated a warm breeze through the open window. She felt assured. Or at least she tried to convince herself she did.

Brad flicked on the turn signal and exited the freeway. Five minutes later he found a parking space next to the curb outside the medical center, and wheeled into it.

Rebecca glanced into the mirror on the back side of the visor, swept her long brown hair behind her ears, checked her make-up and made a mental note to lose ten pounds.

"You look fine," Brad said from habit.

"I'm fat," she responded.

"You weigh exactly what you weighed when we got married."

Rebecca studied her heart-shaped face in the mirror. "I'm fat," she insisted.

"Your name?" Dr. Morris's pretty, young receptionist asked Brad from behind the glass window of the reception room.

"Brad and Rebecca Lindsay. We have a consultation appointment with Dr. Morris at three."

"Sign in, please," she said as she spun the clipboard around and handed Brad a pen. "The doctor will be with you shortly."

They found two chairs near the single lamp in the dimly lit waiting room and sat down. The clock on the wall read 2:55.

At three twenty, a neatly dressed woman in her forties stuck her head out of the doorway that led to the examining rooms. "Mr. and Mrs. Lindsay?"

Brad rose to his feet and offered his hand to Rebecca. They followed the nurse as she led them down a long hallway past floor-to-ceiling shelves with rows of file folders, a set of scales, and several sterile rooms. At the last door, she stopped and nodded toward the room beyond, a cheerful office with a massive oak desk in front of a neatly arranged bookshelf.

Brad and Rebecca sat down in the two comfortable conference chairs. "Dr. Morris will be with you shortly," the nurse said, detached but courteous, and then shut the door as she left.

Rebecca squeezed Brad's hand. She loved him for being strong. She needed it now more than ever. Her brown eyes filled with tears and she looked away.

All her life, all twenty-eight years of it, all she ever wanted was a family. While her friends planned careers, she only wanted to be a wife and mother, an oddity in today's world.

And when all her friends were earning degrees in business or marketing, she dropped out in her second year to marry Brad. She was not sorry. It was what she wanted.

The door opened and a bearded and bespectacled Dr. Morris entered with a clipboard under one arm. "Good afternoon," he said as he extended his hand, first to Brad and then to Rebecca. "How are you today?"

"Fine, thanks," Brad said.

Dr. Morris sidestepped around the corner of the desk and sat down in a big leather office chair. "Now let's see," Morris said as he studied his notes on the clipboard. He paused for a moment and then looked up. "Well," he began, "as you know, we've ruled out a number of things. We know Brad isn't the reason."

Rebecca grimaced.

Dr. Morris continued. "And you, Rebecca, have no medical history that would indicate any problems." His eyes went back and forth between the clipboard and Rebecca. "You ovulate regularly; in fact, quite consistently it appears. You've had no abortions, which is good. That sometimes creates problems. And, let's see, we've ruled out infection." Dr. Morris paused to read. "You don't seem to have any thyroid problems, Becky."

"Rebecca," she corrected.

"Oh, yes, forgive me, I forgot. No short cuts!" Morris smiled warmly.

"What about the tests you ran last week?" Brad asked impatiently.

Dr. Morris sat back in his chair, tapping his teeth with his pen. "I was hoping to have the results before you got here today. But the lab is backed up so we may not have the results for a few more days. Frankly, I don't think we're going to find anything. This is not uncommon. We can't always find a medical explanation. Sometimes women just don't conceive easily. I'm sure you've heard some of the tales that make the rounds from time to time—women who try for years, and then either give up or adopt and…bang!" Dr. Morris snapped his fingers. "A baby!"

Rebecca was sullen. "I just wish we could be sure."

"Let's wait and see what these latest tests show, but for now the best thing the two of you can do is settle down—relax! Take one day at a time. I know that's not very helpful, but believe me, it'll be better for both of you in the long run. And who knows, maybe it will happen when you least expect it."

"That offers little comfort," Brad said. "She—we—want a baby more than anything in the world."

Dr. Morris smiled. "I know. I wish I could offer you more. As much as we doctors hate to admit it, it's in the hands of the Almighty. Sometimes there's very little any of us can do about it unless you want to try something as sophisticated as artificial insemination—which can be very expensive—or fertility drugs—which are risky. But if I were you, I wouldn't give up just yet. There's still hope."

Brad stood to leave. "We'll try to keep that in mind."

Dr. Morris rose and extended his hand. "We'll have those tests back in a few days, and my nurse will call you."

Sunlight shimmered across the surface of the waters of the great Pacific Ocean in the early morning where golden rolling hills met the sand along the beach a few yards from the breaking surf near Santa Barbara, California. An old Victorian style home stood guard on the highest hill a few miles from the highway.

Wilhelmina Dawson—"Billie" to her friends—was up before the sun as she had been every morning for the last sixty years of her adult life. She savored the brisk walk that took her down to the water, along the beach, and then up the path by the cliff near the pier to follow the road back home. She stepped sprightly up the long driveway, stopping to inspect the roses that were in bloom. She pushed the sleeves of her gray sweat suit up to her elbows and reached down to pull a few weeds. There were very few, but she tolerated no clutter, and she always made it a habit not to let something go that could be dealt with at the moment.

At seventy-eight, her infectious vitality was well known, and she refused to give in to the years. With a few meager traces of auburn in her graying hair, she easily could pass for a woman fifteen years younger.

Billie carried the handful of weed pickings with her and deposited them in the waste can near the rear door to the kitchen. An old, gray tabby cat rubbed against her leg.

"C'mon, you," she said as she leaned down and scooped her up. She carried the cat inside and let her slink from her grasp to the floor. The cat landed on her feet and went straight to her dish by the cupboard.

Billie went to the sink, washed her hands, and then reached into the cupboard for a coffee mug. Her Bible lay on the countertop. She poured herself a cup of coffee from the pot on the counter, tucked the Bible under her arm, and carried everything with her to the table and sat down.

It was her morning routine. She had done it without deviation for all the years she had been married and the five she had been a widow. When Mr. Dawson was alive, they did it together. It was harder now. She sipped from the cup as she thumbed through the Bible until she came to the passage in Ephesians 6:12 she had been studying.

"For we wrestle not against flesh and blood, but against principalities, against powers, against the rulers of the darkness of this world, against spiritual wickedness in high places."

The words were true. She had believed them all of her adult life—or a good part of it anyway—and all her prayers reflected the conviction that forces she could not see worked their mischief to do harm to the earth's inhabitants. But it was times like these, early in the morning and alone in the big, old house, that the words offered little comfort in her loneliness. Mr. Dawson always had read the Scriptures while she sat listening to his voice resonate through the kitchen, bringing life to the words. She missed those times—and him.

When she'd finished her reading, she bowed in silent prayer, remembering each one of her friends, family members, and, of course, Rebecca. When she was through, she quickly washed the cup and set the Bible on the counter, ready for her evening reading. She went upstairs, showered, dressed, and then bounded out the door like a young schoolgirl on her way to her first date. Moments later, she wheeled Mr. Dawson's old Ford onto the highway toward town.

"Over here, Dear!"

Wilhelmina squinted against the sun to see across the parking lot of the Sand Crab restaurant. It was Helen Bradley. She was a jolly woman, a little overweight and always smiling. She stood with the others, Meg and Alva, both gray-haired, thin and stooped at the shoulders. They referred to themselves as the "BAG ladies": Bifocals, Aching joints, and Graying heads.

"Morning, girls!" she said as she joined them.

"Morning, Billie," they said nearly in unison.

The four women walked casually toward the main entrance, talking and laughing. Inside, their usual waitress seated them at their usual table and brought them their usual round of orange juice, coffee, and tea without their asking for a thing.

"How are you, Dear?" Helen asked Meg. "We missed you yesterday."

"Oh, I'm fine. I had to take Raymond to the doctor."

"Nothing serious, I hope?" asked Alva.

"No, no. He's been having some trouble with his phlebitis."

"I'm sorry to hear it. We'll have to add him to our prayer list," Helen said.

They all agreed.

"How is your niece, Billie?" Meg asked.

"Rebecca? She's fine. I haven't heard from her in a few weeks, but she's fine."

"It's too bad she's so far away," said Helen.

"It's only a couple of hours to Orange County," said Meg.

"Yes, but I don't like to drive at night," said Billie. "And if I drive home the same day, it doesn't leave much time to visit."

"Can't they put you up for the night?" asked Alva.

"Yes, I suppose," said Billie, "and they've offered. But I have so many things to do here. I—"

"Well, I don't see why they can't come here for a visit," said Alva.

"Brad's job keeps him pretty close to the city."

They all nodded and then sat in silence, sipping their coffee or tea.

"At least they're only a few hours away," Meg said a moment later. "My two are half a continent away. I never see my grandkids."

"At least you have grandkids," Alva said. "I don't think my Bobby will ever get married."

"No prospects?" Helen asked.

"Oh, all kinds of prospects. He just can't seem to make up his mind!"

Meg turned to Billie. "What about Rebecca and Brad? When are they going to start their family?"

Billie shrugged. "I wish I knew," she said softly.

"Do they plan on having a family?" Helen asked.

Billie fidgeted in her seat. "I think they'd like to have kids someday."

"Well, I hope they don't wait too long," said Meg. "They don't want to be raising their family when they're our age!"

"Oh, don't be silly," Helen said. "They have plenty of time. Besides, they won't know what they're doing until they're our age!"

Meg chuckled. "And by that time it'll be too late!"

They all laughed.

"Well," said Helen, "we can keep praying for them. They're not saved, are they, dear?"

"No," said Billie. "And, of course, that's my first concern."

Alva reached over and patted Billie's arm. "In His time. We'll keep praying. Would you like us to pray for children as well?"

"I think that would be fine," Billie said.

An hour later, Billie left the others still chatting on the sidewalk in front of the restaurant. These morning breakfasts were special. It was good to have friends, but they were more than friends—they were prayer partners. They had known each other for many years. Helen was the youngest. She had joined them about ten years ago. The others had grown old together in the same small church, in the same town on the California coast. It had always been a small church, but over the years it had gotten smaller—and grayer. Still, there was a core group of faithful warriors committed to the Lord and His service.

Billie climbed behind the wheel of her car and started the engine. She had a couple of stops to make before she went home. She backed slowly out of the parking spot and turned onto the highway, stopping at the boulevard stop and then crossing it as the light turned green. She continued for a block and turned left. It was slower this way, but she hated driving the main street through town with all that traffic.

A few blocks later, she pulled up to the curb in front of an older stucco home. The roofing was worn and the concrete driveway was cracked with sections that had been lifted by the root system of a massive elm tree in the front yard.

She knocked at the door and waited patiently.

"Morning, Billie," said the frail old gentleman who answered the door.

"Good morning, Charles. Is she up?"

"Oh, yes. She's been waiting for you to come. The pain's been worse the last couple of days. But it seems some better today."

Billie made her way down the hall to the bedroom at the end and knocked softly on the door. "Ellen. It's me."

"Come in," said a sandpaper voice from inside.

Billie opened the door and went in. "How are you?" Billie asked.

"Oh, fine," Ellen said from her bed as she extended her hand. "I've had some trouble sleeping. I couldn't get to sleep last night until two."

Billie took her hand. "Has the nurse been by?"

"She came by yesterday," said Charles who was leaning in the open doorway. "We've got an appointment with the doctor in the morning."

"Thursday," said Ellen.

"In the morning," Charles corrected. "Tomorrow is Thursday."

"No, tomorrow is Wednesday. Isn't that right, Dear?" She looked at Billie for affirmation.

Billie started to answer, but Charles interrupted her. "Today is Wednesday! Tomorrow is Thursday!" He pushed away from the wall and went into the other room.

Ellen sighed in disgust. "He never listens to me anymore. Tomorrow is Wednesday. Isn't that right?"

Billie squeezed her hand. "Today is Wednesday," she said tenderly.

"It is?" she said weakly and then shrugged. "I don't know what's wrong with me lately. I don't know how I'm supposed to know what day it is, shut up in this room all the time."

"Would you like to move into the living room?"

"No, I'm fine."

Charles came back, holding a glass of water in one hand and two small tablets in the other. "Come on. It's time for your medicine," he said as he sat on the edge of the bed.

He opened his cupped hand and waited patiently for her to take each tablet between her frail fingers. She put them in her mouth one at a time, taking the water glass each time, sipping from it, and then handing it back to her husband.

He waited a few seconds longer. "That enough?"

She nodded. He stood and walked slowly out of the room.

"He's such a dear," Ellen said.

"Yes, he is," Billie said, but she was thinking how tired he looked.

"The doctor says I'm a little stronger this week, and he says the cancer has slowed. They didn't think I'd make it this long, but I've fooled them all."

Billie smiled and gently squeezed her hand. Ellen responded, but her hands were frail and weak.

"The doctor says if I keep on like this for a few weeks more, I can go to church, maybe next month."

"We all miss you."

"I miss you too. Of course you're the only one who comes to see me. And the pastor. He's been by a few times, but it gets mighty lonely just sitting here."

Billie gave her a half smile. "I know."

"But I'm fine."

Ellen's eyelids began to droop, and Billie could see the pain medication Charles had given her was beginning to take effect. "Well, I'd better be going and let you get your rest."

Ellen nodded, but her face fell. "Thank you for coming. Would you pray before you go?"

"Of course."

Billie offered up one of the traditional prayers for the occasion. She prayed that God would help Ellen, that He would give her strength, that He would heal her in His own time, and that He would build up her faith through her trials. And then she stood to leave.

"Billie?"

Billie turned at the door.

"Thank you for coming."

Billie nodded and then closed the door behind her.

"Thanks for coming," Charles said at the front door.

"She seems in better spirits today," Billie said.

Charles shrugged. "She's lost a lot of her strength in the last few days, and she gets confused. It was all I could do to prop her up this morning. I just can't lift her anymore."

Billie said goodbye and then slid in behind the wheel of the old Ford. She started the car and pulled away from the curb, headed in the general direction of home. She stopped at the market to pick up something for dinner and a birthday card for the pastor's wife. When she pulled into her own driveway it was a quarter of one. She stopped at the mailbox for the mail, sorted through it briefly, and then set it on the seat next to her as she drove up the driveway.

After parking the car in the garage, she closed the big door behind her and walked slowly into the house. She was tired, more so than usual.

The house felt cool and comfortable. Brad kicked off his shoes just inside the door on the raised tile entry and plopped down in his favorite chair. He put his head back and closed his eyes. Rebecca went into the kitchen.

"Get me a beer," he called out.

"You want it in a glass?"

She always asked. And his answer was always the same. "No, thanks."

She brought it in and set it down on the end table next to him.

"Thanks."

Rebecca bent down over the back of the chair and kissed his forehead. "What do you want to do for dinner?"

Do? Rebecca always asked one of two questions when it came to dinner. There was the traditional question: "What do you want for dinner?"—the one she asked nine nights out of ten that was routine and had no lilt of double-meaning. But then there was the other question, the one that carried all the weight and force of double-entendre. The one that let him know she expected a reprieve from her role as the traditional housewife: "What do you want to *do* for dinner?"

"I don't want to go anywhere tonight," he said without opening his eyes.

She slipped her arms around his neck without responding.

"I love you too," Brad said, eyes still shut.

Rebecca stroked his forehead with her finger. "You should never have married me," she said.

Brad straightened in the chair, grabbed her wrist, and pulled her around in front of him.

Rebecca giggled as she fell across the arm of the chair and into her husband's lap. "Be careful!" she said. "Do you want to break the chair?"

"And what about my lap?"

Rebecca giggled like a schoolgirl, but her solemn expression returned as she wrapped her slender arms around her husband's neck. She studied his eyes for a moment and then kissed him.

"I've got what I want," he whispered softly. "No regrets."

"You deserve better," she said.

"That's probably true," he said playfully as he leaned forward to meet her eyes.

Rebecca knew it wouldn't work. Brad never let her feel sorry for herself very long. A smile crept across her face. They both laughed. "OK," she said. "No more pity parties!"

"Good. Let's not have any more of this talk about who'd be better off without who. OK?"

Rebecca nodded. "It's just that I know how much this means to you. And I want you to be happy!"

Brad put a finger to her lips. "I am happy. I've got you," he said as he pulled her close.

"But you don't have a son."

"And what if I want a daughter?"

Rebecca jabbed her husband in the ribs. "OK, Mr. Smarty! You don't have one of those, either!"

"But I've got you. That's the only little girl I need."

Their eyes met. Rebecca put her head on Brad's shoulder and he held her close.

"It'll happen. You said so yourself. Maybe the tests will show something. Maybe it's something simple."

Rebecca nodded as she brushed away a tear that was just forming in the corner of her eye. "Maybe I need vitamins."

"Or maybe I do. Or maybe something else just as simple. And if not, well, we'll do what we have to do."

Brad kissed his wife. "Let's not have any more of this talk about marrying someone else. All right, Mrs. Lindsay?"

"Yes," she said, brushing her fingers against the day-old stubble on his chin.

"Maybe it's time we considered our options," Brad said after a moment. "We've talked about it before, but maybe—"

"Not yet!" Rebecca said before she could stop herself. "I'm sorry. You know I didn't mean to snap."

"I know. It's OK."

"It's not that I'm opposed to adoption. You know that. But I just want to try it this way first. It's important. At least, it is to me. I can't explain it. I just—"

Brad shook his head as he held up his hand. “It’s all right. I understand.”

Rebecca stroked her husband’s forehead. “Family is important to me. I can’t explain it, but I want children. And I want to have my own. I think I could love one that wasn’t born to me, but I want to carry one here.” She patted her stomach.

“I’d like to put it there,” Brad said with a gleam in his eye.

“Only you,” she said softly as she stroked the short bristles of his close-cropped hair. “You and no one else.”

Rebecca shuffled into the bathroom early in the morning. A yellow Post-It was stuck to the mirrored door of the medicine cabinet where her face should be:

Don’t forget the air conditioning!

Brad had left early in the morning. He had a meeting in Palm Springs, and the drive there could take a couple of hours or more if traffic was bad.

She pulled the sticker from the glass, crumpled it into a ball, and tossed it in the waste can in the corner. Her reflection in the mirror reminded her that her chin was too big and her cheeks should be a little higher. Brad thought she was pretty, and more than a few heads turned when she passed, but still....

She tried not to hurry as she went through the daily ritual of makeup and a curling iron. It was after seven thirty and there was much to be done today, starting with the car.

By eight thirty, she was headed for the freeway. It was ten miles to the auto shop where Brad had arranged to have the car fixed. But it was within walking distance of shopping, and shopping would be good therapy to get her mind off what troubled her.

“What’s it doin’?” Fred, the mechanic, asked as he wiped his meaty hands on a shop towel.

"I don't know. It just doesn't cool the car. My husband said something about 'freezon' or 'Freon' or something like that," Rebecca said, trying to be helpful.

"We don't use Freon no more," he said as he turned to his companion standing in the doorway of the shop. "Pull this in next to the hoist. We'll do it first." He turned back to Rebecca. "We'll have it done in a couple hours. You can pick it up about noon."

Rebecca looked at her watch. A couple of hours was eleven. But she didn't argue with him. "I'll be back. Thank you."

Fred nodded indifferently and then turned and walked back to his shop. Rebecca watched helplessly as her car disappeared into the black hole of auto repair. She turned and walked to the street corner. When the light changed, she followed the sidewalk that headed north toward the mall, stopping occasionally to peer into one of the small shops along the way. But the contents of the display cases and aisles of clothing or knickknacks were lost on her. She was deep in thought.

It was funny how something, the same something, could be so important both to her and the man she loved, and yet for totally different reasons. She loved family. She loved her family. She felt warm and secure knowing who she was and where she came from. She knew who her relatives were for six generations, and it gave her comfort. It never seemed to matter or even to occur to her that the knowledge was not really hers. Aunt Billie knew. And the information was available any time she wanted it. Somehow, since her parents had died, it was even more important—as though it were up to her to keep the flame alive.

She continued walking along the sidewalk toward the mall four blocks away. There were shops all along the street and Rebecca took her time. It was hot again today, too hot to hurry. She stopped in front of a men's clothing store and peered in at the rows of suits. Brad would look so good in that one!

Family was important to Brad too. But it was different. He knew very little about his family. His mother was alive, but he didn't know about his dad. His folks had separated when Brad was in junior high school and Brad's mother didn't like talking about it. In fact, she refused. Brad was never allowed to talk about his father after he left, and even now his mother forbid the mention of his father's name in her home.

It didn't seem to matter to Brad, not knowing where his father was. He was never close to him when he was at home. The old man never said much when he was around. To Brad, it just made him seem all the more exalted and unapproachable. And then one day his father was just—gone.

His departure left Brad with a longing for some sense of connection—of belonging. It was a tough thing to put into words, but not knowing about his father, and wrestling with the inner demons of self-doubt about his own worthiness to be loved by him, left Brad with a feeling that he was an intruder in an ordered world. Other people, his own wife for instance, knew who they were. They could find their own little twig on the branches of a family tree. They could know, good or bad, where in the universe they fit in. They could claim a tether from which to reach out, and to look back to, as they sought to make whatever mark they were destined to make on the world. Somehow he felt a family of his own could give him that anchor.

Rebecca knew these things, as much from her own instinct about the man she loved as from the times he had opened up and told her of his childhood, and it made her want to give him the family she was sure he craved all the more. She felt despair creeping up on her again. She couldn't let herself think about it. The guilt of knowing what Brad wanted, and her belief that it was her own failing that was preventing it, was more than she could endure.

The entrance to the mall was a high arch that towered overhead. Busy shoppers hurried in and out of the long row of glass doors. Rebecca followed a young couple through one of them. Cool air caressed her arms and face as she passed through. She made her way along the mall's corridor, stopping at one of her favorite shops to try on a blouse.

At about ten thirty, the mood struck her to get a bagel and some cream cheese. Remembering a little shop on the middle floor that sold them, she started toward the escalator, but as she approached it she slowed her pace, remembering something else. She paused for a moment, looking down the long promenade as she considered the other escalator at the farthest end of the mall.

She was only a few feet away from this escalator. As she stood before the conveyor, she looked over her shoulder again toward the other end of the mall. No, it was too far and she was acting silly. There was no good reason to go all the way around. She would go this way and that was that!

As she stepped onto the escalator, she gripped the moving banister tightly. She was committed now. There was no turning back. At the bottom, she walked briskly, looking straight ahead. The little shop with the bagels was only four doors away, but between it and where she walked, a brightly painted entrance and a cheerful sign announced "The Baby Store." It was a cheerful place with bright colors, but Rebecca saw it only as an antagonist taunting, ridiculing and reminding her of her failure.

She stopped at the entrance. Inside the store, a young mother held her toddler in her arms as she leafed through tiny dresses hanging neatly in a row. Near the front, rows and rows of cuddly stuffed animals lined the wall. The young mother looked up and smiled. Rebecca returned the smile, but her anguish must have registered in her face because the young mother lingered for a moment before turning away. Rebecca turned and walked away.

At the bagel shop, Rebecca sat in the booth, sipping a cup of coffee and nibbling on a bagel, but the pleasure they should have brought her was missing.

"More coffee, Ma'am?"

Rebecca looked up. "Hmmm? Oh, no, thank you," she said to the young waitress as she held her hand over her cup. "I'm almost through."

The girl nodded and walked away toward the next table. Rebecca watched her as she worked. She wondered if she had children. She wondered if she wanted any.

She looked around the room. There were people in several of the booths. A couple sat silently near the door next to the cash register. *They are probably in their thirties*, Rebecca thought. *They could have children.*

Another couple, much older, sat across from where she was sitting. *They probably have children—and maybe grandchildren.*

She watched as scores of people passed outside the shop. Many, if not most of them, she thought, probably had children.

It seemed so unfair. All were busy with their own meaningless pleasure: shopping! To watch them, none seemed to appreciate the children who followed, led, or scampered about as they went their different ways. Rebecca longed to savor even the most trivial moments with her own child.

"Do you know Jesus?"

Startled, Rebecca turned sharply in her seat. The waitress was standing next to the table with a quizzical expression.

"I beg your pardon?" Rebecca said a little indignantly.

"I said, would you like some more cream cheese—you know, for your bagel?" she said as she motioned toward the half-eaten bagel on Rebecca's plate.

"Um, no. No thank you." Rebecca watched as the waitress turned and went back behind the counter, unsure if she had heard what she thought she had, or if it was her imagination. Maybe the acoustics in the room caused her to hear what had not been said. Yeah, that must have been it. Ha! It was funny, now that she thought about it. How silly!

Rebecca smiled as she sat staring at her plate. Her mind soon returned to her troubles. It seemed so unfair. She would make the best of all possible mothers. So many women take the special gift they have for granted. Some even throw it away. Why was she being denied? And the doctors could find nothing wrong so far, which made it even more frustrating to her. If there was a problem, something tangible that she could see and understand, then she felt she might be able to deal with it. She could fight it, or know why she should look elsewhere for her happiness. But there was no reason! Just...nothing!

An old but familiar sense of despair returned. Prayer was not something to which she was accustomed, but her heart ached, and she felt the need to reach out as she never had felt it before. It was almost as though an unseen ally was pulling her along. She resisted for a moment, but each time she pulled away, a renewed sense of urgency tugged at her heart.

Tears rolled down her cheeks. Her head bowed slightly, more from the weight of her burden than from any acknowledgment of tradition, and her lips formed the words that were spoken in her mind.

"Dear God, help me. I don't know what to do. I've tried everything. I've...I've...Dear God please, just...just ..."

As she prayed a prayer without words, unseen forces began to orchestrate events many miles away on her behalf. Rebecca began to sob. Next to her, the Centurion held his shield firmly and stood his ground with the resolve of one assured of victory.

Rebecca felt better after her brief prayer. She shook off the weight of self-pity threatening to pull her down again. She knew better than to let herself wallow in pity. It did no good and it only would make her suffering all the more intense. She finished her bagel and slipped out of the booth, leaving enough money on the table for the tip and the bill.

Outside, the summer air smelled good. A breeze drifted in from the ocean only two miles away, carrying with it the scent of salt water. Rebecca drew in a deep breath and held it for a moment.

Walking briskly in the warm California sun, she looked at her watch. It was almost eleven thirty. By the time she walked back to the garage it would be noon—time to pick up the car. She felt better now. The fresh air and sun washed over her, giving her a new outlook. Brad was right. It was too early to give up. Besides, she was a fighter—from a long line of fighters. She chuckled to herself as she thought of Aunt Billie. Better not let her hear any talk of quitting!

It had been months since she had seen her aunt. The forceful and strong-willed Wilhelmina Dawson was the closest thing to a mother Rebecca had. There was a bond between them. Billie had no children of her own. Rebecca often wondered why. Billie relished children.

Billie had a knack for lifting a person's spirits. And right now, Rebecca needed that more than anything. She knew what she would do. She and Brad would drive up and see Aunt Billie for the weekend.

Brad wouldn't like the idea. It was a two-hour drive, and Brad hated to drive on the weekends if he didn't have to. But she could talk him into it. She needed it, and she would just have to make him understand.

Rebecca edged into the driveway as far to the left as she could to give Brad room enough to pull his prized Plymouth into the garage. The air conditioning in the Toyota was working great again, and it felt good on this warm afternoon. She shut off the engine and hurried inside. Setting the handful of shopping bags down on the kitchen counter, she went straight to the phone.

"Hello?" came the voice on the other end after several rings.

"Aunt Billie? It's Rebecca."

"Oh, hi, Honey! It's so good to hear your voice! How are you?"

"I'm fine."

"Are you in town?"

"No, I'm at home. I was just thinking about you, and thought I'd call."

"Oh, how nice. And how is Brad?"

"He's fine."

"Good. And is everything going well with you?"

"Oh, yes. Well, pretty well. You know, same old stuff, work and sleep."

Aunt Billie chuckled a polite laugh. "Well, maybe you two need to get away more. You know I'm always telling you that you need to play more. And you're always welcome here. I'd love to have you come stay with me for a few days."

Rebecca smiled. Aunt Billie always made it so easy. "To be truthful, I was hoping you'd ask. Could we come up for the weekend?"

"Oh, of course! I'll have your room ready as soon as you get here. Are you leaving now?"

"No. Brad isn't home from work yet. And, well, I haven't actually talked to him about it yet."

"Ah, well, the two of you discuss it, and I'll be waiting for you when you get here." Aunt Billie paused for a moment. "Rebecca?"

"Yes?"

"Is everything all right?"

Since she was a little girl, Rebecca never could hide anything from her aunt. "I just…need to get away and think for a while…I guess."

"Is everything all right between you and Brad?"

"Oh, yes, everything is fine. It's just, well, I'll tell you about it when I see you."

"All right, Honey. Drive carefully. Bye."

Rebecca put the receiver back in its place. She felt better already, just knowing she'd soon be in the warm, cozy setting of Aunt Billie's home. As far back as she could remember, the old house represented retreat—and sanctuary from whatever troubles the world was throwing at her at the time. Aunt Billie had a way of making it so.

Rebecca grew more eager by the minute. Now there was only one thing left to do, one minor hurdle to cross. She would have to convince Brad.

It was a warm afternoon. Billie hung up the phone in the kitchen, fixed herself a sandwich, and then sat down at the table to eat. Her spirits were higher than usual. Rebecca was coming. She thumbed through the stack of mail, discarding those addressed to "occupant," and put the bills in a pile of their own. When she finished her sandwich, she washed her plate and put it away before wiping down the countertop with a dishrag. She hurried upstairs to change her clothes. Then she bounded down again and out the back door.

Her garden was small, encircled by a white plastic picket fence a foot or so high. It was placed strategically between the house and the garage so that it took full advantage of the sunlight. Each row of assorted vegetables was neatly spaced, and the loamy brown soil was flawlessly tilled to perfection.

She stepped easily over the fence, picked up a hoe, and began working the ground. She loved to come here in the warmth of the afternoon, dig into the earth, and feel the sweat on her brow. She used it as a time to pray. She could think—or not think if she chose, but mostly she prayed—to the steady, mindless rhythm of the hoe. The weight of the world lifted, and she sensed a comforting hand on her shoulder as each care, each concern, each burden—whether her own or someone else's—was placed before the throne of heaven.

She prayed for Ellen and Charles. She prayed for Helen and Alva. She prayed for Meg and her husband. She prayed for her church and the pastor. She prayed for hurting children, those she knew and those she didn't know, and she prayed for broken homes. She prayed for the missionaries who spoke a few weeks before on a Sunday evening. She prayed for those in positions of power and authority, that God would give them wisdom and guidance. She prayed for the nameless little boy in the supermarket with the dirty face—the one whose mother looked gaunt with hollow eyes and a perpetual sniffle. She prayed for the man who delivered her mail. But mostly she prayed for Rebecca.

When the afternoon sun disappeared behind the house, she set the hoe in the corner of the garden by the garage and stepped out onto the sidewalk, brushing the dirt from her hands and the front of her denim trousers. Starting toward the house, she remembered something and turned back to the garden. She stepped gingerly over the fence and stooped down to pick a head of lettuce, a couple of tomatoes, and a bell pepper. She climbed over the fence and carried her harvest into the house, setting it on the counter next to her Bible.

Her back felt sore. She stretched, leaning backward with her hand in the small of her back, and then rocked side to side as she walked slowly to the stairs, counting each one as she ascended them. As a young girl she bounded up and down these same stairs without a second thought, but now they represented her greatest challenge. For the last few months, though, in the evening the burden was almost unbearable.

She showered, letting the warm water caress her aching joints and muscles, and then slipped on a clean pair of sweats. A shower always invigorated her, and the stairs were easier going down. She went to the kitchen and fixed a quick salad. Then with her Bible under her arm, she went into the living room and sat in her favorite chair. She laid the Bible on the table next to the chair, held the salad plate in her lap, and reached for a magazine, flipping through it as she ate without thinking.

She read a couple of the articles before reaching for her Bible. It was several hours later when she awoke with a start as the Bible slid from her lap and landed on the floor. She rubbed her eyes with her fingers and looked around for a moment. Then slowly she went upstairs to bed.

An invisible golden shield covered the old house, just as it had done for her entire life. The bearer of the shield smiled down on his charge. His time here was short; a new mission waited. The house and its occupants had been under his care ever since the old woman had been a little girl. The family had enjoyed his unseen protection for generations, almost since the beginning of time. Now a new assignment soon would require the Centurion's attention. He knelt down. His eyes flashed his unwavering perseverance, and his steady hand held the shield with vigilant resolve.

CHAPTER THIRTEEN

"COME IN! COME in!" Aunt Billie said with childish delight. "Oh, it's been so long since I've seen you!"

Rebecca beamed as she stepped into the entry of the old Victorian home. She gave her aunt a kiss. "I know it has. We really should get up here more often."

Billie turned to Brad and gave him a warm hug. "How are you, Dear?"

"Fine."

"It's so good to see you!" Billie said again.

"It's good to be here," Rebecca said. "I miss this old place." She looked around, letting familiar smells fill her nostrils. The dark oak paneling and the way each footstep echoed through the house brought a flood of memories. As a young girl she would run through the great rooms and hallways, enchanted by the echoes, and imagine herself in a great castle. She loved to run down the hallway that led to the billiard room, lunge headlong onto the little throw-rug, and slide along the old oak floor as far as she could.

"And this old place misses you," Billie said with a wink.

Brad smiled politely. All he could see was the weathered siding and the tattered roof. It smelled like an old house too. Brad was used to the smell of new carpet and paint with a hint of potpourri, and he saw nothing charming or nostalgic about a dusty old house.

Aunt Billie slipped her thin, bony hand into Rebecca's. "Come on, you two. Let's go into the sitting room. I'll make some tea." She turned to Brad. "I baked some goodies when I found out you were coming."

"I never turn down food," Brad said.

The sitting room was large and spacious, with tall windows on three sides that reached the ceiling, drenching the room in sunlight. There were small tables and knickknack shelves everywhere, bearing the collections of a lifetime. The old sofa's mahogany trim glistened in the sunlight and the upholstery could have been new yesterday if it weren't for the fabric's dated pattern. William's telescope sat in the corner, as if waiting faithfully for him to return. Next to it in a bookcase along the wall, pictures were scattered about, beginning with old and faded black-and-white photos and ending with new color prints. They filled the entire bookcase. On the top shelf was an old photo of a young couple in dated clothing posing for a wedding picture. Beside it a picture of William in his heyday—crisp business suit and neatly trimmed moustache—sat reverently in a place of highest honor behind a single dried carnation, a reminder of the day Billie buried him. Beneath it, on the very next shelf, was a whole row of pictures of Rebecca from the time she was a baby until her wedding day a few months before William died.

"You kids make yourselves comfortable while I start the water for the tea." Billie disappeared for a moment as Brad and Rebecca sat on the sofa.

In another moment, she returned.

"Will you stay the night?" Billie asked as she settled back in her favorite chair.

"I'm not sure," Rebecca said. "We haven't discussed it yet." She shot a pleading look at her husband.

Brad was cornered and he knew it. "Well…I thought we were—"

"Oh, could we?" Rebecca said. "It would be so nice to stay here again."

"Well, sure. I suppose we can," Brad said, trying to infuse a measured amount of displeasure in his voice.

"Oh, that would be wonderful!" Billie exclaimed. "I have your room all ready! Do you have your things?"

"We have a suitcase out in the car," said Rebecca.

"Fine, fine! Then we're all set!" Billie settled back, pleased with herself. "So how is work?"

"Fine," said Brad. "We've been working on a project out in the desert. It's keeping me pretty busy."

"And how is the house? Did you get the backyard landscaped yet?"

"I've been working on it myself," said Rebecca. "But I save the heavy stuff for Brad."

"That's what a man is for," Billie grinned. Her eyes went to the picture on the shelf.

"I'm pretty sure that's why she keeps me around!" Brad said.

From the other room, the high, shrill whistle of the teapot brought Billie to her feet.

When she was out of earshot, Brad leaned over and whispered, "You planned this."

"Now, Honey. We hardly ever come. It won't hurt us to spend the night."

"Yeah?"

Rebecca leaned close. "Please?"

"I thought we were going to go someplace, just the two of us."

Her eyes pleaded. "I know, but—"

Brad sighed. "Yeah, I suppose," he mumbled.

"Do you take sugar?" Billie called out from the kitchen.

"I do!" said Rebecca. She turned to Brad and whispered, "I love you."

"You should."

A moment later, Billie came in, carrying a large tray with two china pots. "I know Brad likes his coffee, so I made both."

She set the tray down on the coffee table in front of the sofa and hurried off to the kitchen again. She returned with another tray piled high with crackers, cheese, and a few cookies.

"So tell me what's happening with you two," Billie said as she sat down again. "Is the Lord treating you OK?"

Brad shifted his weight. Aunt Billie always managed to bring God into everything. It wasn't that he was opposed to religion—in its proper place. He was even sympathetic toward it, politically speaking, but Billie always managed to talk about Jesus—and talk of Jesus made him uncomfortable.

"Oh, yes," said Rebecca. "Everything's fine at home. We couldn't be happier."

"Well, that's good to hear," said Billie. "I do worry about the two of you down there all by yourselves."

"We have a few friends," Brad said.

"Oh, I know. But there's no family nearby. You should be close to family."

Brad didn't like where this was headed. "We have friends close if we need anything."

"Mm-hmm. More coffee?"

"No, thanks. Well, maybe just a little to warm it up."

"How about you, Dear? More tea?"

Rebecca held out her cup. "Thank you."

"You know," Aunt Billie said as she set the pot back on the tray, "someday this house will be yours."

Rebecca felt uneasy.

Brad sank back on the sofa at the thought of someday spending his Saturdays painting and fixing the old house.

"That day is a long way off," Rebecca said, more to assure herself than her aunt.

"Maybe," Billie said. "You can never tell. I do wish you lived closer, though."

"Maybe you should move to the city," Brad offered. "It would be a lot easier for you, and then we would be near."

Billie looked around. "I couldn't leave this house."

"I imagine there are a lot of memories here," Rebecca said.

"Yes," Billie almost whispered.

"It's a lot to take care of," said Brad.

Billie looked into her cup.

"You know," said Rebecca, "my earliest memories are here. I can remember Uncle Bill taking me for a walk down by the water. I remember he usually had to pick me up and carry me halfway home."

"This old house has been a part of our family for many years," Billie said. "My father built it when he came here from Oregon in the early thirties. Some of my earliest memories are here too."

Rebecca sat forward. "I always knew that Grandpa Jakes built the house, but I didn't know he came from Oregon. I always thought the Jakeses came from Pennsylvania."

"They did—originally. But your grandpa's great-grandfather went to the Oregon Territory first and settled there. We left there when I was very young. When I married your uncle, I just couldn't bring myself to leave this old house. By then both my folks had died and left the house to my brothers and me, so Bill and I bought out your father and your uncles."

"I'd hate to have to take care of it," Brad voiced his thoughts. Rebecca jabbed him with her elbow.

"It can be a great deal of work," Billie mused.

"But it's so pretty here," said Rebecca. "I can see why Grandpa would want to move here."

Billie set her cup on the table next to her chair. "Well, yes, but that wasn't why he moved here."

"What do you mean?"

"Well, there was some trouble—superstition really, but my father believed it, and he left."

"What kind of superstition?" Brad asked.

"Oh, silly notions." Billie shifted nervously, eager to change the subject. "I still own some of the land they settled on."

"Really?" Rebecca asked. "I didn't know that."

"Mm-hmm. I haven't been up there since I was little, but I still pay taxes on it. I don't even remember much about it really. I can recall the house...and the basement, of all things to remember. I don't know why, but I do. Even that's a faded memory. I remember putting coins in a jar and hiding it in the basement, behind a wall. Oh, it seemed like it was miles high! I remember climbing the wall—it was stone, I think—by putting my toes between the stones. I was holding the jar tightly under my arm for fear it would fall and break and I'd have to explain to my father why there was glass all over the basement floor." Billie chuckled to herself at the memory. "I suppose it would be smarter to sell the old place, but I just never got around to it."

"You oughta sell it and this old house and move closer to us," Brad said. "Then you wouldn't have to hassle with it."

Billie took her cup from the table, sipped long and slow, and then set the cup back down. "I suppose so," she said. She straightened in her chair and drew a deep breath. Then she smiled. "I was hoping I could talk you into helping me with one of those 'little hassles' while you're here. The upstairs bath has a leak under the sink. Do you suppose you could fix it for me? I really hate to ask, but I tried to fix it myself, and I just couldn't do it. I'm afraid I'm not as strong as I used to be."

"Sure," Brad said, trying to muster some enthusiasm. "Do you have some tools?"

"In the garage along the west wall," she said, pointing in the general direction of the garage and making a circle in the air with her finger. "And there are a few plumbing…things in a drawer under the workbench."

"Things?"

"Yes, you know those little round black things."

Brad raised an eyebrow. "Washers," he said as he headed for the front door.

When he had gone, Billie turned to Rebecca. "What say we go for a walk?"

"Sounds good."

The two women strolled along the walkway that led to the beach in silence. They were almost to the pier before Billie spoke. "So do you want to tell me about it?"

"About what?"

"You said on the phone you had something to tell me. Is everything all right?"

Rebecca took a deep breath. "It's nothing, really. I mean, it's no big deal. It's just that Brad and I would like to have a family, and—"

Billie waited for her to finish, but Rebecca was silent. "So what's stopping you?"

Rebecca shrugged. "I just don't seem to be able to get pregnant."

"That doesn't sound like nothing. Is there a problem?"

"We don't know yet. The doctor is still running some tests."

"I see."

They continued to walk until they came to the pier. "You know," said Billie as she took Rebecca's hand and squeezed it, "I love you more than my own life."

Rebecca looked down at the ground.

Billie continued. "I've always felt that way. But after your folks died, well, I've always felt that in a way you were sort of my daughter too. I never had children of my own. I wanted them desperately. In many ways you fill that gap in my life."

Rebecca's eyes glistened with tears. "I'm sorry," she said as she wiped them away. "I shouldn't be such a baby. It's just that it's so important to me—to us! We want a family more than anything."

"I know, Honey," Billie said softly.

"We've been to the doctor. I'm so sick of tests! And they can't seem to find anything wrong!"

Billie breathed a heavy sigh and slipped her hand under Rebecca's arm as they continued along the beach. "I don't know about such things, but I do know that God can help."

"I know," Rebecca said from reflex. "It's just that we never have time for church, and Brad doesn't like any of the ones we've been to."

Billie nodded politely. "Well," she said as she tried to think of the best way to say what was on her mind, "church is fine. I mean you should go to church, but that's not really what I was talking about."

Rebecca knew what was coming. All her life, Billie had talked of Jesus and the need for a relationship—whatever that meant. Rebecca believed in God. She prayed. And her Bible was very important to her, although it never left the shelf in the den. Religion was never important to her parents. The only time she ever went to church was when Aunt Billie took her on one of her summer visits.

"I've prayed," Rebecca said apologetically.

They continued walking.

"I don't know what to do," said Rebecca. "We've tried everything."

"Well," Billie said, "maybe God isn't ready for you to have a baby yet. But I want you to know that I've been praying for you, and I'll keep praying as long as I live."

"I hope it helps," Rebecca said through tears.

"God always answers prayer, Honey. He may not always do it the way we want or even in ways we know about—sometimes He does it without our knowledge—but He always answers."

"I'm willing to try just about anything at this point."

Billie shook her head. "God isn't something you try, like trying on a new blouse. I don't know what He has in store for you, but I know He loves you. When you trust in Him, you give your life to Him—and everything that goes with it, including babies."

"Sort of like 'the devil may care,' huh?"

Billie smiled warmly, but the disappointment she felt showed on her face. "Not exactly. The devil has no power over those who love Jesus, Honey. Just don't give him a foothold in your life. I wish I'd learned that a little sooner."

Rebecca nodded obediently, but the words meant little to her. She had heard her aunt talk of the devil and demons as though they really existed and had power. But this was the twenty-first century and such notions, though quaint, had no place in modern thinking.

Wilhelmina Dawson knelt by the side of her bed as the late afternoon sun streamed in through the open window that faced the sea. Rebecca and Brad had taken a stroll after lunch. Billie had come to her room under the pretense of taking a nap.

"Dear God, please help them. I know You love them. And I know of your great sacrifice. Please, Lord, touch them through the power of your Holy Spirit and bring them both to their knees in true worship of your Son."

The Centurion stood nearby, but something beyond Billie's bed held his attention. He knelt down on one knee in reverent obedience and nodded his affirmation of new orders.

Saturday morning, Brad and Rebecca slept until almost eleven. They finally woke to the distant sound of the sea and the smell of salt air. The window had been thrown open. Billie must have come in some time in the morning, just as she had when Rebecca was a little girl, and opened it.

"Good morning," Brad said as he opened his eyes and noticed Rebecca was studying his face as he slept.

"Good morning," she replied.

"What time is it?" he asked.

Rebecca raised her head to see the clock on the stand. "Ten fifty-five."

Brad stretched and yawned. "Did you sleep well?" he asked.

Rebecca shook her head. "Not very. I tossed and turned all night. How about you?"

"I didn't sleep much either. Someone kept kicking me."

"I'm sorry," Rebecca said. "I suppose I was restless."

"What was the matter? You have something on your mind?"

Rebecca shrugged. "I don't know. I just couldn't sleep."

"Mmm." Brad closed his eyes as Rebecca began stroking the side of his head.

"You like?" she said a moment later.

"I like."

Rebecca studied his face. He was strong. She liked that in her man, but now, lying here with his eyes closed, he seemed almost helpless. "You're cute," she said.

"I am, huh?" he said, opening his eyes.

Rebecca nodded. "I could stay here all day."

"Yeah, me too." Brad sighed. "But it's getting late. We'd better get moving."

They quickly dressed, packed, made the bed, and tidied up the room before going downstairs. Brad set their suitcase near the front door. The smell of frying bacon lured them to the kitchen.

"You kids hungry?"

Brad was always hungry. "Sure am."

"Sit down and I'll have some bacon and eggs for you in a minute."

Billie finished her chore at the griddle and served them. When they were through, Rebecca picked up the dishes and carried them to the sink.

"Just leave them, Honey, I'll take care of it later," Billie said.

"Oh, no," Rebecca said. "I can't leave you with a mess."

"Nonsense! You're my guests and guests don't do dishes!"

"But I—"

Billie shook her head. "I won't hear of it. I'll take care of it. You two are in a hurry. You go on. I'll tend to it later."

Rebecca gave in. "All right. But I feel funny about it."

"No need. I insist."

Brad followed as Billie and Rebecca lead the way to the foyer. Aunt Billie walked close to Rebecca and held her arm. "You know, Honey, I don't know how much time I have, but I want you to know that I love you with all my heart."

"Is there something you're not telling me?" Rebecca said.

"Can't I tell my favorite niece that I love her?"

"Of course. It's just that—"

Billie shook her head. "Just the musings of an old lady. Don't pay any attention to me."

"You're not sick, are you?"

"No!" Billie said. "Nothing like that. It's just that I'm getting older, and no one has any guarantees. I just wanted you to know, that's all."

Billie's words frightened Rebecca. She pondered them on the way home.

"What's the matter?" Brad asked an hour later as the car headed south along Highway 101.

"Huh?"

"I said, 'What's the matter?' You seem a million miles away."

"I'm sorry," she said, but her mind was elsewhere.

Brad reached over and took her hand. "Where are you?"

Rebecca sighed. "I'm sorry," she said again. "I just can't get Aunt Billie out of my mind."

"Something wrong?"

"I don't know. She didn't seem the same to me. Didn't you notice? She seemed frail."

"That's never been a good word to describe your aunt."

"No. But she seemed that way today."

Brad hadn't noticed. But he knew his wife. "You want to go back?"

Rebecca didn't answer.

"Sweetie?"

Rebecca shook her head. "No. It's probably silly of me. I'll call her in the morning and make sure she's OK."

As Brad and Rebecca pulled out of the driveway onto the road, Billie shuffled back toward the house with a sense of urgency. Somehow she felt as if time were suddenly a luxury she could no longer count on. She knew what she must do. She must go to the attic.

The leather pouch with the papers—and the unfinished business.

But now, as she mounted the stairs, she stopped to rest. She wasn't as young as she used to be, and those stairs posed an ever-increasing challenge. Tomorrow would be soon enough. Tomorrow morning she would go to the attic—first thing.

Brad flipped on the headlights as the sun disappeared into the magnificent Pacific Ocean, shimmering in the last few rays of sun outside the passenger-side window.

"Would you like to stop for the night?" Brad asked.

"Don't you have to work Monday?"

Brad shrugged. "It's only Saturday. We've got time. Let's take tomorrow and play. If we don't make it back by Monday morning, I'll call in."

Rebecca slid over next to her husband and slipped her arm under his. Brad was impulsive. She hated it, usually. She hated impulse. She wanted to know where everything was and where it was going. She didn't like surprises. She liked the world to be ordered and planned. But there were times, like now, when impulse had its advantages.

She rested her head on his shoulder. "Sounds wonderful."

Brad turned off the freeway at the next off-ramp and headed for the little bed and breakfast he knew was just up the road. The circle driveway that led to the front of an old Victorian house was lined with neatly trimmed primroses. A weeping willow tree gracefully cast its boughs over a manicured lawn and the salt air, mixed with roses, gave the old house a sense of magic that hinted at grand ballrooms and southern belles and noble gentlemen in carriages. A neatly painted wooden sign near the road announced rooms were available and breakfast was at eight thirty.

A middle-aged woman met them at the door. She was a short, odd-looking woman, stooped shouldered, and her head seemed to have been placed too far forward for her body. Her mousy brown hair was streaked with silver gray and she shuffled when she walked.

"Can I help you?"

"Yes. Do you have a room for the night?"

"Yes, we—"

"The one on the west corner," Rebecca interrupted. "The one with the ocean view."

The old woman raised a brow as the corners of her mouth curled upward slightly. "Oh, yes. I remember. You've been here before, haven't you?"

"Yes." Rebecca beamed. "On our honeymoon five years ago."

"I thought so," the woman cackled. "I never forget a newlywed couple. We get them here all the time. I never forget!"

"We'd like the same room if it's available," Rebecca pressed.

The old woman nodded with a wink. "Yes, I think it is," she said gleefully. "You kids come with me."

The old woman turned and shuffled toward the stairs at the end of the large foyer. Rebecca and Brad followed her. Brad, impatient with her slow pace, rocked back and forth, mocking her plodding. He straightened with embarrassment as she turned to see if they were still with her. When the old woman looked away again, Rebecca poked him in the ribs and gave him a scolding look.

"Here we are," she said as she pushed open the door, revealing a large, open bedroom with a mahogany canopy bed. The bureau was the same—ornately carved mahogany. The oak floors creaked as Rebecca walked to the polished brick fireplace in the corner.

It was just as she remembered it. "Can we get wood for a fire?"

"Firewood?" the old woman questioned.

"It's not cold," Brad said.

"I know, but I love a fire." Her eyes pleaded with him.

Brad shook his head. "Whatever the lady wants."

The old woman nodded. "I'll see that some is brought in. Breakfast is at eight thirty. Will you be joining us?"

Rebecca and Brad looked at each other.

"We're not sure," Brad offered, turning to the old woman. "Better not count on us."

The old woman nodded again. "You two kids enjoy your stay," she said and then shut the door and was gone.

Rebecca fell back on the ruffled comforter that covered the bed. "Oooh, I love it. Let's live here!"

"And who'll pay for it?" Brad chided as he settled in next to her on the bed.

Rebecca put her long, slender arms around his neck. "The most handsome man in the world!"

"And why would this 'handsome man' want to pay for our room?"

Rebecca smiled. "Shut up and kiss me! Mmm, not bad."

"That's what they all say!"

Rebecca reached down and pinched the flesh of Brad's side.

"Owww!" Brad held Rebecca tightly and began tickling her.

"Noooo! Stop!" Rebecca giggled as she struggled to free herself.

Brad stopped tickling her but held her close, his fingers poised to resume the torture at the slightest provocation.

"That's enough!" Rebecca said, trying to sound sincere.

"No more pinching?"

"No more pinching," she affirmed.

Brad released her. She rolled over on the bed next to him. "Sooo—what are we going to do?" She said as she folded her arms behind her head.

"I don't care. Whatever you want. Tomorrow is our day. I want us to forget everything—babies, tests, and mortgage payments—everything. Let's just have fun and be together. OK?"

Rebecca put her arms around Brad's neck again. "I love you," she said.

Brad grinned his devilish grin. "And with good reason."

Rebecca giggled, but then her face darkened as she lay thinking for a moment. "You know, I always thought Aunt Billie never wanted children."

A knock at the door interrupted them. Brad pushed himself off the bed and went to the door. A young man of twenty or so stood in the hallway with a heavy burden of chopped wood. "You the ones that wanted firewood?"

"That's us," Brad said as he stood aside to let him in.

"Not too many people want firewood this time of the year," he said as he set the bundle down next to the fireplace. "Guess you folks get cold, huh?"

"Well, one of us is a little crazy," Brad said under his breath. He handed the young man a five-dollar bill at the door, closing it behind him, and then joined Rebecca on the bed again.

"Maybe she didn't."

"Didn't what?"

"Your aunt. Maybe she didn't want children. Maybe she's just now realizing that she missed out."

Rebecca shook her head. "No, I don't think so. She always knows what she wants. Once she makes up her mind, it's made up for good. No, I think she wanted them. And besides, she said she wanted them."

"I wonder why she didn't have any then."

"I don't know," Rebecca said. She rolled to her side and put her head on her husband's chest. "But I know I don't want to be old and have that look."

"What look is that?"

Rebecca unbuttoned the top two buttons of Brad's shirt and stroked his chest with the tips of her fingers. "The look she had this afternoon when she was talking about having children—or not having them."

"I didn't notice."

"You weren't there, silly! It was when we were walking along the beach. Anyway, she's lonely, I could tell. Her eyes said it all. They were sad. And I think I know why."

"Why?"

"Because she wanted children and couldn't have them. I think she didn't have children because she couldn't, and that scares me."

"Why would it scare you?"

"Because ..." Rebecca paused, fearing to hear the words she was thinking, "because I'm afraid it might run in the family."

"Nonsense! If it was something hereditary, why are you here?"

"I don't know. Maybe it skips generations or something. Maybe—"

"I think you're letting your imagination run away with you."

"Maybe."

Brad knew that tone. He reached down and began gently stroking her hair. She loved to have her hair stroked and he hoped it would be enough. "Don't give up. There's still hope," he said softly as he kissed the top of her head.

The next morning, Rebecca woke to the distant sound of the sea through the open window. Delicate draperies fluttered in the soft breeze as salt air filled the room, and for a moment the magic and charm of the romantic setting pushed her troubles aside. She stretched and yawned, and then rubbed the sleep out of her eyes. Brad was not in the bed next to her.

"Honey?" Brad didn't answer. She swung her feet out of the bed and sat on the edge, trying to work up the energy to go to the bathroom. The clock on the nightstand said 9:30. She felt as if she could sleep another hour, and any other day she might have, but not today.

"Honey? You in there?" she called out toward the bathroom.

Brushing her long hair out of her face with her hand, she shuffled toward the bathroom door. It was standing open a crack, and she pushed it open. Brad was not there either. *Must have gone for a paper.*

She quickly slipped on a dress and then busied herself with the daily ritual at the mirror. She wanted to be ready when he returned. This was going to be a fun day. And she needed a fun day—free of care. This was just the place to do it, here along the coast with the sea air, the rolling hills, and the quaint little shops.

She studied her face in the mirror. It was a good face. It was the face of a mother. She'd make a good mother. She knew she could. Why in all the world, with all the mothers who didn't appreciate motherhood, who abused their children, even killed them in the womb, why couldn't she be a mother? To hold a tiny person, to nurse it at her breast, yes, even to rise early in the morning—to sacrifice, to give of herself, the thoughts tugged at her heart. It wasn't fair. It wasn't right.

"About ready?"

"Oh!" Rebecca put her hand over her heart. "Honey! You gave me a start! I didn't hear you come in!"

Pleased with himself, Brad tossed a newspaper on the bathroom counter and stood behind her with his arms around her waist. She put on the last bit of lipstick and quickly brushed out her hair. "There! All set!"

She turned around to face him and slipped her arms around his neck. "You look great," he said, and then kissed her. "Mmm, let's stay here," he said as he started to unzip her dress.

"No, not now. You promised me a day. There'll be time for that later."

"Doesn't seem like a very good policy for baby making," he said.

Rebecca pulled him in close. "Don't you worry, Mister," she said. "I won't let you get very far away."

Brad kissed her again and reached around for the zipper. Rebecca gently pushed him.

"Yeah," he said, a little disappointed. "So do you want to eat here or go someplace?"

"Let's go someplace. I feel like something nice."

"Your wish, m'lady," he said as he bowed low and swept his arm across the room, striking the bathroom door with his knuckles.

Rebecca giggled. "Let's go, silly."

The day went quickly for Rebecca, as good days often do. After a seafood breakfast in one of the local restaurants that overlooked the ocean-side cliffs, they spent the morning hitting some of the local shops. Around noon, they bought a couple of sandwiches at a local cafe and strolled out onto the pier to eat. At two, they decided to go for a walk on the beach. The salt air and the gentle breeze had a soothing effect and they soon forgot the time, finding themselves several miles away from the car. It was dark by the time they walked to the car and drove back to the bed and breakfast, so they decided to stay another night.

As they entered the room, Rebecca fell back on the bed. "Did you enjoy yourself?" Brad asked.

"Ohhh, it was wonderful!" Her eyes found his. "You were wonderful," she said softly as she held out her hand.

Brad crossed the room and sat on the edge of the bed. She took his hand and held it in her own as she stroked the back of it with the other.

"Wait right there," he said as he pulled away. He stepped over to the lone chair, pulled a small package from the pocket of his windbreaker, and sat back down on the bed.

"What is it?" Rebecca asked.

"Open it and see."

"When did you get this?" she asked as she pulled at the wrapping.

"Today, when you weren't looking."

"But how—"

"Never mind. Just open it."

Rebecca removed the paper wrapping to reveal the small box inside. Slowly and reverently, she lifted the lid. Inside was a small, delicate ornament. It was a reindeer surrounded by Christmas holly. Sitting on the reindeer was a baby, smiling and happy. The inscription read, "Baby's First Christmas."

A teardrop fell, moistening the baby's face. Rebecca looked up at her husband. He reached down to hold her face between his hands and studied her eyes.

"Because there is hope," he said. "Because there is always hope."

Wilhelmina Dawson set the receiver back on the hook. Rebecca and Brad were not home. She wondered if they had decided to spend the night somewhere along the way.

She hated those infernal answering machines, but as much as she detested talking to them, she had to admit it was nice to know Rebecca would receive the news as soon as she came home. And she had to know—know all of it. The papers, the leather pouch, all of it. Billie knew the truth, but she had to see that Rebecca knew it, too. All of it. And Billie knew she had to be the one to tell her—to make sure she understood.

Her Bible held the key, as she knew it would. Ever since Brad and Rebecca had left, Billie's spirit would not let her rest. She began a search for something she knew by heart, but couldn't immediately find. Her brief study unlocked the fragmented memory as she read:

> For I am convinced that neither death nor life, neither angels nor demons, neither the present nor the future, nor any powers, neither height nor depth, nor anything else in all creation will be able to separate us from the love of God that is in Christ Jesus our Lord.

The papers in the leather pouch would point to a different truth. Yet it was time for Rebecca to know her heritage. Billie gripped her left arm as a pain shot down to her fingertips. A strange feeling washed over her as her mind struggled to remain focused.

Billie picked up the phone. She felt a need to call that was strangely urgent.

Rebecca should be home by now. Oh, of course she would be. It was yesterday she was here, not today. But was it today I went into the attic to look? Yes, it was this morning. But Rebecca was here today—no, yesterday.

Drat! Why couldn't she keep it straight? The phone looked strange in her hand. What to do? The dial–but there was no dial, only buttons. Now when did that happen, and how?

William would know. But he is at the beach with Rebecca. He should be home by now. Rebecca's mother would be here soon to pick her up and tomorrow was a school day. No, that's not right either.

The phone slipped from Billie's hand, landed on the table, and then fell to the floor with a crash. The echo reverberated through the old house, but the sound fell on deaf ears.

The Centurion looked down with a smile, took up his shield and moved on.

Rebecca held Brad's arm as he drove home, her head resting comfortably on his shoulder. In her other hand she clutched the little ornament, studying its every detail and reliving the moment he gave it to her. There was hope. She felt it. There must be hope. Brad believed it too, and it gave her strength.

Rebecca sighed deeply.

Brad shifted his weight. "You awake?"

"Mm-hmm," she said as she pulled away from his shoulder and sat up. "I was just thinking."

"That's encouraging."

Rebecca poked him in the ribs with her finger. "You think so, huh?" she said playfully, and then snuggled in close again.

Brad silently swung his arm over the back of the seat and softly brushed the bare skin of her shoulder with his hand.

"So what were you thinking?" he said after several minutes.

Rebecca inspected Brad's day-old growth. It was a good face. "I was just thinking what a good father you'd make."

Brad smiled. "You can tell, I suppose?"

"I can tell."

It was late Monday afternoon and traffic was light by Southern California standards. They should be home in half-an-hour. Brad let his mind drift as the car followed the broken centerline that snaked along the rolling hillside. Soon they merged with freeway traffic as they drew closer to Los Angeles.

"I've been thinking too," Brad said. "You know, about what your aunt said about not having kids and wanting to."

"What about it?"

"I don't know. I was just wondering, why the big secret?"

"I don't know what you mean. It's no secret."

"Well, yeah, not having them, sure. But I mean the part about wanting them."

Rebecca shrugged. "That's not a secret either."

Brad shook his head. "Maybe not. But you said yourself you didn't know about it, and you're as close to her as anyone. Closer maybe."

Rebecca shrugged again. "So what's your point?"

"I don't know. I'm just thinking out loud. But you know, maybe we should talk to the doctor and ask if there could be something to this idea that it could run in the family."

Rebecca recoiled at the thought. She had been struggling all along with the possibility that it was her fault she couldn't conceive. Now there was a new wrinkle, and somehow it seemed to make it worse. If it was something "in the family," how could she overcome it? Infections and thyroid problems were one thing, but what if it was something that was part of her—her very makeup as a woman? She couldn't begin to guess or understand the medical or physiological reasons why it might be true. She only knew the idea frightened her.

"Let's talk about something else," she said.

CHAPTER FOURTEEN

THE RED LIGHT of the answering machine flashed its silent alarm that someone had called. Rebecca kicked off her shoes and watched them slide across the entry tile and stop a few inches from the wall underneath a small table. It felt good to be home again.

Rebecca took a step toward the hallway and the bathroom. Brad, when he saw what she was doing, began moving in the same direction. Their eyes met. They paused for a moment, each waiting for the other to make the first move, and then made a collective dash for the hallway. Rebecca braked a few feet away and slid in her stocking feet into the hallway entry, beating her husband by only inches. He pulled up short as she turned and back-pedaled toward the bathroom, giggling.

"You win that one," he said, laughing, "but there will be others!" He turned to walk back toward the living room sofa, stopping at the entry table where the answering machine continued to flash its silent announcement, and punched the play button.

Gotta remember to push save, he reminded himself. He hated this new machine. The old one saved all messages automatically, but with this new one, the save feature had to be done manually as soon as the messages had been played. Brad made the mental note.

"Hi." It was Aunt Billie. "Hope your trip home was pleasant. Call me as soon as you get in. I have something important to tell you. I was going through some old papers in the attic and I found something that I think you should know. I know this is going to sound silly, but—"

Just then, the phone rang. Brad reached down and lowered the volume control on the side of the answering machine.

"I'm not sure how to say this, but I may have something that you should consider... ." Billie's voice trailed off as the volume lowered.

"Hello? Yes? Oh, hello, Clay. No, not yet. I'll pick it up on the way to work tomorrow. Yeah, we did. It was great to get away. Yeah, weather was good. Ha! You, too. Yeah, see you in the morning."

Click.

Brad hunted for a pencil and paper. He found neither on the table by the phone, so he went into the kitchen and dug a pencil out of the drawer by the refrigerator and quickly scribbled a note to himself on the Post-it pad by the kitchen phone: "Pick up wiring diagrams for Clay." When he was through, he headed for the bedroom and stuck the Post-it on the nightstand next to his bed, where he would see it in the morning.

Brad stood in the doorway to the bedroom for a moment, thinking. There was something else he didn't want to forget. But his mind wouldn't cooperate. What was it? He walked back into the room, hoping that retracing his steps would trigger the memory, but...nothing.

As he walked back into the hall, Rebecca was just emerging from the bathroom. They exchanged a kiss as they passed in the doorway. Rebecca went into the kitchen to get a drink. Brad went into the bathroom and shut the door.

In the entry, the red light of the answering machine flashed as a message panned across the tiny screen: "Do you want to save messages?"

In another moment, the machine clicked, paused, and clicked again. The screen flashed: "Erasing messages."

The next morning, Rebecca slept in. When she opened her eyes, it was nine thirty. Brad was gone. She slipped out of bed and went into the bathroom to shower and dress. She was about to blow dry her hair when the phone by the bed rang. It was Cheryl.

"Oh, just drying my hair," Rebecca said in answer to Cheryl's question. "Uh-huh. We got back last night.... Yeah, it was great! It's so pretty there.... Yes, she's fine. I worry about her, though. I wish she were closer.... No, I don't think we could talk her into it. In fact, Brad suggested it, but she'll never sell that old house.... This morning? Sure! Sounds great! I'll put on a pot.... Half an hour then? Great! See you then!"

Rebecca set down the receiver and went back to the bathroom to finish dressing. She dried her hair and then went downstairs to start a pot of coffee. She pulled a couple of frozen breakfast rolls from the freezer and popped them into the microwave. The doorbell rang just as she was setting two empty cups on the dining room table.

"Morning!" Cheryl said as she handed Rebecca the newspaper she had picked up on her way in. "How about that for service?"

"Thanks," said Rebecca as she threw it on the sofa. "C'mon. Coffee's almost ready."

Cheryl, twenty-eight and pretty with short brown hair, stepped confidently into the entry, slipped the shoulder-strap of her delicate purse off her shoulder, and tossed it onto the sofa next to the newspaper.

"Brad at work?" Cheryl asked as she headed for the dining room table.

Rebecca followed her. "Yes. He left early."

The *plurp, plurp* of the coffeepot echoed in the background from the kitchen as they both sat down at the table.

"Do you have to be at work this morning?" Rebecca asked.

"Yeah, but not for a couple of hours. I have to drive out to the valley this afternoon to make a presentation, and I have to stop at the office first and pick up a couple things. So, how was the trip?"

"It was fun," Rebecca offered. "It was nice to get away for a few days. Brad has been working so hard, and, well, we've both been under a lot of stress lately."

Cheryl looked down into her cup. "The baby thing?"

"Yeah, the baby thing," Rebecca said.

"How's that going?"

Rebecca shrugged. “It isn’t.”

“That sounds final. You’re not giving up, are you?”

“No,” Rebecca said. “I just get down sometimes, but I’m fine. Don’t pay any attention to me.”

“Have you gotten the results from the doctor yet?”

Rebecca shook her head. “No, not the latest, but it’s only been a few days. He said we shouldn’t expect to have them for at least a week.”

“Oh.” Cheryl tried to avoid eye contact. She reached down and picked up the ornament Rebecca had laid on the table the night before.

“What’s this?”

“Brad found it in one of the shops by the beach.”

“Stick the knife in and twist it, huh?”

“No, no. Nothing like that,” Rebecca said as she took it and held it in her hand. “It means there’s hope.”

“Yeah, well, there is, I suppose.”

Rebecca set the ornament on the table and went into the kitchen to get the coffeepot. “I thought it was sweet,” she said as she poured Cheryl’s cup to the brim.

“Do you have cream?”

“Just milk. I’ll get it.”

“So what are you going to do if the tests are bad?”

Rebecca returned with the carton of milk. “I don’t know. I don’t even want to think about it.”

“Why don’t you try in-vitro or something? I mean, hey, what’s the big deal?”

“Brad’s insurance won’t cover most of it. And, I don’t know, it just seems so drastic.”

“Yeah, well, maybe. But you gotta do what you gotta do. I mean sometimes you gotta take charge. Right?”

“I suppose.”

“Maybe you should go back to work to, you know, take your mind off things. I never did understand why you quit anyway.”

Rebecca shrugged. “Brad makes enough for us to live on. And we just felt that we could focus better if I weren’t tied to a job.”

"And Brad likes the 'little woman,'" Cheryl scratched at the air with her fingers for emphasis, "at home, right?"

"It's not like that. It was my decision, and I can go back any time I want. But right now, I want this."

Cheryl shook her head. "Yeah. I suppose I'd like a family someday, but I can tell you this, it isn't going to interfere with my career."

Rebecca felt a familiar twinge of guilt. "I can still have a career. But right now a baby comes first. There's still time."

Cheryl couldn't hold back the disapproving look. "Well, don't wait too long. After all, you don't want your life to pass you by. And besides, like I told you before, a job could take your mind off things."

Rebecca took a long sip from her cup. Cheryl was a good friend. But somehow the subject of careers always came up, and it left her feeling a little guilty. She was eager to change the subject. "So how have you been? Any hot prospects?"

Cheryl shrugged. "I've got to make a presentation this afternoon. And then next week I hope to sign—"

"I meant in the romance department."

"Oh, yeah, right. Well, no one new. I think you met the last guy. What a loser!"

"Jason, right?"

"Yeah, Jason!"

"I thought he was nice."

"Too nice! He'd never make it in the real world—he had this idea to move to Idaho and raise ostriches. Idaho! Can you see me in Idaho? Yeah, right! Anyhow, I quit seeing him a few weeks ago."

There was an awkward silence as the two women sipped from their cups. Rebecca fidgeted with the ornament. Cheryl looked around the room at the walls.

"So your aunt was well?"

"Mm-hmm," Rebecca nodded. "She's doing fine, I guess. She's always such a boost to my morale." Rebecca studied the ornament. "Cheryl?"

"Yeah?"

"Do you ever go to church?"

"Church?" Cheryl said as if she had been offered bugs for lunch. "Not if I can help it. Why?"

Rebecca shrugged. "I don't know. I was just wondering."

"Beats me what going to church has to do with having a baby." Cheryl sneered, and then laughed. "Seems to me the time could be better spent doing what makes a baby."

Rebecca gave a weak smile.

"I'm sorry," Cheryl chuckled. "I don't mean to rain on your parade. If going to church makes you happy, you should go. I mean, everybody should do what makes them happy, right?"

Rebecca sighed. "Sometimes I don't know what I want."

"Well, if a baby is what you want, I'd put my money on medical science if I were you. They can do a lot if you've got the money. So what if the insurance doesn't cover it? You could always find a job with insurance that would cover you. Did you ever think about that? You might have to hunt around, but hey, if it's what you want, go for it!"

"Can I get you more coffee?"

"No, thanks. I've gotta get going." Cheryl pushed away from the table and started for the door. "Think about what I said, you know, about going back to work. It would be the best thing for you. Believe me, I know what I'm talking about."

Rebecca noticed her head was starting to hurt. "I will," she said at the door.

She waved as Cheryl climbed in behind the wheel of her new sports car, and then closed the door as she drove away. She went straight to the bathroom for an aspirin and then into the kitchen for a glass of water, standing at the sink as she popped the tablet into her mouth and following it with a swallow of water. She was about to clear the table when the phone rang.

"Hello?"

"Hello, Dear. This is Helen Bradley. I'm a friend of your aunt."

"Yes, Mrs. Bradley, I remember you. We met a few years ago at my uncle's funeral."

"Yes. That's right. Listen, I'm afraid I…I have bad news. I wish there was an easy way to tell you this but…well, several of us, including your aunt, have been meeting for quite a few years every morning, and, well, your aunt didn't show up this morning. So I went over to her place to see if she was all right, and, well, I found her on the floor by the phone."

A moment passed as Rebecca let the words sink in, holding the phone close. "Is she all right?"

"Listen, I don't know any other way to say this. When I found her, I'm afraid she was dead. The doctor says it was probably a heart attack."

Rebecca could feel the blood drain from her face as she let the receiver rest on her shoulder for a moment. "I…I …"

"Listen, Honey," said Helen. "Are you all right? Is your husband there?"

"No. No, he's at work right now. I…I'm…." She began to sob.

"Are you all right? Do you want me to call him from here?"

"No. No, I can call him."

"Is there someone there with you?"

"No," Rebecca sobbed weakly, "but I'll be all right."

"All right, Honey. Listen. I'll call you this evening and give you the details. All right, Honey? I'm so sorry. I know you were close. I'm very sorry."

Rebecca set the receiver back on the hook. Her knees were weak, and she stumbled as she made her way to the sofa to sit down.

"Dear God, no!" she whispered under her breath. She buried her face in her hands. "Dear God, no! Help me, dear God! Please help me!"

The darkness of despair settled around Rebecca's heart. She felt alone and helpless. But next to her in the entry, unseen, the Centurion knelt down, his sword in its scabbard, his shield held at the ready. Beyond him in the living room, and visible only to him, stood a Lamb without blemish and with wool white as snow. His eyes burned brightly with the fires of truth and love. The Centurion bowed low in reverent worship.

CHAPTER FIFTEEN

REBECCA STARED OUT the passenger-side window as the car pulled into the long driveway that led to Billie's home on the hill. Through the dense fog that draped the countryside this early morning, she could just make out the outline of the house. Several cars were parked in the drive out front.

Brad reached over and took her hand. "You OK?"

Rebecca squeezed his hand. It had been three days since the news. She had worked her way through the shock, then the sadness, then the anger, then the guilt, and then the emptiness as the knowledge her aunt was gone for good began to settle in. Now the sight of the old house brought it all back.

"There she is," Brad said. Helen Bradley stood near the front door, clutching a handkerchief. When she saw them, she walked to the edge of the driveway and waited for the car to come to a complete stop.

"Hi," she said as Rebecca swung her legs out of the car. Mrs. Bradley put her arms around her and hugged her. "I'm so sorry. I know this must be hard for you."

"Thank you. I appreciate your meeting us here."

Helen smiled. "She was a good friend."

Brad got out, reached into the back seat to grab his suit coat, and draped it over his arm.

"I brought you these," Helen said, handing Rebecca a ring of keys. "I'm not sure which ones are which, except this one." She held one of them out from the rest. "It's for the front and rear doors. The rest are probably to the garage and the gates and, of course, the car."

"Thank you," Rebecca said through the tears she had been fighting all morning. She stood holding the keys for a moment, as though she was unsure what to do with them. "This doesn't feel right."

"I know, Dear," Helen said, giving Rebecca's hand a squeeze. "But it's yours now. Your aunt wanted it that way." She turned and led them toward the front door.

"Come inside for a few minutes. You'll want to put your things away before we go."

Rebecca followed obediently while Brad popped the lid to the trunk and hoisted the two suitcases onto the driveway. He shut the lid and then followed with his load.

"We don't have to be there for an hour or so," said Helen, "if you want to rest for a while."

"Will it be at the church?" Rebecca asked.

"Yes," Helen said. "Did you talk to Mr. Stephens?"

"I did," Brad offered. "But all he said was that Billie had taken care of everything and that we should be here by eleven."

"Yes, that's right." Helen looked at her watch. It was ten fifteen. "He said he'd try to meet us here before the service."

"Will it be a long service?" Rebecca asked.

"Not too long," said Helen. "Usually less than an hour."

"I suppose there will be a small service at the cemetery afterward," Brad said.

"Why, no. Didn't Mr. Stephens tell you?"

Brad shook his head as at the same time Rebecca said, "Tell us what?"

Helen looked surprised. "I suppose I should let Mr. Stephens tell you. That's really his department."

Rebecca was impatient. "Tell us what?"

Helen shook her head. "Mr. Stephens can fill you in on all the details. I know he wanted to talk to you," she said, looking at her watch again.

"There are papers for you to sign, and a few loose ends that must be attended to."

"What kind of loose ends?" Brad asked.

Helen patted Brad on the arm. "Mr. Stephens will fill you in. You two run upstairs and freshen up a bit. When you're ready, you can follow me to the church."

Rebecca mounted the stairs slowly, running her hand along the slick surface of the banister—and remembering.

Brad followed her up the stairs, carrying the two suitcases. He set them down in the corner just inside the bedroom door. Rebecca went to the window.

"Pretty, isn't it?" she said as he came up behind her and put his hands on her shoulders. The fog was beginning to lift, exposing the lush hillsides that met the sea.

"Mm-hmm."

"I used to love this window when I was a little girl. I could sit and watch the waves for hours."

Brad slipped his arms around her waist and held her close. He could feel tears falling on his arm as they stood together, watching the waves in silence.

"I just can't believe she's gone," Rebecca said after a moment.

Brad wanted to have an answer—something meaningful that would comfort. "I know," was all he could think to say.

Neither of them spoke for a long time. Rebecca let the memories and the soothing sights of the sea filter through her mind: long walks on the beach with Uncle Bill, summer picnics on the grass, Billie's comforting words after her parents' deaths.

A soft rap on the door brought them both back to the present. Brad went to the door and opened it.

"Mr. Stephens is here," Helen said.

"We'll be right down," Brad said. He turned to Rebecca. "Come on. It's time."

Helen waited at the bottom of the stairs beside a distinguished looking gentleman in his fifties, tall, and wearing a meticulous suit.

"This is Mr. Stephens," Helen said as Brad and Rebecca joined them at the bottom of the stairs.

"Nice to meet you," Brad said as they shook hands.

"I'm sorry it had to be under these circumstances," Stephens said as he turned to take Rebecca's hand. "Your aunt was a fine lady."

"Thank you," Rebecca said.

Stephens reached for the briefcase under his arm. "I was hoping I could catch you here at the house before the service. I know this is a bad time, but there are some things we need to take care of. Is there some place we can sit?"

"Why don't we go into the study?" Helen said, motioning with her hand.

Helen led them through the study doors. It was a large, open room with rich paneling and endless shelves containing a lifetime's accumulation of books. There was a dated sofa at one end and a small, mahogany conference table in the middle surrounded by four comfortable chairs. Stephens set his briefcase on the table, pushing aside an ornately embossed leather pouch that was doubled over and tied with a string. It looked old.

Stephens motioned to one of the chairs. "Won't you sit down?"

Rebecca obliged. Stephens sat down next to her and cleared his throat. "I suppose you know of the provisions your aunt made for dispersing her property?"

Rebecca shook her head. "No, not really. She told me she was going to leave me the house, but we never really discussed it."

"I see. Well, briefly, your aunt put everything into a trust. It's a quick and easy way to transfer property without having to go through the court system, and it also helps avoid a good portion of the inheritance taxes, which saves you quite a bit of money. She's left you everything—this house, some land holdings, and a rather sizable chunk of money. No great fortune, I suppose, but certainly nothing to sneeze at. At any rate, I have some papers for you to sign," he dug into his briefcase, "and also some documents, the deed to the house, title to the car, things like that. I also have a list of things you may want to go through in the near future: checkbook, insurance policies, whatever she had that could affect your financial standing.

"And, of course, I'll need your signature," he said as he spread a piece of paper out on the table, "here and ..." he reached into the briefcase and pulled out another piece of paper, "here."

"What are these?" Rebecca asked.

"This one," he said, pointing with the pen, "is a form that the airlines require for transport. And this one authorizes them to release it at the other end."

"What are they transporting?" Brad asked.

Stephens looked up at Brad and then at Helen. "You didn't tell them?"

Helen shook her head. "I thought it was best to let you handle it."

Stephens looked annoyed. "Your aunt had her will drawn up about five years ago, a new one, that is, in which she made some changes."

"I knew she had a will drawn up," said Rebecca.

"And she told us the other day that she had left everything to Rebecca," said Brad.

"Hmm," Stephens grunted. "Well, to get to the point, your aunt made arrangements to be buried in the same cemetery as her father and mother."

"Where is that?" Brad asked.

"Up north—Oregon. A little town called 'Creek Junction.'"

"Creek Junction?" Brad said.

"But isn't that—" Rebecca started.

"It's about six hundred miles from here—a few miles over the state line."

Rebecca sank back in the chair. "But—"

Brad had settled back in the old sofa. Now he sat forward. "Why on earth would she want to be buried so far from home?"

Stephens shrugged. "She didn't say, and I didn't ask. It was her wish, and I took care of the legal necessities."

Helen stood back, nervously wringing her hands. "Did you know about this?" Brad asked her.

Helen nodded. "I'm sorry," she said. "I didn't know how to tell you. It didn't seem right on the phone, and then when you came—"

Stephens handed Rebecca a pen. "There is no reason to worry. The airlines know how to deal with these things. They do it all the time. There will be people to handle things at the other end."

"She'd be all alone," Rebecca said softly.

Brad suppressed the urge to tell her Billie wouldn't care.

"But there won't be anyone there who knew her—loved her," Rebecca continued.

Brad stood next to his wife. She reached out and took his hand. "I don't know what to do."

"Well, there's really nothing for you to do," Stephens said. "Your aunt took care of everything before she died."

Rebecca slumped. "But Uncle Bill is buried here."

"Yes, I know," Stephens said. "But her will is quite clear. The plot is bought and paid for. I made the arrangements myself. She wanted to be buried next to her mother and father."

Rebecca sat back and sighed. "Why? Why would she want to be buried in a place she hadn't even seen in seventy years?"

Brad reached down and picked up the leather pouch, fumbling with it absentmindedly. "Beats me, but it seems to me it would be wrong to go against her wishes."

Rebecca rubbed her forehead. "I don't know what to do," she said.

"Well," said Stephens, looking at his watch, "I suppose we could do this after the service, but it will complicate things."

"And we really should be going," said Helen.

Brad set the leather pouch back on the table.

Stephens motioned to the papers. "I'll need these after the service if the casket is going to be transported. It's scheduled to be delivered to the airport immediately after. I hate to rush you, but—"

"I wish I had known," Rebecca said, more to herself than to Stephens.

"Yes, well, I'm sorry about that," he said, avoiding a look in Helen's direction. "I suppose I should have made sure that you knew."

Rebecca took the pen in her hand. She felt betrayed, as if she were losing her aunt all over again. She touched the point of the pen to the paper, held it for a moment, and then signed her name.

Stephens quickly shuffled the papers together and stuffed them into his briefcase. He looked at his watch. "I have to get back to the office. You should be going as well. We'll need to get together sometime soon—say in the next week or so. In the meantime, if you have any questions, please call my office."

"Thank you," Rebecca said as she shook the hand he offered her.

In a moment, Stephens was gone.

Rebecca still held the ring of keys awkwardly in her hand. She followed Helen and Brad out the front door, locked it behind her and then slipped the keys into her purse.

The drive to the church took only a few minutes. Rebecca sat in the passenger seat staring out the window, but she saw very little of the countryside between Aunt Billie's and the church. She felt sick. Aunt Billie was the most caring, most giving person she knew. Why would she do this to her? Surely she knew how important this would be to her.

The parking lot of the small church was full. Crowds of people mulled around the entrance and stood on the walkway that led to it. Most were older, but Rebecca was surprised to see how many people there were. The curb was lined with cars with a space near the entrance marked "Reserved." Brad, at Helen's direction, pulled into it and stopped. A middle-aged man with a full head of gray hair, whom Rebecca recognized as the pastor, greeted them as he opened her door.

"Hi," he said. "I'm Pastor Romberg."

Rebecca took his extended hand as she climbed out of the car. "Yes, I remember," she said. "We met at my uncle's funeral."

"Yes, yes, of course."

Brad grabbed his coat and joined them. The pastor extended his hand. "Pastor Romberg," he affirmed before Rebecca could introduce them.

Brad shook his hand.

"Why don't you come with me?" Pastor Romberg asked. He was a confident man, and his words sounded more like a command than a question. "We have a room where you can be alone before the service."

He smiled warmly and Rebecca felt at ease with him. "I think I'd like that," she said.

"Good," he said as he moved between them and took each by the arm. "Come this way. The service won't start for a few minutes. You have some time. I know you must be tired. Did you drive up?"

"Yes," said Rebecca. "We just got in about a half-hour ago."

"Will you stay for a few days, or are you driving back right away?"

"We figured to stay a day or two and then drive back," said Brad.

"We want to go through some of my aunt's things while we're here," said Rebecca. "And we have to decide what to do with the house."

"Yes, I know these things can be difficult. I'm sure this has been rough for you."

"We were very close," said Rebecca.

Pastor Romberg smiled a fatherly smile. "I know."

He led them to a long, narrow building behind the church. "Here we are," he said as he opened the weathered door into a small room with a desk at one end and a few meager chairs at the other. "This is my office. You two make yourselves at home."

He turned to Helen, who had been following quietly behind them. "Will you stay with them? I have to check with the organist."

"Of course, Pastor."

The pastor left, but before the door was completely closed, Alva and Meg swept into the room and hovered around Rebecca. Helen introduced them.

"We're so glad to meet you," said Meg.

"We loved your aunt very much," said Alva. "We met every week for prayer for years. We're the BAG ladies!"

"I remember my aunt telling me about you. You met for coffee, isn't that right?"

"Five times a week for more than twenty years!" said Meg. "We feel like we know you already!"

"Closer to thirty," Alva corrected.

Rebecca felt comforted.

"We're so sorry," Alva said as she patted Rebecca's hand. "We know this must be hard for you."

"Your aunt loved you very much," said Meg. "She talked about you all the time."

"Thank you," Rebecca said through tears.

Helen sat down next to her. "She loved the Lord, Honey. This really is a time for celebration."

Rebecca looked down at her lap. She knew Helen meant well, but she didn't feel much like celebrating. She felt empty, and a little betrayed that God could take someone so close to her. There was comfort in the solace of these three little ladies; their tender concern shown through on their wrinkled faces. She could see they had genuine peace, and she longed to have such peace.

The service lasted less than an hour, but Rebecca heard very little of what was said. She sat with her handkerchief in her hand, looking forward, trying not to look at the casket. It was a beautiful thing, glistening in the unnatural light of a small lamp near the head, but the sight of it tormented Rebecca. It seemed so cold. She only half noticed Brad's occasional gentle touch as he stroked the back of her hand.

After the pastor finished speaking, people began filing past the casket and in front of the place where Rebecca was sitting, offering her words of comfort. A few reached down to hug her and whisper in her ear. Pastor Romberg stood off to the side, waiting patiently. As soon as the last well-wisher had moved on, he took Rebecca by the hand.

"Thank you," she said. "It was a beautiful service. I know my aunt would have been pleased."

Romberg smiled. "I understand that a few of the ladies have prepared lunch. They have things set up at your aunt's house."

"That's right, Dear," said Alva, who was standing a few feet away. "Everything is taken care of. We've seen to it. You just go on over to the house and let us handle the details."

Rebecca wasn't sure she was up to company. "Oh, you shouldn't have," she said.

"It was no trouble. And besides, a lot of the folks want to get a chance to know you a little bit. But don't you worry. We'll take care of everything. By this evening, you won't even know we were there."

Rebecca looked at Brad and then at Alva. "How many people are coming?"

"A few of her close friends," Pastor Romberg interjected. "It's sort of a tradition here. Your aunt approved it in a way."

"That's right, Dear," Meg said. "She told us she'd like to have all her friends get together and celebrate when she was gone."

Rebecca bit down on her lip and smiled weakly. This was the second time someone had mentioned celebration to her. She wanted to scream.

Pastor Romberg gestured toward the door. "Why don't you ladies go on over to the house, and we'll meet you there?" he said. "We'll be along in a few minutes."

Meg and Alva hurried off toward the main door.

Romberg turned to Rebecca. "I know this may not be in your plans, but it would mean so much to the people here who loved your aunt."

Rebecca nodded.

"Maybe we can find some time, a little later on, to talk," Romberg continued. "There are some things I'd like to talk to you about. Things I promised your aunt."

"Of course," Rebecca said.

Brad took her arm, and they walked slowly toward the door.

Romberg watched as they made their way to the car. He took a deep breath and sighed. He could see the pain in her eyes. He'd seen the look before—many times—and he was sure she had no comfort, no peace. At least not the kind that mattered, the kind that passed understanding.

He locked the office door behind him, and then headed for his own car.

Brad closed the passenger car door as soon as Rebecca was inside. He hurried around to the other side, slid in behind the wheel, and took her hand. "Hang in there."

Rebecca nodded.

"You can go upstairs when we get there if you want. I'll entertain them for a while."

Rebecca shook her head. "I'll be all right."

Brad turned the key and put the car in gear. "Well, let me know if you want me to run them off."

She reached over and took his hand. "I'll be fine," she insisted.

The driveway was already full when they got to the house. One space near the front walk had been left open. Brad pulled into it and stopped.

The house was full. People mulled around, talking and nibbling on the hors d'oeuvres the ladies had made. Helen greeted Brad and Rebecca at the door. "Come in here," she said, motioning toward the study. "I kept the doors closed so no one would use it. You can sit for a while."

"How long will this take?" Brad asked, nodding toward the crowded foyer.

"Not long," Helen reassured. "They'll be gone in a couple of hours. Give them time. They loved your aunt. That makes you very special to them, even though you don't know them. They just want a chance to show you."

"We don't mean to seem ungrateful," Rebecca said. "It's just that it's been a long drive, and we're very tired."

"I understand," Helen said. "You just sit down and relax. Everything is taken care of. Don't worry about a thing."

She disappeared, returning a few moments later with a tray of food. Meg followed with another tray of various kinds of soft drinks and a pitcher of lemonade. They set them down on the table, pushing aside the leather pouch.

"Would you like anything?" Meg asked.

"Not just now, thank you," Rebecca said.

"How about you?" said Meg, turning to Brad.

"Nothing right now,"

"Well, it's all here if you want anything."

The two ladies left. Brad walked over and plopped down on the sofa. Rebecca sat at the table.

Brad rubbed his eyes with his fists. "Man, I'm beat!"

Rebecca sat in silence, running her fingers over the embossing of the old leather pouch. "I depended on her for so much," she said softly.

"You hardly ever saw her."

"I know, but I always knew she was here. She always gave me a sense of security—spiritual security. She was always there if I needed an answer."

"Yeah. She was pretty religious."

"Yeah," Rebecca said softly.

Brad got up from the sofa and began rubbing Rebecca's shoulders.

"I'm going to miss her," she said.

Brad dug his fingertips into the muscles between her shoulder blades, the way she liked it.

"I know," he said. "But hey, she's probably better off now. And they said she went fast—didn't suffer. Sounds like a pretty good way to go if you ask me."

"Yeah," Rebecca sneered. "Let's all celebrate."

Brad pulled up the chair next to her. "Now, c'mon. They didn't mean any harm. I suppose if you're religious, you could think of this as a time to celebrate. Anyway, they're just trying to make you feel better."

Rebecca stroked the side of Brad's face with the back of her hand. She studied his eyes. "I know," she said. "I'm just feeling sorry for myself. Don't pay any attention to me."

"No problem," he said softly. He took her hand and held it in his own. "I'm sorry."

"What about?"

Brad shrugged. "Just…everything."

"I suppose this hasn't been easy on you either, has it?"

"I'm tough," he smiled. "You know, in some ways I envy you."

"Envy me?"

"Yeah, you know…your family and the way they are—or were."

Rebecca swallowed hard. Billie was gone. Uncle Bill was gone. Mom and Dad were gone. The only people left were two of Billie's brothers, but they were on the other side of the continent. She hadn't seen them since she was little.

"Everyone is gone," she said.

"I know. But you had something special—still do."

Rebecca looked around. "I did."

"I'm not talking about the house. I mean you still have something—I wish I knew how to say it—something of your aunt. You still have everything she gave you, the things that make you who you are. You still have memories." He paused. He knew what he wanted to say, but the words failed him. "I know I'm not saying it very well, but I always wanted what you have."

Rebecca could feel the tears coming again. She was tired of crying.

"I know this isn't the best time to talk about it," Brad continued, "but I suppose that's why I want a family. I want to feel connected."

"I never thought about it," Rebecca said. "I suppose *connection* is a good word for it."

"You and your aunt were more than just close. You had something: a bond that gave you a foundation. I could see it in the way you talked to her, the way you relied on her for strength."

"Yes," Rebecca said, "I suppose I did." She sat forward at the table and began fumbling with the old leather pouch. "Honey?"

"Yeah?"

"I can't let her go."

"You've got to let go. She's gone, and you can't change that."

"No, I mean I can't let her go to her grave alone with no one there who loves her. I can't leave her alone. I know it seems silly, but I want to go with her."

Brad thought for a moment. "What about work? We start work on that new project in a few days."

Her eyes pleaded. "You could drive home. I'll catch a plane and be home in a few days."

Brad's practical side surrendered to her pleading look. "Well, I suppose if you're determined—"

Rebecca wiped away the tears that forced their way down her cheeks. "I wouldn't be gone long. I could leave tonight and fly home as soon as I'm sure everything is taken care of. I might even beat you there."

"All right, but I'm not letting you go alone. We'll both go. I'll call work and get a few days off."

Rebecca turned to face him. "Oh, Brad, it would mean so much! I know it's silly, but it would mean so much to me."

"All right," Brad said. "And we might as well take the car. If we leave in the morning, we can be there by tomorrow night. I'll call Mr. Stephens and get all the information."

For the first time in days, Rebecca felt a measure of reassurance. "I love you," she said as she met his open arms.

"I love you too," he said, holding her close. "You know, this thing about the burial still bugs me. I just can't understand why your aunt would want to be buried six hundred miles from her friends and family—and especially her husband."

"I don't know. I can't figure it out. She never said anything about it."

"She did the other day. Remember? She talked about some property she owned."

"What does that have to do with where she's buried?"

"I don't know, but it seems strange that she'd mention it after all these years only a day before she died. It's almost as if she wanted us to go there for some reason."

"I don't know what it could be."

"I don't either. But it seems strange."

Rebecca held her husband close. His strong arms surrounded her, and she felt safe.

CHAPTER SIXTEEN

IT WAS ALMOST dark by the time the last guest left the old house. Rebecca and Brad eventually had opened the study door and a throng of Billie's friends soon had joined them. Person after person wished them well and told Rebecca how much they loved her aunt and how sorry they were for her loss. Her emotions were rubbed raw. And three days with very little sleep made forcing a smile more exhausting by the minute.

Brad could see in her eyes that her head was beginning to hurt. He pulled her aside. "C'mon, let's go upstairs."

"But what about—"

"They'll keep. You need a little time."

They lay back on the bed with the intention of resting for a few minutes, but soon fell asleep.

Downstairs, Meg, Alva, and Helen busied themselves with the business of cleaning and vacuuming.

"I'm almost done here!" Helen called back to Alva.

Helen flitted around the sitting room, picking up paper plates, plastic forks, and napkins that littered the delicate furniture, stuffing them into a large, plastic trash bag. Then she wiped her hands on her apron. The last few days had been hard for her—finding Billie on the floor next to the phone in the kitchen and struggling with her own sense of loss. She had welcomed the necessity of organizing and planning. The pastor depended on her for so much. She found that staying busy and seeing to other's needs helped keep the image of her longtime friend lying on the floor out of her mind. But it had been a long day, and she was tired.

Alva stuck her head in the door. "I'll see to the living room."

"Fine. If you see the pastor, send him in. I have a trash bag that needs to be taken out."

"Where is it?"

"Right there in the corner, but I'm on my way to the kitchen now. I'll set it by the back door."

"I'll tell him," Alva said, and then turned to leave.

Helen stuffed her hand down into the large plastic bag, pushing the contents as far down as she could, and then twirled the bag as she held the opening. She tied a rough knot and carried it into the kitchen, where she set it near the back door.

"About done?" Meg asked as she wiped down the countertop next to the sink.

"The sitting room is done," said Helen. "All I have to do is vacuum. The kids asleep?"

"I saw them go upstairs about an hour ago. They looked beat. Poor Rebecca. This has really been hard on her."

"Well, I'll hold off on the vacuum for a while. Is the pastor still here?"

"Right here," Pastor Romberg said from the open back door of the kitchen.

"Oh, good! I need this taken out," Helen said, pointing to the trash bag on the floor by his feet.

"Yes, ma'am," he said and then hoisted the bag and cradled it in his arms. "Anything else you need?"

"Yes," said Helen. "You can come help me in the study."

Pastor Romberg nodded and then disappeared with his load. Helen hurried off to the study with an arm full of cleansers and cleaning rags, as well as an empty trash bag. She picked up a napkin from the floor just inside the door and set it, along with all her cleaning implements, on the conference table. She quickly skirted the room, picking up a few paper plates and napkins and setting them on the table too. She pushed aside the leather pouch.

Helen wiped down the tops of the end tables, using the last of the furniture polish, and then set the empty can on the tabletop in the middle of the room. She went to the sofa, adjusted the cushions, and then bent over to pick up a candy mint from the floor. Satisfied that the room had been restored to its former state, she hurried off toward the living room where Alva was hard at work. Pastor Romberg passed her in the foyer.

"Anything else?" he asked as she brushed past him.

"Yes. There's a pile of trash on the table in the study. Could you put it in the trash bag I left on the table and take it out?"

"Sure thing," he said. He stood in the study doorway for a moment with his eyes on the stairway. He had been waiting all day for a chance to talk to the two kids, but there just never was a good time for it with a house full of people. Now that the crowd was gone, he hoped to steal a moment or two.

He loved to tell people about his Lord and Savior. But there was more to it this time. Billie was a good friend. She had been there for him on many occasions, ministering to the sick and helping with almost anything the church needed as long as she was physically able. She never wanted recognition, though, and she refused it whenever she had the chance. Yet her faithfulness was well known. He would miss her, not just for the things she did, but for her faithful, steadfast example. She gave him strength and he owed her something. He knew it might be his last chance to keep a promise.

The upstairs bedroom door was closed. He hesitated for a moment, listening for any sound of stirring that would tell him Brad and Rebecca were awake. When he heard none, he went into the study, but his ear was always toward the door.

A pile of debris sat in the middle of the table where Helen had left it. He stood for a moment, puzzling on the best and fastest way to transfer the pile of paper plates and napkins from the tabletop to the trash bag. He unfurled it and held it down by the table's edge, holding one side of the bag with his hand and the other with his raised knee against the tabletop while he scooped everything from the top of the table with his free hand. He set the bag on the floor, stooping to pick up the few items that had fallen. Then he walked toward the kitchen with the bag in hand.

"Is that everything from the study?" Helen asked as they passed each other in the foyer.

"Yep!" he said cheerfully.

"Did you get everything from the table?"

"Clean as a whistle! Anything else?"

"Go ahead and take it out. I have some things for you to do when you get back."

"Yes, ma'am!" he said, whistling as he bounded happily into the kitchen toward the back door.

Helen disappeared into the study. Seconds later, she darted out again. "Pastor!" she called out toward the kitchen.

Pastor Romberg turned at the back door.

"Did you see a leather pouch on the table when you cleaned it?"

"Nope, sure didn't. Why?"

"It was there earlier."

"Let me check," he said as he untied the knot in the trash bag. He rummaged around for a moment. "This it?" he said, holding it up.

"I was afraid of that," Helen said.

"What is it?" Romberg asked.

"I don't know," Helen said. "It was there in the study the day…the day we found her."

"Looks like it has papers in it," Romberg said, turning it over in his hand.

"Yes, well, it must be something she found. I've never seen it before."

"What do you want me to do with it?"

"Just set it there on the drain board. I'll take it back into the study in a minute."

Romberg nodded obediently and set the pouch next to the sink as Helen had directed before continuing on his mission with the trash bag.

Helen finished what she was doing and then went into the kitchen. She went to the sink to wash her hands and then busied herself putting away the clean dishes that sparkled in the drainer.

"I've got some more trash here," Alva said as she set another bag near the rear door. "I couldn't find any of those twisty things. And I can't tie a knot with this arthritis."

"Just leave it. I'll have the pastor tend to it as soon as he comes back in."

"All right," said Alva. "I'll see if the kids are awake yet."

"Good. Oh! Could you take this into the other room?" Helen said, reaching for the leather pouch.

"What is it?"

"I don't know. Probably some old thing Billie found on the beach. Just put it in the study."

Alva put the pouch under her arm and went back the way she had come. As she passed by the living room, Meg called to her.

"What is it, Dear?"

"Could you help me move this?" Meg said, motioning toward the sofa. "Somehow it got moved out from the wall."

Alva made her way across the living room and dropped the leather pouch on a sofa cushion.

"What's that?" Meg asked.

"I don't know. Some old piece of junk that Billie found on the beach."

"Oh," Meg said, turning her attention to the sofa. "Can you push on that end? I think we can do it if we push together."

"My goodness!" Alva said. "It's so heavy!"

The two women pushed together, moving the sofa a few inches.

"Is that it?" Meg asked hopefully.

Alva looked down at the carpet. "No. We need a couple of inches more. Why don't we wait for the pastor?"

"No, we can do it! Besides, I want to get it done!"

"All right," Alva said.

They pushed again, this time moving the sofa legs into the depressions in the carpet where they had been before. "Goodness!" Alva said.

Pastor Romberg stood in the doorway. "Do you need help?"

"Not now," Alva said as she straightened.

"Are the kids up yet?" he asked.

"I don't know," said Alva. "I was just on my way upstairs to check on them."

"Well, tell them I'd like to see them before I go. Will you?"

"Sure thing, Pastor," Alva said. She hurried out of the room and headed for the stairs.

"Tell them I'll be in the study," he called out to her, and then turned to Meg. "Anything I can do?"

"No, I'm almost through in here," she said.

Romberg nodded an acknowledgment and went back into the study. Meg straightened the end table by the sofa and dusted its top. She stood back to survey the room. Everything met with her approval except the pouch on the sofa cushion. She picked it up and headed for the kitchen.

"The living room is done," she said to Helen, who had her head under the sink. "What are you looking for?"

"I thought Billie always kept an extra can of furniture polish under here, but I can't find it."

"Maybe she ran out," Meg said, looking down at the trash bag by the back door.

"Well, I suppose," Helen said as she continued to rummage under the sink. "But I'd really like to do the table in the study."

"I've got some more trash," said Meg, holding up the leather pouch.

"Just put it in the bag by the door," Helen said without looking up. "I'll have the pastor take it out later."

Meg looked down at the trash bag again. "Oh, it's all right. I can do it," she sighed. She stuffed the leather pouch deep into the trash bag, gave it a twirl, and hoisted it up in front of her. "My goodness, this thing is heavy!"

"Well, let the pastor do it!" Helen scolded from under the sink.

"Never mind," Meg said as she pushed the door open. "I've got it."

From the comfort and security of the delicate bedding of Aunt Billie's guest room, Rebecca began to stir. She reached over and stroked the side of her husband's face as he slept. "Hi," she said softly when he opened his eyes.

Brad drew a deep breath and stretched his arms. "Hi, yourself." He rolled over on his back and folded his arms behind his head. "What time is it?"

Rebecca looked at her watch. "Five thirty."

"Do you think they're gone?"

"I don't know. I don't hear anything." Just then, as if to answer her, someone rapped softy on the door.

Brad slid out of bed and went to answer it.

"I'm sorry to disturb you," Alva said from the hallway when Brad had opened the door. "We're just about to leave and the pastor said he wanted to see you before we left."

"Is everyone gone?"

"Just about. We're almost through cleaning up. The pastor's in the study."

"We'll be right down," Brad said, and then shut the door.

Rebecca stretched and yawned, kicking the bedding to the floor at the foot of the bed.

"You OK?" Brad asked.

"Yeah, I'm fine."

"C'mon then," Brad said, holding out his hand. "It's time for the sermon."

"Oh, don't be cynical! I think he's nice. And they've all been very good to us."

"Yeah, well, we'll see. But I'll bet we're in for it."

Rebecca swung her feet onto the floor and slipped on her shoes. "A little religion never hurt anyone, so you be nice!"

"Don't worry," he said as he put his arms around her. "I won't embarrass you."

"See that you don't, Mister!" She leaned close and kissed him.

"C'mon," she said, pulling away and taking his hand. "I want to see Helen before she leaves. If we're going to go to Creek Junction, I want to see if she can look after the house for a while."

Brad let her hand slip from his and reached for the doorknob. "I suppose this means you've made up your mind?"

"It's something I have to do," she said.

"Just thought I'd ask," he sighed, and then opened the door.

The sun hung low on the horizon. At the foot of the stairs, the study door was open. From the study, light streamed through the western window and cast its beams through the open door across the entry floor. Pastor Romberg sat reading a book.

"Ah! Come in and sit down," he said when he heard them. "Did you sleep well?"

"Yes, thank you," Rebecca said.

Brad shuffled over to the sofa and slouched down into it with his leg over the arm.

Romberg smiled his fatherly smile. "I'm sure it's been a long day for both of you."

"Alva said you wanted to see us," Rebecca said as she sat down next to him.

"Yes," said Pastor Romberg, folding his hands on the table in front of him. "The ladies are just about through, and we'll be going in a few minutes, but I did want to talk to you before I left.

"I wanted to see Helen before she left," Rebecca said, only half-listening.

"Did I hear my name?"

Helen stood in the doorway, holding a cleaning rag in her hand.

"Come in and join us," the pastor said, motioning.

"Oh, I don't want to interrupt," Helen said as she crossed the room. She began wiping the tabletop with the rag. "Just one second, and I'll be out of your way." When she was through, she dug into the deep pocket of her apron and held out her hand to Rebecca. "I wanted to give you this."

"What is it?"

"It's my key to the house. I've had it for years. I kept it for today, but I won't be needing it anymore."

Rebecca took Helen's hand in her own and closed Helen's fingers over the key. "There's no hurry. And besides, I'd like to ask you something. I was hoping I could get you to do me a favor."

"Of course, Dear. If I can. What is it?"

"Well," Rebecca said, looking in Brad's direction, "we've decided to go with Billie…to see this through. And I was wondering if you would take care of the house until we get back. There wouldn't be much to do, really, just feed the cat and check up on things every so often. We should only be gone a few days."

Helen's eyes filled with tears. "Oh," she said, "I've been so good up to now!" She dug into the pocket of her apron again, pulling out a rumpled handkerchief and dabbing at the corners of her eyes. "I used to take care of things around here every time Billie went out of town. Oh! This is so silly!" She sniffled and then smiled weakly. "I'd be happy to."

"You've been a good friend," Rebecca said, squeezing her hand.

Helen straightened and gave one of her warm smiles. "Don't worry about a thing. I'll see to things here while you're gone. Take all the time you need." She gave the room one last critical inspection. "Well, I think that takes care of about everything."

She leaned down and kissed Romberg on the cheek. "It was a wonderful service, Pastor. Billie would have been pleased."

"Thank you," he replied.

Helen leaned over and gave Rebecca a kiss and a hug. "God bless you, Dear," she whispered.

"Thank you," Rebecca said, fighting her own tears.

Helen sighed. "Well, I suppose I'd better see if the girls are ready to go."

"Let me see you to the door," the pastor said. He rose from his chair and followed Helen out of the room. Alva and Meg were waiting just inside the living room.

"Are we ready?" Alva asked as she and Meg met them at the door.

"Yes, I think so," Helen said.

"How are the kids?" asked Meg.

"They'll be fine," said the pastor. "You ladies just remember to pray for them."

"Oh, we will," they all agreed.

"Every weekday morning," Helen said with reverence.

"We owe her that, I think," Meg said, looking down at the floor.

There was a brief silence.

"Everything looks very nice, ladies," said Romberg. "You did yourselves proud."

"It went very well, don't you think?" Meg said.

"And such a turnout!" Alva added.

"I hope we didn't wear out those poor kids," Helen said.

"I'm sure they appreciated everything you did," Romberg reassured. "And it will mean so much to them later on—to know that so many people cared."

The ladies all nodded their agreement.

"Well," said Meg, "I'd better be going. Raymond is probably wondering where I am."

"Can I get a ride with you?" Alva asked. "I came over with the Johnsons and they left an hour ago."

"Of course."

"Thank you. Let me get my purse. Now, where did I leave it?"

"Right here," Helen said, bending down to pick up the purse that was sitting next to the front door.

"Oh, thank you," Alva said as she slipped the strap over her shoulder. "Well, good night, Pastor."

"Good night, ladies," he said, waving as they made their way down the sidewalk. He watched until they were in the car and then shut the door. He turned back to the study, whispering a little prayer to himself.

Pastor Romberg settled back into the comfortable old chair in the study. Rebecca sat across from him. She looked tired. Romberg felt a nervous flutter in the middle of his stomach as he leaned forward with his hands folded in front of him.

"So," he began, "when are you leaving?"

"We're going to drive up in the morning," Brad said from the sofa.

"That's fine," Romberg said. He paused for a moment, took a deep breath, and slowly let it out. "You know," he began, "Your aunt was a fine lady."

"Yes, she was," said Rebecca.

"She was also a good friend," Romberg continued. "I knew her for many years and, well, there are a few things I think she wanted you to know."

Rebecca sat forward in her chair, but Brad sank back, bracing for what he was sure would be religious talk.

Romberg paused for a moment as he collected his thoughts. "You know," he began slowly, "I don't know of anyone who was more willing to sacrifice than your aunt. She was a very giving woman."

Rebecca nodded. She remembered how Billie was always thinking about others— like the times she had taken her shopping. She remembered how Billie made a game out of learning. She always made things fun.

"She liked to help people," Rebecca said.

"Yes, she did," said Romberg. "Did you know she had a list of people—"shut-ins" we call them—that she visited every day?"

"No," Rebecca almost whispered. "But it doesn't really surprise me. It sounds like something she would do."

"Well, I'm not surprised that you didn't know," said Romberg with his usual warm smile. "She didn't go looking for recognition or a pat on the back. She was one of those rare people who just go quietly about their business helping others."

"Yeah, well," said Brad, "if anyone could make it to heaven, I'm sure she did."

Romberg looked down at the table. "I have no doubt," he said almost to himself.

Rebecca held back the tears. "I'll miss her," she said.

Romberg reached across the table and put his hand on Rebecca's. "I know your aunt talked to you about spiritual matters." He paused to let the words sink in. "But I wonder if you truly understand why she is in heaven."

Rebecca shrugged. "She was a good person. You said yourself she was always helping other people."

Brad felt suddenly defensive. "She always thought about other people," he said, his voice rising slightly. He caught himself and then said, "Seems to me that God would have to let a person like her in."

"Many people believe that," Romberg said with a smile. "But Billie didn't believe it. She wasn't counting on her own goodness."

Rebecca nodded respectfully, but Brad began to fidget in his chair. He didn't trust people who smiled too much.

Brad clasped his hands behind his head. "I think we make our own heaven and hell right here. Life is what you make it."

Romberg didn't answer him. It was Rebecca who wanted—who needed—to hear. "I'm convinced that your aunt is in heaven this minute," he said, "but there is only one reason. She's in heaven right now because many years ago she gave her life to Jesus Christ."

"I know," Rebecca said automatically. "She used to tell me about it."

"Yes, I know," Romberg said. "She told me. But do you understand?"

Rebecca shrugged. "I suppose so. I suppose she decided to live a good life."

Romberg shook his head. "No," he said softly, suppressing frustration. It seemed so simple. And yet so many people twisted the good news of a free gift until it met their selfish need to accomplish salvation by their own deeds.

He looked at Rebecca and waited for her eyes to meet his own. "It means," he said as he studied her face, "that she understood that living a good life isn't enough. It means that she knew she couldn't meet God on her own terms. It means that she surrendered everything to Him. It means that she gave her life to Him. It belonged to Him—belongs to Him."

Rebecca nodded as though she understood, but the truth was none of it made sense to her. She had heard it before, though not the same words exactly, from her aunt. But to her it sounded like a lot of religious rules. Yet something was different. Something tugged deep within her. She felt as if she were on the brink of something but she didn't know what. Though it frightened her, she felt as if she were standing before a bridge, and that something, or someone, beckoned from the other side.

"She used to talk about religious things a lot," she said.

Romberg smiled. His warm eyes reassured. "I know this has been a tough day for you. But I can't leave without telling you what I know your aunt would want you to know. She loved you very much. And more than anything she wanted you to know God in the same way she did."

Rebecca felt a sudden goading of curiosity. Curiosity? No, it was more than curiosity. It was as if something inside her had awakened—as though, like the early morning shadows of consciousness that reveal faint images, she was beginning to see something she never had seen before. A question, one that had never occurred to her before, began to form in her mind. She resisted. To ask it would mean to take a step she was unsure she wanted to take. It would require some degree, though measured and slight, of acquiescence. She was certain Brad would not approve. She started to ask, and then hesitated. She could see her husband sitting on the sofa with a disapproving look. But the question demanded an answer.

"Why do we need Jesus?" she asked.

"Because," Romberg began slowly, "we are all under a curse—the curse of sin and death. And only Jesus has the power to break the curse."

Brad had had all he could take. He didn't like this kind of talk and the pastor was beginning to annoy him. But a frontal attack would only serve the preacher by giving him Rebecca's sympathy. "Curses, foiled again," he said, just above a whisper.

Romberg and Rebecca both turned. There was fire in Romberg's eyes as his smile disappeared, but Rebecca was diverted. She hid the smile at her husband's wit, fearful the pastor might see.

Brad sat back, pleased with himself. He had felt a flush across his face in that awkward moment when they both had turned. It was worth it, though—that moment of embarrassment—because he had succeeded. The mood was broken.

"Believe me," Romberg said, trying not to let his anger show, "God can give you a peace that passes all understanding if you turn to him in repentance."

Rebecca pulled away as old fears rushed to the surface, fear of religious words like *repentance* that conjured up images of wide-eyed fanatics in her mind. Brad shifted nervously on the sofa. Pastor Romberg sent up a quick prayer. He could see the look in Rebecca's eyes, a look he'd seen before, many times.

"God loves you," he said, "but He is also a holy God. He's made a way for us, but He doesn't let people in through the back door. You have to make the decision to follow Him yourself. I know your aunt would want you to consider what I've said."

"I'm sure you're right," Rebecca said to her folded hands resting on the table in front of her.

Brad stood and walked over to his wife's side. "We'll think about it," he said.

Romberg sat back. "Good," he said. "I hope you do. Why don't you let me pray with you before I go?"

"Sure," Brad said.

Romberg took each of them by the hand and bowed his head. "Father, I want to pray for these two young people right now. I ask that You would help them through this time of trouble in their lives. Lord, I know they are struggling with many things, and I pray that You will help them as they search for answers. Give them protection and keep them safe from the enemy's grasp—"

Pastor Romberg hesitated for a moment as a thought entered his mind. He felt sure, though he couldn't be sure why, that God was giving him something specific to pray for.

"Bless them as they travel and help them through the ordeal that lies ahead. In Jesus' name, amen."

Rebecca felt as though the pastor could see into her soul. His words cut deep, and they seemed as though they were meant only for her. She was struggling—and hurting. It was more than losing Aunt Billie, more than not being able to conceive. She felt empty and alone, and she didn't know why.

Brad let go of the pastor's hand and stood next to his wife, waiting.

"Well," Pastor Romberg said, "I suppose I should be going." He turned and started toward the door. Rebecca and Brad followed.

"Thank you for everything," Rebecca said at the door as she extended her hand. "We really appreciate all you've done."

The pastor shook her hand and then Brad's. "I hope you'll consider what I've said. I want you to know that I'll be praying for you."

"Thanks," Brad said and then went into the living room. Rebecca waited at the door until the pastor climbed into his car. She waved as he drove away and then shut the door.

Brad was sprawled out on the sofa in the living room with his leg over the arm. "That was close," he said.

Rebecca walked over to the chair by the window and sat down. She was sullen.

"You OK?"

Rebecca shrugged. "Yeah, I guess."

"Don't let him get to you. He's harmless."

"It's not that," she said.

Brad chuckled to himself. "Well, at least he didn't hit us up for money."

Rebecca stiffened. "I thought he was nice!"

"Hey, take it easy! I'm on your side!"

Rebecca sat back in the chair, looking up at the ceiling. "You didn't have to be so rude."

Brad shrugged. "He'll get over it. Besides, I don't like all this talk about religion. What's the big deal, anyway? You're not getting into this religious stuff, are you?"

"Of course not," she said. "It's just that—"

Brad waited for her to finish. "Just what?"

"I don't know," she said. "I just...don't know." She got up out of the chair and started across the room.

"You going upstairs?"

"I'm tired. I think I'll go to bed."

"All right," said Brad. "I'll be up in a bit."

"Fine. Don't forget to put the trash out by the curb in the morning."

"I won't."

Rebecca turned toward the door and then paused. "Do you think God cares about what happens to people?"

"I don't know," he said without looking up. "I never thought about it."

Rebecca felt strange and alone. Her head hurt, and she was tired. She leaned against the doorway. "I don't. I think He can be very cruel."

She turned and went upstairs to bed.

CHAPTER SEVENTEEN

THE NEXT MORNING was bright and cheerful. Rebecca felt good as she lay in bed, the warm covers snuggled up against her chin. Brad was already up.

She opened her eyes to a cool breeze blowing in from the open window and burrowed down under the heavy blanket. She could hear Brad in the bathroom, brushing his teeth. The bathroom door opened, and a moment later the bed rocked as he sat down next to her. He began stroking her hair.

"You awake?" he said in a low voice.

Rebecca drew a deep breath, stretched her arms over her head, and then shook her head. "Huh-uh," she teased.

"How do you feel?"

"Better," she said after thinking for a moment.

"I was worried about you last night," said Brad. "It's not like you to get so down."

She reached up and stroked his face with the back of her hand. "I'm sorry. I guess I was feeling a little sorry for myself."

"You're entitled. It was a rough day."

"You're sweet," she said.

Brad's eyes twinkled. "I know." He leaned over and kissed her. "C'mon. We should get going."

"If you insist," she sighed in mock displeasure. She swung her feet out of bed and started toward the bathroom.

"I'll meet you in the kitchen," Brad said as he headed for the door. "I'm going to run the trash out to the curb. I don't want to miss the pick-up."

Rebecca went into the bathroom and shut the door. She could hear Brad's fading voice mumbling something about the neighborhood dogs and trash bags that were left out for days.

She showered and dressed quickly. It was amazing, she thought, what a good night's sleep could do. The night before, she had felt the weight of all that had happened in the last few days bearing down on her. But now she felt refreshed. For now, the cool air and the bright day made her feel as though she could handle anything.

She bounded down the stairs—suppressing a sudden urge to slide down the banister—and went straight to the kitchen. Brad was just coming in the back door.

"Did you get it all?"

"Yeah. Four bags! I had to make two trips—three, counting the one to pick up what fell out of the bag that tore, but I made it."

"Good. How about some cereal?" Rebecca went to the cupboard and grabbed two boxes from the shelf.

"Sounds...like home! I'll get the milk."

Rebecca opened the cupboard next to the cereal and picked up two bowls. "How much time do we have?"

"No more than an hour," Brad said, looking at his watch. "It's at least an eight-hour drive, and I don't want to be looking for a motel in the middle of the night."

Rebecca set the cereal box on the table and sat down. "I thought you said it was ten hours."

"If we drive all the way to the airport, it probably is. But I thought we'd drive up to the border and find a room for the night. We can drive the rest of the way in a couple of hours tomorrow. That way we don't have to look for a room after dark in a strange town."

"You're so smart. You think of everything." She poured two bowls full of cereal.

"What are husbands for?"

"Well, that and carrying things," she grinned.

"And maybe one or two other things," he said as he reached up and stroked her hair.

"Eat your cereal."

"Yes, ma'am."

When they had finished, Rebecca took the bowls to the sink, washed them, and put them away.

"I'll finish packing," she said. "It'll only take a few minutes."

"Great! I'll pull the car up to the front walk. Where are the keys?"

"They're in my purse. I'll get them."

Brad followed her upstairs. The purse was lying on the floor under the pile of blankets at the foot of the bed. She picked it up and rummaged through it, slowly at first, and then more franticly.

"Oh, great," she muttered.

"What's the matter?"

"I can't find them."

"What a surprise," he said.

"They were here," she said. "I remember dropping them into my purse when we got here yesterday afternoon."

Rebecca pawed through the contents of her purse again and then dumped them onto the bed.

"It doesn't look to me like they're here," Brad said in a condescending tone Rebecca had grown to detest.

"Well, they were!"

Brad kicked the bedding aside with his foot to inspect the floor. He bent down and picked up the blankets, shaking them out.

"They're not here," he said.

Rebecca was down on her hands and knees, looking under the bed. "I don't see them here either."

Outside, a distant, faint rumble reverberated through the house. Neither of them noticed at first.

"Did you leave them in the car?" she asked.

Brad shook his head. "You just said you remembered putting them in your purse."

"Well, maybe I was wrong! Go look!"

"How can I find them if the door is locked?"

"You can look in the window and see them, can't you?"

"All right, all right! I'm going!" Brad started toward the door. "You didn't leave them in the bathroom, did you?"

"I'll check," she said.

Brad hurried downstairs and through the front door. The car sat in the driveway where he had parked it the day before, just a few feet away from the walk. He went around to the driver's side and peered in through the windshield. The keys were not in the ignition. He gave the floorboards a quick search.

In the distance, a heavily burdened diesel engine labored up the winding road, stopping every so often and then straining to regain its momentum anew. Brad looked at his watch and went back inside.

"Did you find them?" Rebecca asked as he entered the bedroom.

"Nope."

"What about the study?"

Brad shrugged. "I'll check."

"Is that the trash truck I hear?"

"Yeah, I think so. I'm glad I got up when I did. I'd hate to have all that garbage next to the garage for a week."

Rebecca sat down on the bed. "What could I have done with them?"

"I don't know, but we'd better find them soon."

Rebecca felt the finger of accusation poking her in the side. She clenched her jaw.

"What about the kitchen? You didn't leave them in there, did you?"

She shook her head. "I know I had them when we came in. I heard them when I threw my purse on the bed."

"You're sure?"

"Yes! I'm sure!"

Brad bent down and squinted to see under the bed again. "They're not here."

"Well, maybe they're downstairs!" Rebecca said.

"All right, all right! I'll check the study."

Rebecca followed Brad down the stairs. "Look behind the sofa."

"Yes ma'am!"

Rebecca went into the kitchen. She searched the countertops, running her hands along the surface of the tile. She looked under the table and along the cabinets, and then stood in the middle of the room with her hands on her hips. She went over to the cupboards and opened them, not really expecting to find anything, but she was getting desperate. She looked under the sink, rummaging through the wastebasket Billie kept there.

"Any luck?" Brad called out as he came into the room.

Rebecca stood with her hands on her hips, shaking her head, more from frustration than in answer to his question. "I've looked everywhere. I even went through the trash. Nothing."

The sound of the diesel engine was growing louder as it crested the hill and stopped at the stop sign on the corner.

They looked at each other. "The trash!"

Brad made a mad dash for the front door with Rebecca right behind him. As they passed by the car, they could see the truck coming into view. They ran to the end of the driveway just as the truck pulled up to the curb and stopped. A burly man in city overalls jumped down and reached for the first bag of trash.

"Hold on!" Brad called out.

The man, who had not noticed them before, looked up.

"We think we may have lost our keys," said Brad.

The man dropped the bag in his hand. "Happens all the time," he said.

Brad took the bag the man had dropped and opened it. "This will only take a minute," he said.

"We can wait a minute," said the man.

Brad rummaged through the contents of the bag. "Take that one, Honey," he said to Rebecca. "Watch the bottom. It's torn."

Rebecca took the bag and opened it. She looked down inside, hesitating to put her hands into it, and then gingerly scooted some of the dirty paper plates to one side.

Brad picked up the bag he was searching and shook it, hoping to hear the sound of keys jingling.

The burly man in the city overalls looked at his watch.

"Shouldn't take too long," Brad said as he shoved his hand inside the bag.

Rebecca followed Brad's lead and shook the bag.

"I don't hear anything," she said.

"Well, dump it out!" Brad said, turning his own bag upside down.

The burly man looked at his watch and then at his partner, who had just come around the back of the truck.

"Lose something?" the man asked.

"Car keys," the first man said.

The second man nodded with a knowing look toward the sky. He stepped over the debris through which Brad was busy digging, and took a third bag and opened it. He rummaged around, poking his nose down into the bag, pushing dirty plates and napkins to one side and then the other.

"Don't see no keys," he said. He thrust his hand deep into the bag. "Is this something you folks want?"

He pulled out his hand. In it he held an old leather pouch covered with cake frosting and dried gravy. A stale piece of lettuce clung to one corner.

"That was on the table!" Rebecca cried.

The man threw it onto the curb and continued his search.

"I don't see no keys!" he said after a few minutes.

"Neither do I," Brad said.

"They're not here," Rebecca declared as she began shoving the contents of the bag back into it.

Brad quickly gathered up all the trash and stuffed it into his own bag. The two men loaded the bags onto the truck and soon were on their way.

"Now what?" Rebecca asked as they sat down on the curb.

"I don't know," said Brad.

Rebecca took his hand. "I'm sorry I snapped at you." Her eyes pleaded.

Brad smiled and squeezed her hand, then reached over and picked up the pouch. "I wonder what this is?"

"And I wonder how it got out here?" said Rebecca.

"Looks like it has papers in it," said Brad.

"Well, they're not helping us find the keys," she said. She stood and reached down to give Brad a hand up.

"I'll take it in and clean it up a bit. It must be something of your aunt's."

"I never saw it before."

"It was in the house. It must be hers."

The pouch was bundled and tied with an old string. He slipped the string toward one end and carefully let it fall into his other hand.

"This thing is really old," he said as a few brittle pieces of paper flaked away and fell to the ground.

"Be careful."

Brad gently unfolded the pouch. It was large and shaped like an oversized billfold, folded over into thirds. It was stuffed with old papers, brittle and brown from the years. He fingered some of the papers to the side so he could see inside.

"Looks like some letters, and some kind of legal stuff. And there are some pictures."

"Pictures of what? What does it say?"

"I don't know. Looks like a letter addressed to your uncle." Brad thumbed through the bundle. "And some pictures of a couple of little girls on a horse."

"What else?" Rebecca asked as she peered inside.

"I don't know," said Brad. "Let's take it into the house." He refolded it and replaced the string.

They walked back to the house arm-in-arm. Brad set the pouch on top of the suitcase just inside the door.

"We still have to find the keys," he said.

"I don't know where they could be," said Rebecca. "We've looked everywhere."

"Well, they've got to be around here someplace. Are you sure you had them when we came in?"

"Yes. I remember hearing them jingle in my purse."

"When?"

"When we went upstairs. I know I heard them when I threw my purse on the bed."

"Well, they didn't walk out by themselves. They must still be there."

"I'll look again," Rebecca sighed, "but I don't know what good it'll do. I've searched the whole room twice."

Brad went into the living room as Rebecca headed up the stairs. He sat down on the sofa, but then remembered the pouch and went back into the foyer to retrieve it. He carried it into the kitchen and wiped it off with a damp dishtowel, taking care not to get the edges of the papers wet. On his way back to the living room, he resisted the urge to slip the string from it and peek inside. He settled back on the sofa and tossed the pouch on the coffee table at his feet.

Rebecca stood in the doorway to the living room jingling her keys.

"Where did you find them?"

"They were in the blanket—right where you looked! I just picked it up, and there they were."

"Must be gremlins," Brad said, shaking his head.

"Gremlins who wanted us to find that," Rebecca said, pointing at the leather pouch.

Brad picked up the leather pouch and turned it over in his hand. "Yeah, weird," he said.

He inspected the embossing and then slipped the string off again.

Rebecca sat down beside him. "Why don't we look at it on the way?"

"Yeah, OK," he said only half listening. "Just a minute." He opened the pouch and spread it out on his lap. Two black-and-white, faded photos fell out and landed on the sofa between them. Rebecca picked them up. Frozen in time by the camera lens was a picture of an old man in overalls and a scraggly gray beard. He was holding a small child. The other was of two little girls in long dresses standing next to a Model-T Ford on a dirt road in front of an old house with dingy wooden siding. Tree-covered mountains rolled gently away to meet the distant horizon. Smoke drifted from the rock chimney. A swollen, muddy creek cut through the meadow behind them.

"I wonder who they are," Brad said.

"I think this one might be Aunt Billie," said Rebecca, pointing. "She looks like the same girl as the one hanging on the wall in the sitting room—next to the picture of my Uncle Bill."

"Who's the other one?"

Rebecca shook her head. "I don't know."

"They must have been about two or three years old there."

"What a beautiful place," Rebecca said.

Brad lifted the papers out of the pouch.

"Be careful," Rebecca said, reverently.

He put the papers on his lap and set the pouch aside. "This one's a letter," he said as he lifted the first delicate piece of paper. It was a handwritten, single page. "It's addressed to Effie. Who's Effie?"

"I don't know. Who's it from?"

Their eyes went to the signature at the bottom of the page.

"George," Rebecca read. "It must be Grandpa Jakes."

Brad began to read:

Dear Effie,

I reckon you heard about all the trouble we been having. I don't know what I'm going to do. I'm at the end of my rope. I read yesterday where the Lord don't give you no more than you can handle. But I ain't so sure. The children ain't give up, but it pains me some to see them planting on played-out ground. I got more to say on the matter when I see you.

Your loving brother,
George

"I wonder what that was all about?" said Rebecca.

Brad shrugged as he laid the letter on the sofa. He leafed through the stack—a couple of old handwritten receipts, one for a horse dated 1905, and one for a woman's dress two years earlier. He flipped through a few more.

"Here," said Rebecca with her hand outstretched, "let me have a few."

Brad separated the pile into two roughly equal parts and handed her the one from the bottom. She laid it on the sofa and began sifting through it.

"Ohhh, look!" Rebecca said, holding up a tattered and fragile parchment. "It's a marriage certificate!"

Brad leaned close to her and read out loud, "'George and Lydia Jakes, 1877.' That can't be your grandpa, can it?"

"I don't know."

Brad cocked his head, eyebrows raised. "If he got married in 1877, that would make him pretty old when your father and your aunt were born. Your aunt was born, what, in the early thirties?"

"1932, I think."

"That would make it more than fifty years later. Doesn't seem likely."

"Hmmm." Rebecca set the parchment on the sofa. "Here's another letter."

"What's it say?"

"It's from 'Ruth' to somebody named 'Clayton.'" Rebecca paused as she read silently.

"What's it say?" Brad asked again.

Rebecca held up her hand. "Just a minute."

Brad scooted closer. He peered over her shoulder and began to read:

> I wish I could begin to explain the awful circumstances that bring us to this dreary day. You've read the diary, or at least those passages that concern our proposed union, and you know of my fears. I know you believe them to be unfounded superstition, yet I cannot, in good conscience, allow the warning to go unheeded.
> I shall always love you.

"Man, these people sure were cryptic!" said Brad.

"I wonder what it's all about?" said Rebecca. She leafed quickly through the rest of the papers. "There is so much here. It'll take hours to go through it all."

"Well, we don't have hours." Brad looked at his watch. "We'd better be going now. C'mon, you can look at this stuff in the car."

They gathered up the papers and put them back in the leather pouch, taking care not to damage them. At the front door, Brad grabbed the suitcase and opened the door for his wife. Rebecca clutched the leather pouch close to her as if it were her most valued possession.

As they pulled out onto the highway, Rebecca stared out the passenger-side window as the house disappeared from sight. "You know," she said a few minutes later, "when she died, I felt so empty." She looked down at the pouch in her lap. "But now I feel as if I have a piece of her here with me."

She opened the pouch and pulled the papers from it, setting them in her lap. The pouch slid to the floor.

They drove in silence for several hours. The only sound was an occasional sigh from Rebecca as she waded through the old papers and photos. It was almost dark when they stopped for the night at a motel along the road. She hardly noticed when Brad got out in front of the office and went inside to pay for the room. When he came back, she was still reading.

"Must be good stuff," he said.

"Hmmm," she said without looking up.

Brad pulled the car around back and parked. "You want me to bring you a blanket?"

Rebecca looked up. "Huh? What?"

"I thought maybe you wanted to spend the night in the car," he said sarcastically, motioning toward the papers in her lap. "It must be pretty intriguing stuff."

"It is," she said. She gently scooped the papers into a neat pile and held them close to her as she stepped carefully out of the car and waited for Brad, who was grabbing the suitcase from the trunk, at the door to their room.

Inside, Rebecca set the papers on the small table in the corner.

"So what did you find?" Brad asked.

"I don't even know where to begin," she said. "There is so much here, so much of her, so much of me."

Brad sat down next to her.

"Look at this," she said, taking a large, faded, black-and-white photograph in her hands. "It's dated 1916."

She turned it over quickly to show Brad the date written in the corner on the back. In the upper left-hand corner was a list of names.

"See here," Rebecca pointed to the list. "It tells who all these people were."

She flipped it over again. There were two rows of people. Some were old—men in fedoras and women in long, drab skirts. Some were young children. All were standing except for a gray-haired woman, frail and petite. Yet her eyes were strong and resolute. She was seated in the middle of the front row.

Rebecca pointed to a young man in the back row. "See," she said, "that's my grandpa, George Jakes. And this one," she pointed to an older man standing next to him, "is his father, George Senior."

"Who are these?" Brad asked, pointing to two of the women.

"This one is Mary," she said, tapping the photograph with her finger. "She's George Senior's sister. And the one next to her is Effie."

"The one who received the letter?"

"It must be."

"So, she's also George's sister?"

"Mm-hmm."

"And Mary's sister?"

"Right."

Brad shook his head. "Just trying to keep it straight."

"These four," Rebecca said, tapping the photograph as she explained, "are brothers and sisters. Effie, Mary, George—my grandfather's father, and John. It seems there was another brother, but he died just before this was taken."

"So who's the old lady?" Brad asked, pointing at the woman seated in the middle.

Rebecca drew a deep breath. "That's their mother, Katherine Jakes," the softness in her voice betrayed her sense of awe, "the year before she died."

"That's really something," said Brad. "Your whole family is wrapped up in that little pouch. And to think it almost went to the dump!"

"But there's more," Rebecca said. "I've read most of these letters and there seems to be one theme running through them all. None say what it is, but they all talk about 'the trouble' and how none of them know what to do about it. And here, look at this." She handed Brad a tattered old letter.

Brad took it and spread it out on the table. It was addressed to Wilhelmina Dawson and signed by a woman named Ruth.

"Who is Ruth?" Brad asked.

"I think she was my grandfather's sister—George Senior's daughter. That would make her my aunt's aunt."

Brad began to read:

Dear Billie,

Let me begin by congratulating you on your marriage. I regret that I could not be with you on the happy day, but I'm sure you are aware that my own father is gravely ill and in need of constant attention. I must tell you I was distressed to hear that you wanted to read the diary. I know the trouble that has plagued us for too many years. I am, perhaps, more acutely aware of it than you realize. My advice is that you should forget about what is, I am sure, an old superstition, and forget about the diary. There is surely nothing to it, and if there be any truth found in its pages, know this, that all that could be done has been done to no avail. Do not allow it to affect your life the way it has mine.

Affectionately,
Ruth

"Ruth," Brad said. "Isn't that the one who sounded so cryptic this morning—something about not being able to marry?"

"Mm-hmm. The letter to Clayton. But this one was written much later—about thirty years, I think. I don't know what it all means, but it seems to center on a diary. But," she waved her hand over the stack of papers, "no one says whose diary it was, or where it is now."

"Probably long gone by now," Brad said.

"Probably," Rebecca agreed.

"So what do you think it's all about?" Brad asked.

"I have no idea, but there's something else that doesn't make any sense to me." Rebecca shuffled through the papers until she found what she was looking for. "Here. Look at this."

She handed Brad a letter.

Brad took it. It was a letter from Aunt Billie.

Dear Jonathan …

"That's your dad, isn't it?"

"Mm-hmm. It's dated the year I was born."

Dear Jonathan,

Let me congratulate you on the birth of a healthy daughter. My prayers are with you, and I hope that God will richly bless the three of you. I was pleased to hear of your choice of names. I have always liked it. It is with some regret, and an abiding sense of guilt, that I feel I must bring up the awful business again. You asked me if I think it is real. My answer is yes, I do, but not in the way you think. Knowing your propensity for self-reliance, as well as your rejection of the faith that holds me up, I know you will not believe me, but I feel it is my duty to point it out, nonetheless. I know you regard it as silly superstition and the product of ignorance. While I agree that it has no real power over us, I still must insist that dark forces may be at work. That does not mean what you may think it means. Just as having someone hold a gun to your head would be terrifying, it could be just as awful to think someone is holding a gun to your head. A perceived threat can be just as debilitating as a real one. Why have so many in our family suffered? I can't answer. I am sure you will remember the agony that my husband and I experienced in the early days of our union. Perhaps not. You were so young, an unfortunate consequence of your unseasonable arrival so late in our parents' lives. Bitter though they were, those days served as a catalyst to bring me closer to my Savior than I ever thought possible. Those events that have shaped not only my own life, but those of all the Jakes family for many generations, seemed to have escaped your awareness. But they shaped us in ways you probably don't understand. All I know is that "all things work together for good for those that love the Lord and are called according to His purpose." I know, I know, you don't want to hear it. Yet you asked what I think. I believe that God has His own purposes for the events of our lives. Bill and I accept His will for our lives and trust that He has a good plan for your new daughter. What that may be only time will tell. I only know that I will pray that He will pour out a measure of His grace on our new little addition and end this "trouble" and its hold on us once and for all. May God bless and keep her.

Your loving sister
Billie

"Wow!" Brad said.

"Yeah. I wish I knew what it was about."

"I don't understand this part," Brad said, running his finger back through the page until he found what he was looking for. "This part about your dad being so young."

"My father was quite a bit younger than his brothers and his sister. He was almost seventeen years younger than Billie. She was born in 1932. My father wasn't born until 1949."

"So what's this part about darkness?"

"I don't know. And there's nothing in the rest of this that explains it," she said, waving her hand over the stack of papers.

"A weird letter," Brad said.

"The whole thing is a little strange," Rebecca agreed.

"That's putting it mildly." Brad motioned toward the papers. "What else is here?"

Rebecca shrugged. "Just some old documents and more letters and a few photos. The strange thing is that everything here—all the letters refer to the diary or 'the trouble,' but none say what it is.

"Something else is strange too. Some of the letters are obviously answers to other letters, or answers to conversations that someone had with the person he or she was writing to. But there are no letters that don't refer to 'the trouble.' My aunt seems to have collected all the things that had to do with whatever it is they're talking about."

"Except the diary," Brad said.

"Except the diary," Rebecca agreed, "but there is no mention of what 'it' is, which is strange. Why would my aunt keep all this stuff?"

"I don't know."

"Something else bothers me," Rebecca continued. "Why was the pouch on the table when we arrived?"

"I suppose because your aunt put it there before she died."

"Yes, but why?"

"I don't know. Maybe she—" Brad threw up his hands. "I don't know."

Rebecca shook her head. "I don't know either, but I've never seen it before. It wasn't anywhere in sight the other day when we spent the night before she died."

"I still can't figure out how it got in the trash."

"One of the ladies must have thrown it there by mistake. Anyway, I'm curious why it was out in the first place. Aunt Billie must have had a reason."

"Maybe she was reminiscing, you know, about old times."

Rebecca had her doubts. "I suppose. But something she said the other day still bothers me, and I wonder if this letter has something to do with it."

"And what was that?"

"We were walking along the beach and talking—you know, about things like not being able to have a baby. Anyway, things turned to religion like they always do with her. But this time it was like she was making a connection. She said something about not praying enough. And not letting the devil get a foothold—I think that's what she said. Then she got a funny look on her face and said, 'I wish I'd learned that a little sooner.'"

Brad wrinkled up his nose. "So what's your point?"

Rebecca shrugged again. "I'm not sure. But it was the way she looked. Remember what I told you?"

"Yeah, I remember. You said she wanted kids, but I don't see the connection."

"I'm not sure I do either," Rebecca said, looking down at the letter in her hands. "This last part is obviously talking about me. It almost sounds like the trouble has something to do with me."

"That's ridiculous!"

Rebecca was silent. She couldn't argue with Brad. It did sound ridiculous. She wondered if she'd ever know the answer, but something tugged at her heart. She felt as though there were answers—answers she needed, answers she wanted, and answers she felt she must have—somehow.

CHAPTER EIGHTEEN

THE SIMPLE ONE-TERMINAL airport in Medford, Oregon, rested in a quiet valley surrounded by distant mountains and green trees—a stark contrast to the busy freeways, glittering offices, and myriad of cookie-cutter homes of Southern California. Brad parked the car to the din of massive jet engines as a 707 lifted from the runway less than a hundred yards away. Near the terminal entrance, a hearse waited with the back door open and faced the parking lot. Elegant lettering on the door announced "Garvey and Sons Mortuary." Two men in business suits stood a few feet from the car, leaning against the building and talking. Occasionally, they laughed. Rebecca looked away.

As she and Brad stepped out of the car and walked briskly along the sidewalk toward the terminal, a third man in a dark suit joined the other two. He was tall with flawlessly trimmed silver-gray hair that swept neatly back from his face. He spoke to the other men, who stopped laughing and straightened when they noticed him approaching. One of the men nodded obediently as the man with the silver-gray hair spoke. They all looked suddenly grim.

Rebecca held her eyes straightforward as they walked past the hearse. Brad held the door to the terminal for her and then followed her inside. The man with the silver-gray hair finished his business with the other two and followed Brad through the door before it completely closed.

He hurried through another door behind a gate with a sign that said, "No Admittance."

Brad walked up to a pretty attendant standing behind a high counter. He glanced down at the slip of paper with the information Mr. Stephens, Billie's lawyer, had given him over the phone.

"Excuse me," he said. "We're supposed to meet Mr. Garvey. Can you tell me where I can find him?"

The girl turned to the window behind her. "That's him," she said, pointing to the man in the dark suit with the silver-gray hair. He was standing next to a man in an orange jumpsuit, having what looked to Brad like a heated discussion.

"You'll have to wait until he comes back in," the girl said.

Brad smiled, thanked her, and then joined Rebecca, who sat in one of the chairs that lined the wall along the back of the terminal. She stared without blinking out the great wall of glass facing the runway.

"That's him over there," Brad said as he sat down, pointing to the man in the dark suit.

Rebecca did not answer.

"You OK?"

Rebecca rested her head on Brad's shoulder without answering. He stroked her hair.

Mr. Garvey finished his conversation with the man in the orange jumpsuit and marched through the same door he had exited. The girl behind the counter motioned to him and then whispered something as he leaned over the counter. She pointed at Brad and Rebecca. Garvey strode, businesslike, over to where Brad and Rebecca were seated.

"Hello," he said, cool and professional with a hint of measured compassion. "I'm Richard Garvey. I understand you're looking for me?"

Brad stood and took his extended hand. "Yes," he said, glancing back to acknowledge his wife, "we are. Did Mr. Stephens call?"

The man looked puzzled. "No?" he said. It sounded like a question.

Brad hurried to explain. "My wife is the niece of the woman who—"

He paused in an awkward silence, and then motioned toward the hearse.

Garvey's eyes widened.

"No one told me you were coming!" Garvey said just above a strained whisper. He quickly regained his composure. "That is, I would have made arrangements to meet you."

Rebecca stood. "We're sorry. We didn't know until yesterday that we were coming."

"Mr. Stephens was going to try to contact you this morning," said Brad.

"I haven't been to my office yet," Garvey said. "And I don't have cell service here."

"It's no problem," Rebecca said. "We didn't expect any fanfare. We just came to see this through for my aunt."

Garvey turned white. He shot a quick glance at the hearse outside. "There ..." he paused, wishing there were words benign enough. "There is a problem."

Rebecca and Brad exchanged glances. "What kind of problem?" Brad asked.

"Well," he began slowly, "the airline—" Garvey hesitated. "It seems that there has been a mix-up."

Rebecca braced herself.

"I'm afraid your aunt's casket has not arrived as scheduled." He cleared his throat.

"What do you mean? Where is it?"

"It seems it is en route...somewhere. We're not exactly sure at this point."

"You mean you lost it?" Brad's tone accused.

Garvey's jaw tightened. "For the moment, yes."

Rebecca felt the tears returning. She had spent the last four days with her face in a handkerchief and she was tired of it. Finding the leather pouch had been a welcome diversion, as well as a comforting link to her aunt. The drive up had been pleasant, even fun, as she discovered things about her history and her family she had never dreamed she could know or even care about. Now she felt a knot in the pit of her stomach at the thought of losing her aunt all over again.

Something else had bothered her ever since the night of the funeral, when she had gone to bed leaving Brad on the sofa wondering where her sudden burst of cynicism had come from. She felt so down, so completely defeated then. By the time she went to bed she was sure she was alone in the universe and the butt of some big, cosmic joke. She felt if there was a God, He surely must be cruel and uncaring. Worse still, she had voiced it. She had called Him cruel. She wondered—she feared—that God was punishing her now.

Brad's rage, spawned by some deep protective instinct, boiled just below the surface. "How do you lose a coffin?" he demanded.

Garvey maintained his air of professionalism. He answered slowly, taking care not to sound flustered. "It happens sometimes, unfortunately. But it is only a minor problem. We know which flight it was supposed to take from California. We just have to find out if it was transferred to the wrong flight by mistake, or if it was loaded on the correct flight and simply wasn't unloaded when the plane landed here. Someone is checking now. As soon as we know the flight number that it was loaded onto in California, we'll know where to start looking. It should only take a few minutes, an hour at the most."

"We were supposed to be at the cemetery at ten," Brad said. He was calmer, but not much. "Will it be here in time for that?"

Garvey felt his face flush. "Well, no, probably not. You see, we can locate it, but getting it back here may take a little longer."

"How much longer?" Brad demanded.

Garvey cleared his throat. "We hope...that is, I'm certain we can have it here in a day, maybe two."

Rebecca felt sick to her stomach. She hated hearing her aunt referred to as "it."

Brad was losing what little patience he still had. "Is that the best you can do?"

Garvey cocked his head and shrugged. "At the moment, I'm afraid so." He waited for a response. "Would you like me to arrange a room for you for the night? We have several fine hotels a mile or so from here."

"No," Brad said. "We can manage."

"Well, if you need anything, please call me," Garvey said, handing Brad a business card. "My home phone number is the one on the bottom. Please feel free to call."

Brad took the card. He had no way of knowing whose fault all this was—this man's or someone else's—but he didn't care. Someone blew it, and he wanted that someone to pay. "Yeah, fine," he said.

Garvey smiled weakly, excused himself, and then hurried through the glass door and stopped at the rear of the hearse. He said something to the two men and then started across the parking lot. One of the men shut the big back door, while the other one slid into the driver's seat and waited for the other to get in before starting the engine. Garvey walked quickly across the parking lot and got into a silver-colored SUV. Brad and Rebecca watched as both vehicles drove away.

"Now what?" Brad asked.

Rebecca felt the words as if they were dead weight in her arms. Her knees felt weak as she sat down in her chair.

"You OK?" Brad asked, sitting down beside her.

She nodded, fighting tears. Brad felt the rage of helplessness a man feels when someone he loves is injured or threatened and he has no power to do anything about it. He took her hand.

Rebecca felt the warmth of his skin as their fingers interlocked and their palms met. She rested her other hand on his.

"Well," Brad said, "there's no sense waiting around here. What do you want to do?"

Rebecca didn't want to think about it. She wanted someone to lead her, to show her the way, and she would follow willingly.

Brad sighed. "We might as well drive up to Creek Junction. It's only a few miles from here, and we can call the mortuary when we get settled and let them know where we are."

Rebecca gave a longing look toward the runway. "What about Aunt Billie?"

"There's nothing we can do here." Brad wished he could soften what he said next. "The man said it could be days. Besides, the cemetery is in Creek Junction. We might as well go on up and wait there. It'll give us a chance to check out the property your aunt told you about."

"That'll take four or five hours." Rebecca said. "What are we going to do after that?"

"Oh, I don't know," Brad said, leaning close to her with an impish smile. "Maybe we could work on a family."

Rebecca pulled away. She felt alone and empty and the last thing she wanted, or needed, was unwelcome and poorly timed advances from the very one who should have been providing comfort and assurance.

"Don't," she said.

Brad pulled away. "I was only trying to cheer you up."

"I don't feel very cheerful."

"I'm sorry," Brad said. He held her hand in his and stroked the back of it gently with his fingers. They sat in silence for several minutes.

"So what do you think?" he asked.

Rebecca shrugged. "I don't know. You decide. I'll do whatever you say. Just tell me. I really don't feel like making decisions."

"All right," he said as he stood, holding her hand and pulling her to her feet. "C'mon."

He slipped his arm around her waist and pulled her close to kiss her.

She stiffened her arms against his chest for a moment and then submitted, but only for a moment, and then she pushed him away.

"Not now," she said with a chill in her voice Brad rarely heard—and hated the few times he had.

"All right," he said, infusing an equal amount of coldness of his own. "Shall we go?"

The callousness of his response was not lost on Rebecca. It was something he rarely did. But at the moment, she didn't care. She brushed past him and pushed open the door before he could open it for her. She strode across the parking lot, defiantly burying her hands in her pockets when Brad tried to hold her hand. When they got to the car, Brad hurried to open her door.

"Thanks," she said coldly.

Brad went around to the other side and climbed in. He turned the key, the motor responded, and he pulled the shift lever into position. Then he waited. After a moment of chilly silence, he pushed the lever up into "park." He hated admitting he was wrong. Even more, he hated saying it when he was convinced he was right. Not that his actions were totally appropriate. He knew Rebecca was hurting, and he tried to understand. But her anger was way out of proportion to the offense.

His jaw clenched as he sat debating whether to apologize. He had done nothing for which to apologize. He had been the picture of understanding through this whole thing. She should understand and appreciate that.

Brad drew a deep breath. “I’m sorry,” he said.

Rebecca stared silently out the passenger-side window. Brad reached over and took her hand. She pulled it away.

All right, fine! he thought as he pulled the shift lever into gear again and backed out of the parking spot. The car rocked side to side as it rolled from the parking lot to the street and sped toward the onramp to Interstate Five. Brad looked over his shoulder as he made the transition from the onramp to the freeway. The freeway seemed almost uninhabited compared to what he was used to, a pleasant surprise. He kicked it up to seventy, and then backed off, letting the car settle in at sixty-five. He reached down and set the cruise control.

Rebecca sat with her arms folded for several miles, barely noticing the pristine scenery that panned by the side window as the freeway ascended out of the valley and into the surrounding mountains. She was angry and she didn’t know why. Brad’s show of affection was nothing new. She liked it—usually. But she couldn’t think about it right now.

Her life had changed abruptly. Billie was gone and she’d hardly had any time to adjust to it. She had felt like a failure before, not being able to give Brad a son or a daughter, and she felt instinctively that Billie could have helped her. Billie always knew the answers, even though Rebecca had not always listened. Billie had a direct line to God, it seemed. She prayed about everything, even little, insignificant things.

Rebecca never really had thought about it before, but she realized she had been holding out some inner hope that if she asked Billie to pray, God would answer her. Now that secret hope had died with Billie. And if that weren’t enough, to come all the way up here to find that Billie’s casket had been lost. It was too much. Brad should understand.

Outside the window in a meadow a few hundred yards from the freeway, a deer grazed near the tree line. Rebecca hardly noticed. As she sat rigid and stubborn, she wondered why there had to be so much pain in the world. Life handed out so many dirty deals and gave so little comfort. If there was a God, why did He allow so much suffering? She felt angry and at the same time a little ashamed that she could compare her own petty problems to the misery of the world—and yet her problems weren't petty to her. And even if they were, why couldn't God, with all that power, wave His hand and fix them along with every other problem in the world? What, after all, was the big deal to God?

She didn't know the answer. She had tried prayer. She had prayed for a baby. A lot of good that did! She couldn't remember one thing prayer had ever gotten her. Instead, God took away her only source of security and spiritual comfort—Aunt Billie. Somehow knowing Billie was praying for her made her feel as if God would make allowances for any past indiscretions, as well as any and all present imperfections.

But now Rebecca was alone.

As she sank into depression, she felt the weight of her circumstances bearing down on her. She felt lost, really lost, and helpless to do anything about it. Brad, her one source of strength, couldn't help her. When she married him, she had felt secure and safe—not the same security Billie offered, but the security a man gives a woman (real or imagined) just by being a man. She looked to him for guidance. She relied on him for security. She wanted to trust him with the feelings that oppressed her now. Instead, he mocked prayer, the one thing that, deep down, she still hoped could give her the answers she craved. It was more than she could take.

Rebecca trembled as she prayed a simple prayer from the poverty of her heart.

The Centurion took notice of the cry that went out from her soul. He smiled knowingly and then acknowledged the directive that came down from on high in response to her plea. Then he bowed low in worship before the Lamb.

It was mid-morning when Brad reached the off-ramp at Creek Junction. He turned right at the bottom of the hill, followed it to the intersection, and turned left onto the main street that ran through town. Battered clapboard buildings lined both sides of the street. A mom-and-pop market in need of paint, with a sign over the facade that read "Doucets,'" sat in the middle of the block. Next to it was a small café, and across the street two or three antique shops hunched together under a common mansard roof with weathered shingles.

Down a little farther was an auto parts store, and across the street a small shop with a banner that announced, "Chain saws. All makes and models." Behind the row of stores and shops hidden by lush trees and truculent berry vines, the river issued up soothing sounds as it caressed a rocky bed.

Brad followed the road slowly, looking for a motel.

When they had gone three or four city blocks, the road narrowed just past an intersection marked with a sign that identified the small creek that flowed into the river beyond a two-lane bridge. It said: "Walker Creek."

They continued to follow the road for almost a mile. Just outside of town, a modern casino, slick and new, stood in stark contrast to the sleepy little town. It beaconed potential customers with a glittering "Indian Bingo" sign. Next to it was a large, modern hotel with an adjoining parking lot. A narrow greenbelt separated the two.

"That OK with you?" Brad asked, pointing.

Rebecca nodded. She'd had time to cool off a bit, and she no longer felt like arguing. Yet her outburst and cool attitude toward her husband for the last hour made reconciliation awkward.

Brad turned into the driveway and stopped under the high roofed canopy at the front entrance. "I'll be right back," he said as he slipped out of the car.

Rebecca watched him as he walked around the front of the car and into the hotel lobby. He was gone for a few minutes. When he reappeared, he was holding a key in one hand and a credit card slip in the other.

"I got us one on the ground floor," he said.

"Good," she said softly.

Brad started the car and drove around to the back. He parked in front of the room with a number on the door corresponding to the one on the key. He handed Rebecca the key.

"Open the door, will you?" he said. "I'll get the bags out of the trunk."

Rebecca took the key and said nothing. She climbed out of the car, went to the door, and opened it just as Brad met her with their suitcases.

The room was spacious and new. Rebecca felt the crunch of new carpet under her feet as she set the key on the dark wood Formica finish of the table in the corner. There were two double beds side by side and the customary bureau with a television bolted to a swivel platform. A small open closet and a door that led to the bathroom were at the far end of the room.

Rebecca took a deep breath. "Smells new."

"Yeah," Brad said. "The guy at the desk said they've only been open for a few months. The casino has really changed things around here."

"I'm sure," she said, not really caring.

Brad hoisted the suitcases onto the table and then surveyed the room. "I think I'll take a shower."

Rebecca nodded. "OK."

Brad turned to her and put his hands on her shoulders. "Care to join me?"

"Not now," she said, softness returning to her voice. "Maybe later."

Brad stroked her shoulder. "All right," he said, measuring his own tone. He turned and walked toward the bathroom.

"Brad?"

He turned at the door.

Rebecca studied his face, strong and confident. "I love you."

Brad smiled. "I love you too."

They lingered for a moment, sharing unspoken intimacy. "I'll be back," he said and then disappeared behind the bathroom door.

Rebecca sat on the edge of the bed. There was a television guide on the bedside table next to her. She picked it up and thumbed through it, wrinkling up her nose at the offered selections, and then set the guide back on the table. She kicked off her shoes and swung her feet up onto the bed, stretching out with her hands behind her head. It had been a long day. She felt drained of energy and wondered what she was doing here a thousand miles from home—and for what?

She remembered the pouch, got up, and went to get it from the car. When she returned to the room, she stretched out on the bed again, unfolding the pouch and taking the contents from it. She set the empty pouch on the bed next to her. There were two documents in the pouch, but with the excitement and mystery of the letters, she hadn't paid much attention to them and had placed them together at the bottom of the pile. The first was the marriage license for George and Lydia Jakes dated 1877. After reading the letters, she discovered they were the son and daughter-in-law of John and Katherine Jakes.

Beneath the marriage license was another tattered document that was dated 1852 with an official looking seal that said, "Donation Claim." It included a legal description of a piece of property. John Jakes was listed as the recipient of the claim.

Brad came out of the bathroom, rubbing a towel over his wet hair.

"That was fast," Rebecca said.

"Comes from years of practice," he said with a grin.

Rebecca chuckled.

"More good stuff?" he said, motioning toward the papers on the bed.

"Just some documents—the marriage license you saw the other day, and something called a 'donation claim,' whatever that is."

"Did you call the funeral home?"

Rebecca shook her head. "It's probably too late," she said as she looked at her watch. "I'll call first thing in the morning."

Brad tossed the towel on the floor and fell back on the bed next to his wife. "How about dinner?"

"Sounds good to me. What did you have in mind?"

"Oh, I don't know. Why don't we find a little restaurant and then go to the casino afterward?"

Rebecca stretched her arms. "I'm kind of tired. Why don't we just have dinner and come back here?"

"All right," he said as he leaned down to kiss her. "I'll get dressed and be ready in a few minutes."

A few minutes later, he was ready to go.

"All set?" Rebecca asked.

"Yeah, let's go."

Brad held the door for her and then hurried to beat her to the car door. "Thank you," she said, sliding into the car.

They drove through the little town until they came to the small café next to the market. It was neat and clean on the outside with a sign in the window announcing the day's special. Brad pulled up to the front and parked.

Once inside, they waited for the waitress, a pretty young woman of about twenty, to seat them. She handed them their menus and smiled, her eyes lingering on Brad.

"What's good?" Brad asked.

"Everything's good," she teased.

"Is it?" Brad said.

"Mm-hmm," she said with a sly grin. "Some of the best isn't on the menu."

Brad smiled and then looked down at his menu, avoiding Rebecca's cold stare.

"Why don't you just bring us the specials?" he said.

"Sure," she said, but there was more to it than simple acknowledgment. She took the menus and sashayed toward the kitchen with a quick glance over her shoulder.

Brad suddenly wished he were alone.

CHAPTER NINETEEN

"YOU DIDN'T SEEM to mind too much!"

Rebecca and Brad had returned to the room after what turned out to be a lonely dinner.

"What was I supposed to do? She smiled! I smiled back! What's the big deal?"

"I saw!"

Brad threw his hands in the air. "I don't know what you expect from me."

Rebecca was silent for a moment.

"I just don't like it," she finally said.

Brad put his arms around her. "You know you're the only girl for me."

She stiffened. "I'd better be," she said. But then her heart softened a bit.

Brad held her close. She relented and slipped her arms around his neck.

"Truce?" he pleaded. Their eyes met.

Brad smiled his boyish smile. She never could resist it.

"Truce," she confirmed.

Brad held her close and kissed her. She felt safe in his arms for the moment, the feeling of betrayal subsided. Maybe he hadn't done anything wrong, but he was handsome, and he had smiled back at the waitress—no matter if she smiled first. There was no such thing as innocent flirtation, not where her husband was concerned, not when it was he who was being pursued.

"Just the same," she said, "let's find another place to eat while we're here, OK?"

"All right. If you insist."

"I do."

It wasn't that she didn't trust him exactly, but no woman could feel safe when another woman had an eye for her man. And she knew Brad's eyes could wander, especially if he thought she wasn't looking.

They undressed and settled into the bed, Brad in his boxer shorts and Rebecca in an old T-shirt. Brad flipped off the light.

Rebecca felt restless as she lay staring at the ceiling in the dark, and she was sure she would have trouble falling asleep. But the next thing she knew it was light outside and the muffled sounds of people leaving their rooms and talking just outside the door woke her. Brad was just beginning to stir.

She rolled over and snuggled close against his back, draping her arm over his shoulder. After a moment he rolled over and put his arm around her. She rested her head on his chest and stroked it gently with the tips of her fingers.

"What time is it?" she asked.

Brad glanced at the clock on the nightstand. "Quarter 'til eight."

Rebecca closed her eyes. It felt good to lay quietly with her head on Brad's strong chest, feeling the warmth from his body. She wanted it to last.

"We'd better get up," he said when a few minutes had passed. "We've got a big day ahead of us."

He rolled out of bed and slipped on his pants.

"Do you think they've found her?" The slight quiver in her voice betrayed her inner fear.

"They better have." he answered.

Rebecca pulled the sheet up to her chin.

"Don't worry," Brad said. "I'm sure they've found her by now. We'll call in a few minutes." He looked at his watch again. "Why don't you get dressed? I'll give it a few more minutes and then I'll call Garvey."

Rebecca pulled herself to a sitting position, sat for a moment, and then made her way reluctantly to the bathroom. She stood in front of the mirror, studying her face. The lines around her eyes seemed deeper than they had a few days ago.

When she had finished dressing, she rubbed lotion on her arms, brushed out her hair, and then applied lipstick and mascara. She studied her face in the mirror. It was a nice face, she decided—not perfect, but a nice face. She opened her eyes wide, forcing the crow's feet beginning to form at the corners to disappear. She could see, for the first time, her mother's eyes in her own.

Today would be a good day. She would will it. No concerns about families or babies or...somehow the pain of losing Billie was less intense today and she refused to let her loss get the best of her.

She quickly straightened the bathroom counter—a force of habit—and turned out the light as she left. Brad was standing next to the bed with his cell phone in his hand. He looked up at her.

"I see," he said into the receiver. "All right. Thank you."

Rebecca could sense the anger in his voice. "What's up?"

Brad clipped the phone onto his belt. "It's not good," he said, clenching his jaw.

Rebecca braced herself. "Well?" Her eyes pleaded.

"The airline still doesn't know where your aunt is."

"You mean they've lost her?"

"Garvey says it's nothing to worry about. They'll find her. It just may take a few days."

"Days?"

"That's what he said."

"He told us it would only be a few hours!"

"I know. I reminded him of that, but there doesn't seem to be anything we can do about it."

"But—" Rebecca felt her fear turn to hopelessness in an instant. She sat down on the edge of the bed. "There must be something we can do."

"Yeah," Brad muttered. "I'll call the airline."

He grabbed the phone book from the drawer beside the bed, flipped through it until he found what he was looking for and then punched in the number on his cell phone.

"Hello? This is Brad Lindsay. I'd like to speak to someone about—about lost cargo." He hated the way it sounded, but it was all he could think of. Rebecca sat on the edge of the bed. Her hands were trembling.

The voice on the other end asked him to hold. He heard canned Muzak before he could agree. In a moment, another voice, a man's voice, answered. Brad repeated his request.

Rebecca waited. Her hands trembled as she tried to decipher the conversation from Brad's end of it. But all she could make out was that Brad was not happy with what he was hearing. He gave whomever he was talking to the phone number of the hotel and their room number, and then he hung up.

"What did they say?"

Brad was grim. "Not much. They think they've traced it to somewhere on the east coast. But they don't even know for sure yet."

"How could they not know?"

Brad's jaw tightened. "I don't know."

"What do we do?" she asked.

Brad drew a deep breath, sighed, and shook his head. "I suppose we wait."

Rebecca sank back at his words.

"Don't worry," he said. "They'll find her. In the meantime, we might as well find something to do. Why don't we take a drive and see some of the country?"

"I don't really feel like sightseeing."

Brad sat on the bed next to his wife and put his arm around her. "We're here," he said with resignation. "We might as well make the best of it. You said you wanted to see the old homestead your aunt told you about. Why don't we see if we can find it?"

Rebecca felt hopeless. "How do we find it? I wouldn't even know where to begin."

"I suppose we could go to a real estate office and ask," Brad offered. "I'm sure they'd know how to find it. It's worth a try."

Rebecca's curiosity was piqued. Her self-pity gave way to curiousity and a sense of adventure. "All right," she said, "where do we start?"

Brad stood and walked back to the other side of the bed. He flipped through the phone book again.

"Here we go," he said as he ran his fingers down the page of listings for real estate agents. "Heh—small town. There are only three listings."

He dialed the first number.

No answer.

He dialed the second and got an answering machine. He left a message, hung up, and then dialed the last number.

"Hello?"

Brad gave his name and explained briefly what it was that he wanted. "Ten minutes? Yeah, that would be fine. Thanks."

"Let's go," he said as he hung up the phone.

Frank Downs wheezed as he struggled to pull himself from behind the wheel of his four-wheel-drive utility vehicle. He'd arrived at the office a few minutes late and found the phone ringing as he turned the key in the lock. He had lumbered across the room to answer it, dropping his keys on the floor. He'd tried to bend down to pick them up, but then as the phone rang again decided it wasn't worth the considerable effort and waddled across the room to pick up the receiver.

A couple of kids were up from California and wanted to look at some property, just the kind of prospect he liked: some yuppies with money to burn on a back-to-nature kick. As he set the receiver back on the phone, he realized he had left his briefcase in the car. He went out to get it, bending down on his way across the room to retrieve his keys with great difficulty.

As he grabbed the briefcase from the passenger-side seat, he noticed the gum wrappers and wadded pieces of paper that littered the floor.

He strained over his rather large paunch to gather them up in a wad. With his briefcase in the other hand, he squeezed out past the steering wheel.

He strutted back to the office, brushing the string of too-long hair over the top of his domed head, pushing the door wide and letting it thud against the wall.

Those kids will be here any minute. They said they were staying at the new hotel next to the casino a few blocks away.

He wanted to straighten up a bit before they came, so he gathered up the clutter of papers that covered his desk and shuffled them into a neat stack. Then he grabbed the vacuum cleaner from the closet and quickly vacuumed the floor—something he'd not done in more than a week. As he was putting the vacuum cleaner back in the closet behind the door, a late model Toyota pulled into the dirt parking lot and stopped next to his own car. A young man in his twenties got out and went around to the other side as a pretty young woman about the same age in jeans and a sleeveless top opened the door and joined him. The two of them headed for the door.

Nice! Frank thought as he eyed Rebecca.

Frank Downs ran his hands around his belt, tucking in his oversized shirt. The door opened.

"Hi, folks! Frank Downs! How are you?" He took Brad's hand and pumped it.

"Fine, thank you. This is my wife, Rebecca."

"Hi, Becky! Glad to meet you! Here, sit down, will you? Can I get you something—soda, coffee?

"Coffee would be fine," Brad said.

"Two coffees! No problem!" Frank lumbered over to the coffee pot on a narrow shelf by the copy machine.

"I'll just rinse this out," he said, taking the dingy pot with yesterday's last brew to the sink where he poured it out.

He filled it with water and poured it into the machine, dumping coffee into the filter without measuring it. He hit the start button.

"Be ready in a jiffy!" he said as he sat down behind his desk. "Now, what can I do for you? Are you two looking for a nice little cabin or maybe a little land you can build on?"

Rebecca pulled the tattered donation claim from her purse and handed it to her husband.

"We'd like to find a piece of property," Brad said. "We're not sure where it is, but it should be under the name of Wilhelmina Dawson. It's an old claim. I think the property was one of the original land claims from the 1850s."

Downs looked befuddled. He liked routine, and real estate was usually nothing but routine. No one had ever handed him an old document and asked to find the property before.

"This is really old!" He studied it for a moment. "Nathan Walker. That rings a bell. Do you know who he was?"

"I'm not sure," said Rebecca. "All I know is that my aunt said she owned some property up here that belonged to her family. This was in with some papers she had."

"Hmmm," he said, looking over the top of his glasses. "It couldn't still be valid, but I suppose we can try to track it down with the legal description."

"We hoped you could," Rebecca said.

Downs studied it for another minute. "Well, Becky" (he prided himself on his ability to remember names), let's find out."

Rebecca hated to be called Becky. She bit down on her tongue.

Downs hoisted himself out of his chair and waddled across the room to another desk, old and marred with drawers that fit askew on broken down runners. Sitting on its weathered surface was a brand-new computer. He sat down at the keyboard.

"Just got this thing," he said, and then added almost to himself, "Now, let's see if we can figure this out."

Rebecca could hear him clicking the mouse and muttering to himself.

"Ah!" he said a couple of times, and then "Ah …!" as if he caught himself before uttering a profanity.

"Hmmm," he said a couple of more times—and then, "Here we are!"

He looked down at the document in his lap and then back at the computer screen. He was glad the desk faced away from the two kids, or they might see what he was sure was a look of disbelief and even horror on his face.

He could hardly believe it. After all these years, someone was finally asking about it. He could feel his face flush as he read the information from the computer screen.

"Yes. Here it is," he said, hoping his voice didn't give away his alarm. "It's a piece up on Walker Creek about six miles from here. Let's see…it's not one piece anymore, though. Looks like from the description on this," he looked down at the claim, "it started out as about six hundred acres. But it's been split. About three hundred of it is owned by one of the big lumber companies. I think I know that piece. It was harvested about thirty years ago—got a good stand of fir on it right now.

"The rest is in the name of someone, let's see. It seems to be held in trust. Wil-hel-mina Dawson," he read slowly.

"That's my aunt!"

"Well, looks like she still owns it," Downs muttered as he read through the information on his screen. "That's really something. I didn't know there were any original donation claims left."

"My wife's aunt died a few days ago," Brad explained. "All her property was left in trust to Rebecca."

"Well, Becky, looks like you've inherited a chunk of Oregon's finest. It fronts the creek and there's a good deal of it that is tillable land."

"It's 'Rebecca.'"

"Sure, sure! I remember!" Downs grinned. "Now, would the two of you like to see it? I can drive you out there if you'd like. We'd only be gone an hour or so."

"We don't want to waste any of your time," Brad said.

"Nonsense, that's what I'm here for! Always ready to welcome new folks into our little valley! Besides, one of these days you may want to sell it and when you do, you'll remember ol' Frank, won't you?" He smiled. It was true. He'd love to have the listing if it came to that, but he had another reason for wanting to go with them.

Brad looked at his wife and raised an eyebrow. "We've got time. Whaddya say?"

"I think I'd like that."

"Good! Good!" Downs swung the chair away from the computer terminal and jumped to his feet. The dated printer in the corner next to the computer clicked and clattered as it spewed out a piece of paper.

"Just let me get the info," Downs said as he grabbed the paper. "I'll need the address. And some of this data may come in handy."

"There is one other thing," said Brad. "Can you find out if a person owns property with just a name?"

"Well, to tell you the truth, I'm not sure what I can do. We just got this new computer, and I'm still learning to use it. But I suppose we could give it a try. Who are you looking for?"

"Well," Brad said, "we knew that my wife's aunt owned property up here. But we don't know if this is all she owned. I was hoping you could tell us if she owns another piece somewhere close by?"

"We can give it a try," Downs said. "Do you know what county?"

Brad looked at Rebecca for confirmation. "She just said Creek Junction, didn't she?"

"Mm-hmm." Rebecca nodded. "Creek Junction."

"All right," Downs said, sitting down at the computer terminal again. "Let's see what we can find out."

He clicked the mouse several times as he studied the screen. "I'm hoping that I can ..." He paused as he read. "Let's see, Dawson, Dawson. You folks wouldn't be related to a Henry Dawson, would you? There's a Henry Dawson listed with property in the southern part of the county."

"No," said Rebecca, "I have no other family."

It wasn't a lie, at least not an intentional one. Except for the two uncles who lived in the east, she had no relatives, and she hadn't seen them since she was little. They didn't seem like relatives, and she didn't really think of them that way.

Downs nodded and made a mental note as he continued his search. "Yes. Yes, I think this is it." He read some more. "I've done a cross-reference with the tax records and her name. I see the property out at the end of Walker Creek Road, but that's all—no other listings under that name."

"That must be it then," said Rebecca.

Downs shrugged. "Must be." He pushed away from the desk and stood. "Shall we go take a look?"

Brad and Rebecca stood. Downs started toward the door and then remembered the coffeepot. He stood a moment looking a little befuddled. "Let's see, you folks didn't get your coffee," he said. "Would you still like some?"

"No. No thanks," Brad said, relieved that he wouldn't have to find a tactful way to refuse coffee from the dingy pot.

"Fine!" Downs seemed relieved himself. "We can have some when we get back. Shall we go?"

Downs climbed in behind the wheel of his four-wheel drive. Brad held the rear passenger door for his wife and then climbed into the passenger seat next to him. Downs backed out and started down the road through town.

"This is a nice little town," he said as they rolled slowly along, turned right at the intersection before starting across an old concrete bridge. He stopped in the middle of it.

"That's our river," he said. "If you look down that way," he pointed downriver, Brad followed his finger, "you can see a creek that runs into it. That's Walker Creek. Just beyond it you can see an old log building."

Brad and Rebecca strained to see through the dense growth of berry vines that overran the edge of the creek. Visible through the vines was a log wall and part of a roof, obscured by the dense foliage.

"That's the original town—or what's left of it. Built in the 1850s. That was the old trading post."

"I'm surprised it's still standing," said Brad.

Downs shrugged. "There's not much left but what you see. And it's not in very good shape." He gestured with his hand to a point a few yards farther on. "Over there you can see four foundation stones. They say that was the first church. Some of the folks around here, mostly the ones from California, have tried to get the whole place declared a—what do you call it?—a 'historic site.' Most folks around here don't think much about it. But everything's pretty much gone now."

"That's too bad," Rebecca offered from the back seat.

"Yeah," Downs said, trying to sound sincere. "That creek," he said, pointing, "runs right in front of your property. The road follows it all the way up."

"Walker Creek?" asked Brad.

"Yep."

Rebecca was holding the donation claim in her hand. Brad reached across the seat and flipped one corner of the paper up so he could see it.

Rebecca looked down. Brad tapped the document with his finger under the name "Nathan Walker." She nodded her silent acknowledgment.

"How far is it?" Brad asked.

"About six or seven miles. The road follows the creek most of the way. Some of the locals tell me that in a few places down closer to the creek you can still see some of the old road that was used more than a hundred years ago."

Downs drove for several minutes in silence. The road followed the creek, crossing it a couple of times on old concrete bridges. There were a few homes scattered along the way, separated by a half-mile or more. Some were older frame houses surrounded by wire fences. Others were single-wide mobiles with abandoned cars scattered about. A few were big, modern, new homes with manicured lawns.

Rebecca sat back, listening to her husband and Downs talk and laugh as they exchanged information about interest rates and political positions. They joked about sports figures and blonde women. She tuned them out when the subject turned to hunting and timber yields. The mountains were so beautiful, lush, and green, and the trees seemed like silent sentinels watching over the whole valley. Their majesty and beauty seemed like a perfect testament to a creative will. The serenity around her made her suddenly remember the longing deep within her—a longing to know peace.

Her thoughts returned to the conversation in the car as Downs braked in the middle of the road. He pointed out the passenger-side window. “Look there!”

Rebecca followed his finger to the clearing a few yards from the road. There was a stand of oak trees at the far end.

“See?” Downs said.

In the shadows of the trees, Rebecca detected movement. “What is it?”

Downs didn’t answer. Rebecca strained to see. “I don’t see anything.”

“There!” Brad exclaimed. “I see them!”

Just as he said it, six large elk, five cows, and a bull with a full rack—holding his head in princely fashion—entered the light of the clearing from under the canopy of trees.

“Oh! I see them!” Rebecca said.

The cows, unconcerned with a vehicle so far away, ambled out into the clearing, grazing peacefully. The bull turned, proud and aloof, and then looked away.

“American elk,” Downs said. “Or ‘Wapiti.’ It’s an Indian name. I don’t remember which tribe.”

Brad and Rebecca sat in silent awe for several minutes. Downs let off the brake and the car began to move slowly forward, idling for a few yards before he pressed down on the accelerator. Rebecca watched through the rear window until the herd was out of sight.

“They’re all over,” Downs said. “The government’s been managing them pretty closely for several years and they’re coming back. Time was when they’d all but disappeared from this part of the country, but we see quite a few of them now.”

“They were so close!” said Rebecca. “I didn’t think they’d stay so close to the road.”

“Oh, yeah. Sometimes they get to be a real nuisance. Some of the local ranchers have a fit because they damage their fields. But they’re good for the tourist trade.”

Rebecca sat back, filled with the wonder of creation.

The road continued along the creek for another mile before it swung away in an unnatural turn near a wide S-bend in the creek. From there it climbed to the ridge of a small hill and followed it for almost a quarter-mile, before returning to follow the creek. A few minutes later, Downs slowed to a stop at the end of the road.

A long dirt drive, well-worn but overgrown from non-use, began where the road ended. The broken-down remnants of a few wooden fence posts protruded through the tall weeds on either side. To the right of the driveway was a small natural pond. At the far end, a few rotten boards lying in the grass hinted that there once had been a pier. The water was dirty green.

Beyond it, at the end of the driveway, sat an old, two-story wood framed house. The siding was worn and devoid of paint. Many of the old boards were loose and some had fallen to the ground. The rock foundation was cracked, something Rebecca could see even from the road, and one side of the house seemed to sag. The windows were broken and the front door hung askew from a single hinge. The rich, beveled glass that once had adorned it had disappeared many years before. But the roof was new.

Rebecca sat forward as the light of recognition hit her. "That's the house in the picture!"

"Picture?" Downs asked.

"We found some pictures of my wife's aunt when she was a little girl with the claim you took the legal description from." Brad nodded toward the house. "One of them was taken in front of that house."

"Ah," Downs said, trying to sound interested.

Brad pointed at the roof. "Looks like someone is fixing it up."

"Could be," said Downs. "Maybe your aunt was having some work done."

"That doesn't seem likely," Brad said to himself.

Downs started up the drive. The ruts were deep from past use, but weeds grew abundantly, making it difficult to make out exactly where the road ended and the open field began. The only clue was the rotten fence posts that were visible in the tall grass on either side. Weeds and brush scraped along the door of the car as it rocked back and forth.

To the right, mosquitoes buzzed over the green surface of the pond's water. Downs stopped in front of the old house.

"Well, this is it," Downs said, trying not to reveal his doubts. He'd learned a long time ago that property was property, and it didn't matter what he thought of a piece of property. All that mattered was what the client thought of it.

Brad and Rebecca got out of the car and stood together. Downs walked up behind them.

"I'd guess that the property line follows that fence," he said waving his arm toward the hillside to his left. "You can see where the land was cleared at one time. The property line must follow that ridge along the back. Three hundred acres would probably take it somewhere on the other side of the ridge."

Rebecca hardly heard him. A sense of awe engulfed her as she stood in front of the old house. All her life she had nourished a sense of family. She had always felt, since she was a little girl, that the ties she shared with other human beings gave her a right to claim a place in the world. Family was the strongest tie she knew. Here in front of her stood a silent witness to a tie that predated anything she had imagined until this very moment.

She slipped her arm through Brad's. "Can we go inside?"

Brad had his doubts. "I'm not sure it's safe."

She held his arm. "Please?"

"Let's look around first," he cautioned. He took her hand and started to walk around the house. Weeds grew in abundance. Scattered around the yard were the remnants of life in an earlier time. The rim of a wagon wheel lay half-buried in the dirt near a massive and ancient oak tree a few feet from the house. Behind the tree was the rusted hulk of an old Hudson automobile, web-shaped cracks radiating out from three small bullet holes in the windshield.

The broken frame and rusted wire mesh of what appeared to be a chicken coop sat in ruins behind an old barn beyond the remains of a fence that once had encircled the yard.

"How long has it been since anyone has lived here?" Rebecca asked.

Downs shook his head. "No one has as long as I can remember. I don't think anyone has lived here for more than fifty years."

"How old is the house?" asked Brad.

"My guess is around the turn of the century," said Downs. "Maybe older."

Near the rear corner, Brad discovered the cause of the sagging roofline. The rock foundation had crumbled and fallen away from the building. There were rocks in a neat pile a few feet away. A new hammer sat on top of the pile, and it looked as though someone had been knocking away mortar from the rocks and setting them in a separate pile.

"I thought you said no one lived here."

Downs came up from behind them. His eyebrows rose. "No one does that I know of."

"Looks like someone is doing some work on the old place," Brad said, nodding toward the pile of rocks.

Downs scratched his head. "You'd know more about it than I would. Maybe your aunt was figuring to rent the place out." Downs leaned back and shaded his eyes from the morning sun. "Looks like it's got a new roof. Somebody's been fixing things up."

"Looks like a waste of money to me," Brad said.

Brad led Rebecca around the house. Cellar doors sat askew beside the darkened opening that led beneath the house. Rebecca peered in.

"Stay back," Brad cautioned. "We don't know if it's safe."

"Been standing for most of a century," said Downs. "I don't figure it's going to cave in just now."

"Let's look around a bit more first," Brad said.

He took her hand and continued around the house until they had come full-circle. They stood at the bottom of the steps that led up to the high front porch. Brad took the first step up.

"Watch your step," he warned. He stepped gingerly over a broken plank, testing the reliability of the creaking lumber with each step. "Looks solid enough."

Rebecca followed as he entered the house.

It was not a big house, but the living room seemed more spacious than the exterior had promised. A small sparrow fluttered out from the flue of a massive rock fireplace, made a hard turn, and flew out the glass-less window next to the door.

Rebecca held her hand over her heart. "Oh!"

The floor was littered with chunks of plaster from the ceiling, which was giving way to the elements and time.

"What a mess," she said.

Brad was amused. "Always the woman's perspective."

He looked around. "It doesn't seem to be too bad, though, except for a few things like that," he said, pointing to the hole in the ceiling. "Except for that one spot where the foundation is damaged, the structure looks pretty good."

"I wouldn't trust it," Downs said from the front porch.

"We're fine," said Brad. He turned to Rebecca. "C'mon."

He took her hand and led her through the door at the far end of the room. A few sticks of the oak wood cabinets along the wall beneath a window were all that was left of a turn-of-the-century kitchen. An old cast-iron sink rested on its top in the center of the room.

"Notice anything?" Brad asked.

"Like what?"

"Look at the walls."

"So?"

"What's missing?"

Rebecca took another look. "I don't see anything."

"Of course not. Not even electrical outlets."

"I wonder why?"

Brad shrugged. "Well, it was obviously built before there was electricity, or at least before it was common."

"I wonder if this is the house that Aunt Billie lived in."

"I don't know."

Rebecca felt a chill as goose bumps crept over her arms. "This must be it," she said softly.

Brad nodded. "I wonder if she was born here."

That hadn't occurred to Rebecca. The thought filled her with warmth. "I wonder," she said softly.

To his right, Brad noticed a door, scarred and beaten, with a new padlock that barred entrance. Brad lifted the lock in his hand and then let it fall against the door. "Someone's doesn't want company," he said.

"Can't you break it?" Rebecca asked.

I could, he thought, *or at least kick it loose from the screws bolting it to the door.*

"Let's wait," he said. "We can come back another time. I don't want to go tearing up someone's property. After all, someone may have a legitimate reason to be here."

Rebecca smiled to herself. Brad had resisted this whole idea of coming to Oregon. And he'd mentioned several times he needed to get back to work. She was sure he'd want to head home as soon as the funeral was over, but now he was talking about "another time."

It sounded good to her. She was just beginning to know her family and her history, and she wasn't ready to leave.

High on the ridge overlooking the house, a lone figure on horseback, hidden by trees, watched through the scope of his rifle as the man and woman walked back to the car with the real estate agent. His dark Indian eyes held fast to the car as it backed around and then headed out the way it had come. He did not like this particular real estate agent, this Frank Downs.

He lowered the rifle and returned it to the scabbard under his left leg. He wondered what interest the couple could have in the old place and why Downs would be showing it to them since he knew full well the place wasn't for sale. Whoever they were, intruders were not welcome.

He ran his hand over his bristle-short, crew cut hair. It was a lucky thing, he thought to himself, that he happened along when he did, especially since it wasn't his usual day for a ride.

Reining the horse around, he headed up the mountain slope to the ridge above. He knew what he must do. He'd ride home, get the truck and head into town. He'd follow the two tourists and see what they were up to. If it turned out they wanted to buy the old place, well, it *could* be innocent. They *could* have just wandered up the road and discovered the place innocently enough. Some Californian was always looking for a good deal on a summer getaway. Yet the man on horseback couldn't help but wonder if Gil Doucet had put them up to it.

In the mean-time, Frank Downs had some explaining to do.

Frank Downs took the turns a little faster than he had on the way out to the Walker place. He was in a hurry. It was clear these two kids from Southern California didn't intend to sell right away, so there was no need to waste more time than he already had. There was always that fine line between spending too much time with a client and wearing out your welcome, and cutting things short and losing a prospect because you didn't stroke him or her enough.

He was confident, though. He'd made his contact. He'd spent time establishing a relationship of sorts. He'd talked. He'd listened. He'd laughed at the husband's jokes. If they ever needed an agent, he felt sure that they'd call on ol' Frank. But for now, he just wanted to get back to the office as soon as possible. There was a phone call to make.

Frank rested his foot on the brake. The car slowed for the turn that lead away from the S-bend in the creek.

From a vantage point on the mountain across the valley, something ancient and evil watched. It had been a long time, but something stirred deep within as an old memory pushed its way to the surface. There was recognition. There was danger in the car below on the road. It was an old danger and an old enemy—familiar and feared. And with it, the threat of defeat, the stealing away of an old victory. Victories were sweet, but they had a nasty habit of withering away just as it seemed nothing could deny a sure triumph.

Smoldering hatred.

It wasn't fair. The enemy had no right. Boundaries had been established. He had no right at all.

Swiftly, the presence skirted the boundary until it hovered over the S-bend in Walker Creek. It eased for the moment. The boundary held. All was secure—for now.

CHAPTER TWENTY

"GIL? FRANK DOWNS.... Yeah.... Hey, listen. You said to let you know if anyone showed an interest in that old place at the end of Walker Creek Road. Well, someone just did.... Nope. They already own it.... No, I didn't say a word.... Yeah, OK. You bet.... Any time."

Gil Doucet set the receiver back in its cradle on the phone on his desk.

So, it had finally happened. After all these years, it had finally happened. All these years of watching and waiting, only half believing the stories he'd heard since he was a small child, stories handed down from who knows how long ago. And, then, as the years went by, not really believing them at all. He did the watching and waiting more out of tradition, or perhaps habit, than from any conviction of veracity.

Now all of that had changed with one simple phone call. Just to pick up the receiver and say, as he did countless times every day, "Doucet's Market" and have everything change. But for what? The stories had been handed down from his mother, like those told to other children at their mother's knee. Only other little children heard the harmless tales of fairy princesses or little boys who conquered dragons. But not the Doucet children—he and his sister, since before they could remember, were spoon-fed stories of duty and of the flame that must be kept alive, at any cost.

This is silly. After all, one inquiry does not a prophecy make.

Gil tapped the top of his desk with the tip of his pencil. His eyes narrowed as he tried to sort it all out in his mind. He picked up the phone and dialed.

"Marty? Get her for me."

Sara Doucet slouched against the leather cushion of a booth in the darkest corner of the Red Crown Saloon, her slender arm draped over the back of the seat with a bottle of beer held loosely in her hand. She threw back a swig and set the bottle on the table. Country music blared from the jukebox in the corner.

"You're cute," she said to the tall, rugged lumberman across from her. He was new in town, something of a rarity in the small town of Creek Junction, and new faces, especially good-looking ones, always caught Sara's eye.

He smiled. She was great to look at, dark and slender. Her long, black hair down to the middle of her back shimmered in the dim light. "Have another?"

She smiled back, cat-like and all knowing. "You don't need to do that."

"I don't mind."

She gave him a come-on look, took his hand, and slid out of the booth. "No, I mean, you don't need to do that."

She led him across the room toward the door.

"Sara!" Marty shouted over the music from behind the bar. He held up the phone. "It's your brother!"

Sara sighed as she dropped the young man's hand. "Don't go away. I'll be right back."

"Yeah?" she said into the receiver before she had it all the way to her ear. She listened, her interest growing only slightly as Gil explained. "Now? I'm kinda busy." She winked at the young man standing close to the door. "All right! All right! I'll be there!"

She swore as she handed the receiver back to Marty, and then turned to size up the young man waiting for her by the door. He was tall and handsome. He smiled at her through perfect teeth. He had an innocent look about him, something that excited Sara. She liked them innocent.

She smiled back as she started toward the door. Gil could wait. An hour or so wouldn't hurt him. And besides, what could he do but threaten and yell? She was used to that, and it might be worth it—just to see the veins on his neck stand out.

Marty watched her leave as he poured two beers from the tap and slid the glasses down the bar to eager, waiting hands. She looked good, with her long black hair and her brown, supple skin. She was good for business. She attracted men like flies on a carcass, and men on the prowl were always thirsty. But when it came to men, Sara was also careless.

Marty had no feelings for her, unless the occasional venture into animal lust counted for feelings, but if anything happened to her, there was no telling what Gil would do.

He picked up the phone and punched in Gil's number.

Brad slipped behind the wheel of the Toyota, turned the key until the motor responded, and then pulled it into gear. As he backed out of his spot in the dirt parking lot of Downs Real Estate, he could see Downs through the window talking on the phone.

The car rocked on its suspension as it made the transition from the parking lot to the street.

"How about some lunch?" Brad asked.

"Sure," Rebecca said.

"Where to?"

"I don't care. How about we drive up the freeway and see what's up the road?"

"Sightseeing?"

Rebecca caught the twinkle in her husband's eyes as she remembered their conversation earlier in the morning when she'd told him she didn't feel like sightseeing. "Mm-hmm," she said as she loosened her seatbelt and leaned over the console to be close to him. She did feel better. And the beauty and majesty of the mountains was intoxicating, drawing her into its splendor.

Brad turned the corner and passed by the restaurant where they had had dinner the night before. His eyes lingered on the window as they passed.

Rebecca pretended not to notice.

Brad entered the onramp. In a moment, they were cruising north on a deserted section of the I-5. "I could get used to this," Brad said. "Look at this! No traffic!"

"It beats the mess at home," Rebecca agreed. She let her mind wander as open pastures with grazing cattle panned by her window. It felt good not to think. She'd had so much to think about in the last week.

She sighed. The old house had intrigued her. Exploring it made her feel like a little girl again, tramping around in dusty corners to discover someone else's past. It brought back memories of venturing through the many rooms of Aunt Billie's big old house in Santa Barbara. She was struck with a sense of adventure that she hardly could contain. She wanted to go back.

Brad let off the accelerator and pointed to a sign on the side of the road indicating gas and food ahead. "That OK with you?"

"Fine. Anything is fine."

Brad left the freeway at the off-ramp and turned into the parking lot of a converted Denny's, apparently sold a few years ago when the corporation decided to streamline its operation, and now under local ownership. The sign said, "Country Cafe."

Brad pulled up to the front row of parallel parking spaces and stopped. He got out and started around the car to open his wife's door, but Rebecca met him at the curb. "Can't wait for me, huh?"

"I'm hungry."

Brad smiled. "Ah, the ravages of feminism!"

Rebecca slipped her hand through Brad's arm. "Don't count on it, Mister. I like to have my doors opened for me. I'm just hungry."

Neither of them noticed the four-wheel-drive pickup with oversized mud tires and a gun rack bearing two rifles that pulled in and parked on the other side of the parking lot. A dark-skinned man with crew-cut hair climbed down from the cab.

Brad held the restaurant door for Rebecca. "Well, that's a good sign. You haven't eaten enough in the last week to keep a bird alive. Does this mean I'm going to get my wife back?"

Rebecca swept past him and then waited near the sign that offered a polite command to do just that until the waitress could seat them. Brad came up behind her and rested his chin on the top of her head.

"I suppose I haven't been much company lately."

Brad said nothing but squeezed her shoulder.

"Two?" the waitress said as she grabbed two menus. "Come with me, please," she said, not waiting for a response. Brad and Rebecca followed her to a booth and sat down. Rebecca faced the door.

"So! You're hungry, huh?"

"Mm-hmm," she said, studying the menu. "Hungrier than I've been in days. All of a sudden I feel like I could eat a horse!"

"Maybe you're eating for two," Brad kidded.

The smile left Rebecca's face.

Brad reached across the table and took her hand. "I'm sorry. I didn't mean to bring it up."

Rebecca shook her head. "It's OK." She took only a passing notice of the big, dark-skinned man with coarse black hair as he came in, went straight to the counter, and sat down. He looked over at her and then looked away.

"So what did you think of the property?" Brad asked, hoping to lift her spirits.

"I'd like to go back and see it again," she said without hesitation.

"If we have time. But what I meant was, what are we going to do with it?"

Rebecca sighed. "I don't know. I really don't want to think about selling it. Not yet."

"You know," said Brad, "we really should do a little more checking before we do anything. We could take a trip to the county offices and check the records."

"Is that really necessary? I mean, we already know it was Billie's, don't we?"

"Yes, but it wouldn't hurt to have more information. And if I can get a current legal description and a tax number, I can call Stephens and have him check a few things for us."

"Like what?"

"We can get a copy of the deed that is current. That way we know how much land is there. We can also find out its assessed value to get an idea what it's worth."

Rebecca felt threatened. "I don't want to sell it."

Brad held up his hands. "We don't have to do anything right now, but we have to consider the practical side of this. We can't take care of property up here. Now that your aunt is gone, we'll have to pay taxes on it. And I hear that Oregon's property taxes are high."

Rebecca started to protest but she was distracted. She noticed the man at the counter was staring. He was young, maybe late twenties, lean and fit, with broad shoulders that tapered down to a narrow waist. Faded jeans molded to his rugged hips and thighs, and the long sleeves of a denim shirt were rolled up past his elbows.

"What's the matter?" Brad asked.

"That man at the counter," Rebecca said into her coffee cup. "He keeps staring at us."

Brad attempted a discreet glance over his shoulder. He failed.

"Don't turn around!" Rebecca whispered. "He'll see you!"

"He's probably just a good judge of woman flesh," Brad said with a twinkle and a grin. "I've caught myself staring at you a few times too."

"Well, he's making me nervous."

"Do you want to trade places?"

Rebecca shook her head. The man glanced over in her direction again, saw that she had caught him looking, and turned away.

"No. Let's not make big deal about it."

"I wasn't."

"I know! I just don't want to be obvious about it. Let's just forget it."

"Forget what?" Brad said with a twinkle.

Rebecca kicked off her shoe and gave him a love tap under the table with her bare foot. Brad grinned his boyish grin.

They ate their lunch in silence, Brad because he was hungry and Rebecca because she didn't want to talk about selling the property.

When they had finished, Brad held the door for her as they left the restaurant and then he hurried to beat her to the car door. Rebecca slid in without a word.

Brad started the car and headed for the freeway. He took the onramp heading north, away from Creek Junction.

"Aren't we going back to the room?" Rebecca's voice almost challenged.

"I thought we were going to the recorder's office?"

Rebecca's brow furrowed. "I thought we talked about it. I didn't know you decided without me."

"We have time. It won't hurt us to have the information. Besides, what else are we going to do for the rest of the day?"

"I never thought that was a problem for you. You can always think of something to do," she said with sarcasm, double entendre, and innuendo all rolled neatly into the carefully placed lilt of her voice.

Brad clenched his jaw. He'd tried to be patient with her. She'd been through a lot. But his patience was wearing thin, and now she seemed to be looking for fault, for things to pick at. Didn't she appreciate his sacrifice?

Rebecca looked away. She knew she'd stepped over the line, but she wasn't ready to admit it—at least not to him. Sometimes she felt as though she was just his plaything, an object meant solely for his pleasure. Sex wasn't an obligation. She enjoyed it. But sometimes she wished she could be sure it meant more to Brad than physical fulfillment.

"We might as well go," Brad said softly. "It's only a few miles from here and the information can only help us make a better decision."

Rebecca was silent the rest of the way.

Only a few minutes had passed when Brad parallel parked at the curb in front of the aging, white, three-story county building. Brad shut off the engine and waited.

"Listen, it doesn't mean we have to sell it," he said. "I just think we should check it out."

Rebecca looked away. She bit down on her lip.

Brad sighed. "Look. We don't have to do this if it's that big a deal. I just thought—"

"We're here," she said. "We might as well see what we can find out."

Brad climbed out and waited by the curb for her. Rebecca met him with folded arms. It was a long, silent walk to the high marble portico at the top of a dozen wide steps. Brad held the massive glass door for her and followed her inside to the framed directory that hung on the wall.

"'County records,'" Brad recited. "'Third floor, room 334.'"

He tried to take her hand as he turned toward the elevator, but she pulled away. The ride up to the third floor was solemn.

"Down this way," he said as they stepped off the elevator.

Rebecca followed him through the door at the end of the hallway. There were rigid chairs along the wall opposite the high counter. She sat with her arms folded as Brad went to the counter to ask for help.

She felt threatened and she didn't know why. Brad's decision was reasonable. She knew that. And it wasn't really any objection to his chivalrous act of decision-making or any resentment to what some might consider an assault on her feminine sovereignty that made her angry. She liked to have him make the decisions, though she had learned the art of feigning indignation in the presence of her peers.

But now she felt threatened. She was on the verge of discovery—discovery of something she had known all her life she wanted: her own history. Yet things weren't working out the way she had imagined. In fact, nothing had worked the way it was supposed to for as long as she could remember, it seemed. It was bad enough to want and need a baby. It was bad enough to lose the one person who meant so much to her—the one who could give her the answers she craved about who she was and how she could find the peace she wanted. It was bad enough someone had managed to lose the casket, as though that person was determined to play the cruelest of all practical jokes on her and was standing a few feet away, hiding behind a door laughing at her pain. It was bad enough that the man she loved, the one to whom she looked for guidance and comfort, the one to whom she should be able to turn in her need, would reject any attempts to lift the veil of his heart and reveal the spiritual void within.

As if all that weren't bad enough, she felt as though she was not being given control over the last thing she had to link her to a past she hoped could give her answers. She didn't understand. All she knew was a secret had been hidden—a secret she felt affected her directly. She didn't know why, but she felt sure the house held the answers.

She watched as Brad followed the instructions of the young man behind the counter and opened the swinging gate that led to the rows of identical cubicles demarcated by half-walls in a tight grid. The man led him to a desk at the rear by the window and motioned for him to sit. Brad complied and was soon engaged in pushing and clicking the mouse and staring at the computer screen. The man returned to the counter.

Rebecca felt a pull that had become common for her in the last few days. For the first time, she was aware it was becoming a fixture in her thinking. She bowed her head, nervous at first that someone might see, and began to pray.

The Centurion knelt down beside her, unseen, as if to comfort, pleased with the knowledge that soon his services would be needed.

Across the street from the county building, a four-wheel-drive pickup with oversized mud tires and two rifles mounted on the gun rack in the window sat next to the curb. The driver's eyes never left the portico. He would wait. He knew they were on the third floor. He had followed them into the building, waited until the elevator doors had shut, and then counted as the light over the door remained lit. Count to four, second floor. Count to eight, third floor. He'd learned that when he'd worked there as a janitor while he was in college.

He knew it would be easy to find out why they were there too. There were only two offices on the third floor, Department of Public Works and County Records. The rest of the floor was storage and private offices. So it would be easy. He'd simply go to one of the two departments and ask if a young couple had just come in for something. If it wasn't one, it had to be the other. The people who worked there knew him. They'd never give a second thought to answering his questions. And if they did, he'd say he thought he recognized them, that was all. With any luck, he might even be able to get their names.

"Why would anyone do this?" Rebecca asked in disgust. She stood in the hotel parking lot with her husband, looking down at the Toyota's four flattened tires. They had returned from the county offices in the late afternoon. They lay down on the bed together, watched a little TV, and then dozed off for a short nap. When they'd awakened, Brad had gone out to the car for a map he'd picked up at the gas station.

"You got me," Brad said. He reached across the hood and snatched the piece of paper stuck under the windshield wiper. It was folded once; he opened and read it.

"'Go home, Yuppie.'"

Rebecca wrinkled up her nose. "What's the big idea?"

"I don't know," said Brad. "Sounds kinda unfriendly, doesn't it?"

Rebecca folded her arms. She didn't think it was at all funny. Someone deliberately had let the air out of the tires—no damage that they could see, just inconvenience, but she felt violated. "Now what?" she asked.

Brad shrugged. "I suppose we'll have to call a garage and see if someone can bring out some air. Either that or we'll have to have it towed in. C'mon," he said as he took her hand and started toward the hotel lobby, "let's go see if we can find a phone."

"Where's your cell?"

"I left it in the room."

"So where are we going?"

"To the lobby!"

They entered the lobby to a computer-chip chime, triggered by the opening of the door. A young man and woman standing behind the front desk in white shirts and bow ties greeted them with animated smiles.

"Good morning, folks!" the woman said with a zesty bounce. "Can we help you?"

Brad leaned on the counter with one elbow. "We have a little problem. Can you recommend a good garage?"

"Are you having mechanical problems?" the young man asked.

"Well, sort of. It seems that someone has let all the air out of our tires."

"You're kidding," the woman said with genuine astonishment.

"Is the car damaged?" asked the young man.

Brad shook his head. "I don't think so. I'm pretty sure they just let the air out."

The young man picked up the phone and held it to his ear. "I'll make a call for you if you'd like."

Brad shrugged. "Sure. Thanks."

"Do you have any preference?"

"Just someone who will take Triple-A."

"Well, that'll be easy," said the young man. "There's only two shops in town. Bill's is the only one that takes Triple-A." He punched the buttons on the keypad, clearly knowing the number by heart.

"Hi," he said after a few seconds. "This is the hotel."

Brad tried not to let the smile he could feel creeping across his face seem too obvious. *The hotel*—it struck him as amusing. No explanation. No other identification. Just "the hotel."

You're really in hicksville now.

"We have some folks here with a mechanical problem," the young man said. "No. Not if you can bring a compressor or something to air up the tires."

He paused. "Yeah, that's right.... Someone just let the air out.... No. No other damage that they can see," he said, giving Brad a quick look for confirmation.

Brad nodded.

The young man hung up the phone. "They said they'd send someone out within the hour." He set the phone on the counter and handed Brad the receiver. "But you'll have to talk to Triple-A yourself and have them call the garage to confirm."

Brad took the receiver and reached for his wallet to dig out the card. He dialed the number for AAA and acknowledged the voice on the other end, but then was silent.

"They put me on hold," he said.

Rebecca motioned toward the door with her hand. "I'm going to wait by the car," she almost whispered.

Brad nodded as the AAA operator came back on the line.

Brad's voice faded and then disappeared as Rebecca leaned against the lobby door and then let it swing shut behind her. She walked back to the car.

It was a pitiful sight, resting as it did, low to the ground with the rubber of the tires spreading out under the wheels as if they had melted into a puddle of black. The feeling of violation returned. She half hoped she would see a bobbing head hiding on the other side of the car, and that the prankster or pranksters had returned to finish the job. She imagined cornering them and holding them for the police, and then felt a flush of fear at the thought that it really could happen. She opened the driver's door, peered into the back seat, and then sat down behind the wheel.

"They'll be here in a few minutes," Brad said as he walked up to the car.

"Good."

"Why don't we wait in the room? We can leave the door open. Then we can see them when they come."

Rebecca shrugged. "Why not?"

The parking lot was large and spacious. It was divided by a narrow greenbelt with young trees planted only a few months before. There were parking places on the other side of the divider, used mostly by patrons of the casino. Rebecca noticed a large four-wheel-drive pickup with over-sized mud tires parked several rows away. Its motor was running. A man sat inside.

"What's the matter?" Brad asked.

Rebecca's brow furrowed. She tossed her head in the direction of the truck. "That man."

Brad followed her eyes to the truck. "Yeah? What about him?"

Rebecca could just make out the man's outline through the glint of the afternoon sun on the windshield. "He looks like the man at the restaurant. You know, the man who was staring at us."

Brad turned and looked again, shading his eyes with his hand. "Yeah? How can you tell?"

Rebecca clenched her jaw. "It's him! I know it's him!"

"What if it is?"

Rebecca felt uneasy. "He was staring at us. And now he's here…and we have four flat tires."

Brad looked back toward the truck. It didn't make sense. Why would the guy follow them? And for that matter, why would he let the air out of their tires? But then again, none of it made any sense.

"Maybe I'll have a talk with him," Brad said. He started toward the truck.

Gears clunked as the man put the truck into gear and backed out of the parking space. Brad held up his hand as he sprinted toward him. The truck's engine raced as gears ground and the truck lurched forward. The tires squealed as the dark-skinned man sped out of the lot.

Brad bounded across the greenbelt to the pavement on the other side. He yelled for the man to stop, but the truck turned the corner at the end of the parking lot and sped down the street.

Brad stood helplessly for a moment and then walked slowly back to the car.

"He was sure in a hurry," Rebecca said.

"Makes you wonder," Brad said. "Makes him look kind of guilty."

"Do you think he flattened the tires?"

Brad shrugged. "I don't know. But he sure seemed to have something to hide."

They both turned to the street again at the sound of a truck's engine as it entered the parking lot. It was a tow truck.

The driver hesitated at the curb and then started across the lot and pulled to a stop behind the lame Toyota. The door opened and the long, slender, jeans-clad legs of Sara Doucet descended from the high cab.

"You the folks with the problem?" she asked, nodding toward the car.

"That's us," Brad said with a skeptical eye on the young woman. He and Rebecca met her as she surveyed the four tires.

"Is ..." Brad hesitated, looking for a polite way to say it, "is anyone else coming?"

Sara was used to male resistance to a woman behind the wheel of a tow truck. "Nope. What you see is what you get," she said with a smile as she turned back to the car. "Yep. You've got a problem all right. What d' you want me to do?"

"Can you just put air in them? I don't think they're damaged."

"You sure?"

"I don't see any damage on the outside," Brad said as he leaned down and inspected the tires again.

"Well," Sara said, "we can try."

She unfurled a long hose that was coiled up near the rear of the truck and walked backwards to the first tire, bent down next to it, and pressed the nozzle onto the valve stem. Brad and Rebecca watched the rear of the car rise as the tire filled with air. Sara repeated the ritual three more times in silence.

"There!" she said as she returned the hose to its place. "All set!"

"Thank you," Rebecca said.

Sara gave her a catty grin. "I'll have to fill out the work order. It'll be a few minutes. Then I'll need you to sign it." She leaned against the side of the truck as she wrote.

"You folks here on vacation?" she asked casually.

"We came up for my aunt's funeral," Rebecca said.

"I'm sorry to hear that," Sara said.

Rebecca was sure she didn't mean it.

"Be in town long?" Sara asked after a brief pause.

"Not long," said Brad. "We thought we'd do a little sightseeing while we're here."

"Good place for it," Sara said, handing Brad the clipboard. "Sign here," she pointed.

Brad took it, found the place for his signature, and touched the pen to the paper. "You don't see many women driving tow trucks," he said.

Sara smiled. "I work in the office and help out with deliveries mostly. But I bug the ol' man to let me drive once in a while. He doesn't like it, but sometimes when they're busy they don't have much choice. I just happened to be there when the call came in." She smiled at Brad and cocked her head. "Lucky me."

She took the clipboard and tore out a copy, handing it to Brad.

"I suppose," Rebecca began slowly, "that you know most of the people in town?"

"It's a small town," Sara confirmed.

"Do you know anyone who drives a four-wheel-drive pickup with a couple of guns in the back window?"

Sara laughed. "A couple o' hundred! Why?"

Rebecca felt the color rise in her cheeks. "Oh, it's nothing. I just…never mind."

Sara gave her a wry look. "Sure thing, Honey." She cocked her head and smiled at Brad again. "I guess you'll be on your way, huh?"

"We'll be around for a few days. We have some business to take care of."

Sara eyed him up and down. "Maybe I'll see you around," she said.

Brad smiled back. Rebecca felt color in her cheeks, but this time it was not the color of embarrassment.

Sara climbed into the cab of the truck. She turned the key, and the engine came to life. She winked at Brad. "See you," she said, and then gunned the engine. The tow truck lumbered out of the parking lot.

Across the street and down a block, the four-wheel-drive pickup with over-sized mud tires sat under the shade of a large fir tree. The driver watched as the tow truck left the parking lot and headed back to town.

He couldn't make sense of what he'd just seen. He knew Sara and what a conniver she could be. One way or another, she was up to no good. But what about the couple? Were the flattened tires merely a clever way for them to meet Sara without drawing attention? After all, Sara probably knew what he'd been up to out at the Walker place. Secrets didn't stay secrets long in a small town. If she knew, perhaps she and Gil had hired someone to front for them in an attempt to buy the Walker place. If she wanted to meet with them without risking discovery, flat tires and road service might be one way to do it.

He wondered why they had gone to the county recorder's office. He knew after talking to a couple of old friends there that they'd gotten tax records and checked the deed.

But he couldn't get the most valuable piece of information: their names. His friend only could remember the man's first name, Brad, but his friend had forgotten the guy's last name, and he'd never talked to the woman. All he remembered was she had nice legs and a pretty face.

The man started the four-wheel-drive truck and pulled away from the curb. There was no use hanging around there. The couple had gone into their room and closed the door. But there was someone who might be able to help. As much as he detested the thought, he knew Frank Downs probably could answer his questions. He didn't like the idea for two reasons. One, Frank was a pompous jerk. And two, whatever he said to Frank he was sure would get back to Gil Doucet. But it was a chance he'd have to take. He needed to know.

"It was stupid!" Gil Doucet shouted, aiming a thick finger across the small office in the back of his grocery store.

"Careful, Gil," Sara said. "You'll disturb the customers."

Gil opened his mouth to answer but stopped short. His dull eyes blustered a silent warning as he creaked back in the antiquated office chair, forcing it almost to the breaking point.

A big man with thick arms, Gil cared nothing for customers. He was not a man given to compassion. He understood little of the world, beyond his own needs and wants. His only driving passion was the simple dislike he nurtured for his fellow man. Unfortunately, customers were a major source of income.

"You said you wanted to know," Sara said, "and since the old man has the only tow truck in town—"

"What did you find out?" Gil interrupted and then hurried to answer his own question. "Nothing that I didn't already know from a two-minute conversation with Frank!"

Sara shrugged. "No big deal. I didn't hurt anyone. And besides, I wanted to get a look at him."

"That's all you think about, isn't it?" Gil said.

Sara sat down and leaned back on the old sofa Gil used for afternoon naps. "Sometimes I think about getting high."

Gil sneered. "And how would you have explained it if they'd caught you letting air out of their tires?"

Sara shrugged. "They didn't catch me."

Gil shook his head. "I don't know what I'm going to do with you." He sat down in the swivel chair and folded his hands on top of the desk. "I really don't."

Sara smiled. It was a wicked smile, and one often interpreted by most of Creek Junction's male population as one of feminine favor. But to Gil it only meant trouble.

"So what are we going to do?" she asked.

Gil huffed as he leaned back in his chair. "I don't know. I haven't given it much thought."

Sara laughed a mocking laugh. "You haven't given it much thought?" She sat forward. "We've been hearing about this for as long as either of us can remember. Don't give me that nonsense! You've given it plenty of thought!"

Gil sighed. "I don't know what difference it makes."

"I'll tell you," she said, pointing her finger across the desk. "I'll tell you exactly what difference it makes."

Her voice lowered and her eyes narrowed, betraying her bitter resolve. "We owe it! It's a debt! One that has been handed down to us!"

She leaned back again and crossed her legs. "We can't ignore the past. We can't ignore who we are. And we can't ignore—" She hesitated to say the word. It was never used in all the years she'd heard the story. Yet it never had the feel of anything else. She knew. And Gil knew. It had been handed down from generation to generation with reverent awe, and the weight of it carried the full gist of the word she now found on her lips. "We can't ignore the prophecy."

Gil sank back. He felt as though a strong current were sweeping him along and he had no power over it. He was a practical man—a businessman. He was a man of the twenty-first century. He had no desire to be the Don Quixote of past obsessions.

Still, there was the practical side. There was the timber to which he hoped to one day obtain the rights. There was also that other little matter, the clearing far above the road and beyond where only a few had ventured. Deep in the hills, but within the boundary of the Walker place, there was a cultivated field of contraband—a profitable business deal that made the paltry earnings of a two-bit grocery store tolerable. Yes, there was the practical side.

"All right," he said, "but from now on, don't do anything until I say so."

CHAPTER TWENTY-ONE

REBECCA SAT EXPECTANTLY, nervously wringing her hands as the car slowed at the end of Walker Creek Road early the next morning.

She hadn't slept well. She'd tossed and turned much of the night. Any little noise outside the hotel door gave her a start. It was unsettling, this business with the tires and the dark-skinned man in the truck with the big tires and the guns in the rear window. She couldn't get the thought out of her mind.

And the house. She kept thinking about the house. It held a fascination for her. She wanted to see it again. All night long she found herself staring at the ceiling as a narrow shaft of light assaulted the darkened hotel room through the crack between the draperies. Then, in the early hours of morning, she had noticed Brad's eyes were open.

"Hi," he had said.

"Hi, yourself."

"Can't sleep?"

Rebecca shook her head.

"Me either."

Rebecca studied Brad's face.

"Why don't we drive out to the house this morning?" she asked. "You know, spend the morning just looking around."

Brad smiled his teasing grin. "You're dying to know what's behind that locked door, aren't you?"

"Well," she said, feeling the intimidation of Brad's insight, "it is ours. And, well, yes, I suppose I am curious."

Brad reached across the bed and stroked her hair. "I suppose we can, but we should call the funeral home first."

Rebecca looked past Brad's shoulder to the clock on the nightstand. "Isn't it too early? He won't be there yet, will he?"

"He gave us his cell phone number, remember? And, with all the trouble they've caused us, I won't feel the least bit guilty if I wake him up." Brad rolled out of bed and slipped on a shirt. "Why don't you go take your shower? I'll call."

Rebecca got up and went into the bathroom.

A few minutes later, she came out with a towel wrapped around her head turban-style and another around her torso. Brad closed his cell phone. She braced herself as her eyes met her husband's. "Was that Garvey?"

Brad was solemn. "Yeah. They've found her."

Rebecca sat down on the bed. "Where? When?"

"Apparently the airline called him about a half-an-hour ago. He was waiting to call us. Said he didn't want to wake us."

"Where did they find her?"

"Miami, Florida."

"Miami?" Rebecca shook her head in disbelief. "Miami!"

"That's what he said."

"How did she get to Miami?"

"He didn't say. He just said they found her this morning, and that they'd be sending her back as soon as they could arrange it."

"Miami," Rebecca said again, shaking her head. "She always wanted to go to Florida."

"Well," said Brad, "she'll be back soon enough. Garvey said it should only take a day or so."

Rebecca felt the same sense of helplessness that had plagued her for days. "What should we do? Should we wait here? How long—"

Brad was shaking his head even before she finished. "There's nothing for us to do. We might as well drive out to the house like you wanted and look around. I'd like to get a better look at it anyway, to see what it's going to take to fix it up. We'll need to know if we decide to keep it—or for that matter, if we decide to sell it."

Minutes later, they were on the road out of town. Neither of them noticed the four-wheel-drive pickup with the oversized mud tires as it pulled away from the curb in front of the café next to the grocery store in the middle of town.

A few minutes later, Brad slowed to a stop at the driveway entrance that led to the lonely old house in the middle of the clearing. It offered Rebecca a sense of comfort in an odd sort of way. She touched his arm. "Don't drive down yet. Wait here for a moment," she said softly. She could hear the creek babbling softly to her right a few yards from the car.

"Needs a lot of work," Brad said after a while.

He let the car roll forward down the dirt road past the pond, stopping a few feet from the house. He reached for the notepad on the seat next to him and then opened the door. Rebecca met him at the front of the car.

"I don't even know where to begin," she said, gazing at the old house.

"Yes you do," Brad said.

Rebecca smiled sheepishly. "I'm curious. Aren't you even a little curious?"

Brad chuckled. "Yeah, I suppose I am. Let's go."

Brad led the way up the steps to the front door, through the living room, into the kitchen, and to the padlocked door. He reached out and took the lock in his hand as he had the day before.

"I suppose I can kick it in," he said. "It's pretty old."

Rebecca held his arm. "No, don't!" Her eyes pleaded. "Don't hurt it."

"It won't feel a thing."

"I know, but it doesn't seem right somehow. Can't we just take the lock off?"

"You make it sound so simple," Brad said. "I suppose we could find something to pry it loose. Would that suit you?"

Rebecca nodded.

Brad looked around. The only thing in the room was the sink lying in the middle of the room. "Wait here," he said. "I'll be right back."

He hurried from the house and returned a few moments later holding a tine—a long, curved piece of flat, rusted steel—from a farmer's harrow. "I noticed this out in the yard the other day. It'll do."

He stood staring at the door with his chin resting in his hand. Then he wedged the tine between the door and the frame. He heaved once, then twice, before the lock gave way. The door shuddered on its hinges as it swung against the wall. Brad held up his hand to stop it from swinging back. Beyond it in the dim light was a stairway that ascended to the attic.

"Now why would anyone want to go to all the trouble to lock a door that goes nowhere?"

"How do you know it doesn't go anywhere?"

"It's just the attic," he said with a wave of his hand.

Rebecca stood behind her husband, gripping his arm and peering up the stairs. "Why don't we go up and see?" She gave Brad a little nudge. "You go first."

Brad took her hand. "C'mon."

They started up the stairs, floorboards creaking with each step. Brad was the first to peer over the top step into the attic, dimly lit by a single, small dormer window that protruded from the slope of the roof facing east. Beneath it was a window seat. He stopped.

"Hmm," he said to himself.

"What is it?" Rebecca asked from below him.

"C'mon up and take a look," he said as he took her hand.

Rebecca followed him the rest of the way up the stairs.

The attic room was small and the roof's pitch left just enough headroom to stand upright near the center and a few feet in either direction. The walls and ceiling were covered in pine board, once lacquered to a glossy finish, but now dark with age. Water stains spread here and there where the roof had leaked. There was a horse harness hanging from a nail across from the window, as well as several ancient hand tools. Beside them, a dusty bookcase from another era held a meager library of tattered readers and spellers and a copy of Mark Twain's *Pudd'nhead Wilson.* A dust-covered stack of magazines sat on the bottom shelf.

Beneath them on the floor was a new cross-bed toolbox, the kind construction workers mounted in the backs of their trucks.

"Someone's been using this place for something," Brad observed.

He went to the toolbox, bent down in front of it, and pressed the button to open it. The lid flung open.

"What's in it?" Rebecca asked from the stairs.

"Just a lot of construction stuff—hammers, tape measures, saws—that kind of stuff."

"I wonder whose it is?"

"I don't know. But it seems kind of out of place, doesn't it? I mean, the whole thing—the tools, the patching and fixing. Someone's sure going to a lot of trouble on this old place."

"You don't think it could be transients, do you?"

Brad motioned toward the toolbox. "Where would transients get something like this?"

Rebecca shrugged. "Well, if my aunt was having work done, it seems to me that Mr. Stephens would know, and he didn't say anything about it."

"Humph," Brad said. He closed the toolbox lid.

Rebecca, drawn by the promise of intrigue ancient books offered, moved to the bookcase and bent down in front of it. She cocked her head to the side to read the cover of the magazine at the top of the stack on the bottom shelf. She reached down to wipe away the dust, reverently at first, and then with the excitement of a child on Christmas morning. It was a copy of Look magazine dated 1912.

Rebecca picked it up and thumbed gently through it, taking care not to damage its delicate pages.

"Whaddya got?" Brad asked as he sat down on the toolbox and crossed his legs.

Rebecca held it up. "It's really old," she said with awe in her voice.

"More stuff to be hauled to the dump," Brad said.

Rebecca frowned. "You just keep your hands to yourself!" she scolded. "This isn't junk!"

"Yes ma'am," he said indifferently as he looked around.

Rebecca put the magazine back on the shelf and looked around the room. She couldn't help but imagine her aunt as a little girl, playing on the floor with a favorite doll. She wondered if it even could have been her room.

"Nice view," Brad said from across the room. He had moved to the dormer window and stood with his hands in his pockets, looking out. Rebecca joined him.

It was a nice view. The timbered mountains seemed peaceful. Their majesty offered a sense of security and comfort.

"I think I could get used to living here," Rebecca sighed.

"I think I could get used to hunting and fishing if I didn't have to work." Brad rested his foot on the window seat and leaned forward on his arms. He hardly noticed the boards creaking under his feet.

Rebecca began stroking his back with the tips of her fingers. "Wouldn't it be a great place to raise a family?" she said.

Brad's jaw tightened. "Yeah, maybe."

Rebecca could hear the tautness in his voice. She continued stroking his back in silence. Brad shifted his weight to one foot.

As he did, he felt as the floorboards in front of the window seat gave way. A hundred years of faithful service came to an abrupt end. He felt his body react to the sudden burst of adrenalin that called upon every instinct, muscle, bone, brain cell, and synapse to instant action for survival. But it was too late. The weight of his body, working against him, pulled him down. His arms flailed in desperation as he crashed through the ceiling over the kitchen. He caught himself on the now-exposed timbers of the attic floor.

Rebecca screamed. She hesitated in a brief moment of indecision, and then fell to her knees and reached to grab his arm. She caught the corner of his sleeve with one hand and grabbed for the window seat with the other. Friction between the palm of her hand and the dusty surface of the pine board seat was her only grip. "Oh, God!" she cried, half-praying.

She held on with all her might as Brad struggled to pull himself up through the hole in the floor. As he did, Rebecca grabbed the belt loop of his pants and heaved. In a moment, he was sitting on the floor, panting and wheezing.

"Are you all right?" Rebecca asked, her voice quivering.

"I'm fine," Brad said as he struggled to catch his breath. Without thinking, he rubbed his bruised leg. He looked down through the hole to the kitchen floor below. "What a rush!"

Rebecca slapped his arm. "Don't scare me like that!"

"I'll try to be more considerate next time," he said as he stood and turned around to inspect the hole. As he did, he picked up a piece of the splintered wood. "This whole piece is shot. It's rotten."

He turned his attention to the ceiling above the hole. "Look at this," he said, pointing to a ringed water stain on the ceiling's pine boards. "Well, now we know why the roof was fixed. Now if we only knew who fixed it and who authorized it."

Rebecca looked around her, suddenly afraid to take a step. "Is it safe up here? Maybe this whole thing could fall."

"I think it's OK," said Brad. "The rest of it seems solid enough. The water must have dripped down here and rotted this section." He pointed to the hole and made a circle in the air with his finger. "Must've been leaking for years."

"You're sure?"

"I'm sure. The rest of this isn't in bad shape at all."

The flooring had pulled away from the bottom of the window seat as Brad fell, leaving a gap between the wall and the floor. Rebecca noticed a piece of paper protruding from under the seat as if it had fallen down from the inside.

"What's this?" she asked as she reached for it.

She gave it a gentle tug, but it was wedged between two of the boards.

"Just a minute," Brad said. He put his foot against the boards and pushed. "See if you can get it, but be careful not to tear it."

Rebecca pulled gently on the paper and slid it out from under the wall. "It's an envelope," she said as she stood. She slipped her fingers into the open end to pull out the contents, a folded piece of paper. Reverently and carefully, she unfolded it.

"What is it?" Brad asked.

Rebecca's eyes never left the paper she held in her hand, but her face turned pale as she read.

"What is it?" Brad said again, impatiently this time.

Rebecca looked down at the window seat and then back to the paper. "It's—" she started, and then paused as she continued to read.

"It's what?" Brad said.

"It's a letter."

"I can see that! What does it say?"

"It's from Ruth."

"Who is Ruth?"

"She's my grandfather's sister. Remember the letters in the leather pouch? The one who sounded as if she couldn't, or wouldn't, marry someone named Clayton? And the other letter is to my aunt, telling her not to worry about the diary."

"Ah, yes. The ones that sounded so cryptic. So, what does this one say?"

Rebecca's eyes went back to the page. "It's written to my Grandpa George."

She paused. "I'm...I'm not sure what to make of it, but—" Her eyes went to the window seat.

Brad reached out and took the letter from his wife's hand. He began to read:

> Dear Brother,
>
> I received your letter today with the news of Billie's impending marriage. You asked me what I thought you should do. I can only tell you that it is my firm conviction that the awful trouble will continue and that nothing can be done about it. But I have had a lifetime to consider its consequences, and I can tell you that I believe with all my heart that it is fruitless, as well as faithless, to allow it to affect our bids for true happiness. You, of course, are aware of its terrible influence on my own life.
>
> It is because of this, and because I now believe that we must all seek our own course in faith without regard to the phantoms of misfortune, that I can finally say without reservation, "Burn it!" Burn the awful thing and be done with it! And let the rivers of history flow where they may.

I cannot know what may happen in regard to your daughter's impending marriage, but I have written to her and instructed her, as I do you, that it is best to forget the superstition of the past and destroy the thing that holds it ever before us. I know that you have it. I know that you have guarded it with great care. You have not spoken of it in many years. Yet I know that you have it still.

And so I say, take it from its hiding place! Take it and burn it, and with it the vexation that haunts us! Do this and let your kin and their kin after them live in peace.

"Man!" Brad said as he handed the letter back to his wife. "Your family sure is—"

"Is what?" Rebecca asked.

"I don't know," Brad shrugged. "If all these letters weren't written before TV, I'd say they'd been watching too many movies. What's it all about?"

"I don't know for sure," Rebecca said as her eyes went back to the window seat. "But—" She wagged her finger at the seat. "How did that letter get inside that?"

"I don't know," Brad said as he went to the seat. "Sometimes these things had a storage area underneath." He grabbed the pine facing of the seat and gave it a little tug. "It's nailed down."

"Can you pry it loose?"

Brad rubbed his chin. "I'll be right back," he said as he headed for the stairs. He returned a moment later with the tine he had used to pry open the locked door. He stooped in front of the window seat, straddling the hole in the floor.

"Let's see if I can wedge this under here," he said, forcing the tine under the wooden plank of the seat. He lifted the tine, slowly at first and then with more force as the plank gave way. Nails creaked as the plank lifted and then fell to one side. Brad dropped the tine on the floor and picked up the plank, tossing it aside. He quickly pried the remaining boards from their place.

They both peered into the space beneath the window. It was lined with the same pine boards that finished the room, but the protection of the seat had shielded them from the elements and time. They looked new, except that the lining nearest the front had pulled away when Brad had fallen through the floor, leaving a crack through which the letter had fallen. In the center of the compartment, neatly placed as though put there with reverence and care, was a bundle, wrapped in sheepskin and tied with a leather cord.

Rebecca reached in and picked it up. She carefully untied the knot and dropped the cord to the floor before unfurling the sheepskin. Her face betrayed her astonishment as she stood silently, gazing down at the package in her hands. She somehow knew without looking further what it was she held. She knew before she opened the first page of the tattered, leather-bound volume that she held the answers to all the questions from the last few days.

"It's the diary!" she said with awe and wonder.

"You're kidding," said Brad. "You mean *the* diary?"

Rebecca nodded as she turned back the cover to the first leaf. "Oh!" she said softly. "Oh my!"

Brad leaned close, tilting his head to get a better look. There was an inscription in the upper right-hand corner.

Katherine Walker,
from Mother and Father,
on her 14th birthday,
October 6, 1850

As she ran her fingers over the inscription, Rebecca felt as though she were reaching across space and time. The corners of the page were smudged and worn from regular use, and as she touched the page she felt a closeness, a kinship, to the one who had written down her intimate thoughts and desires over a century-and-a-half before. She wondered what secrets it contained.

"Wow! That thing's really old," Brad said. "I wonder how it got there?"

Rebecca carried the diary over to the toolbox and sat down. A thousand thoughts and feelings vied for her attention. She remembered the letters. She thought of Aunt Billie and the things she had said before she died. She had wondered about the diary, and even allowed herself to daydream about finding it. But now she held it in her hands. She was sure the answers to questions that had nagged at her for days were within its pages. Somehow she felt there was more.

Brad sat down next to her.

"Look at this," Rebecca almost whispered as she turned to the first page. She read the first entry:

> October 6, 1850
> Dear Diary,
> Today I am fourteen years of age. Mama and Papa have given me a diary which I shall treasure all my life. I feel certain that I shall share with it my deepest secrets, and that it shall afford me the greatest of comfort when I am able to look back to its pages when I am old. God bless Mama and Papa.

Rebecca thumbed through several pages, pausing to read a few entries, and then turned a few more pages. Some of the entries were a page or two long. Others were only a line or two. With rare exception, there was an entry for every day.

"Oh, look," Rebecca said as she came to an entry that caught her eye.

> May 18, 1851
> Dear Diary,
> The wagons are ready, and Papa says we will leave Independence in the morning. It is to be a long journey. I look upon the new adventure with an eager heart, yet I cannot help but wonder what it is that God has in store for us. Papa likens the new land to a ripe plum waiting to be picked. Yet all my friends are here.

"How sad," Rebecca said.

> May 19, 1851
> Dear Diary,

> The sun has not yet risen, but we have been on the trail for almost an hour. Papa's new friend, Mr. Elam, says that we shall travel long hours to ensure that we cross the Rockies before the Fall snows. Mr. and Mrs. Elam are very nice. Mr. Elam has had some experience with horses, so the wagon master assigned to him the task of seeing to the sick. Mr. and Mrs. Elam are nice, but their three boys are horrid! I wish they would leave me alone! There is an abundance of children on the wagon train, but so far as I can see, no girls my own age.

Brad read along with Rebecca. "Hmm," he muttered once or twice.

She turned several more pages, paused to read, and then turned several more. There was an entry for November 2, 1851, that told of an early snow that had forced them to winter at a place called "Fort Bridger." Several entries lamented the lack of companionship on the lonely trail. Rebecca turned several more pages and stopped to read:

> May 29, 1852
> Dear Diary,
>
> We saw cabins today. Papa is heading for them, and our long journey may be coming to an end. I only wish I knew for certain. It has been a strenuous trip, and I had begun to fear that I should never see another human face besides those of my own family again. Yet here we are, a full year since our departure, on the brink of a green valley in the vast Oregon Territory. Papa says that our new home is surely less than a two-day journey. Thank God for His mercy!

"Hmm," Brad said again.

Rebecca flipped through a few more pages. "I don't see anything here about any trouble," she wondered aloud.

She turned a few more pages.

"Wait," Brad said as he stuck his hand in the way of the pages and leafed back until he saw what had caught his eye.

March 8, 1854
Dear Diary,

God, in His mercy, opened a window today! I had begun to doubt His great purpose, or even that He cared for me, but then, when hope seemed at its greatest distance from me, John Jakes came and took my hand in the churchyard today. He is the most handsome man I have ever seen! I believe with all my heart that he is the one for me and that we will one day wed. It is a wondrous day, and I can hope again!

Addendum:

We met the strangest family today on the way to church. They have settled along the creek near where it makes the bend. Papa says they are Creole. There is a mother, a father, two boys somewhat older than me, and a girl about my own age. I have longed for female companionship, someone with whom to share my innermost thoughts, but I fear that our relationship is not to be a close one. I felt at once that there is something sinister there! I can only hope that I am wrong and that my first impressions were in error.

"Hmm," said Brad. "Interesting."

Rebecca said nothing but flipped through a few more pages.

July 28, 1854
Dear Diary,

A wondrous day! John has asked me to marry him! God is so good! I shall make him the best wife possible, and with God's help I know we can make the journey along life's road together, my hand in his. I am sure that Kyra plans more mischief, though John has told me of the circumstances of that other business, and I believe him. But she is not one to give up so easily that we should consider the matter closed.

"Hmm," Brad said. "Who is Kyra?"

"I don't know." Rebecca began flipping forward a few pages.

September 20, 1854
Dear Diary,

The day is here at last! It is my wedding day and my beloved awaits! Mama is busy at this very moment making a few last minute alterations to the dress that was hers. It is beautiful! I am beside myself with joy!

addendum:

It was a beautiful wedding. Everyone said so, and I am pleased to tell you, Diary, that I am Mrs. John Jakes. It was a wondrous day; it was all that I could have hoped it would be, and even Kyra and whatever mischief she had planned could not dampen my spirits. She was there, at least according to Mrs. Elam, but stayed a respectable distance away. I am somewhat perplexed, I confess, since respectability has never been Kyra's habit. Yet the day has come and gone without incident. Perhaps we have heard the last of Kyra and her wicked purpose.

"Well," said Brad, "what's the big deal? I still don't see anything worth all the fuss. Where's the big mystery?"

Rebecca held the diary up to compare the two halves. "We're not even halfway through yet," she said.

"Well," he said as he stood, "I think I'll leave you to your dime store romance. I'm going to look around and take a few notes—see what we need to fix-up the place."

Rebecca frowned. She resented Brad's belittling attitude toward what she considered a sacred moment. Brad disappeared down the stairs.

February 4, 1860
Dear Diary,

Kyra continues to be a thorn in our side. She has claimed, to no avail since no one seems willing to listen to her, that John is the unlucky father of the child that she bears. I am among those who do not believe her. Yet it has caused me some grief, which I dare not show, lest my husband misinterpret my sadness as distrust of him. I feel certain that her latest ruse is the result of her own frustration, since I now have three fine children. If the rumors be true, she must surely be in a state. Poor thing! I pity her. We heard that she has been having birth pains since yesterday morning. Mr. Elam rode out yesterday about noon to see if there was anything he could do to help, a tangible sign of the new man that Mr. Elam has become by God's grace, but Mr. Doucet ordered him to leave at gunpoint. I continue to pray for Kyra, though circumstances and my own propensity to sin make it a burdensome task, and I hope that one day she will come to know the Savior. My burden has eased somewhat in the last few weeks as I grow more certain that maternal joys await me once again in the fall.

Rebecca thumbed through the diary, shifting her weight on the toolbox to relieve the slight pain in her back. She straightened, stretching her muscles, and then turned her attention back to the diary. The last entry she had read was less than halfway through. She thumbed forward to about three-quarters of the way through and began to read:

December 6, 1864
Dear Diary,

I have sad news for you today. It is the strangest thing. John was riding out to Mama and Papa's place this morning. When he was no more than a stone's throw from the Doucet cabin, Mrs. Doucet came running out of the house with Kyra's young son in tow, screaming that Kyra was gone! The poor boy, unable to keep up with her, fell several times, but she paid him no mind as she ran to the barn and then along the road. I fear she may have gone mad. John said he nearly lost his mount when she rushed up to the horse and caused it to rear. When John dismounted, he tried to console her, but she would have none of it and said that John was responsible for Kyra's disappearance. John offered to get the sheriff, but she only became more enraged. It was then that she confirmed the awful rumors we have heard since the day of our wedding, as well as the details that, up to this day, have been hidden from us. Kyra, in her demented lust and thwarted efforts to possess what could never be hers, pronounced a curse

> on the offspring of our union, more specifically, the female offspring. We had some idea that she had done this vile thing, but we assumed it would be to cause me barrenness. It seems this is not so, and that she intended for the curse to perpetuate itself in the Jakes line by allowing sons to father children and thus continue the name of Jakes, but preventing any daughters born to us from bearing living children. It seems that the full weight of the indignity of the curse is aimed at me. I know not whether there is any merit to curses, but I trust that God will work all things to good for those that love Him and are called according to His purpose.

Rebecca closed the diary. She felt her strength drain as the words hit her with all the weight of certainty. She was dumbfounded. It couldn't be! And yet how could she explain it? Billie could not bear children. According to the letters, neither could any of her female relatives as far back as a hundred years. So far, she and Brad had been unable to conceive. And now this! The trouble, the dark secret, was the curse!

She sat back and leaned against the wall. How could it be? This was the twenty-first century. She couldn't believe in curses. How could she? She felt helpless and alone. It weighed heavy on her shoulders, and she felt as though not even God could help her now.

The Centurion raised his shield and placed his hand on the butt of his sheathed sword. He stood ready for battle.

CHAPTER TWENTY-TWO

REBECCA STOOD, BUT her knees felt weak. For days she had wrestled with conflicting emotions. When Billie died, Rebecca had been as low as she could remember ever being in her whole life. With the discovery of the leather pouch and the wonderful mystery the letters contained, she had been as high as she could remember in a long time. Then the more she learned about the "trouble" and began to fear that it could be something that affected her, the more she experienced an emotional tug-of-war as she grappled with her burning curiosity and her fear that to go further in her search could lead her to knowledge she was not certain she wanted.

The diary had taken away any chance of turning back. Instead of satisfying her curiosity, it only served to give her a piece of the puzzle on which she had not counted. She felt helpless to know what to do or believe. Her head told her one thing: she was a product of the twentieth century, and there were no such things as curses. How could anyone in this day and age believe in something so archaic and backward? She felt shame and embarrassment that she could even consider it.

Yet her heart told her something different. She knew there was a spiritual side to her. She knew deep down that what Billie and Pastor Romberg had told her was the truth. Yet she could not shake the feelings of guilt that haunted her. She had rejected God. She knew what she should do. She had known for a long time. But she resisted, and with her resistance came the guilt. And with the guilt came the feeling that she deserved to be cursed. The discovery of the diary and its contents only served to confirm in her mind that what she feared must be true—somehow.

She made her way to the attic stairs, bracing herself with an unsteady hand against the wall as she descended. Brad was not in the kitchen. She made her way through the living room and onto the front porch. Brad was standing near the corner of the house, looking intently up at the eaves and busily scribbling notes to himself on the pad of paper in his hand.

Rebecca staggered down the front porch steps toward him on the verge of tears and visibly shaken.

"What's the matter?" he asked as he held out his arms. She fell into them, weeping softly.

"What's the matter?" Brad asked again as he held her close. She was trembling. He noticed she was holding the diary. "What's going on?"

Rebecca didn't answer. She sobbed quietly into his shirt.

Brad felt a sudden burst of anger from the seething cauldron of indignation that had been brewing for several days. He could sense Rebecca was going through more than the emotion and turmoil of losing her aunt. Something more was happening, and though it may have been the catalyst, her aunt's death was not the cause. He had sensed it before at home, and then on the weekend at Billie's before she died. Then there was that preacher! Brad swore to himself at the memory of the preacher's little speech and the effect it had had on his wife. It picked at the scab of his deepening resentment.

"Hey," he said softly and trying to sound conciliatory. He pushed her away gently and met her eyes. "What is it?"

Rebecca trembled. She wanted to tell him. She needed to tell him. But she was afraid. How could she tell him? It was silly! Yet she believed. She desperately needed someone to tell her what she feared was not true, and everything would be all right. More than anything at the moment, she needed to hear reassuring words from the man she loved and trusted.

But words of condemnation or ridicule would not comfort her. Brad's skepticism was obvious when it came to spiritual things, and she knew he would not understand. It was hard enough to get him to go to church once or twice a year. He had no interest in God or anything having to do with the exploration of what was deeper than his own comforts and ambitions, and his best and only defense had always been to mock.

Bible study and prayer were one thing, but this business with curses was akin to cave-dwelling, flint-making, belly-scratching witch doctors who manipulate their peers with wide-eyed fear and bullying. Rebecca knew he never would believe it or understand, and she was afraid of his reaction.

Brad's eyes went to the diary. "What have you been reading?" he almost demanded.

She opened her mouth to speak, but the words wouldn't come.

"C'mon," Brad said as he led her to the front porch steps.

Rebecca sniffled as she sat down.

Brad sat down next to her. He reached for the diary under her arm.

"No!" she said as she pulled away.

"I just want to look at it," Brad said without taking his hand away.

Rebecca reluctantly let go.

Brad tucked the diary under his arm. "Now tell me what's wrong."

Rebecca took a deep, quivering breath. "I know you're not going to believe this, but I know why we can't have children!"

The lines in Brad's forehead deepened. "What?"

Rebecca's eyes met Brad's. She needed him. She needed him to understand. Her eyes pleaded an unspoken request to hear her out. "There is a —" The word stuck in her throat. She looked down at the diary. "There is a curse!"

Brad wrinkled up his nose and frowned. "You're kidding?"

Rebecca shrank back. Tears forced their way down her cheeks. "It's true!" she said.

Brad tried to pull her close and give her a patronizing pat on the shoulder, but she pulled away.

"It's true! I know it's true! The diary explains everything! Aunt Billie! Ruth! Us! Everything!"

Brad shook his head. "Don't you think you're getting a little carried away? C'mon, listen to yourself! Curses? What's next? Ghosts and goblins? Haunted houses?"

Rebecca pulled away. "It's not funny!" she sobbed.

"All right, all right!" Brad said. "I'm sorry! But you've gotta listen to yourself. There is a rational explanation for what we're going through and it doesn't involve curses. Now c'mon, get a hold of yourself."

"I know it sounds silly, but you have to listen!"

"All right," Brad said as he took her hand. "I'm listening."

"It's all in here," she said, resting her hand on the diary. "I know what happened. There was this girl who made a lot of trouble for Katie and John, you know, my great-great-grandmother and grandfather. She cursed them! And no Jakes woman has had children since!"

Brad winced with obvious disbelief. "I think you've been reading too many of those letters," he scoffed. "You're letting your imagination run away with you."

"It's true! I know it's true!"

"All right," Brad said as he pulled her close. He held her for several minutes as she sobbed. After a moment, he pushed her away gently and held her arms at the shoulders. "I think we'd better go, don't you?"

Rebecca shook her head and sniffled. "I want to stay and look around."

"We haven't been here half-an-hour and you're a basket case! I don't think this place is good for you—at least not right now. I think we should go back to the room and let you rest. We can come back another time."

Rebecca shook her head. "I want to stay."

Brad was getting angry. "I don't think —" he began, raising his voice slightly.

"I'm not leaving." She couldn't leave, not yet. She felt as though there was more here to discover. She knew she had to stay. "I'll be fine," she said to Brad's skeptical frown.

"Well, all right. But no more talk about curses?"

"I'll be fine," she said, turning away.

"All right," Brad said. He stood and reached down to give her a hand up. "But I'm sticking close, so don't run off. All right?"

Rebecca nodded through tears.

"So where do you want to look first?"

"I don't know," she said as she took the diary and tucked it under her arm.

Brad planted his feet. "Well, this is your party. You decide. I'll follow you."

Rebecca nodded again. "C'mon," she said as she took his hand. She tiptoed slowly through the tall grass across the yard and around the house. Brad followed, taking notes and muttering to himself. Rebecca came to the cellar doors.

"Could we look down there?" she asked, wiping away the last of her tears.

Brad bent down and tested the weight of the doors by lifting one of them a few inches. He grunted as he lifted and then flung the door over, letting it fall to the ground. They both peered into the darkened void below them.

"Got a match?" Brad said, half-kidding.

"I have a penlight on my key chain. Will that do?"

"Yeah. Get it."

Rebecca went back to the car for her purse and returned with her keys in one hand and purse in the other.

"What did you do with the diary?" Brad asked as he took the key ring and flicked the penlight switch. He took a step into the darkness.

"I left it in the car," she said.

High on a ridge overlooking the old house, the neglected meadow, and the stagnant pond, a presence, filled with a lust for vengeance and death, watched the young couple as they peered for a moment into the basement's darkness and then descended the steps. It hesitated for a brief and cautious moment and then started down the mountain, covering a great distance in milliseconds before coming to rest just outside the clearing. It pondered the young couple, looking for weakness as it kept an ever-vigilant lookout for the real source of danger.

The young couple was off-limits, but there had to be a way. It hated them. There was no reason. Logic and reason were foreign. It only hated.

Yes, it would find a way.

It was not safe here. The danger was real and the consequences for breaching, or attempting to breach, the boundary would be swift.

The presence moved away from the house in the direction of the S-bend in Walker Creek, to home and safety—and willing servants.

Yes, there was a way. It was an old way, a tried and true way, and very effective.

Brad ducked low as he swept the penlight across the narrow cellar's stone walls. Above the chest-high walls, a shaft of light peeked through the house's cracked outer foundation and severed the darkness. Dust particles danced magically through it. The cellar was empty except for two wooden posts that rested on large boulders in the middle of the floor to meet the rugged beam of the ceiling just above their heads.

"It smells," Rebecca said, wrinkling up her nose.

"It's musty—damp. Look at that rock," Brad said pointing to one of the boulders. "See the water line? This thing must take in water in the winter. It's still damp, even now."

"Mmm," Rebecca said as she remembered something. She ducked under the beam and went to the far wall, leaned against it, and peered along the top.

"What're you looking for?"

"I'm not sure. I just remembered something my aunt said —" She started to reach over the top of the wall, and then jerked her arm away quickly.

"What's the matter?" Brad asked.

Her eyes pleaded her damsel-in-distress plea, and then she sniffled. "Would you do it?"

Brad joined her at the wall. "What do you want?"

"Could you reach over here," she said pointing along the wall, "and see if there is a jar there?"

Brad peered over the wall and back at Rebecca. "Why can't you do it?"

"What if there are spiders?"

His eyes widened. "Yeah, what if?" He peered over the wall again. "Time for the cavalry, eh?"

"Is it there?"

Brad reached over the wall and felt along the back of it with his hand. "Just a minute," he said. He pulled out a small, mud-caked Mason jar and handed it to Rebecca.

Rebecca held it reverently. "It is here," she whispered with wonder. "Aunt Billie told me about it that day we walked along the beach. I'd forgotten about it until just now."

"What's in it?"

Rebecca strained to twist the lid. "I can't do it."

"Here. Let me," Brad said as he reached for it. He took the jar and heaved against the lid, but it wouldn't budge. "Curses, foiled again!"

Rebecca frowned.

"All right, I'm just kidding."

He shifted his grip and tried again. The rusted lid gave way and fell into two pieces. Brad let it fall to the ground.

"Watch out for spiders." Rebecca warned.

Brad reached in with two fingers. He lifted the rotted remains of an old handkerchief halfway out of the opening, and then turned the jar on its side and shook it. A dozen coins jingled into his open palm.

"Just as she said," Rebecca said softly.

Brad sifted through the coins—all pennies. "They're all dated in the early twenties. But how did you know?"

"Don't you remember? She told us about it that day at the house just before we went for a walk on the beach. She said she didn't remember much about the house or living here. But this was one thing that stuck in her mind. She remembered hiding her little treasure here in the cellar. She couldn't have been more than four or five."

Brad had clicked off the penlight as soon as their eyes had adjusted to the dim light of the cellar. As they studied the coins in the palm of Brad's hand, they turned automatically toward the light coming from the open cellar door. But as Brad fingered the coins from side to side, the light dimmed. They looked up.

Near the bottom of the stairs, the dark-skinned man stood grim-faced, cradling a rifle comfortably in his arms. He was lean and fit. His broad shoulders tapered down to his narrow waist, and his dark, commanding eyes pierced the cellar's dim light, sending shivers of fear down Rebecca's spine even as she noted how handsome he was. In his free hand he held the diary.

"Oh!" Rebecca gasped.

The man's eyes accused as he motioned toward the jar. "Do you usually take things without asking?"

Brad moved slowly between Rebecca and the man. He could feel the blood draining from his face. "Who are you?" he asked.

The man hefted the rifle to make a point. "I think I'll ask the questions." He nodded toward the jar. "Why don't we let the lady put the jar back where she got it?"

Rebecca took the jar and the coins from her husband, dropped the coins inside and set the jar on the wall. Her eyes never left the rifle.

"Thank you," the man said. "Now why don't you tell me who you are, why you're trespassing, and where you found this?" He held up the diary.

Brad felt a sudden surge of bravado mingled with indignation. "Trespassing?" he demanded. "You've got a lot of nerve!"

The man raised an eyebrow. "If you don't mind?" he said, raising his index finger as he gripped the diary.

"We found it upstairs in the attic," Rebecca said.

"In the attic? Where in the attic?"

"It was hidden under the window seat."

Surprise registered on the man's face as he rolled his eyes. "The window seat! Of course. I should have thought of that."

"This place belongs to us!" Rebecca exclaimed from behind her husband. "And so does that diary!"

"Suppose you tell me who you are," the man said, "since I know who owns it, and I don't know you."

"Why should we tell you anything?" Rebecca challenged.

"Because I have, as they say, the upper hand." The man glanced down at the rifle.

Brad clenched his jaw. "My name is Brad Lindsay. This is my wife."

The man studied them for a moment. "I don't know you," he replied.

"We've never been here before. We just came to look at the property."

"Never?" the man demanded.

"Never before this week," Brad affirmed.

The man studied them in silence for a moment.

"But we recognize you!" Brad continued, his fear of the rifle and the stranger giving way to righteous indignation. "And we resent being threatened!"

The man's eyes flashed. "Threatened? No. But until I find out who you are and why you're here, you may consider yourself under citizen's arrest. As soon as we get to my truck, we'll make a call to the sheriff." He swung the barrel of the rifle around, motioning toward the stairs. "Let's go."

Brad felt a sense of relief. The law sounded good to him. They could straighten out this mess. But Rebecca was enraged.

"This is my property! You can't go around pointing guns at people and ordering them around!"

The man gave a half-smile. Spunk. He liked that. "You should notice, ma'am, that I have not once pointed this gun at you, and no one named 'Lindsay' has ever owned this property."

"Well, I own it! It's been in my family for generations. My aunt willed it to me, and that makes it mine!"

The man's eyes softened. He stood silent for a moment as he studied his two captives. "Rebecca?" he questioned, even as he silently chastened himself for tipping his hand so quickly.

Rebecca was startled. "Yes. How —?"

The man held up his hand. "You'll forgive my cautious nature, but I trust you have proof?"

Rebecca's jaw was set. "In my purse." She opened it and rummaged around for the wallet with her driver's license. She pulled it from its plastic holder and handed it to the man.

"Well," the man sighed as he lowered the rifle and let the butt rest on the ground beside him. He handed Rebecca's license back to her. "I am sorry. I hope you'll forgive me. My name is Sam Michaels. I am a friend of your aunt's." He took a step forward and extended his hand.

Brad hesitated and then took it with a wary eye on the man and his gun. Sam offered his hand to Rebecca. "I'm very pleased to meet you," he said with a warm smile. "I feel like I know you."

"Why all the melodrama?" Brad asked.

Sam Michaels cocked his head to one side. "I'll be happy to explain. But first, could you explain something? You said your aunt willed you the property?"

Rebecca nodded. "She died last week."

Sam face fell. "I hadn't heard. I'm sorry."

Rebecca could feel the tears coming again.

Sam could see her grief. "Come. Why don't we get out of this dreary place?"

Sam handed Rebecca the diary as they followed him out of the cellar and walked around the house to their car. Sam's pickup sat next to it. He walked around to the back and opened the tailgate. "Please sit," he said as he motioned with his hand.

Brad stood next to his wife as she sat down. "You still haven't explained why all the melodrama—or why you let all the air out of our tires."

Sam held up his hand. "It wasn't me who let the air out of your tires, but first things first. Tell me about your aunt. What happened? How did she die?"

"A heart attack," Brad said. "Very sudden."

"We were with her the day before and we had no idea," Rebecca added.

Sam nodded. "Mmm. She was a remarkable woman."

"You knew her?" Rebecca asked.

Sam nodded. "Yes, as I said, most of my life, in fact. And I feel like I know you too. Your aunt talked about you often."

"But how did you know her?" Brad wanted to know. "She told us she hadn't been here since she was a little girl."

"That's true enough," said Sam. "I never actually met her face to face. We communicated by letter, and once or twice by phone."

"So you didn't really know her?" said Rebecca.

Sam dropped his head. "I wouldn't say that. I suppose it sounds odd, but we became good friends. We had a common bond."

"So why are you running people off at gunpoint?" Brad asked with renewed confidence.

"Well, that's a long story. I made a promise to your aunt that I'd keep the place up and watch out for things around here."

"So you're the one who has been fixing things up?" asked Rebecca.

"Yes. I wrote your aunt that the roof leaked and she sent the money to fix it. I started doing a little work on the foundation a few weeks ago."

"But why?" Rebecca asked.

"To keep a promise," Sam said.

"But why did you let the air out of our tires?" asked Brad.

Sam shook his head. "It wasn't me."

"But we saw you there."

"I was there, yes, but it wasn't me. But I think I know who did."

"Who?" Brad and Rebecca asked at the same time.

"I have my guesses, but I'd prefer not to say until I'm sure. I have this thing about spreading gossip."

Rebecca still wasn't satisfied. "Why were you following us?"

Sam smiled and shook his head. "I suppose I'm going to have to work on my tracking skills. It just won't do to have an Indian who can't sneak up on someone, especially a white man." He chuckled at his private little joke. "You're right, of course. I was following you. I had to know who you were and why you were hanging around this place. I followed you to the county building, but the friend I have there didn't get your name. I had planned to see Frank Downs last night, but he wasn't in his office. He usually goes to the café for an early breakfast, so I was on my way to see him this morning when I saw you leave your hotel room. So I followed you here."

"I still don't understand," Brad said. "Why all the need for the cloak-and-dagger stuff?"

Sam became solemn. "There are those in this valley who want this property. Your aunt wouldn't sell and these people will do almost anything to get it."

"Why?" Brad asked. "What makes this broken-down old place worth so much attention?"

Sam was silent as he studied their faces. There was much to tell in time. But for now…"Many reasons," he said with a cock of his head. "Perhaps it is because the land is good for farming. Or perhaps it is that there is a good stand of timber on the other side of that ridge."

"Then why not sell them the timber and be done with it?" Brad asked.

"Because they want the land."

"What's so important about the land?" asked Rebecca.

"That's tough to answer. You'd have to know the history of this valley."

"Are you the one who padlocked the door to the attic?"

"Yes. I didn't want prying eyes to go snooping around too much. Around here, theft isn't too much of a problem, but I didn't want certain people to go digging around up there. I've always had a sneaking suspicion that the diary was somewhere up there." He laughed. "I could kick myself for not thinking of a place as obvious as the window seat!"

"What people?" Brad asked.

Sam drew a deep breath. "Have you read any of that?" he asked, pointing to the diary.

"Some," Rebecca said.

"Have you read about the curse?"

Rebecca and Brad looked at each other.

"I see you have," Sam nodded. "How much have you read?"

"Just a few pages," said Rebecca. "I've read the entry about the wedding, and a couple about someone named Kyra." Rebecca's eyes narrowed. "How do you know what's in it if you've never seen it?"

"Well, I've never read it, of course, but I've heard the stories for as long as I can remember. And it's as much a part of me as it is you."

"Don't tell me you believe in curses too?" Brad chided.

Sam shrugged. "Whether I do or not, the story is very much a part of both our lives," he said, nodding toward Rebecca. "It involves both our families as far back as the history of this valley."

"You mentioned people," Brad reminded.

Sam nodded. "The other family in the diary was Kyra's family. Maybe you noticed the little market as you came into town? Doucets'? It's their market—Gil and his sister Sara. They're direct descendants of Kyra Doucet."

"Sara!" Rebecca exclaimed. "Wasn't she the one driving the tow truck?"

"That was her. A real conniver. I'm pretty sure she's the one who let the air out of your tires."

"But why?"

Sam shrugged. "I'm guessing, but I think she probably knew who you were and why you're here. She probably wanted to get a close look at you—maybe find out what you intended to do with this place."

"Why didn't she just ask?" Brad wondered.

Sam shrugged. "Well, in any case, I didn't actually see her do it."

"Why does she care so much about this place?" Rebecca asked.

"Her brother probably put her up to it, although I really thought he'd be more careful than that. And, to answer your question, they want to own this place."

"Sounds like a deal in the making to me," Brad said.

"Why?" Rebecca asked Sam.

"Well, that's hard to figure. I think Gil wants it for the timber. This place has a small fortune in lumber sitting on it that's mature enough to harvest any time someone has a mind to. There's also a patch of contraband back in those hills," he said, tossing his head behind him, "that I'm pretty sure is his. I've seen it a time or two when I was hunting. It's a pretty big operation—probably close to three hundred acres scattered here and there. It probably makes more money than the store."

"How do you know it's his?" Brad asked.

Sam shrugged. "Small town. What can I say?"

"How does he keep from being caught?" asked Rebecca.

"The only people who ever go back in that far are hunters—locals like me and sometimes the game warden. But he's an old pothead buddy of Gil's from high school. He just looks the other way. Besides, the laws have relaxed so much in the last ten years that no one really figures it's worth much effort. Anyhow, it's a good source of income for Gil, and the seclusion makes it a perfect place. It could go on for years.

"But I don't think any of this interests Sara. All she's interested in is the newest pair of jeans in town—and I don't mean she likes to go shopping. She's a strange one—has been as long as I can remember, since grade school. In a way, she's responsible for my being here."

There was something about the way Sam looked away that caught Rebecca's attention.

"Why is that?" Rebecca asked.

Sam shrugged. "We had something, once."

There was an awkward silence. Finally, Sam broke it.

"As long as I've known her, she's been talking about the curse. No one ever paid much attention to her when we were kids, but she was always talking about it and how it was up to her to 'carry the burden' as she used to say. And, well, the task of keeping an eye on this place just sort of fell to me."

Sam could see the puzzled look on both Rebecca's and Brad's faces.

Rebecca sighed. "I still don't understand how you became involved."

Sam looked at his watch. "I have to be somewhere in a few minutes. Can we meet tonight for dinner? I'd like to answer all your questions and I have a few of my own."

Rebecca looked at Brad, who was less than enthusiastic. "I think we can manage that," she said, turning to Brad. "Is that all right with you?"

Brad shrugged. "Yeah, I suppose."

"Fine," said Sam. "I'll meet you at the café next to the Doucet market at six o'clock. You know it?"

"Yes," said Rebecca. "We had dinner there the first night we were here."

"Great! I'll see you then."

Gil Doucet pulled off the main road and onto the dirt driveway that led to the clearing at the S-bend in Walker Creek. He stopped his ten-year-old Ford pickup at the gate and waited for the dust cloud that followed to pass by before opening the door and pushing against the steering wheel to get out. He had to lean back and suck in, holding his breath to get his oversized beer-belly past its resting place on the bottom of the steering wheel.

He braced himself, through force of habit, by hanging his weight on the doorpost as he swung out of the cab. He walked to the gate and flipped the latch, then walked back to the truck cab as the gate swung open and bounced against the single wooden fencepost that had been anchored in solitude for that sole purpose.

He hoisted himself into the cab and started down the driveway. The clearing was not visible from the street thanks to his grandfather's clever cunning many years before when the county decided to pave the road. He'd insisted to county officials that the family owned the property where the road sat. The lie was made easy by the fact that he had a friend who worked for the surveyor who had mapped out this whole valley—a friend who owed him a favor. He'd simply changed a few figures on a couple of documents one night, and moved a single surveyor's stake when no one was looking.

So when the time came to begin construction, the old man, influential in the valley then, raised such a stink that the county was forced to relent in the face of the evidence and built the road so it swung away from the S-bend in Walker Creek. It gave the Doucets an extra twenty acres of land. But the old man never told anyone of the ruse, not even family, so as far as Gil or anyone else knew, the land was rightfully theirs.

Gil followed the driveway over the bridge, made from an old flatbed railroad car that had been stripped of its wheels and hoisted with a crane into place and then surfaced with heavy beam planks. At the far side was a clearing nestled behind a ribbon of fir and yew wood trees that encircled it just beyond the S-bend. The Doucets liked their privacy.

The clearing offered an odd collection of assorted curiosities. It butted the mountainside that rose abruptly a few yards beyond the abandoned shack built by Gil's grandfather—abandoned, unless the few sacks of chicken feed that were stored there counted for use. A naked doublewide mobile home—no skirting, no patios or walkways, nothing to give it the feel of home—rested on jack stands in the middle of a patch of dust devoid of vegetation.

A rusted hulk of an old military dump truck, minus wheels and tires, sat on blocks beside the old shack. Only a few patches of army-green paint remained on it's rusting hulk. A Ford tractor that appeared to be in worse shape than the truck sat in tall weeds on the other side of the driveway. The only thing to give away its serviceability was the newly worn path of flattened weeds that led to the rear tires. The rest of the yard was littered with various wheel rims, old motors, rusted farm equipment, and an old hay-bailer Gil had not used in ten years.

A few feet into the ribbon of trees between the mobile home and the S-bend in the creek, four weathered gravestones had all but disappeared under the layers of time and winter mud. Only one of the stones still stood upright.

Gil used to play among them when he was young. The names were known to him, handed down along with the stories. They were the original family that had settled here in the valley—or most of them anyway. There were the two brothers, Yves and Veré, murdered, one by an Indian and the other by a backstabbing, two-timing woman. Gil knew the names and the dates even though they were no longer visible. He'd spent an afternoon as a boy many years ago removing the layers of dirt and brushing them clean to see.

The other two markers were those of the two boys' parents, Andre and Maud, larger than the other two and newer. The family had placed them there almost forty years after they had died in an attempt at veneration.

Yet there was a name not to be found among the monuments to the past—a name that had also been handed down in stories to the family's children. And there was a reason. It had always been the plan, for several generations of Doucets, to place a marker. It was a legacy as strong and as much a part of them as any legend or prophecy, and Gil and Sara had talked of it themselves. There was a difference, though, between this name and the others. The sense of connection that the other graves brought, a bridge across the years, a tether to patriarchal authority, a link to bring meaning and substance to the stories, was missing—missing because the owner of the name was not there.

Gil knew the story well. He knew of the love of a woman for a man, and the conniving and treachery of another woman. He knew of the unlawful death of the two brothers and the scorn and betrayal of a man. And the curse!

He knew of his own heritage—a woman stricken with grief and anguish over lost love, turned to another. The woman conceived and bore a child, and the family had carried her name instead of that of the father. He knew that over the years jealousy and rage had turned to bitterness and apathy, and that one day she had disappeared into the mountains, leaving her young son to be raised by his grandparents. Such was the fate of Kyra Doucet. For years, the family talked of putting up a marker in her memory, but it never seemed to get done.

Gil slammed the truck door and strode toward the mobile home. His heavy boots thunked on the wooden front porch. He went inside, brushed past the eager greetings of Sheba, his Australian Shepherd, and went straight to the phone on the stand by the dirty, worn sofa. He quickly dialed the familiar number of his old friend Frank Downs.

"Frank? Gil. Hey, I've got a little job for you. No, no. Nothing like that. It's right up your alley. You might even make a few bucks. Yeah. I thought that'd get your attention."

CHAPTER TWENTY-THREE

FRANK DOWNS PUT on his best and brightest smile as he knocked on the hotel room door just before noon.

"Hi!" he said to Rebecca when she answered. "Remember me?"

"Of course," she said as she glanced over her shoulder to see if Brad was out of the bathroom yet. "Mr. Downs, right?"

"Right! Right! Say, do you mind if I come in? I have some news that I think might interest you!"

Rebecca said, "My husband is in the shower. Could you come back another time?"

Downs peered over her shoulder as the bathroom door opened and Brad stepped out, minus his shirt. "Who is it?" he asked as he grabbed a shirt from the suitcase on the foot of the bed.

"It's Mr. Downs," Rebecca said, "but I told him you were busy."

"What is it?" Brad asked Downs at the door as he shoved his arm into his shirtsleeve.

"Like I was telling your wife, I think I have some news you'll want to hear if you have a minute."

"Now is not a good time."

"It'll only take a minute," Downs assured him, "and I know you'll want to hear what I have to say."

"All right," Brad said reluctantly. "C'mon in."

Downs settled into the chair Brad offered him and asked, "Are you two enjoying your stay in our little town?"

"Yeah," Brad said. "Nice little town."

"Good, good! Say, listen, like I was telling your wife, I have news that may interest you." Downs made sure he had on a perfect smile. "I was talking to a client of mine who's always looking for investment property and I told him about your place. Now I know you said you hadn't decided what you were going to do with it yet, but I think you'll be interested in what he's willing to offer. Like I was telling him, this could work out for both of you."

Downs hesitated for a moment to let what he said sink in. "The thing is, he's willing to pay top dollar, and not just top dollar for Oregon prices, but top dollar! You kids could really make a bundle!"

"We're not —" Rebecca began.

"How much?" Brad said. Rebecca shot him a cold stare.

"Well, like I said, top dollar. He figured maybe, oh, as high as four thousand an acre."

"We're not —"

"We'd have to get it appraised before we'd consider any offer," Brad said.

"Fine, fine," Downs said, trying to hide his disappointment. "I think I can get one set up for you, if you'd like."

"We have someone who can do that for us," Brad said.

Rebecca gave him a questioning look, wondering who it was he had in mind—if there was really anyone he had in mind. Brad avoided her stare.

"I see," said Downs. "Can I tell my client that we have a deal?"

"We'd also need to see an offer in writing," said Brad, "before we'd even consider it. We may want to have the timber appraised as well."

"I see," said Downs. His smile faded but quickly returned. "I don't think that'll be a problem. Why don't I —"

Rebecca was becoming impatient and more than a little miffed at Brad. "We're not interested in selling at any price."

Downs looked at Rebecca, then at Brad, and then back at Rebecca. "But I thought I understood that you would entertain an offer. I'm sure that once you —"

"We're not interested in selling at any price," Rebecca insisted as she glared at her husband. "The property is not for sale."

She stood and opened the door, waiting for Downs to leave.

"I see," Downs said. His polyester smile had disappeared. "Well, you seem to know what you want, but my client will be most disappointed."

"We're sorry," Rebecca said, "but I'm afraid we won't change our minds."

Downs lumbered out the door and Rebecca shut it behind him. Brad's jaw was tense.

"Just like that!" he said as she settled onto the bed and reached for the TV remote. Rebecca flicked on the television without answering. Brad grabbed the remote from the lamp stand where she had set it down and flicked it off again.

"What's the big idea of stepping all over me in front of a perfect stranger?"

Rebecca glared. "What's the big idea of treating me like 'the little woman' in front of a perfect stranger?"

"What's that supposed to mean?"

"You! You were ready to make a deal without even consulting me!"

"It was simple cat and mouse. Nobody signed anything. Nobody agreed to anything. What was the harm in finding out if there really was a buyer or how much he might be willing to offer?"

"I told you, I don't want to sell!"

"And what are you going to do with it? It's a mess! Who's going to fix it up? Who's going to take care of it?"

"We can work that out later!"

"Oh, but we can't consider unloading it—now or later—is that it?"

"You were negotiating without me! You treated me like I wasn't even here! Just 'the little woman' who doesn't understand business or finance!"

"Someone has to take the lead."

"Oh, really? Why does it have to be you?"

Brad looked hurt for a brief moment, but then the veins in his neck began to stand out as his face turned red. He glared at Rebecca, considering his next words, but then grabbed his razor from the suitcase on the bed and stormed back into the bathroom.

Rebecca's anger was the only thing keeping her from bursting into tears. She was angry all right, but what she felt most was betrayal. The pain of it cut to her heart. She felt as though she were alone at a time when she needed most to be with someone who cared and understood. She wanted to throw her arms around Brad's neck, hug him, and tell him she was sorry if only he would forgive her—and she wanted to throw the nightstand lamp at him at the same time.

She reached for the remote again and started to turn on the television set, but the thought of watching some mindless sitcom, or a chatty talk show, left her feeling empty. She set the remote on the nightstand and pushed it away in disgust.

As she lay on the bed with her arms behind her head, staring at the ceiling and rehashing her argument with Brad, something occurred to her. It was a strange thought; she wondered what would make her think it.

Take the Bible out of the nightstand.

Before she knew it, the drawer was open and the Bible was in her hand.

She opened it and flipped through it, but the thick volume of thin pages seemed daunting. Several times she stopped to read a passage, but the words were strange and meaningless to her. She continued to surf until a passage in red caught her eye: "Come unto me, all ye that labor and are heavy laden, and I will give you rest."

The words offered comfort. She longed to have the kind of peace she imagined the verse to mean. She wondered if Aunt Billie had that kind of peace. She wanted peace. It seemed like her whole life had become a playground for turmoil and conflict. She never had doubted there was a God, but she wondered if He could, or would, hear her if she prayed. Lately, it seemed so many people had told her she needed Him. She didn't doubt it.

Her own attempts at happiness were futile. She wanted someone to take the pain of the last few weeks, and for that matter the pain of her whole life, and crush it into dust. She wondered if God could do that for her, and she wondered if there could be more words of comfort like those she had just read.

She flipped a few more pages. The Bible fell open to a book called "Ephesians." Her eyes went to the top of the page. "For we wrestle not against flesh and blood, but against principalities, against powers, against the rulers of the darkness of this world, against spiritual wickedness in high places."

Rebecca's eyes froze on the words. The weight and force of them hit her as though they were written only for her, and she felt suddenly as if someone were watching her. The words were true, she knew, but the only thing she could think of was the terrible consequences and awful truth of the curse. She felt no comfort. She saw only the confirmation of her worst fears: there were powers beyond her own understanding, there was spiritual wickedness, and there was darkness in the world. And somehow she was sure they meant there was a curse!

Rebecca closed the Bible, held it close, and sobbed quietly as she curled up on her side with her knees drawn to her chest.

Brad came out of the bathroom. "You hungry?" he said to her back.

She shook her head as she wiped away the tears before he could see.

Brad's heart had not softened, but a slight twinge of guilt forced him to offer the smallest sprig of an olive branch. "I am. You want to go?"

Rebecca shook her head.

Brad noticed the Bible held tightly against her chest. To him it was a symbol of his own failure as a man. He was proud and wanted to feel like he was all his woman could need or want. She used to turn to him for answers. She used to turn to him for comfort. He liked it. But lately she couldn't find her answers with him, and he knew it was because he didn't have them—not the ones she wanted anyway. This business with the baby had been going on for a long time, but lately she had seemed to want more.

This was Billie's fault. And the preacher's. All religion had ever done for him was clutter up a perfectly good day. Now his wife clung to the

Bible as if it could warm her on a cold night. He felt threatened, but it only took a second for his fear to turn to anger.

"I'm going out," he said. "Don't wait up."

Rebecca didn't look up. "Sam Michaels is coming by, remember?"

Brad opened the door. "Your property. Your family. Your problem. You go."

He shut the door and was gone.

Frank Downs pushed his way through the swinging glass door of Doucets' Market and wheezed his way down the middle aisle toward the back of the store. He let himself into Gil's office and made himself at home on the dirty sofa in the corner. A few minutes later, Gil came in.

"What's up?" he said without bothering to say hello.

Downs dismissed Gil's gruff manner with a wave of his hand. "Not much."

"Whaddya mean? Did you get it?"

"Well, no."

Gil gave him a hard look. "Why not?"

Downs shrugged. "They don't want to sell."

"Did you tell them how much?"

"Yeah, I told them. They don't want to sell—at least she doesn't."

Gil's eyebrows rose. "Whaddya mean, 'she doesn't'?"

"I was pretty sure we were getting somewhere. I mean, the guy seemed agreeable enough. We dickered back and forth, and I thought he was going to go for it. But then his wife butted in and said the place wasn't for sale."

"They're playin' good cop/bad cop with you," Gil said with confidence as he settled into the chair behind his desk. "Just playin' games. They'll come around."

Downs cocked his head. "Maybe, but I don't think so. I could hear them arguing before I got to my car. I don't think she's gonna sell."

"Well, go around her! Talk to the guy again! What is he? Some kind of a wuss? Is he gonna let his wife tell him what to do? You ask him that! He'll come around."

Downs shook his head. "The property doesn't belong to him. It's hers. Her aunt willed it to her."

Gil slammed his fist on the desk. "I don't care! I want that property!"

The outburst startled Downs. Gil was a powerful man in the town, physically as well as financially. Frank liked to imagine himself one of Gil's closest confidants and friends.

"Look," said Gil, more composed, "I want you to try again. You can do that, can't you?"

"Sure, Gil. I'll try."

"Good. Get back to me as soon as you can, will you?"

"Sure, Gil, sure." Frank got up and started for the door, but turned around halfway to it. "Tell me again why you need the land? There's so much of it around here. It just seems like it'd be easier to find something that's already for sale. I know it would be cheaper."

Gil drummed his fingers on the desktop. He'd only told Frank why a dozen times before. Frank was many things: loyal, to a point, reliable, also to a point, but limited by his incompetence. But he was also someone whom Gil could control, even though sometimes he tried his patience. He really did.

"I need the land," he began slowly as he got up from the desk and made his way across the room, "because it's situated in a convenient place. It's secluded. It's at the end of the road, which makes it less likely to have visitors. And since I'm already using it, it would save me a whole lot of time and effort if I didn't have to move everything. Do you understand?"

All of Gil's reasons were the truth, but they were not the whole truth. The truth was that Gil probably didn't know the whole truth if someone were to ask. Buried deep within, beyond what he himself was able to understand or be fully aware of, were the pressures, teachings, and beliefs of a lifetime—more than a lifetime: many lifetimes. He was driven, and nothing, not anything, would stand in his way.

"Yeah, Gil, I understand."

"Good," said Gil as he put his big hand on Frank's shoulder. "Now don't you have something you're supposed to do?"

"Yeah, Gil. I'll get right on it." Frank twisted the doorknob and was gone.

Gil shut the door behind Frank, went back to the desk, and sat down, giving himself a mental chastening for his outburst. It would serve no purpose to alienate someone as handy to have around as Frank. And Frank was handy, if a trifle dense. He'd have to be patient. Getting the two kids to sell would be the easiest and safest way to get what he wanted. And, if that didn't work, he always could do it the hard way. But he didn't like the hard way. There was too much risk, and Gil didn't like risk. He'd wait. A few days wouldn't hurt. Then he'd see about taking more drastic measures.

It was late afternoon when Rebecca awoke to the sound of Brad's cell phone ringing on the nightstand next to her head. An hour before, she had cried herself to sleep.

"Hello?" she said into the receiver as she pushed up on her elbow. It was Stephens, Aunt Billie's lawyer.

"I'm returning your call," he said. "I got your message, and let me apologize for taking so long to get back to you. I understand you've had a little difficulty up there."

"Yes," Rebecca said.

"Well, I just wanted to let you know that I've done a little electronic running around from here, and I think we have things squared away. I called the mortuary and the airline. I talked to a Mr. Garvey, and he tells me that your aunt's casket is due to arrive up there tomorrow morning. They assured me everything has been taken care of and that the service can be held tomorrow at ten in the morning. Is that suitable for you?"

"Oh, yes. I think so," Rebecca said, still half asleep.

"Good. Now about that other little matter, the land that you asked about. I went through your aunt's file, just to make sure, and to answer your question, since the property was held in trust and is in your name, you can do with it as you please. My advice would be to consider selling it, unless you plan to move onto it, in which case I'd recommend selling Billie's house here. But that's up to you, of course. In any case, the taxes on both would be high."

"Yes," Rebecca said. "I'll give it some thought." She thanked Stephens for returning her call and for his offered sympathy at the way things had turned out. Then she said goodbye and hung up.

She had given Brad's number to several people and told them she'd be using his cell while they were gone. She punched in the code to retrieve her messages.

"Hi. It's Cheryl. Just wanted to see how you guys were doing up there. Hope everything is fine."

Rebecca deleted Cheryl's message and then brought the phone back up to her ear.

"Hi. This is Helen. I hope everything is going well. I just wanted to see how you're doing and to let you know that we're all still praying for you down here. God bless! Bye!"

There were two messages from Brad's office, one asking where he put the file for the Lambert project and one from his boss wondering how much longer he'd be gone. She grabbed the complimentary notepad near the phone, scribbled down a quick summary, and then set the pad on the nightstand on Brad's side of the bed.

The last message was from the young receptionist for Dr. Morris, Rebecca's gynecologist.

"This is Dr. Morris's office calling with a message for Rebecca Lindsay. We have the results of your tests. If you'd care to give us a call between nine and five, Monday through Friday, we can discuss them with you. Thank you."

Rebecca looked at her watch. It was almost five-thirty—too late to call, yet hope would not let her wait. She dialed knowing she was unlikely to get an answer. It rang twice before she heard the click at the other end.

"Yes?"

"Oh, hello! Is this Dr. Morris's office?"

"Yes. This is Dr. Morris."

"Oh, Dr. Morris! I didn't expect to find anyone there! I just got the message from your office and thought I'd take a chance. Your receptionist said you had the results of my tests."

"Oh, yes," Morris said. "Can you hold for a moment while I get them?" Rebecca could hear him set down the receiver, walk across the room, walk back, and pick up the phone again. "Yes, here it is, Mrs. Lindsay. We got the tests back from the lab today and, to make a long story short, there still is no reason why you can't conceive—at least, no medical reason. I know you were hoping to find something concrete that we could treat, but I'm afraid it isn't going to be that simple. On the other hand, as I've told you before, the best medicine may be to just relax and quit worrying about it. If it's going to happen, it will, when the good Lord gets good and ready for it to happen. In the meantime, I'd like to see you in my office when you get back so we can discuss this further. I know this isn't very helpful, but my advice is to not let the whole thing get you down. Believe me, the best thing for you and your husband is to pace yourselves and let nature take its course."

Rebecca wasn't sure what to think. "Thank you, Doctor," she said as she hung up the phone. She lay back on the bed with her hands behind her head. She felt troubled and lonely. Her mind felt full, as though it would burst if just one more thing, one more bothersome thing, tried to intrude on her life. She could feel the tears as they rolled freely down her cheeks and onto the bed. She tried to pray, but there didn't seem to be words to express what she felt. She wondered if there really was a God who could hear her.

Brad ambled along the quiet streets of the little town with his hands in his pockets. He had cooled off some, but now he needed a measured amount of anger he could mislabel as "righteous indignation" to justify what he was thinking.

When he left the hotel, he didn't know what he was going to do or where he was going to go. He stormed out without taking his car keys, so unless he wanted to risk another confrontation with Rebecca or, worse, risk losing the drama and the effect of the moment by returning too soon, he was afoot.

He walked for about a half-hour before he found himself in the same café where he and Rebecca had dinner two nights before. He tried to tell himself that the reason was no more degenerate than the satisfaction of the hunger pangs that assaulted his stomach. Yet he was hardly through the door before he had found himself scanning the room for the waitress who flirted with him as he and Rebecca ordered dinner.

It hadn't taken long to find her. She was the only one working the floor on this particularly slow night.

"Hi," he said as he sat down at the bar.

"Hi, yourself," she answered with a coy look that enticed. "What can I get you?"

Brad savored the passion he felt when she asked it, suppressing the little voice in his head that warned him he was crossing a line.

He ordered. When she brought him his plate of food, she lingered, making small talk and flashing that big, beautiful smile.

Dana. Her name was Dana. Her perfume served its purpose well, filling his mind with a lust for more.

"Where's your wife?" she asked.

"Somewhere else," he answered dryly, hoping she hadn't noticed his face turn slightly red. She only smiled.

When he paid his tab a couple of hours later, she handed him back his change.

"What do you do for excitement around here?" he asked before he had time to consider the consequences.

"I usually get off around nine," she said. "I'll probably go to the casino for a little while." She cocked her head and smiled. "Maybe I'll see you there?"

Now as he walked along the street, his mind fought and argued with itself. So what if he went to the casino? What was wrong with a little harmless flirting? She might not even be there. But something tugged at his heart. He fought it.

He rubbed his eyes with the flat of his hands. Things weren't working out the way he'd planned. This whole trip seemed like a waste. It wasn't just the property or Rebecca's stubborn resistance to simple logic that bothered him. It was the whole business with Rebecca's childish propensity toward religion that aggravated him most. She always had leaned toward religious things. There were religious symbols in the house, little crystal angels and cutsie little sayings in delicate frames that hung on the wall. And she was always trying to find some hidden meaning in everyday things, like why it was raining and how maybe it was a sign that they should stay home that day and enjoy a fire. Or how maybe she couldn't get pregnant because of a dusty old curse.

Brad's face darkened. He hadn't minded the religious knickknacks, or the sayings on the walls, or even the search for meaning in little circumstances. But religion was not for him.

It was only a few minutes later that he found himself standing at the glittering entrance to the casino. He entered with a nod to the doorman and then stood in the vast foyer, wondering where he should go from there. The bar was directly in front of him. He went to it.

"Can I get you something?" the muscular bartender asked as he poured a beer and pushed it across the bar to the cocktail waitress, who carried it off to one of the tables next to the band.

"G and T with a twist."

"Gin and tonic with a twist of lime. Anything else?"

"Nope," Brad said as he dug into his pocket for his wallet.

"Three bucks," the bartender said, setting the glass in front of Brad.

Brad slapped four one-dollar bills on the counter. As he sipped his drink, he noticed his hands were shaking. He tried to convince himself he was only there to look around and have a little fun.

"Hey!" he heard from across the room. Dana was already halfway across the floor before he could respond.

"Hi, yourself," he said, his heart racing. She smiled as she sat down next to him. "What are you drinking?"

"Beer," she said to the bartender.

"So! What are your plans for tonight?" she asked with a coy grin.

Brad shrugged, but the question went straight to his heart. "Oh, just to have a good time." He hoped she hadn't noticed the slight quiver in his voice.

"Me too," she said with a smile. She threw down a swig from her bottle. "Why don't you ask me to dance?"

Brad smiled weakly as he slid off the barstool and took her hand. They made their way through the crowd to the dance floor and the mellow tune the band was playing. She turned and put her arms around his neck and held him close as they swayed to the music. Brad wished there was a graceful way to dry his sweating palms.

When the song was over, the music stopped and the band took a break, but Dana lingered, holding Brad close as they stood in the middle of the dance floor.

Brad had a thought. What if Rebecca came looking for him? He glanced nervously around the room. His eyes found the doorway. He couldn't look away.

He put his hands on the young girl's waist and pushed her gently away. "C'mon. Let's go sit down," he said.

He turned to walk away, but she let her hand slip down his arm to his hand. She locked fingers with him as he led her to a booth near the corner of the room. He let her slide in first.

He was about to follow her into the booth, but something held him back. Something struck him—a mood, a fear—something, but he suddenly knew he had to leave. This wasn't right—and it wasn't what he wanted. Or if it was, he needed the security of better planning.

"Listen," he began. "I —"

He looked down at the floor, then at his watch. It was almost ten. He remembered that Sam Michaels was to meet them at the room at six. He wondered if Rebecca had met with him or not. Either way, she was probably back at the room by now and wondering where he was.

"I can't," he said, and then turned and walked away.

CHAPTER TWENTY-FOUR

REBECCA WAS ABOUT to doze off again as she lay on the hotel room bed, when a knock on the door brought her to her feet.

"Brad?" she asked expectantly as she opened the door.

"'Fraid not," Sam Michaels said through a broad smile.

"Oh, hi," Rebecca said without letting her disappointment show. She looked at her watch. "Is it six already?"

"Yep. You folks about ready?"

"Um, why don't you come in?" Rebecca said as she stepped out of the doorway and back into the room.

Sam stepped inside. "I take it your husband isn't here?"

"Um, no—no, he's not. I…I had hoped he'd be back by now, but —"

"I could come back later."

Rebecca was about to say yes, but she suddenly felt defiant. Brad had gone off without telling her anything. He'd already been gone for a couple of hours and now he was late. For all she knew, he'd never show up for the meeting with Sam Michaels.

"No, that won't be necessary. I'll leave a note and tell him where we are. He can join us when he gets back." *If he gets back*. "Where did you say we were going?"

"The little café next to the market, if that's OK with you. They have pretty good food there and we can talk."

Rebecca nodded as she finished the note and left it on the table. "I'm ready. Let's go."

"Do you have the diary? I'd like to look at it, if you don't mind."

"I'll get it." Rebecca grabbed the diary from the table and the two of them headed for the parking lot.

"We can take my car," Rebecca said.

Rebecca drove out of the parking lot and past the casino into town. Sam tried to make small talk, apologizing for the misunderstanding at the old house earlier. He asked harmless questions about where she lived, how she liked it, and how the trip had been. But her mind was not on small talk, and her answers were brief. She forced herself to look straight ahead when she saw Brad walking along the street away from the café, but as they passed him she couldn't help the quick glance to see if he noticed her. If he did, he gave no sign.

Rebecca pulled headfirst into a parking place at the curb in front of the café. She met Sam at the front of the car and they walked together into the cafe. Rebecca remembered the young waitress who had seated them with a pang of jealousy.

"So," said Sam as he gave his menu a cursory once over, "tell me about yourself."

"Oh, not much to tell, really. Brad and I have been married for five years, and we're very happy. We hope to have a family one of these days."

"Mmm," Sam nodded. "Sounds great."

"Have you always lived here?" Rebecca asked.

"All my life. I was born here. Except for a few years in college, I've never been anywhere else."

The waitress interrupted their conversation. "What can I get you?" she asked.

Sam motioned for Rebecca to go first. When she had ordered, Sam said, "Same as yesterday."

The waitress scribbled the order on her pad. "Thanks," she said as she turned to leave, but Rebecca noticed her odd smile. She wondered what it meant.

"Small-town boy, huh?" Rebecca said to Sam when they were alone again.

Sam chuckled. "I suppose so."

Rebecca studied his eyes. They were kind and good and she felt at ease with him. "So where did you go to college?"

"Well," he said, "I went to Oregon State for three years, but I managed to get a couple of scholarships in my fourth year and a grant through a special program with the Bureau of Indian Affairs, so I finished up my last year in two at Harvard."

"A Harvard man, eh?"

Sam chuckled. "Yeah. Anyway, my goals were in business, but my passion has always been history. So I ended up with a double major in business and American history. I came back here, and now I'm working with Indian Affairs. We're trying to piece together some of the history of the local tribes."

"Very impressive."

Sam smiled. "Thank you. It's a living of sorts—and a passion. I enjoy it."

Rebecca nodded. "So tell me, what motivates you to work on old houses and protect old lady's interests when you're not digging up the past?"

Sam turned serious. "That's a very long story, and believe it or not, it has a great deal to do with my job, though not officially, but the two overlap." Sam motioned toward the diary on the table next to Rebecca. "May I see it, please?"

Rebecca handed it to him.

"I've known your family, or of them, for as long as I can remember," Sam said as he gestured with the diary that he held between his thick, dark fingers. "My father worked for your grandfather as a ranch hand. When your grandfather left, my father stayed on to look after the place. He did it for many years, long before I was born. I can remember when I was very young, I used to go with him once a week to feed some of the stock that we kept there. Your aunt was generous enough to let him run a few head of cattle on the place.

"My father sort of took it upon himself to see that the house was kept up and the fences didn't go to pot. I was away at college when he died.

When I got back a couple of years later, I went out to the place just to see it again. It was a mess. I got your aunt's name from the county tax records and wrote her a letter. She wrote back and asked me if I would take care of things for her." Sam lowered his head. "We became good friends over the years."

Rebecca looked down. "Her funeral is tomorrow morning at ten."

Sam nodded. "I'll be there."

"How long have you been doing it—taking care of the place, I mean?"

"Six years," he said as he looked up.

"But why? Why would you take on such a task? It must have taken a great deal of time."

"Well, I like to work with my hands. Besides, I owed it."

Rebecca looked puzzled. "You mentioned that before."

"It's hard to explain, but I was raised with a fierce sense of loyalty. My father was loyal, and he instilled that in me. I don't know, maybe it was partly a nostalgia thing—an attempt to recapture what I had as a kid when my dad would take me to the old place. Whatever it is, it's something that's a part of me. It's difficult to explain, but it all started here." Sam opened the diary. "Perhaps it can explain better than I can."

Sam thumbed through it as if he knew for what he was looking. "Eighteen-fifty..., one, two, three, here we are: 1854."

He thumbed through a few more pages. "Ah," he said softly. "I was sure it would be here." He handed the open diary to Rebecca.

May 29, 1854

Dear Diary,

It has been a wonderful three weeks. John has been to see me every week, and I find that I treasure the few stolen moments that we have when I can be near him. He was here this very morning with news that he had rescued an Indian from certain death. It seems that there had been a skirmish between two of the warring tribes, and one of the young men from the smaller tribe was injured. Silas McCoy says he is from the tribe that travels through the valley in the spring and fall as they traverse between

> summer mountains and winter sea. John found him two days ago and he says that they know very little about the savage, except that he was in a fierce battle, which he communicated through the use of hand gestures and drawings upon the ground, and his name, which is Monteneha. John says that the boys have taken to calling him "Monty," owing to the difficulty that they were having with the strangeness of his name. Mr. Elam says that it is a mark of honor to the savages to have a "white" name, and those bestowed with such an honor wear it with pride.

Rebecca looked up from the diary and gave Sam a puzzled look.

"That 'savage' was my great-great-grandfather," Sam said with pride. "And that's why the diary is so important to me, both as a historian and as a source of personal discovery. I believe it probably has more to say about him and I'm dying of curiosity to know. For me, this is like being in a candy store with a blank check!"

Rebecca looked down at the diary and then back to Sam. His enthusiasm was infectious, and her hunger for knowledge had been stirred, if ever so slightly. "It seems a long way to stretch loyalty."

Sam chuckled. "I suppose so. But my father and his father before him, all the way back to Monteneha, were men of honor. The Jakes family took in a wounded Indian at a time when most whites would have left him to die…or worse. Monteneha never forgot that."

"And so your family has been working off the debt ever since."

Sam shook his head. "Not exactly. It's more than a debt. It's not as cold or hard as all that. A few months later there was a fight. Monteneha killed a white man and disappeared for many years. He didn't come back until John Jakes died in 1896. He showed up for the funeral. By then, most of the people who would remember or care about what had happened had died. He lived the last three years of his life in a little shack a few miles downstream from your property. In fact, I still own the land. The shack is gone, but I found a few rotten logs that I'm sure were part of the walls."

"Who was it he was supposed to have killed?" Rebecca asked.

"Ah!" said Sam, "I was getting to that. Do you remember what I told you this morning about the Doucets?"

Rebecca nodded.

"Well, as I said, the Doucets have been here a long time, since almost exactly the same time my great-great-grandfather made friends with the Jakes. There was a mother and father and three siblings, two brothers and a sister."

"Kyra?"

"I see you've been doing some reading," Sam said with a smile. "Yes, Kyra and her two brothers, Veré and Yves." Sam's eyes darkened as he leaned forward. "Do you remember what I said about all of this involving both our families?"

"Of course."

"Good. Because I think this will interest you. Veré and his brother tried to rape Katherine Walker. They attacked her, and if it wasn't for a horse that kicked Yves to death, they probably would have succeeded, and maybe worse. Veré ran off, but Monteneha was afraid he would come back. He felt a great sense of loyalty. He tracked Veré down and killed him. If you can believe the way it's been handed down, he was only defending himself, but he was sure he'd never get a fair shake in a white man's court, which was probably true. There was an Indian uprising about that time and an all-out effort by some to wipe out the Indians in the area. At any rate, that's the story that has been handed down from generation to generation in my family. But for us, the loyalty goes far beyond a mere payment of a debt. They felt a great responsibility had been placed on them by powers much greater than themselves."

"The great spirit," Rebecca said with skepticism.

"Well, yes, probably at first."

Rebecca began running her fingers through scattered grains of salt that had spilled onto the table. "Tell me something," she said. "Do you believe in curses?"

Sam drew a deep breath. "I'm not sure how to answer that. I suppose a Harvard man should say 'No way,' but the Christian in me says yes. In a way, we're all under a curse."

"You're a Christian?"

"Does that surprise you?"

"Well, I —"

Sam's eyes twinkled. "You never saw a Christianized Indian before?"

Rebecca felt her face flush. "Sorry. I didn't mean —"

Sam smiled warmly and chuckled. "I'm teasing you a little. Don't pay me any mind." Then he continued. "I remember when we were kids. Sara Doucet—she was the one driving the tow truck, remember? She used to talk about the curse and once she let something slip. I don't even know why I remember it, it happened so long ago, but I do. She was about ten, I think. A bunch of the boys, including me, were playing a game of basketball during the lunch recess. We couldn't have been more than twelve or thirteen. Anyway, she came up and wanted to play too. She stood off to the side for a while, just watching. But then one of the guys knocked the ball out of bounds and it went straight to her. She caught it and held onto it. When the guy who knocked it out went to get it from her, she wouldn't let go. Pretty soon we all were standing around her, arguing for her to give us back that stupid ball. But she dug her heels in and wouldn't turn loose of it; and no amount of pleading or taunting would convince her. It didn't take long for the arguing to turn into a shouting match, with us calling names and threatening and her spouting her little diatribes and telling us how she could summon powers if she wanted to. It was really weird. And, of course, it only gave us more ammunition to taunt her.

"But then she did something that seemed strange at the time, still does for that matter. She dropped the ball and let it roll away from her as if it never really mattered in the first place. She looked around at us and muttered something that I'm sure was not English. And then she said, 'So long as the waters course!'"

Sam hesitated, as if waiting for the significance of what he had just said to sink in.

"I didn't know for a long time what it meant. I didn't even think about it for years after. But a few years ago when I met Billie and we started to talk, she told me about her family. Then I remembered Sara's little outburst and got to thinking. It occurred to me that Sara was probably just repeating what she had heard at home."

"How creepy," Rebecca said.

Sam chuckled. "I suppose so."

Rebecca looked down. She was curious about something but afraid to broach the subject. "Can I ask you something?"

"Sure."

"This morning you said that you and Sara 'had something.' What did you mean?"

Sam looked into his coffee cup. "We shared a summer, once."

Rebecca reached across the table and touched Sam's hand.

Sam smiled. "We were young—and it was a long time ago. We just grew into two very different people."

"Did you love her?"

Sam shrugged. "If I did, it's long forgotten."

Rebecca could see pain behind his smile.

Sam was eager to change the subject. "You may recall that I told you this morning that your aunt and I had a common bond."

"Yes, I remember."

"We found that we had many things in common, but none was more compelling, more meaningful, than the bond we shared with the Jewish Carpenter. In fact, my father and his father before him were Christians, due largely to the witness of the Jakes family. Monteneha accepted Christ on the reservation many years after he left here. But part of my heritage is the story that has been handed down for generations: that the seeds of faith were planted by the man who saved his life, John Jakes."

Rebecca smiled. "You still didn't answer my question. Do you believe in curses?"

"I was getting to that." Sam paused and smiled. "I suppose I was dodging it a bit, but the truth is, I'd have to say yes…and no. The Bible does talk of curses. There is a passage in the Bible that says, 'We wrestle not against flesh and blood, but against principalities; against powers; against spiritual wickedness in high places —'"

Rebecca recoiled at the sound of the very words that had caused so much pain only a few hours before as she'd read them in her hotel room Bible. She didn't understand them, but they seemed to offer nothing but hopelessness.

"There are other passages," Sam continued, "in which God promises curses upon people and nations if they don't live according to His standards. So, yes, I believe in curses. But I don't believe that a person can curse another person—or a family—" he looked up and paused to make a point, "to cause them trouble."

"So you don't believe in the curse?"

Sam leaned back as he thought for a moment. "I know that there are forces that work against us, and I believe they have a great deal of power. But frankly, I don't believe they have any power over those who trust in the One who created all things. There's another verse in the Old Testament that says, 'Like a fluttering sparrow or a darting swallow, an undeserved curse does not come to rest.'"

Sam noticed Rebecca's pained expression. "Forgive me for prying, but this seems to hit close to home for you."

Rebecca's eyes glistened with tears. "You have no idea," she said.

Sam squeezed her hand. "Why don't you tell me about it?"

Rebecca trembled. The pain and fears of the last few days, coupled with the anxieties of her struggle for motherhood, seemed to rush to the surface, and she felt as if she would burst if she didn't tell someone. Her mind told her one thing, her heart told her another. Yet at the instant she gave in to her heart and told Sam, she was overcome with comforting relief. She shared with Sam about her struggle to conceive. She told him about the countless and fruitless trips to the doctor. She told him about Aunt Billie and Pastor Romberg. She admitted to him her rejection of Christianity and the terrible burden of guilt that came with it. She opened up to him about Brad and his resistance to anything spiritual. She told him about the fight they'd had.

Sam just listened.

By the time she had finished, Rebecca was sobbing quietly. "I'm sorry. I feel like I haven't done anything but cry for two weeks."

Sam smiled. "I understand."

Rebecca met his eyes. They were gentle and caring. "I suppose all of this stuff about curses sounds pretty silly. I know it does to me when I hear myself say it."

"Not at all," Sam reassured. "I knew about the curse, of course. I can remember hearing about it as a boy. And your aunt and I discussed it in our letters to one another. I know she didn't believe it. And if anyone had reason to believe the Doucet curse had power, it was your aunt."

Sam reached for his cup of coffee and stared into it for a moment as he selected his words. "I don't know, nor do I pretend to know, how everything works in the spiritual world, but I do know that God, and I mean an all-powerful God, is in control of the universe, and that nothing can harm those who love Him. There's a verse that says, 'All things work together for good for those that love Him and are called according to His purpose.' I don't know how everything fits together in this. I can't tell you why you can't have children. Or why your aunt never had them or why any other woman in your family with the name of Jakes since Kyra Doucet uttered her vile words has never produced a living child. I know many in your family believed it was the curse. It is possible that there are reasonable explanations for all of the Jakes women not conceiving.

"I know old George, Billie's father, believed the curse was real. That's why the Jakes family moved back to the old Walker homestead. Old George believed that the land held the key, and that if the curse was to be broken, the family had to have control of the land. But after many years and no kids, the family began to pressure old George to leave the valley. When he left, he swore that he or his kin would be back some day to break the curse once and for all. I don't know if he thought of it as a prophecy, but the Doucets took it that way. I think that's why Sara doesn't want you to have the property. She's afraid you'll find a way to break the curse.

"As I said, I can't explain why the Jakes women can't conceive—why you can't conceive—but I know that nothing happens without God's knowledge. He can overcome anything."

Rebecca struggled to understand—to really understand—what it was that the sovereign Creator of the universe wanted for her. "But why would he allow me to go through something like this?"

"I don't know," Sam said to his cup of coffee. He looked up and met her eyes. "Maybe He wants you to trust Him."

Rebecca felt the sting of his words. She hadn't trusted God and she knew it. She had known it for a long time, but she always made excuses. Brad didn't like to go to church. There wasn't time in their busy schedules. She liked to sleep late on Sundays. Religious people were fanatics. She could worship any way she wanted.

She knew they were excuses, but she always felt there was plenty of time and that she could, and would, deal with it later. But as she sat with her hands folded on the table, she could feel the weight of condemnation for all her excuses, and she knew that her later was now.

Sam waited patiently for Rebecca to respond to what he was convinced was the gentle but firm prodding of God's Spirit in her heart. He saw the pain in her eyes as his words challenged her. She lingered for a moment and then looked down.

"I don't know how," she said.

"What did your aunt tell you?"

Rebecca shrugged. "She always said, 'Give it all to Jesus.'"

Sam nodded his approval. "Then why don't you do that?"

Rebecca nodded through her tears. Sam reached across the table and held her hand. "Would you like me to lead you?"

Rebecca suddenly knew what she should do. The words were not clear, but she knew she could not measure up to a holy God. She knew she was a sinner, and she knew from her Sunday school days during her visits to Aunt Billie's that Jesus had died for her. She knew she needed Him.

She shook her head. "No," she said softly.

Instead, Rebecca bowed her head and offered up her own prayer of repentance in whispered silence, her lips forming the words as she prayed. Tears streamed down her cheeks and fell onto the table.

The Centurion stood on the rooftop above Rebecca, sword in hand, vigilant, ready. The sounds of laughter, applause, and singing reverberated all around him, filling his heart with rejoicing even as he held his ground. Below in the restaurant, the Lamb placed His seal on the girl's forehead as thunderous applause rose to a fevered pitch in the heavens. The Centurion raised his sword in the air in triumph.

What a stroke of luck! Frank Downs thought as he climbed out of his dirty four-wheel-drive vehicle and wheezed toward the entrance to the casino. He was driving by on his way home, wondering how he was going to manage to keep his promise to Gil, when he saw the young man who was causing him so much grief leaving the casino—by himself!

Frank lumbered toward Brad as Brad walked through the parking lot in the direction of the hotel. It was late and Frank wondered where "the little woman" was. It was too good to be true that he could catch this guy alone.

"Hey! Wait up!" Frank called out.

Brad looked up. Frank duck-waddled the last few yards, wheezing and gasping for air when he finally caught up to him. "How ya doin'?" he panted.

"Fine," Brad said. "What can I do for you?"

"Well," Frank said, still trying to catch his breath, "I'm still hoping I can do something for you."

"Yeah?"

"Yes, indeed! I've relayed your message to my client, and he still insists that he'd like to make you kids a deal. I was hoping we could talk it over, you know, man to man."

"The property doesn't belong to me," Brad said. "Maybe you'd better talk to my wife."

Frank Downs smiled on the inside. He was sure he detected a rift. Brad's uneasy answer told him there must have been a difference of opinion, maybe even a fight, between the two kids.

Brad turned to leave, but Downs held his arm. "I thought maybe you could convince her."

Brad clenched his jaw. "Not interested."

Frank heard it again, that little twinge of anger and resentment. It was all he could do to contain his glee. He shrugged, feigning indifference. "Well, if you're not interested in selling, I sure don't want to talk you into something you don't want."

Frank paused, hoping to hear it again.

Brad was growing annoyed with this wheezing walrus for picking at the scab that covered his wounded ego.

Frank continued. "I just thought we could sit down, one on one, and talk it over. After all, there's no harm in talking, is there? Of course, if you have to get permission from your wife —"

Frank paused, shrugging when Brad's hard eyes met his. He hoped he hadn't pushed too hard, but the risk seemed worth it. The girl wouldn't listen, and he was sure she never would. Maybe, if he stirred the pot a little by appealing to this guy's male pride, he could convince him to push a little harder at home.

Frank had his answer a heartbeat later as Brad pulled his sleeve from Frank's grasp. "Good night, Mr. Downs," he said, and then turned and walked away.

Frank watched him go for a moment and then, dejected and disappointed, walked back to his car. Gil wouldn't like this, and he really didn't want to tell him. But he'd have to. He wondered what Gil would say, and he tried not to think about what he might do.

An hour after Rebecca prayed, she said goodbye to Sam at the door to her hotel room and went inside. She was tired, but she felt new and clean. She readied herself for bed and then crawled between the sheets with the covers pulled up around her knees as she sat in the lamp's dim light with the diary in her hands. She couldn't sleep, but it was not the troubled insomnia that had plagued her for so long. She was happy and excited, filled with a joy she could not yet understand or explain. She only knew she felt at peace.

The funeral was to be the next morning at ten. Tired as she was, her mind would not rest. There was so much to know. She set the diary in her lap and reached into the nightstand drawer for the Gideon Bible. Sam had told her she should begin a habit of regular Bible reading, and she should begin in the book of John. She fumbled with the pages, searching unfamiliar territory for the first time. When she found it, she read the first chapter as Sam had suggested, and then stopped. She didn't understand it all, but for the first time she felt comforted by the words, some of which she had heard before from her aunt. They seemed different to her now.

She put the Bible on the nightstand and opened the diary. She felt at peace, but she felt a longing too. She wanted to know about her heritage. She wanted to know about the curse. Yet she approached it with a new sense of confidence and courage. She didn't have all the answers. She felt as though in many ways she had more questions than before, yet she knew, somehow, God was in control and she only needed to trust Him.

She began to read. A few minutes later she looked toward the door when she heard the sound of someone outside. The door opened and Brad sulked in. He avoided eye contact as he went around the bed and started to unbutton his shirt.

Rebecca watched him. She no longer felt angry, and she realized she was seeing her husband in a way she had never seen him before. Somehow their differences, which had seemed so important before, seemed petty and unimportant now. She waited until he crawled into bed before she rolled over and propped her head up on her arm. She began stroking his chest with the tips of her fingers.

"I love you," she said.

Brad rolled over on his side, facing away from her. "I know," he said.

Rebecca felt the sting of rejection. She pulled her hand away and sat up against the pillow behind her back. But she was not angry, and that surprised her a little. She felt sorrow and a little hurt, but she wasn't angry.

"Stephens called," she said in as non-threatening a tone as she knew how to muster. "The funeral is tomorrow at ten."

"Mmm," Brad grunted from under the sheets.

"Good night," she said softly and went back to her reading.

And as she read with a sense of wonder and awe, Rebecca Jakes Lindsay ran the tips of her fingers gently and reverently down the ancient pages Katherine Walker Jakes had held in her own hands more than a century before. She noticed every smudge of dirt, every blot of ink, and every stroke of the pen as she tried to understand the little girl, and then the woman, behind them. It was as if she could reach across the fences of time and space and touch the very same hand that once had held the diary, perhaps with a similar sense of wonder as its author contemplated those who one day would read her most intimate thoughts and feelings.

Rebecca intended to stop after an hour or so, but it was nearly dawn by the time she closed the diary, filled to overflowing with the warmth of kinship and common purpose—and the assurance God would take care of her.

Brad had long since fallen asleep, confident he'd done the right thing. He'd come very close to doing something he'd told himself he'd never do: cheat on his wife. As he patted himself on the back for what he perceived as a moral victory, he wondered what it would have been like. He wondered what the harm would have been if he had done it.

He remembered every detail of the evening as he savored the thought of her arms around him as they danced, and the look in her eyes as she smiled. She wanted him and he liked it. But it had been the right thing to walk away. He was confident the episode was over. But a seed had been planted—a door had been opened, if only a crack, and an invitation had been given. The significance of it was not lost on the unseen enemy that cowered just outside the boundary of divine protection encircling the young couple.

CHAPTER TWENTY-FIVE

"WELL?" ASKED GIL Doucet from behind his desk early the next morning.

Frank Downs towered over him on the opposite side of the desk as he stood with his hands in his pockets, wishing he could say anything but what he had to say. Of the two men, Frank was the more likely candidate to intimidate simply because he was so big. His paunch was much bigger than Gil's, and he stood a full two inches taller. But it was the man seated in the chair who did the bullying.

Frank tried not to think about the reason why. There was a girl. Although twenty years had passed, there was no getting around the facts. He had been a grown man and she had been a minor. He wasn't worried about the legal consequences; it was so long ago. But this was a small town. And Gil had pictures. How he had managed to get them was a mystery, but Frank had seen them, and they were genuine.

"No good," said a grim-faced Frank with a shake of his head.

Gil cursed under his breath and muttered something Frank did not understand, but the message was clear enough.

Frank felt his knees weaken as Gil's eyes met his. "Why not?" Gil asked.

Frank shrugged. "He wouldn't talk. I tried, Gil, but he wouldn't even talk about it!"

Gil shook his head. "Frank, Frank, Frank! What am I going to do with you?"

"It's not my fault, Gil. I can't sell something if they won't even listen to me." Frank's voice pleaded.

Gil slammed his fist down on the desktop. "I want that land, and I don't care how I get it!"

Frank sank back, wishing he were somewhere else—anywhere else. "I found out something, though," he said, hoping to redeem himself. He paused, waiting for Gil to give him permission to speak.

"Well?" Gil demanded.

"I ran into Howard at the casino last night. You know, he's the guy who works for the mortuary. He said that they'd be doing a funeral for the girl's aunt this morning." Frank said it with an air he hoped would convince Gil it *was* really important.

"So what?" Gil challenged.

Frank shrugged again. "I thought —"

"Don't do that, Frank," Gil interrupted. "You'll hurt yourself. You just let me do the thinking." Gil settled back in the chair. "Frank, I want you to use all your real estate knowledge and tell me: what would happen to the property if something were to happen to the young lady?"

Frank shrugged again. "I suppose it would go to her next of kin."

"And who would that be?"

"Her husband, I guess."

"And what if something happened to both of them?"

"Same thing—next of kin."

Gil leaned forward. "They don't have any kids, right?"

"No. No kids."

"Does she have any family?"

"I don't think so. She said her aunt willed her the property. She didn't mention any brothers or sisters, and I'm pretty sure she told me she didn't have any family."

"Find out," Gil ordered as though he were talking to his dog.

Frank raised his eyebrows. "I remember now. When we were looking for property on the computer, she told me she didn't have any family."

"You're sure?"

"Oh, I'm sure!" Frank said with confidence.

Gil sat back. "Good," he said almost to himself. "That'll work out just fine."

It was almost nine o'clock by the time Rebecca opened a reluctant eye to the new day. When she did, the first thing she saw was Brad, standing over the bed, tucking-in his shirt and buttoning his pants.

Brad had slept very little during the night. He'd nodded off as soon as his head hit the pillow, but he'd been asleep only a few minutes when he'd awakened with a start as though something prodded him to consciousness. He had tossed and turned, stewing in the juices of his resentment toward God and attempting to justify his temporary lapse in judgment.

That's all it was, he thought, *a temporary lapse in judgment. It never would have happened at all if Rebecca had not challenged my manhood with her unreasonable and petty demand for autonomy.*

And the Bible on the nightstand had not gone unnoticed when he came in either. She'd been reading it, it was plain to see, and he resented it. She knew he didn't like it, yet she persisted in pursuing this sudden fetish for religion.

It was well after dawn when he had decided to put his indignation on hold and be strong for his wife. He was still angry, but only the worst of all possible heels, he felt, would fight with his wife while she buried someone as close as Billie had been to her.

"Morning," he said with measured indifference.

Rebecca rolled to her side and smiled. "Morning," she said.

"You'd better get ready. The funeral is in an hour."

"All right," she said, swinging her feet to the floor. She stretched and yawned and then started toward the bathroom. She hesitated at the door. She was still exuberant from her experience the night before, and she felt as though her feet hardly touched the floor. She knew for the first time in her life what it was to have peace, and the only thing she wanted now was for Brad to have that same peace. It was a strange feeling, one to which she was not accustomed. An overriding sense of selflessness ruled where selfish fulfillment had been king the day before.

She felt something else too. It was as though something—or someone—was goading her to say something that only a few short hours before would have been unthinkable. She turned to Brad.

"I'm sorry about last night," she said softly.

Brad shrugged. "No big deal," he said with machismo.

Rebecca came up behind him and stroked his back. "I was wrong. Will you forgive me?"

Forgive? Brad turned to face her. That was a new word in her vocabulary and it threw him. For a brief moment, he forgot his empty bravado. He put his arms around her, as much through force of habit and the fact that she stood so close as a sign of affection. He started to answer, but as his eyes met hers, he noticed something. She looked different. He couldn't tell why exactly, but she was different somehow, and it disarmed him.

"Sure," he said, trying to sound in control.

Rebecca stood on her toes and kissed him. *That was different too.* There was a softness to her, a gentleness he couldn't describe.

"I'll be ready in a few minutes," she said, and then turned and went into the bathroom.

An hour later, Rebecca stood with her husband under a giant fir tree at the iron gates to the cemetery, waiting for the hearse as it made its way slowly through the entrance. Behind it, another black limousine followed. It stopped in front of them, and Garvey rolled down the window.

"Good morning," he smiled. "We'll be at the far end of the grounds this morning. Would you like to ride the rest of the way?"

Rebecca followed Garvey's gesture across the field of tombstones to a green canvas canopy and a few chairs only a few yards away. "We'll walk," she said.

Garvey nodded and the limo moved on.

The couple had started toward the temporary pavilion when someone called out to them from the street. They turned to see Sam Michaels sprinting across the street and up onto the curb.

"Good morning, Sam," Rebecca beamed.

Brad felt a twinge of jealousy.

"Good morning," Sam said. He took Rebecca's extended hand, shook it, and then offered his own to Brad.

"Morning," Brad said with the same indifference he'd been cultivating all morning.

"How are you this morning?" Sam asked Rebecca. "Did you sleep well?"

"Hardly at all," she said. "I stayed up all night reading!"

Her tone was not lost on Brad. She seemed almost happy about it. He had expected tears on this of all days, but so far there were none. He gave Sam a wary eye.

"Did you read what I told you?" Sam asked.

"Yes, and after that, I read the diary for hours. I couldn't put it down!"

"Did you finish it?"

"Almost. I have about twenty more pages, I think."

"What did you find out?"

"Oh, so much! I'll tell you about it later."

Brad felt very excluded as they reached the pavilion.

Rebecca was surprised by the number of floral arrangements that had been placed at strategic places around the pavilion and the grave. Garvey seated them on the front row, and then directed the four employees serving as pallbearers as they hefted the casket from the back of the hearse and onto the platform over the grave.

Rebecca fought back tears as she sat staring at the coffin. Soon the tears won and flowed freely down her cheeks. But there was a difference this morning. She was sad, but her sadness was tempered with joy. She felt the pain of loss, but it was not the same pain that had put its stranglehold on her life for the past week or the past five years or her whole life for that matter. There was loss, but there was comfort and contentment, something for which she had longed for so long. She no longer felt hopeless, that life was cruel and heartless, or that she had been robbed and cheated. Her new faith gave her comfort, and she felt—dare she even think it?—like celebrating.

The minister, a bespectacled, frail-looking man Garvey engaged when a family had no church or minister of their own, stepped forward and offered a few brief, inadequate words and a quick prayer before shaking Rebecca's hand and hurrying off toward the exit.

Even Brad noticed how wooden the man's words were, and he expected Rebecca to break down or perhaps scold Garvey for the poor choice of spiritual leadership. Instead, she stood, took a single rose from one of the arrangements, and placed it reverently on the casket. She knelt down and bowed her head as Brad stood uncomfortably, unsure what to do. Sam joined her, knelt down next to her, and began to pray.

Brad felt his cheeks flush, partly from anger, and partly from the embarrassment of not knowing what to do with his hands as he watched his wife and this stranger pray quietly. But the anger won as it occurred to him he had been surrounded, it seemed, by religious people ever since Billie had died. He felt as if he no longer controlled his own life or circumstances, and he feared he was losing what little control he ever had had over his wife.

A few moments later, Rebecca and Sam stood as the mortuary employees began moving flowers to one side and preparing to lower the casket into the ground. Garvey came up to them.

"Would you like to take some of these?" he said, waving his hand toward the flowers. "You may want to read some of the cards as well."

"Where did they all come from?" Rebecca asked.

"They were all sent," Garvey said with a shrug.

Rebecca tiptoed over the moist grass, avoiding the flat grave markers, and took a card from one of the delicate bouquets. It was from Helen. She took another card and read the note. It was from Alva. She went around to each one and read the cards, putting them in her purse, and smelling the flowers. They were all from Billie's church friends, as well as a couple from Billie's brothers who, as the notes explained, could not make it to the service in California or to Oregon for the burial because of their own poor health.

She took another rose from one of the bouquets and held it between trembling fingers. "This is all I need," she said to Garvey.

"Fine," he smiled. "Would you like me to see that the rest are dispersed? We usually take them to some of the rest homes and hospitals. Would that be acceptable?"

Rebecca smiled. It was so like Billie to bring a little joy into the lives of those around her. It seemed fitting that she could do something to brighten a day for some stranger, even in her death. "Of course," she said.

Garvey turned back to the business at hand, motioning to his employees and giving whispered, but confident, orders as they prepared to lower the casket into the ground. Soon they all were standing, arms folded, waiting for the trio to leave before embarking on the unceremonious climax to what for them was routine.

But Rebecca was not ready to leave. "There's something I want to do first," was her answer to Brad's curt question about whether she was ready to go. She tiptoed around grave markers and knelt down next to Billie's grave again, but this time she was not praying. She ran her fingers over the marker next to Billie's casket. Brad and Sam joined her.

"It's his," she said softly.

"Whose?" Brad asked as he cocked his head to read the headstone:

George Jakes

1880-1947

Rebecca stood slowly. "That's my grandpa," she said.

"Humph," Brad said.

"You might want to look there," Sam said, motioning toward a marble shrine a few feet farther down in the same row. Rebecca went to it.

It was a high monument, four feet tall or more, with ornately carved marble vines twining around a weathered spire and capped with a simple cross. There were two names side-by-side, husband and wife. Rebecca felt a chill as she read the inscription: "Katherine Jakes, 1835-1917."

Sam stood beside her. "The author of the diary," he said, more from reverence than a need to pass on information.

Rebecca nodded. "And her husband," she said, pointing. "John Jakes, 1833-1896."

Below the two names was a simple inscription carved into the marble's smooth surface. But the words seemed to have a power that only the day before Rebecca would have read with just passing interest and would have missed the weight of their significance. It said simply:

Rejoicing with the Redeemed

She knelt in front of it on the cool grass.

"They must have been remarkable people," said Sam.

Brad stood to one side. "Yeah. You'd have to be tough to be a pioneer—leave your home and all that—to come out here and start over."

Sam and Rebecca were silent, but they were not ignoring him. After a moment, Sam said softly, "They were more remarkable than that."

Brad's face flushed again at a sudden sense of odd-man-out and the accompanying feeling of jealousy.

Rebecca stood and began walking slowly along the row of headstones. Five flat stones in a row marked the children of John and Katherine Jakes. Closest to the first monument was the one for John, an *infant son*. The next four were for sons and daughters: the first George and his wife and Charles and his wife. There were the two daughters, Mary and Effie. The only indication the two girls had been married was their last names were not "Jakes." Both tombstones announced, after a brief scripture, that the two daughters were childless.

"These all their kids?" Brad asked.

"Yes," Rebecca almost whispered.

"Look over here," Sam said after a moment. He led her to the opposite side of Billie's grave and around the funeral attendants who were still waiting.

"These," he said, pointing along the row, "were George Senior's children. George, your grandfather, and his two sisters, Ruth and Rebecca Jakes. Notice the names? They never married."

"So they never had children," said Rebecca.

"Right," said Sam. "Here's something you might find interesting." He led her to the next row at the foot of Billie's grave. "Two of your aunt's siblings. James, who died about twenty years ago —"

"I remember him," Rebecca interrupted. "He came to visit when I was just a kid."

Sam nodded. "And this one," he pointed. The marker read: "Katherine Johnson." "That's Katie. She died in childbirth."

Rebecca stood. "I didn't even know Billie had a sister." She turned to Sam. "How did you know?"

"Your aunt told me. She told me a lot over the years."

Rebecca didn't know whether to feel jealous that Billie had shared so much with a stranger, things she never had shared with her, or to marvel at the man who seemed to possess a genuine and heartfelt interest in her family. Already he had come, in so brief a time, to be a source of comfort and assurance to her.

Rebecca knelt at Katie's headstone. The words that followed the name and date were weatherworn and barely legible. She squinted to read them, but the only thing she could make out were the words Infant Son.

"How sad," she said.

"And a little creepy," said Brad.

"They were buried together," said Sam, "baby and mother."

Rebecca reached out to touch the marker, running her fingers reverently over the marble. It seemed so sad, a mother and child lying in the cold ground. She wiped away a tear.

Brad grew restless. All this talk of women who couldn't or didn't have children or hadn't born a living child—he knew where it was headed and he didn't like it. It only served to fuel this silly notion of a curse, and the worst part about that was it pulled Rebecca in the direction of religion. He began to dislike Sam Michaels. "You about ready to go?" he asked as Rebecca stood.

"I suppose so," she replied. She took his arm as they walked slowly toward the front entrance, stopping every so often to read a marker. Sam followed.

"That was a pretty lame service," said Brad.

Rebecca smiled. "I suppose. The words didn't really say much about her life, did they?"

"Maybe we should say something to Garvey," Brad said, trying to regain a sense of control.

"It doesn't matter," she said softly. "Billie is safe. Nothing can change that or take it away."

Brad was silent.

As they walked along the rows of headstones toward the exit, there were other names Rebecca recognized. She stopped at a marker close to the fence that surrounded the park:

Silas McCoy

1815-1862

"He's mentioned in the diary," Rebecca said to Sam.

A little farther on, another name stood out from the others. "Look here," she said. "This one is mentioned several times."

"Mmm," Sam nodded. "He opened the first trading post here. He also served as the town doctor for the first couple of years of the settlement."

"How do you know that?"

Sam smiled. "I'm an historian, remember?"

Rebecca stooped down to read, "'Ben Elam, 1806-1867. Repented late, made up for it.'"

Rebecca smiled. "How odd," she said, more to herself than to Sam.

Sam shrugged. "Some of them may sound odd to us. I'm sure they were quite meaningful to the people who loved them."

"Mmm," said Rebecca. She stood and slipped her arm through Brad's as they made their way to the front gate. Brad stiffened.

Out in the street, a dirty white pickup truck pulled up to the curb and stopped. The door opened and Gil Doucet climbed down from the high cab, looked around for a moment, and then spotted the trio as they neared the entrance. He ran his fingers around his belt as he started toward them.

"Morning, Gil," Sam said.

"Morning, Sam," Gil said with the same air of distrust. He turned to Rebecca. "Morning to you."

Rebecca nodded politely.

"My name's Gil, ma'am, Gil Doucet," he said without offering his hand.

"Sorry about your loss," he added as an afterthought.

"Thank you," she said.

"What can we do for you, Mr. Doucet?" Brad asked.

"I'll get right to it, ma'am," he said to Rebecca. "I'd like to buy your property up on Walker Creek."

Rebecca remembered what Sam had said about the Doucets. "How do you know about it?" she asked.

"Small town, ma'am. It don't take long for things to get around. Anyhow, I'm prepared to make you a fair offer."

"The land isn't for sale," Rebecca said politely but firmly.

"Yeah, that's what I heard," said Gil, "but I'm willing to make you a good offer."

"The lady's just been to a funeral, Gil," Sam said. "Why don't you pick a better time?"

Gil gave him a hard stare and then turned to Rebecca. "I know it ain't a good time, but business is business, and I got a deal that's too good to pass up. I figure you folks'll be on your way soon, now that your business is tended to." Gil nodded beyond them to the cemetery. "And I didn't want to miss the chance to have my say."

"I've decided to keep the property, Mr. Doucet," Rebecca said. "And as I told Mr. Downs, I'm not interested in selling at any price."

Rebecca started to walk past Gil, but he sidestepped to block her path. It caught Brad off guard for a brief moment. Sam felt his chest swell with rising anger.

"I'd think about it real hard," Gil said. He smiled, but his eyes were hard. "I'd hate to see you do anything…that is, I'd hate to see you pass up an opportunity like this. That land ain't no good to you at all—just one big tax burden. It'll be more trouble than it's worth." His smile faded. "I can just about guarantee it."

Brad felt his anger rising at the veiled threat. He wanted to sell the land and he wanted Rebecca to listen, but his protective instincts won over. "That sounds a little too much like a threat, Mr. Doucet."

Gil shrugged. "I just think you should consider it, that's all."

"I have considered it," said Rebecca, "and I've decided not to sell. If I ever do, you'll be the first to know, Mr. Doucet, but I wouldn't count on it if I were you. That land has been in my family for a hundred and fifty years. It means a great deal to me, and I intend to keep it."

The determination in Gil's eyes, so evident before, disappeared. In its place was acquiescence, as if he'd resolved a conflict in his mind and made a decision. "Is that your last word then?"

"It is," Rebecca said.

The lines in Gil's forehead deepened. "All right then," he said. He took a step backward and turned to Sam. "Tell her how it is, Sam. You tell her." He turned and walked away.

The three of them watched until Gil was in his truck and headed back toward town.

"What nerve!" said Rebecca. "Who does he think he is?"

"What's going on?" Brad asked. "What was that all about?"

"Oh, he's just a pompous jerk!" said Rebecca. "Sam says he's the one who put Mr. Downs up to making us the offer yesterday. Some people just don't know when to quit!"

Sam looked at Rebecca and then at Brad. "I wouldn't take it lightly if I were you. He can be dangerous."

"Dangerous?" Rebecca asked.

Sam cocked his head. "I don't know what he might do, but Gil has a way of getting what he wants. He's got a lot of friends and a lot of power around here."

"Is that what he meant when he told you to tell us how it is?"

Sam nodded. "Probably."

"No one has that much power. What can he do?" asked Brad, forgetting he wanted to sell. "He can't make us sell if we don't want to."

"Maybe," Sam replied, "but you two should be careful while you're here."

"Careful? What do you mean, 'careful'? What's he going to do?"

Sam shrugged. "I don't know, but like I said, don't take it lightly."

"Marty? This is Gil. Say, listen, I need a favor. You still got any of that dynamite we used a few months back to clear stumps up above Deerlick? Yeah? How much? No, that oughta be enough. Never mind what I want it for. I just want it. Can I pick it up this afternoon? Yeah, thanks. And Marty? This is just between the two of us, OK?"

Gil set the receiver back on the cradle and stood for a moment in the middle of his kitchen, thinking. He didn't like the idea that Marty would know, but he needed the stuff, and Marty was the best one from whom to get it. He was pretty sure he could trust him, and it was better than going through the hassles of proper channels where records would be kept. But he wondered if the mortgage he held on Marty's bar would be enough. Especially afterward.

"What's with the dynamite?" Sara asked from the hallway entrance at the far side of their mobile home.

Gil whirled around, unaware that he was not alone. "Don't sneak up on me like that!"

"I didn't sneak up on you. And what are you so nervous about?"

Gil worked the muscles in his jaw. "Nothing."

Sara knew it was a lie. She sauntered across the room and sat down. "Since when can't you tell me what you're doing?"

"Who said I was doing anything?"

Sara threw her head back and laughed. "You never could lie to me! Even when we were kids, I always knew!"

Gil gritted his teeth. "The less you know the better."

"Are you planning something for our two friends?"

"What if I am?"

Sara shrugged. "Nothing," she said with a wicked smile. "Only he's kinda cute. It'd be a shame to mess up his hair."

Gil went to the refrigerator and grabbed a beer. Sara had flipped on the television. Gil leaned against the doorway as Sara surfed through a couple of channels before settling on a game show.

"Is that all you think about?" he asked.

"Aw, c'mon! I hardly ever watch it!"

"That ain't what I mean."

Sara grinned. "I think he's cute. What's wrong with that?"

Gil sipped his beer. "They won't sell."

Sara reached for the remote, turned off the set, and then stretched out on the sofa. "So what are you going to do about it?"

Gil took a long sip of his beer and gave a half-smile. "I'm going to mess up his hair."

Sara sat up. "What are you going to do?"

Gil shook his head. "Don't worry about it."

Sara smiled. "I thought you didn't believe in prophesies."

"Who said anything about prophesies?"

"Oh, right! You're just going to all this trouble for a little piece of land!"

"It ain't no 'little piece of land.' It's an important piece, and I've got to have it if we're going to keep eating as well as we have been."

"Sure."

Gil felt the jab. "What do you care as long as it gets done?"

"I suppose I don't. Only make sure it gets done."

Gil studied his beer and heaved a deep sigh. "What does it matter?" he said more to himself than to Sara.

Sara was off the sofa in an instant. "You *know* it matters!"

Gil smiled. It was his turn to jab. "What's the matter? Afraid your big brother won't fetch and carry for you like you want?"

"I don't know what you mean."

"Yes, you do. You want me to do the dirty work and get rid of any threat to your precious family honor."

Sara's eyes seared. "Doesn't it mean anything to you? Don't you care that it's finally happening?"

"No," Gil said weakly.

Sara took the beer from him, tossed back a swig, and then returned the bottle to his hand. "I think you do, big brother. I think you believe more than you'd like to admit. Ol' man Jakes said they'd be back. You know it as well as I do. He said they'd come back, and when they did, no one could make them leave. He said they'd find a way to break the curse!"

"All before you and I were even born," said Gil.

"Which makes it all the more disturbing. George Jakes was a tough old piece of gristle according to the stories, and even Grandpa was afraid of him. But he's long dead, and now so is his daughter—dead and buried this morning. No one even remembers. I'd bet those two don't know what's going on—not really. It makes me think that something is working against us."

Gil pushed off the doorway. "You and your spooks," he said in disgust.

Sara's eyes flashed. "Don't mock the power of the spirit world!" she demanded. "There is power, and we cannot ignore a whole lifetime of responsibility to those who came before us! If she is allowed to reclaim the land, you know we could lose everything!"

"How? What can she do?" Gil said. He tried to make his question sound rhetorical, but there was doubt and fear in his voice.

Sara smiled. "Nothing, if you carry out your little plan."

"I intend to," Gil said as he turned and went into the kitchen for another beer. "I need the land."

"Sure," said Sara. "Sure you do." She sat back again and flipped on the television.

"It's a shame," she said. "He's so good looking."

Something evil hovered over the blighted mobile home, pleased with what had just happened and savoring the possibilities. It had been a long time since it had wallowed in the sweet victories of murderous revenge. The prospect was pleasing. There had been some small victories: the departure of the wretched family, the barrenness of their women that had eventually driven them to leave, and the continued control of the mindless dupes who occupied the mobile home in the clearing by the S-bend in Walker Creek. But nothing for a long time had satisfied its fundamental craving for blood.

There was some cause for concern. An old enemy was back and caution would be advisable. He was strong and he had authority. Still, there was hope. A door had been opened, an invitation given. The man. The man was the key. Death was the goal, but in the event that death was not possible, chaos would serve almost as well. And there was nothing more chaotic than a wrecked home.

The evil spread itself over the mobile home and its occupants, engulfing it and them. It surrounded the home, filling every nook and corner, every little space between wood and steel, girder and plywood, molecule and molecule, atom and atom, time and eternity. It engulfed the two occupants as well, holding them and knowing them brain cell by brain cell, particle by particle—understanding them far better than they themselves knew or could even imagine. This was home by invitation and by rights, and the evil reigned supreme—at least for now.

But there was danger. The enemy was near, and only great caution and skill would prevent a disaster. The risk was worth it if it reaped a rich harvest of innocent blood.

CHAPTER TWENTY-SIX

"THANK YOU," REBECCA said to the operator who had just given her Helen Bradley's phone number in California. She waited as the number dialed automatically.

"Hello?" came Helen's familiar voice after a single ring.

"Hi, Mrs. Bradley. It's me, Rebecca."

"Oh, how are you, Dear?"

"I'm fine. I just wanted to let you know we had the funeral today."

"Today?" Helen said with surprise. "I thought it was going to be two days ago."

"They had some problems," Rebecca said. "I'll tell you about them when I see you, but I thought you would want to know everything went fine, and we'll be down in a day or two."

"Are you leaving right away?"

Rebecca could see Brad through the hotel room doorway as he leaned over their car's open hood to check the oil and water. "Yes," she said, swallowing the lump in her throat. "Brad is eager to get home."

"Are you all right, Dear?" Helen asked.

Rebecca sighed a deep sigh. She wasn't sure how to answer. "It's been a hectic week," she said. "I don't know what I am."

"Well," said Helen, "I know it's been hard for you. The girls and I have been praying for you. We met just this morning, in fact. I know you don't like to hear religious talk, but we've felt for days that the enemy was working overtime on the two of you."

Rebecca smiled to herself even as a tear fell. "It's funny you should say that," she said. "I don't know how to tell you this exactly, but I gave my life to Jesus last night."

She started to tell Helen about Sam, the diary, and everything else, but Helen burst out with a shout that startled her. "Oh, thank God! Oh! Oh my! That's wonderful! I'm so thrilled! How did it happen? Oh! Everyone will want to know!"

Rebecca told her about Sam and their meeting in the café. She also told her about the Doucets and the old house, but she left out the part about the curse.

"Oh, I'm so happy for you!" Helen said when Rebecca had finished "And what about Brad? Is he saved too?"

"No," Rebecca said in a lowered voice, as if he would hear. "No, he's not ready yet."

"What does he think about your decision?"

"He doesn't know yet. I haven't told him."

"Ahhh," Helen said knowingly, "I see." There was a pause. "Well," she said, "you just remember that God is in control. You trust Him, and everything will work out. You'll see. In the meantime, I want you to remember that all of us here are praying for you."

"Thank you. I appreciate it very much."

"Why don't you let me pray for you now?" Helen asked. And she did.

Brad tossed the suitcase into the trunk of the Toyota and slammed the trunk lid. He was glad finally to be going home. Rebecca had said very little after the funeral, which Brad interpreted as an emotional low after burying her aunt.

It was nearly noon, check-out time, and he wanted to be on the road as soon as possible.

Sam Michaels had stopped by the room to say goodbye and had left only a few minutes before. Brad was glad to see him go—him and his religious talk.

It hadn't been a good week. The sooner they were home and back into their daily routine, the better.

Rebecca stood in the doorway to the hotel room, closely clutching the leather pouch and the diary.

"You got everything?" Brad asked.

"Mm-hmm," she said, nodding her head.

"Good. You ready?"

Rebecca sighed deeply. To say that she was ready would have been a lie, but she didn't want to argue. She felt helpless. She wanted to stay. The old house. Her newfound, hours-old faith. The beauty of the mountains. She loved it there, and she wanted to stay.

And Billie was there. It was silly, she knew. Billie was gone, and the only thing that remained was an empty shell marked with a slab of stone and a few flowers. Yet there was comfort.

"I'm ready," she said.

"Good. Let's go."

Brad opened his door and climbed in behind the wheel. Rebecca reluctantly shut the door to the hotel room. Once in the car, she buckled her seatbelt and settled back, staring out the side window.

She felt strange. Her new faith made her feel like soaring, and yet at the same time she felt numb. Things were not right with Brad. They'd hardly spoken since the funeral, and then it was only short and to the point. She hadn't even told him what had happened to her the night before when she had prayed. She wanted to. She desperately wanted to, but he was so distant and cold, and she knew he would not be pleased.

So much had happened. She felt as though her head would burst if just one more thing tried to force its way into her mind. She thought about the house. She wanted so much to go there again and see it. It was a part of her, and she felt like it had more to give her than she had gotten the two brief times she had been there. What that might be, she didn't know or even think about. She only knew it was too soon to leave.

Brad backed out of the parking space and let the car roll forward slowly toward the street with his arm draped loosely over the steering wheel. His jaw muscles were tense.

Rebecca felt helpless as the car pulled out onto the street and accelerated toward town and the freeway. As they passed the turn-off for Walker Creek Road, neither of them noticed Gil Doucet's pickup as it made the turn and sped up Walker Creek Road out of town.

"Honey," she said as she leaned over and rested a gentle hand on his thigh.

Brad drew a deep breath. His eyes never left the road. "Mmm," he said from deep in his throat.

Rebecca gently stroked the muscles in his leg and studied his face. "I love you," she said, but her tone pleaded. She turned away and watched the road for a moment, then turned back to the man she loved. "Can't we talk?"

"I'm not stopping us from talking," Brad said.

Rebecca reached up and took his closest hand from the steering wheel and locked fingers with him, kissing his fingertips. "I'm sorry about last night," she said.

Brad sighed. The thought flashed through his mind that it was he who should do the apologizing, but he quickly pushed it aside in favor of righteous indignation. "It's no big deal," he said.

He turned the car at the next intersection and headed for the onramp to the freeway. In a moment, they were on their way south on Interstate Five, headed for home.

Gil Doucet pushed his truck past the speed limit.

He had to hurry. It wouldn't take long, but he'd need a few minutes to do the job right, and since he had no way of knowing when they'd come, he didn't want to take the chance of missing the young couple, or worse, being caught by them. He was pleased when he saw their car coming toward him as he turned onto Walker Creek Road, but his joy turned a little sour when they passed the turn-off and kept going. He hoped they were headed for the café and not for the onramp to the freeway.

He toyed with the idea for a moment: *What if they did leave?*

But he brushed aside the fleeting thought that things could return to normal and he could go on using the land indefinitely if they just would go away. No, that wouldn't do. It would always be hanging over his head. And someday they or someone after them would come again, and he'd have to deal with them, and it, all over again. No, it was best this way, now that he'd made up his mind to do it, to deal with it now once and for all.

And besides, there was still that other little matter, the one Sara was always harping about. He hated to admit it, but deep down he feared that it was all true: the curse, Old George Jakes's prophecy that someone would come to end the curse, all of it. Sara was always going on about spirits and powers beyond human understanding. He always dismissed them and her—at least to her face, at least out loud. But deep down, he only half admitted to himself, he did believe—and he feared.

When he reached the end of Walker Creek Road, he swung a wide U-turn and parked under the bows of a fir tree a few yards from the driveway, where he would be hidden from view. Once out of the cab, he leaned over the side of the truck bed, grabbed a small paper-wrapped bundle, and tucked it under his arm as he hurried down the driveway to the house.

His plan was simple. Marty had only had two sticks of dynamite, but they should be more than sufficient for what he had in mind. The house was old. Everyone knew it was falling apart. The broken foundation was visible from the road. It would come as no surprise to anyone if one day it just collapsed of its own accord. All he had to do was help it along a little.

He figured he could plant the two sticks in the basement at the base of the two wooden posts that supported the floor. The resulting explosion would knock the posts free. Not enough by itself, Gil knew, to destroy the house, but the accompanying concussion from the blast would lift the floor slightly, maybe as much as a foot, he hoped, which would break up much of the structure. Gil reasoned that it would lose most of its structural integrity, but not enough to leave any evidence of a blast.

The same concussion would also break apart the unreinforced rock foundation. If all went well, the old house simply would collapse in on itself, and no one ever would suspect. Even the noise from the blast would not be a problem since the nearest neighbor was Gil's own mobile home more than a mile away.

It was a simple plan, with a simple device. Gil had needed to clear a few stumps from the back of his place a few months ago and he had recruited Marty's help. They had used a simple detonation system that included a remote control, similar to the controls of a model airplane, that sent a signal to a receiver to ignite the dynamite. It was not sophisticated and he would have to detonate it himself, which meant he would have to wait and watch. He figured he could see just about everything from a place he knew on the ridge overlooking the house.

He smiled to himself at the two-birds-with-one-stone efficiency of his plan. Not only would he have a chance to own the property, but he'd level the eyesore of a house that would have to be demolished anyway to clear the land. He hoped that the land, once no heirs were discovered, would revert back to the state, where he could bid on it at auction. But even if that didn't happen and the state retained the title, he still could go on using it for many years.

But most important of all, the Jakes family would be out of the picture forever.

Gil quickly made his way to the basement door and descended the steps into the blackness.

Sam Michaels pulled into the driveway of his modest fifty-year-old home on the outskirts of town. He maneuvered between the chain link fence on the one side and the house on the other and then pulled up to the corral about fifty yards behind the house.

He was feeling a little empty. He'd left Rebecca and her husband at the hotel only a few minutes earlier, and he was concerned. Brad had gotten out of the car and had gone into the room without saying so much as a word to him. By itself that didn't bother him, but he worried for Rebecca, who obviously was upset that her husband could be so rude.

Sam had comforted her. He knew from their conversation the night before that Brad was angry about her new interest in religion. She told him she was afraid to tell Brad about her decision to follow Christ. He told her to remember that sometimes those who protest the loudest were the closest to making that decision themselves. Rebecca had smiled, but he could see in her eyes she did not understand, and he knew she doubted it was true in Brad's case.

He had prayed with her before he left, but something in his gut told him things were not over yet. He was uneasy, and years of experience had taught him that many times an uneasy feeling was a prodding from the Holy Spirit to pray.

Sam shut off the engine and climbed out of the cab. Lancer, his five-year-old bay gelding, pranced and snorted defiantly as he worried the rail fence of the corral.

Sam chuckled to himself. "What's the matter, boy? You ready for a ride?"

The horse gave a low, throaty whinny as Sam approached, nuzzling him and pushing him off-balance. "All right, boy! We'll go!" Sam chuckled again.

Sam opened the gate and led the horse into the ancient wooden barn. A few minutes later, he was mounted in the saddle and headed into the hills—his favorite place to pray and think. He made a habit of doing it at least once a week.

He goaded Lancer up a steep embankment to a trail that followed the crest of the hill, up to the ridge high above the house and barn. He was not headed anywhere in particular, but an hour later he found himself looking down on the stale green pond and decaying old house at the end of Walker Creek Road.

Brad said nothing as he drove, but his jaw was set and his teeth began to hurt from clenching them so tightly. He knew he should feel better now that they were on their way home, but instead he felt a knot in the middle of his stomach, along with a hollow emptiness that would not go away. All his life he'd had a picture in his mind about the way marriage should be. He pictured himself coming home from work and being greeted at the door by well-groomed, happy children and the picture-perfect wife who would meet him with a kiss, a well prepared meal, and a wink-of-promise for later after the children were in bed.

It wasn't that he really expected storybook perfection, but somehow what he had with Rebecca was not what he had expected. The baby thing was a kink, sure, but it was much harder on Rebecca than it was on him. And yet there was more. He couldn't put his finger on what it was exactly. He wasn't even sure that it had anything to do with Rebecca. He felt torn—restless. It was as if he were being pulled from either side, almost as if there were a battle raging inside with two sides vying for control. He had never felt so much turmoil in his life, and he wanted it to go away. But it would not leave.

Rebecca stared out the passenger-side window. "Honey," she finally said as she put a delicate hand on her husband's shoulder. Brad was silent.

"Honey," she began again, "I know this is asking a lot, but —"

She waited to see if he would meet her eyes. When he didn't, she continued. "I ..." she swallowed hard, "I want to go back."

Brad's face reddened almost immediately. "Why the —!" He caught himself before the swear words tumbled out, but his rage was evident.

"I know it's asking a lot," she repeated, "but I just can't leave yet."

"Why didn't you say something a little earlier!" he said. He threw his arms in the air. "We're ten miles down the road!"

Rebecca felt tears streaming down her cheeks. She tried to speak, but her voice cracked. It took her a few minutes to recover. Brad kept driving.

"Please?" she pleaded.

Brad sighed in disgust as he jerked the car hard toward the approaching off-ramp. He hardly stopped at the stop sign at the bottom of the ramp before wheeling to the left and accelerating under the overpass. He cranked a hard left again at the onramp to the freeway in the opposite direction.

"Happy now?" he said as he sped up the ramp.

Rebecca's lip quivered as she tried to fight the tears that were now flowing freely.

Brad's anger and resentment chipped away at her rock of peace. She knew her God and she trusted Him. Yet things were not working out the way she had thought they would. Somehow she believed, or maybe she hoped, that God would work the same miracle in Brad He had wrought in her. She had allowed herself to think that Brad might come back to the room and apologize for the things he had said, that they could talk, that he would break free of his resentment and anger, and that he too would turn to God in faith. Instead, he simply had crawled into bed and gone to sleep.

Then this morning his veiled coldness toward her, as well as toward Sam, was obvious and effective. She felt she should be patient with him and pray that God would work on his heart. And she had. But instead of softening, he had become harder than ever. She rode in silence as she stared out the window, praying without words.

"I love you," she said after a while.

"Yeah?" Brad said.

"You know I do," she said as benignly as she knew how.

She could see the muscles in his jaw working again.

"You've got a funny way of showing it," he said a few minutes later. By now they were back in town, and the car was headed up Walker Creek Road.

Rebecca turned away. Guilt ripped at her insides.

"I'm sorry," she said as she placed a gentle hand on his thigh.

Brad's jaw clenched tighter.

Rebecca sighed. "Can't you understand?" she asked.

"Understand what? That you don't give a rip what I think?"

He continued on with a string of swear words that caused her to reel. She had heard him swear before, but never as profane as he was being now. Her heart broke when he called her a vile name. She bit down on her lip.

"I can't sell it—not yet," she whimpered.

Brad worked his jaw until it felt like he would grind his teeth into powder. "You and your buddy Sam got things all worked out?" he said.

Rebecca sank back at his suggestive remark. There was nothing more than warm friendship between she and Sam, even though she had noticed how handsome he was. Brad's words cut deep.

She sat back, numb. It was only a few short minutes later when Brad pulled off the street and onto the loose gravel by the driveway to the old house. He sat silently, staring out the windshield.

"Are you coming?" Rebecca asked.

"Nope," he said without looking.

Rebecca opened her door and climbed out. She leaned in the open window. "Please come," she said.

Brad dropped the car into gear. "I've had it!" he said. "I don't care what you do, but I've had it!"

"What are you doing?" she asked in disbelief.

"You wanna stay? Stay! Get your buddy Sam to give you a ride home!" Brad dropped his foot on the accelerator, flinging gravel as he sped back onto the road. Rebecca stumbled back but managed to keep her balance. She watched in disbelief and horror as Brad sped off and disappeared around the corner.

Rebecca sobbed quietly in the middle of the road. "Dear God, what have You brought me to?" she prayed.

She turned and walked slowly to the house and sank down on the front porch. "Oh, Lord," she whispered, "help me. I feel so lost. Please help me!"

The Centurion sheathed his sword and took the simple coiled rope handed to him with the solemn humility that accompanies a high honor. With reverent wonder, he turned, knelt before the Lamb, and, with head bowed low, placed the looped end of the rope around the Lamb's neck and then let the rest fall to the ground. When instructed to do so, the

Centurion rose to his feet and backed away, head bowed low, his right arm held tightly across his chest in a humble salute.

Sam sat on the hard ground of the ridge above the old house with the reins of his horse held loosely in his hands, letting his mind wander. A hawk screeched out a lonely cry as it circled overhead above the tops of the trees. Except for that, it was peaceful and quiet there.

But the peace was interrupted by a fast-braking, late-model Toyota as it swung around in front of the driveway and came to an abrupt stop in the middle of the road. Sam recognized the car as the one belonging to Rebecca and her husband. A moment later, the passenger-side door opened and Rebecca got out. She stood as if talking to someone inside, and then almost fell as the car sped off the way it had come. A dejected Rebecca turned and walked slowly to the house.

Sam wondered what was going on. He waited and watched for a moment, unsure if he should interfere, but a minute later he picked himself up, mounted his horse, and started down into the clearing.

Rebecca sat on the front porch, wondering what her life was coming to. She wondered about her marriage—its future, or if it even had one. The hard porch was beginning to work a spot on her tailbone. She stood, turned, and went into the old house.

From the ridge opposite where Sam had been watching Rebecca, Gil Doucet held his cell phone in his hand, fingering the button that would, he was sure, solve all his problems. He watched impatiently as the girl entered the house. He had seen her husband drive off in what appeared to be a huff and he wondered if he'd be back. He doubted it, though, and now he was faced with a decision: should he go ahead with his plan or not? He puzzled on it for a moment and then decided it was too late to change his plan now. He was an impatient man, bent with purpose. He could deal with the girl's husband later, if it was even necessary. No, if he had to divide and conquer, he would.

Sara will be happy, he thought.

He let his mind toy with all the things he'd do with the property once it was his, giving no thought to potential consequences. His plan would work. It must work. He was a man of purpose all right. Even driven. But if his lust for power and money weren't enough, there was the sickening feeling in the middle of his gut whenever he allowed doubt to enter his mind—as if someone, or something, were twisting a knot in his insides any time he considered turning back. It drove him back to the task at hand. He could feel the button under his finger as the pressure increased. Just a second longer and it would be all over.

A second later, the ground shook, and a low rumble echoed through the trees. Gil watched as the weakened frame of the old house shuddered and collapsed to the ground in a cloud of dust that rose up and drifted away in the gentle, afternoon breeze.

CHAPTER TWENTY-SEVEN

BRAD PULLED BACK onto the road about a half-mile from the house where he had stopped to sort things out in his mind.

As soon as he had left Rebecca standing by the old house, a nagging little voice inside him had told him he was wrong. He knew it was true so when he was sure he was out of sight of the house, he had pulled over to try to reason away any argument that pointed to his own guilt. He had quarreled with his conscience, and once he almost had turned the car around and headed back. But stubborn pride and self-righteous indignation dragged his mind back to the pit of self-pity.

Now as he rounded a sharp corner and headed into a long straightaway, he felt a brief vibration through the seat of the car. At the same time, he thought he heard a faint rumble. He had rolled up Rebecca's window and the air conditioner hissed subtly in the background. For a moment, he wondered if he had imagined it. But he quickly dismissed it as a small earthquake and went back to his selfish indulgence in self-pity as he pushed the car above the speed limit.

His anger burned. He slammed his fist down on the steering wheel. Why did things have to change? Why couldn't they stay the same? Why couldn't she?

The car crept up above sixty and at each bend in the old mountain road the tires protested a little louder. Brad kept a steady hand on the wheel and a heavy foot on the accelerator.

She had no right, he kept telling himself. *She had no right at all!*

He could see the change in her, and though she had not said so, he was sure he knew what it was. He cursed under his breath. It seemed as if everyone was against him—Billie, Helen Bradley, the preacher, Rebecca's new friend, Sam—all pushing him to something he didn't want and didn't feel he needed. He liked his world the way it was and he didn't want it to change. And he sure didn't want it cluttered up with fanatical religion!

She had no right! She had no right at all!

Before he knew it, he was back in town at the main intersection, wondering where to go next. Gripping the steering wheel as if he could strangle it and gritting his teeth, he brushed aside the troublesome little voice inside that told him he should go back and get his wife.

She deserved to be left, he argued. Maybe the walk would do her good. Maybe then she'd appreciate him. She could get her own ride, for all he cared. Let that Indian friend of hers give her a ride.

He turned right and headed in the direction of the hotel. It made no sense; they had already checked out, but at the casino entrance he turned in without thinking and headed for the nearest parking place.

When the car stopped, he sat for a moment, working the muscles in his jaw. The war inside heated up for a moment as though two forces battled for control of his conscience. But in another moment, one side claimed victory. He opened the car door and got out.

Inside the casino, he walked past strategically placed slot machines and went straight to the bar, slid onto a barstool, and ordered a drink. He slumped down over the bar with his arms draped possessively around a steady stream of drinks. As he fingered the patterns of the intricate, inlaid oak, he wallowed in self-pity. Day gave way to night, but since it was dark inside the windowless bar, he lost track of time. When he finally looked at his watch, it was nearly nine thirty.

A band had started playing country-western tunes. He slid off the barstool to unsteady feet, made his way around the corner, and leaned against the wall. Couples in cowboy boots and jeans swayed arm in arm to the beat.

He found his way to an empty booth and sat down. Almost immediately, a too-old cocktail waitress in a skimpy black dress greeted him and asked if he'd like another drink. He nodded and went back to watching the couples on the dance floor.

When the music stopped and couples began to wander back to their tables, Brad noticed the sultry figure of Sara Doucet on the far side of the floor, holding the hand of a handsome young man and leading him toward the bar. He wondered how he'd missed her before. She turned as if to say something to her escort, but then noticed Brad across the room. She smiled a come-on smile and winked at him. Then, with the young man in tow, she disappeared behind the wall between the bar and the dance floor. A moment later, she reappeared alone.

She never once acknowledged Brad as she took an indirect path across the room, flitting casually from a couple she obviously knew to an old acquaintance and then to a table with more friends. But as soon as she was abreast of Brad's table, she smiled a broad smile.

"Mind if I sit down?" she said.

Brad could feel the alarms going off in his head as he motioned for her to sit.

"How are you this fine evening?" she asked.

"Great!" he lied. "Never better. How about you?"

"I'm in the mood for a good time," she said through a wicked smile. "Buy me a drink?"

Brad motioned to the waitress. "What'll you have?" he asked Sara.

"Beer," she said.

"Beer," Brad repeated to the waitress, who nodded and hurried off toward the bar.

"So," said Sara, "what are you doing here all by yourself?"

Brad clenched his jaw. "Just came down for a drink," he said.

Sara smiled a devious smile. "Your wife lets you run around all by yourself?" she teased.

"From time to time," he answered, annoyed at her mocking tone.

"Foolish girl," Sara said as the waitress brought her beer and set it down.

Brad smiled coolly with forced confidence. His heart raced.

"Have you finished your business here in Creek Junction?" Sara asked.

"Yeah," said Brad to his drink.

"Then you'll be leaving soon."

Brad nodded, avoiding eye contact with Sara. "Yeah, soon."

Sara leaned closer and rested her arm on Brad's shoulder. "We'll have to make the most of it then, won't we?"

Brad's heart beat hard in his chest. He remembered his little encounter with the waitress from the café the day before, and he wondered how he could find himself in the same circumstances so soon. He had resisted his primal urges and congratulated himself on what he thought was a victory of character. But now he stood once again on the threshold of moral collapse, and he found he didn't care.

He smiled as he took her hand. "Yeah, I suppose we will."

"C'mon," Sara said, leading him from the booth, "let's go someplace."

All her life, Sara Doucet had heard about the curse and the need to keep it alive. There was never any logic to it. No reason was ever given except that it was necessary for survival. Yet it was as much a part of her as any organ or limb. She felt no sense of duty or any other noble or moral unction, nothing so meritorious as family loyalty. There was only purpose, a perverted, driving force within her that told her she must not fail. It never occurred to her to question it.

So when Gil had come home and told her that the girl's husband somehow had gotten away and had not been caught in the explosion, she knew what she must do. She took a certain pleasure in the prospect of using a man and then discarding him as a black widow spider would discard her mate.

She had followed him to the casino, studying him unnoticed from the far side of the room for any little sign of weakness or flaw that would tell her how best to tempt him. It had not taken long. She danced with several men, teasing them with vague, unspoken promises, all the while studying her newest victim and savoring the thought of an encounter.

She was surprised at how easy it was. She had expected some resistance from a married man. Not that most offered any. Most men hanging around alone in a bar had already made up their minds about loyalty, but somehow she had him pegged as a man who flattered himself with visions of moral uprightness. When he had invited her to sit, she was pleasantly surprised.

They left the casino together and got into his car. She laughed to herself as he opened the door for her in a pathetic attempt at chivalry. When he climbed in behind the wheel, she leaned across the console to be close to him with her arm through his, making small talk and laughing at his feeble jokes. She hoped Gil would not be too quick to finish their simple plan. After all, an hour wouldn't make any difference.

Twenty minutes after they left the casino, Brad slowed the car and turned into the driveway that led to the mobile home near the S-bend in Walker Creek. At the front door to the house, Sara leaned up and kissed Brad before she opened the door and led him inside.

Like a lamb to the slaughter, he willingly followed.

An evil presence observed the happenings in the shabby mobile home with serpentine anticipation, gleefully savoring the happy turn of events as the man willfully rejected the enemy's protection and submitted to his authority behind the boundary. It was wonderful, this propensity of the human race to reject benevolent warnings in favor of self-indulgence. All a demon needed do was watch and wait until one of them stepped willingly up to the gallows of rebellion and slipped his own neck in the noose of fleeting pleasure.

The enemy, the servant of the Most High and unseen by mortal eyes, waited grim-faced outside the clearing by the S-bend in Walker Creek, his sword sheathed, as the man unwittingly cast aside divine protection and entered dangerous territory.

The bedroom was dark except for a single candle that burned on the bureau. Brad felt as though his heart would beat through his chest as he started to unbutton his shirt. Standing behind him next to the bed, Sara slipped it from his shoulders and let it fall to the floor. She wrapped her slender arms around his waist. Her soft skin felt good against his and his mind swelled with euphoric anticipation. It was wrong and he knew it, but lust had long since won the battle for control. He turned to face her. They moved closer to kiss, embracing each other passionately.

Brad pulled away just as quickly as heavy footsteps on the wooden front porch were followed by the sound of jingling keys and the turning of the lock.

Sara held her finger to her lips and smiled. "Shhh," she whispered. "It's just my brother. I'll get rid of him."

She turned and pushed past the partially opened door into the lighted hallway.

Brad could hear voices in the other room as he hid behind the door. He couldn't make out the words, but he recognized Gil's voice even though he'd heard it only once before. Both voices rose slightly with each exchange until it was clear they were arguing.

"Not yet!" he heard Sara say, and then the voices quieted in an uneasy hush as they continued their arguing.

Brad suddenly felt sick to his stomach and his hands were shaking. The idea of sex with someone other than Rebecca was not new to him. He'd occasionally found himself thinking about Sheila, the receptionist at work. She was pretty and young and every once in a while a lingering smile suggested more than just friendship. He often had wondered what it would be like and what Rebecca would do if she ever found out. Now, as he hid behind the door of Sara's bedroom, he feared she might. But there was no turning back now.

The arguing had stopped. Brad could hear footsteps as someone came down the hallway toward the bedroom. The door opened. Sara stood in the light, leaning against the doorframe with an unemotional smile on her lips. Behind her and off to the side stood Gil. In his hands he held a rifle, its muzzle pointed in the general direction of Brad's belly.

Brad was terrified.

"Sorry," said Sara. "You win some, you lose some. I guess today I lose."

"And so do you," Gil grumbled. "Let's you and me go for a walk."

"What's going on?" Brad demanded. The quiver in his voice betrayed his disbelief. "What're you doing?"

Gil pushed him down the hall toward the laundry room and the back door. Brad gave Sara a questioning look over Gil's shoulder. Sara only shrugged.

"At least let me get my shirt!" Brad pleaded, stalling for time.

"You won't need it," Gil said.

Brad fought the urge to panic and run. The close quarters of the hallway made escape unlikely with Gil's rifle poised menacingly. His brain raced to find answers as his eyes searched in vain for a way out.

"What are you going to do?" Brad asked.

"Nothing personal. It's just business," Gil said through a twisted grin.

Brad remembered Gil's offer the day before for the land and he remembered what Sam had said: "Don't take him lightly." The words hammered their hopeless and too-late warning in his mind. His brain raced to find answers as his eyes continued their futile search for something to help him.

"Listen," Brad said, the rattle in his voice betraying his fear, "we can work this out. I'll talk to her. She —"

Gil's eyes were hard and cold as he shook his head. "It's too late for that. We'll do it the hard way."

"It's not too late! I'll talk to her!"

Gil shook his head. "I've already taken care of that. Just one more loose end and I'll claim what I want with no interference from either of you."

Brad's heart sank. "What do you mean? What have you done?"

"Through there," Gil said, motioning with the barrel of the gun to the laundry room and the back door at the other side.

"What have you done?" Brad said.

Gil raised the rifle and pointed it at Brad's head. "I've solved the problem with her just like I'm going to do with you."

Brad clenched his fist in a moment of protective bravado. "If you've —"

"Ah, ah, ah," Gil cautioned. "Remember our friend." He patted the rifle barrel with his free hand. "Don't do anything stupid."

Brad felt the burden of guilt and shame as the full weight of what he had done rested squarely on his shoulders in one hideous moment. Grieving disbelief quickly followed. It was his fault, and he knew it. It couldn't be true. She couldn't be dead. She just couldn't, but he knew in his heart that Gil was not one to bluff.

"Get going," Gil ordered again.

Brad turned, back peddling as he tried to think, but Gil pushed him before he could say anything. Brad stumbled backward and fell against the washing machine. As he regained his footing, he realized his hand rested in an open box of laundry detergent. Without thinking, he wrapped his fist around a handful of white powder as Gil pushed him out the back door.

It was late and there was no moon. Beyond the small circle of light that surrounded the mobile home, the blackness of the night engulfed the mountains and trees in an all-encompassing void.

Brad, still shirtless, felt a sudden, deep chill. "Where are we going?" he demanded.

"Just a little walk," said Gil. "Not far at all."

Brad sensed the finality of his words. He knew he had minutes to live unless he could think of something—anything.

Something did occur to him that offered relief in a strange sort of way: Rebecca never would know he'd been unfaithful. His body would be found. The authorities would ask around. They'd find out he was at the casino. They'd find out he had left with a woman—and Rebecca never would know.

Something else struck him at that moment.

"The casino!" Brad said in desperation. "The people there saw me leave. They'll know it was me who left with your sister. The police will know I was with Sara!"

"Sara's always leaving with someone," Gil said. "It won't matter a bit if they don't find you. And they won't. I've got a special place all picked out. No one will ever find you. You'll just disappear."

Brad's fear turned to rage. "What have you done with my wife?"

"I simply arranged a little accident," Gil boasted, "and she will be found. She'll be found and everyone will think that the old house just gave out and collapsed at the wrong time. With you disappearing the way you're going to, if anyone suspects something more than an accident, they'll think it was you. They'll figure you killed her and ran off. Lover's spat—which they'll believe, because Sara will tell them that she saw you that night. She'll say that the two of you left together and came here. But then you left and she never saw you again. Either way, we'll be in the clear." Gil let out a perverted laugh. "I may even be the one who happens to discover your poor wife's body!"

Brad's rage turned to fury. He wanted to wrap his hands around Gil's neck and squeeze the life out of him—even more than he wanted to save his own life. Tears of violent rage formed in the corners of his eyes. He took a step toward Gil and then held for a moment, wishing for something, anything, to use as a weapon. Nothing else mattered.

The detergent.

Gil noticed Brad's clenched fist. "What have you got in your hand?" Gil asked.

Brad clenched his fist tighter. His whole body reacted to the sudden burst of adrenalin that brought every muscle to instant action as he threw the handful of detergent at Gil's face, but Gil dodged to one side and turned away. The detergent hit him on the side of his face, missing his eyes but partially landing in his mouth.

Gil spit angrily as he brought the gun around. As he did, he lost his balance, stumbling to the side. He fell back. The gun roared, echoing through the darkness and sending a bullet into the woodpile a few feet away. It missed Brad by inches.

Run! A voice in his head commanded.

Gil recovered quickly, but Brad had obeyed the voice. As Gil worked the bolt-action of his rifle and raised it to fire again, Brad disappeared into the darkness. Gil fired at the last place he had seen his target, missing him by a fraction of an inch. Brad felt the whiz of the bullet as it passed by his arm.

Gil cursed violently as he ran, working the bolt again. At the edge of the clearing, he heard the noise of his prey running through the dense undergrowth. He knelt down on one knee, raised the gun to his shoulder, and fired. But the rustling sounds of escape in the undergrowth continued on. Then silence. He worked the bolt a third time and pressed the stock against his shoulder.

But there was nothing to shoot at.

Gil lowered the gun, cursing loudly.

"Did you get him?" Sara asked from the back door of the mobile home.

"No!" Gil said, and then cursed again.

"Well, you'd better stop him now!"

"Shut up!" Gil said as Sara ran up to him. "Just shut up and let me think!"

Sara stood impatiently for a moment. "You'd better stop him now that he knows so much."

"I said shut up!"

Gil rubbed his chin with the back of his hand and then uttered another profanity when he saw the white detergent on his knuckles.

"Well, don't think too long," Sara said. "He's getting away!"

Gil's eyes narrowed. "Just shut up!" he said, pointing an angry finger. "Go back to the house and wait for me. You got that?"

Gil set his face toward the blackness of the night. "I'll find him," he said.

Sara nodded to his back as he stormed off and disappeared into the trees. "Sure thing, Gil," she said.

But Sara never did what she was told.

Brad sat in terror with his back against a giant fir tree, wondering how a Southern California city boy could find himself a thousand miles from home in the middle of nowhere, expecting to die at any moment at the hand of a madman he didn't know and had never even heard of two days ago. The pounding in his chest throbbed up into his throat and echoed in his ears. Though he knew it was irrational, he feared Gil would hear it and find him. He took a deep breath and held it for a moment, then let it out slowly with a nervous, wavering patter. He felt sick. He tried not to think about Rebecca.

It was pitch black all around. The only light came from the pale luminescence of a single porch light that dimly bathed the mobile home and a few feet of the clearing in a ghostly pall. He knew he could not stay where he was. Gil soon would follow, he was sure, and Gil had the advantage of knowing the area.

He kept thinking of Billie's old house and what Gil had said about it "giving out." He had to know. The trouble was, in the dark he couldn't be sure which direction it was. But he had to take the chance.

He squinted hard until tears formed in the corners of his eyes as he tried to remember. He was pretty sure it was east. *Yeah, east.* But in the dark, which way was east?

He opened his eyes and looked around him, desperate to get his bearings, but his efforts were met with complete darkness.

There was a noise, a broken branch. A few feet away.

He straightened against the tree and held his breath. He thought he saw movement in the blackness. He could hear Gil stumbling around in the dark and cursing only a few feet away. Terror gripped his throat.

He heard the voice in his head again telling him to run. But this time it seemed louder—and he wasn't at all sure it was in his head.

Gil had moved away. At least there was no more sound.

Somehow he managed to get his legs to move. He could see a dim trail in the darkness a few feet ahead leading away from the clearing and the mobile home. He followed it quickly into the black of a moonless night. Faint shadows threatened from every side. Soon he was at a dead run, stumbling over unsure ground, blind terror at his heels.

The trail led him up the side of the mountain. Up ahead, he could just make out the faint outline of the ridge silhouetted against the night sky. Somehow it offered relief, as if reaching it would give him safety. He ran for it, anticipating the comfort of cresting and then descending the other side, putting an entire mountain between him and his attacker.

He looked instinctively over his shoulder, stumbling again and almost falling, but he managed to keep his feet under him. Gil was not following. Had he lost him?

He looked ahead again to the ridge now only a few feet away—and then froze.

Dimly, black-on-black, outlined against the darkness of the night, a rifle-bearing figure stood menacingly in the trail. Brad froze in an instant of indecision as the figure shouldered the rifle. Brad stood a second longer and then dove reflexively into the dense forest. He heard no sound, but he could feel every movement of his body, as though moving in slow motion, as he tumbled headlong down the embankment. He saw a flash of light that illuminated the silhouette with the rifle for an instant; freezing the image in his mind at the same instant he felt a sting in his forehead.

His shoulder hit the ground. He tumbled.

Vague images filled his mind. Once, he found his feet in mid-roll, but they would not hold him and he fell again, rolling like a rag doll down the hill. He felt strange and couldn't tell for sure if he had stopped his descent. The world swirled around him.

His last thought was of Rebecca. Then there was only the blackness of unconsciousness. But it was not peaceful. He dreamed—a dream that was not a dream, in which grotesque images of vile creatures battled against benevolent warriors with golden shields and bright swords before him, as though battling for his soul.

On the hill overlooking the spectacle, a Lamb with a rope around His neck stood majestically, watching with regal concern for the wellbeing of those who fought in His name. A single shaft of light penetrated the heavens and illuminated the Lamb's head, revealing His stately splendor. Even the simple rope seemed to display the grandeur of royal garb.

CHAPTER TWENTY-EIGHT

THUMP... THUMP... THUMP...

Brad's mind tottered on the edge of consciousness. His head hurt—and there was that constant bumping.

His mind opened a bit, and he blinked hard. It was still pitch black, no shadows—nothing.

Just that constant bumping.

His head hurt.

He fought his way back to consciousness. His nose bumped something in the dark. And then he knew. He was being carried over someone's shoulder.

Rage returned. "Rebecca!" he cried out as he swung wildly at his attacker with a clenched fist, wriggling free and slipping away from the broad shoulders that carried him.

But in another moment, iron arms locked vise-like around his throat from behind, holding firm and restricting his air supply but stopping short of choking. A firm hand clamped over his mouth as they both tumbled to the ground.

"Shhh!" came a familiar but unidentifiable voice from beneath him. "Shut up and don't move!"

Confused and disoriented, Brad obeyed, muscles tense and ready. Footsteps passed by, and then moved away.

"What —?" he mumbled through the man's hand.

"Shhh! Not yet!" the man scolded just above a whisper.

Another moment.

Brad felt the man's hand relax slightly. "Don't make a sound!" the man whispered. "Understand? We're not out of this yet!"

Brad nodded into the darkness as his mind's probe unlocked the mystery of the voice. It was Sam Michaels.

Brad pulled away and sat up as Sam removed his hand. "What…what happened?" Brad demanded. He felt cold.

"Shhh! Not so loud! Just take it easy for a minute."

Brad rubbed his aching head. He felt something wet and warm. "How did you —?"

"Just sit for a minute," Sam said. "You've got a nasty cut."

Brad felt the place on his forehead again. He could feel a deep wound. "What —?"

"Just take it easy." Sam winced. "He almost got you good."

Brad could feel Sam's hand on his forehead as he studied the wound. "Looks like he just missed the bone."

"What happened?" Brad asked. "How did you —?"

"Don't you remember? It's a good thing he's not a better shot than he is or you'd be dead."

Brad tried to remember. Running. Seeing Gil! Jump! Darkness.

"I think…I think I…but —"

"Gil's bullet grazed you pretty good. You've lost a lot of blood. How do you feel?"

"Not so good," Brad said as sudden nausea hit him. He leaned forward as if to vomit, but the urge subsided and he leaned back. His head pounded. "Why is it so dark?"

Sam was silent for a moment. Then he asked, "What do you mean?"

"What do you mean, what do I mean? Why is it so dark?"

More silence.

"Are you still there?" Brad asked.

"I'm here. Can you see that?"

Brad was puzzled. "See what?"

There was another long silence. "I just waved my hand in front of your face. You didn't see anything?"

Brad sat forward and grabbed Sam's shirtsleeve. "Why can't I see?"

"Just take it easy," Sam said.

Brad rubbed his eyes with the backs of his hands and blinked hard, staring into the darkness. "Why can't I see?"

Sam ran his hand in front of Brad's eyes again. "Can you see anything—anything at all?"

Brad grimaced. "No! Nothing!"

Sam bit down on his lip. "All right, just stay calm. Maybe it's temporary," he said, rubbing his chin. "Look, here's the deal. By now Gil knows you're alive since he didn't find you at the bottom of that hill where he thought he left you."

"Was that him just now?"

"Yeah. We can't stay here."

"But I can't see!" Brad pleaded.

"Just stay close."

"But I can't see!"

"Look, I can't carry you up and down these hills. You'll have to walk. We've got a long way to go, so keep your mouth shut and take my arm."

Brad nodded into the darkness. "OK."

Brad started to get up when a hard body blow knocked him on his back. Sam came to rest on top of him, hand clamped over his mouth. "Don't make a sound!" Sam whispered.

Brad lay still, ignoring the twig that dug into the flesh of his side. There was no sound. Only the distant wind in the great trees. But then came the soft sounds of approaching footsteps. The footsteps stopped, and then there was only the faint sound of someone breathing a few feet away.

They waited. Brad held his breath as the thought of discovery nudged him toward panic, and he half-expected to hear the explosion from the rifle and feel the sting of the bullet as it ripped his flesh.

Oh, God, I wish I could see!

There were footsteps again, but then they grew faint.

Then there was no sound.

Brad tried instinctively to wriggle free, but Sam clamped down tighter and held him still.

They waited.

Waited.

Sam's crushing weight bore down on Brad's chest. He needed air, but he could find no room for it.

Footsteps again. They grew fainter until they were gone.

Sam rolled off to one side. Brad drew a lung full of air. "Is he gone?" he whispered, grabbing Sam's arm in the dark.

"Yeah, for now. C'mon. We've got to put some distance between us and him. Man, what I wouldn't give for a gun right now." Sam helped Brad to his feet. "Or my horse."

"Yeah," said Brad without hope.

"No time to fret about it now," said Sam. "We've got to get you out of here, and soon."

"Can we make it to town? Get help?"

Sam shook his head as though Brad could see it. "You'd never make it in the shape you're in. Gil would be on us before we got two miles, and it's a lot farther than that to town."

"What are we going to do?"

"My horse is on the other side of the valley across the clearing from Gil's house. I had to leave him tied up when I found you. There wasn't time to go back and get him. But if you can walk, there's an old log cabin about a mile from here above the Walker place. It's tucked away in a little draw at the foot of Fletcher's Peak. We can hide you there. Once you're safe, I'll try to get to town and get the sheriff."

"What about the road? Can't we flag someone down for help? It can't be that far."

"No good. Gil would surely spot us. Besides, there are only two houses up this far, Gil's and the old Walker place. It isn't likely we'd run into anyone—except Gil."

Sam took Brad's arm and started to lead him away. Brad held back. "He told me he killed Rebecca."

"He dynamited the old house yesterday," Sam said. "I saw it."

Brad's fingers dug into Sam's arm as he chocked back the tears. "It's true then."

"C'mon," Sam said. "We can't stay here."

Gil fingered the trigger of the rifle he held closely in front of him as he surveyed the dense undergrowth of the mountainside below him. Unreasonable and unreasoning hate festered in his heart.

He spat contemptuously on the ground, giving himself a mental chewing-out for allowing the kid to slip away so easily. He had seen blood on the trail where the kid had disappeared over the side of the mountain, and he had felt a calming reassurance that his bullet had found its mark. He'd felt confident enough to go back to the house for a decent night's sleep. Morning was soon enough, he had told himself, to dispose of the body.

Now as daylight broke, he stood over the spot where the kid's body should be. A sickening feeling wormed its way through his gut. There was blood. A lot of it. The kid couldn't have wandered far.

He studied the mountainside below him. *He was still here. Somewhere close.* Sooner or later, he'd find him.

Gil reached for the cell phone that hung from his belt and dialed a familiar number.

"Frank? I need you. Meet me on the ridge above the house—about a hundred yards east of where we bagged that buck last fall. No arguments, Frank! Just get here!"

Gil hung up in the middle of Frank's feeble protest. He had no patience for weakness, and Frank was all weakness. He wondered sometimes why he tolerated Frank's bumbling.

Gil focused all his attention on the mountainside. An unnatural lust for vengeance and death simmered in his mind. He never questioned why. He only felt the cancerous hate that drove him. He only knew what he must do.

He knelt down and touched a darkened spot on the ground at his feet. Fresh blood. A lot of it. It led along the ridge to the east.

Someone must be helping the kid. He'd never have made it this far without it—not after losing so much blood. If the kid were alone, he'd be lost. A city boy in a strange place. Yeah, he'd be lost, all right. But the trail led in a straight line, as though he knew where he was going.

Gil rubbed his chin. *Yep, someone's helping him.* And he was pretty sure he knew who it was: Sam Michaels. If it was Sam, he had a pretty good idea where he'd go. There weren't many places they could go in the direction they were headed.

But there was one place. And even if he was wrong, the kid couldn't get far wandering aimlessly through the woods. It would be easy enough to pick up the trail afterward. The diversion only would lose him an hour. And then it would just be a matter of time before he'd pick up the trail and find him out here in the middle of nowhere—on ground familiar to Gil. Sam, if he was helping the kid, wouldn't be so stupid as to try for the road, and the Walker place was no good.

No place to hide. That left very few alternatives.

With all the cunning of a wild animal on the scent of easy prey, Gil studied his options. Frank would be there in about twenty minutes, and then they'd have a vehicle. He could go get his own truck, of course, but he might need Frank's help. Gil had no desire to tangle with Sam in a fair fight.

The old logging road took an indirect path, but in a four-wheel-drive it still would be faster than walking. The old cabin. The old cabin was his best bet. Frank would be there soon. It was worth the wait.

"I gotta stop for a minute!" Brad wheezed.

Sam looked up from the trail. Brad's face was white. "You don't look so good," he said.

Brad slumped to the ground, exhausted and sick. His head pounded.

Sam knelt next to him. "There's a stream a few yards from here. Just sit tight and keep your head down. I'll be right back."

The sound of Sam's footsteps moved away, and then a few moments later they returned. Sam knelt next to Brad and mopped his forehead with a damp handkerchief.

Brad winced from the coldness of the water and the pain.

"The bleeding has slowed some, but you're going to need stitches."

"I'm going to wrap your head the best I can," Sam said, ripping a long strip from his shirt-tail and folding it into a neat bandage. "That wound opens up every time you move."

He wrapped the cloth around Brad's head and tied a knot in the back. "There. That'll help. I don't want you leaving blood all over the trail. Gil's no fool. He'd spot it in a heartbeat."

"I feel weak," said Brad.

"You've lost a lot of blood." Sam's keen eyes swept across the hillside as he sat back on the ground. "I guess we can rest a few minutes. But keep your voice down."

Brad lay back on the ground. "I can't believe she's really dead," he said softly a few minutes later.

"Mmm," Sam said.

"I loved her," Brad said. "She was everything to me."

Sam's jaw tightened as he picked up a stick from the ground. "It's a terrible thing to lose someone you love," he said, almost to himself.

Brad's conscience wrestled with grief and self-pity. For a brief moment, self-pity won. "None of this would have happened if she hadn't gotten religious."

Sam's eyes narrowed as he snapped the stick in half.

The sound startled Brad. "What was that?"

Sam stood, turned, and walked a short distance away.

"You still there?" Brad's voice betrayed his fear.

A gentle breeze rustled through the boughs of the trees but Sam hardly noticed. "You can't pin this on her."

Brad's anger rose. "Or you?"

"Or anyone."

"I loved her," Brad said. "And now she's gone."

Sam's voice seemed to mock. "Yeah?"

For a moment they both forgot about Gil.

"I loved her! What right have you —?"

Sam had heard enough. "You love your own comfort."

"What do you know about it? We had a good marriage. We —"

"Is that why you were at Sara's place?" The disgust in Sam's voice was obvious.

Guilt replaced Brad's anger. "I…I went to see Gil about selling." It was a weak argument and Brad knew it as soon as he heard it come out of his mouth. "Anyway, it's none of your business."

Sam turned away and tossed the two halves of the stick in his hand to the ground. "True enough."

Brad settled back on the ground. "This is as much your fault as anyone's. If you hadn't talked her into religion —"

"I'm not the one who drove away and left her."

"Shut up! Just shut up!" Brad shot to his feet and swung a wild fist toward the sound of Sam's voice. Sam sidestepped and Brad fell facedown in the dirt. "Just shut your mouth!" he said as he pushed himself up on all fours.

"You can't blame anyone but yourself," Sam said after a minute. "You're the one who left her. What right do you have to dictate what she believes?"

Brad rested his forehead on the ground, sobbing uncontrollably. "I loved her!"

"You don't know what love is."

Brad didn't move for a long time. Then he sat back on the ground, shoulders slumped and beaten. "I don't know what to do."

"I think you do."

"It's too late. She's gone and nothing will bring her back."

"You're more blind than you think you are," Sam said, shaking his head, "and stupid."

Brad felt no hope. "I don't care what you think," he said.

Sam grabbed Brad by the shoulders. "Listen, you fool! How do you think I knew to come looking for you? How do you think I knew where to find you? How do you think I knew about the fight you had with her? Did you ever think of that?"

Brad cocked his arm to take another swing at Sam, but as he did, Sam dodged to the side. Brad lost his balance and fell facedown in the dirt again.

"I wouldn't do that again if I were you. I'm liable to lose my patience."

Brad shot to his feet shouting profanities and charged into the darkness in a rage. Sam easily sidestepped and pushed Brad away. Brad caught his balance, turned, and charged again, but Sam grabbed his arms and held him.

"What she ever saw in you I'll never know," said Sam. "She's ten times too much woman for you. I ought to leave you here and let Gil have you! But I won't. I made a promise and I'll keep it, though I'll be hanged if I can see the sense of it." He pushed Brad away.

Brad stood with fists clenched for a moment. And then it struck him. "What promise?"

"Now you ask," Sam said.

"You…you said she was dead!"

"*You* said she was dead. I only said I saw the house cave in."

"She's alive?"

"She's alive."

"But how? I thought —"

"You can thank the God you're so eager to ignore. It's nothing short of a miracle."

"She's alive," Brad said to himself.

"She's alive," Sam confirmed. "It's better than you deserve."

Brad lowered his head. "I want to see her."

"That's just what I had in mind." Sam took Brad's arm and helped him to his feet. "Think you can make it?"

Brad nodded, wincing from the pounding in his head. "Yeah," he said weakly. "And…I'm….I'm sorry."

"Do you hear that?"

Sam froze, his Indian eyes searching. The two men stood still as stone.

"Sounds like a truck," said Brad after a moment.

"Yeah," Sam said warily, still searching the path behind them.

"Is it him?"

"I don't know," Sam said a moment later. "Could be hunters—or Fish and Game."

The sound grew fainter and then was gone.

"Probably Fish and Game," Sam said, doubting.

"Maybe we could flag them down for help."

"Maybe," Sam said cautiously. "I'll keep my eyes open."

Sam led Brad on in silence for another half-hour. Brad's head throbbed.

"Look," Brad offered, "I'm sorry I lost my temper."

More walking. More silence.

"Does she know?"

"About you and Sara? No reason why she should. But I think you should tell her."

"I don't want to hurt her."

"It's a little late for that. But she's a remarkable woman. My guess is she'll forgive you. Anyhow, it's going to be difficult to explain how you got hurt and how we came to be together without telling her the truth."

Brad shook his head. "I don't want her to know."

"She's not stupid."

"I don't want her to know!" Brad said, but his head hurt. Every step sent a new barrage of pain pounding through his skull.

More walking. More silence.

"How did you know where to find me?" Brad managed to ask after a while.

"I didn't, but I know Gil. And Sara wasn't hard to figure. She only knows one thing."

"Yeah," Brad agreed.

More walking. More silence.

Brad's head continued to pound and his wound started bleeding again. He felt faint. "I gotta stop for a minute," he wheezed as he slumped to the ground.

"For a minute," Sam agreed, "but no more. Gil may not be far behind."

Brad lay back with his arm draped over his eyes. "Did she tell you we've been trying to start a family?"

"She told me."

"She thinks it's because of a curse?"

"We're all under a curse."

"I don't know how to fight superstition."

"I'm not talking about superstition."

"I don't know what else to call it," Brad said. "And I don't see the difference between your religion and voodoo incantations. This whole business of curses —"

Sam interrupted. "If the Jakes family has had no children, it's because it fits into God's perfect plan for those who love Him. Not because of any curse."

"But you said —"

"I said we're all under a curse. But I was talking about the curse of sin—and death. Not the so-called curse on the Jakes family."

"What's the difference?" Brad said. "They're both a lot of nonsense."

"The Jakes women are pretty easy to explain," Sam agreed. "It's not too difficult if you consider the time in which they lived. It's not difficult to understand at all. The other makes perfect sense—and it explains a lot."

"I don't get it."

"Well, first," Sam said, "three of the Jakes women never married. There's nothing sinister about that. And one of them died in childbirth. Again, nothing unusual about that if you consider the time that she lived."

"Yeah, but what about Billie?"

Sam shrugged. "I don't know. Maybe Jakes women don't conceive easily."

"And the other?"

"Look around you. Evil is in the world. Man's sinfulness condemns him. And yours condemns you."

Brad sat up and started to protest. But he hesitated.

"What is it?" Sam asked.

Brad blinked and then rubbed his eyes. "I…I think I see something."

Sam waved his hand in front of Brad. "Did you —?"

"I see it! I —!"

Sam clamped his hand over Brad's mouth. "Not so loud!" he commanded just above a whisper. "Come on. We can't stay here. Let's get moving. The cabin isn't far."

CHAPTER TWENTY-NINE

FIFTEEN MINUTES LATER, Brad and Sam crouched behind a clump of berry vines at the edge of a clearing. "There's the cabin, just ahead of us," Sam whispered, eyes searching.

"I think I can see it," Brad said, pointing. "Is it there?"

"Yeah," Sam said, only half-listening. "Looks innocent enough." But he kept a distrustful eye on the log structure and the surrounding clearing.

The cabin sat mournfully at the edge of a small clearing against the chalk white face of Fletcher's Peak. Berry vines encroached on the clearing, threatening to reclaim it as well as the cabin in a few short years. A broken-down front porch slumped at one corner, where a post was missing. Moss covered what was left of the roof. Only partly visible through abundant berry vines that had all but engulfed it, the rusted hulk of an old panel truck rested without tires and wheels on rotted blocks of wood across the clearing at the base of the sheer face of the peak. Beneath it, buried a few feet below the surface and hidden from mortal eyes, the skeletal remains of a Pinkerton man rested where they had been hastily deposited more than a century before.

In the middle of the clearing, a snow-white yearling lamb grazed peacefully, unconcerned. Someone had placed the looped end of a rope around its neck. The other end trailed along behind it.

Odd, Sam thought. *Where did he come from?* He turned his attention back to the cabin.

Brad was impatient. "She's here, isn't she?"

"She's inside," said Sam.

"Well, let's go!"

Sam held Brad back. "Not yet," he said, studying the clearing.

"What's wrong?"

"Nothing," Sam said, eyes searching. "Nothing's wrong."

Sam studied the mountainside. It seemed peaceful enough. He looked to the top of Fletcher's Peak. An old logging road disappeared around the mountain and ended at the top of the cliff. Tall grass waved gently in the breeze. It appeared safe.

"C'mon, let's go!" Brad prodded. He pushed past Sam's outstretched arm, straining to see in the dim light and stumbling through the tall grass toward the shadowy figure of the cabin.

Sam grabbed for him, calling out in an uneasy whisper, "Wait!" But Brad was already well into the clearing.

Sam looked around once more and then followed cautiously.

Brad stumbled onto the front porch, his shoes thunking on the wooden floorboards. "Rebecca! Rebecca!"

He felt his way to the door and pushed it open.

"Brad!" Rebecca started toward him and then held back.

"Rebecca!" Brad exclaimed as he rushed toward her.

Sam came up behind and stood cautiously in the open doorway.

"Oh, Rebecca," Brad whispered in her ear as he hugged and kissed her, "I thought you were dead."

Rebecca touched the makeshift bandage Sam had wrapped around Brad's forehead. "You're hurt!" she said.

"I'm fine. It's nothing," he said, squinting to see her face.

Rebecca studied his face. "Are you all right?"

"It's nothing," he said. "I'll be fine."

But something was wrong. He could feel it. She was rigid in his arms and she hadn't returned his kisses. He held her face in his hands and tried as best he could to see into her eyes. "What's wrong?" he asked tenderly.

Sam had taken a step into the room. As he did, the door swung closed behind him. He turned to face the unsteady hand of Frank Downs, holding a gun. Frank chortled nervously and motioned for Sam to step away.

"What's going on?" Sam said. "What's this about, Frank?"

"Nothing personal, Sam. We jus' got a little business with these two kids!" Frank cackled more nervously than before.

At that moment, from the darkened shadows at the rear of the cabin, as if on cue Gil Doucet stepped into the light, cradling his rifle. Sam felt the blood drain from his face.

"Hello, Sam," Gil said, arrogantly. "Glad you could make it."

Brad only could see the dim outline of a man, but the voice was unmistakable, and it struck fear in his heart.

"I'm sorry," said Rebecca. "They got here about ten minutes ago. I heard someone coming. I thought it was you. I opened the door without thinking."

"I'm afraid she was disappointed," Gil mocked, curling his lips into an evil grin.

Sam clenched his fists. "This is really stupid, Gil."

Gil gave Sam a cold stare. Mutual mistrust passed between them.

Gil pointed the barrel of the gun toward Brad and Rebecca. "Not as stupid as helping them."

Rebecca lifted the makeshift bandage over Brad's forehead. "Are you all right?" she whispered.

"I'm OK. I'm having a little trouble seeing, but I'm OK."

Rebecca gasped, her eyes filled with compassion and love for her husband.

Brad forced a weak smile. "I'll be OK."

Gil's evil grin widened. "It won't matter for long."

Brad pulled Rebecca close. The anguish of knowing that everything that had happened was his fault, and that whatever consequences were to be exacted were his doing, struck him hard. An accusing knot twisted in the pit of his stomach.

He wondered if she knew.

The bore of Gil's rifle menaced from only a few feet away, threatening death at any moment. Yet somehow the fear that he might have to admit his failure to the woman he loved carried an even bigger threat. He whispered in her ear. "I'm sorry…sorry for everything."

She reached up and stroked the side of his face. "It doesn't matter," she said. "I love you and I forgive you. That's all that matters."

There was more to what she said than the words she spoke—a softness, a hurt, a comforting reassurance. *She knew. Somehow, she knew.*

"Very touching," Gil snarled through a wicked smile.

Sam's anger burned. "This is stupid, Gil," he repeated.

Gil turned to face Sam. His face twisted with rage and unyielding, relentless, irrational hate. His whole life had been defined by it. He could not remember a time when hatred and envy were not the topic around the dinner table, or when all that was wrong in the world had not been blamed on someone else. He could not remember a time when love and acceptance were meted out for anything but espousing the family doctrine of revenge. "We have always been different," his father would say, but he said it as though the difference was the reason for some great perceived persecution.

And though it was never said outright, Gil and Sara knew. Acceptance of the family position was expected, and rejection of the family creeds and traditions would have been met with ruthless judgment and rejection. The curse. The curse was all that mattered. And like a festering wound, the family picked at the scab of bitterness, refusing to let time heal it.

All his life Gil had embraced what he had been taught. But it was not love that drove him to his twisted loyalty, admiration, or duty. Nor was it anything resembling faithfulness. Early in his life, Gil had given unquestioning loyalty to selfish indulgence and ambition. The curse had done its work. But it was not the curse of human pronouncement that twisted Gil's mind. It was the judgment of willful, sustained rebellion, and a depraved and sinful heart turned toward the darkness of blasphemous self-worship.

Gil threatened with the barrel of the gun. "Over there," he said to Sam, nodding toward the far wall of the cabin.

Frank Downs giggled nervously. "Yeah! Over there!" he said. His eyes darted back and forth between the three captives and Gil. "What're we gonna do, Gil?"

Gil's smile twisted even further until it resembled the grotesqueness of a Halloween mask—vulgar, evil, and bent on perverted mischief. "I thought we'd have a little fun with the lady first."

Brad held Rebecca close in fear.

Sam stood his ground, looking for opportunity.

"C'mon! Gil demanded. "Get moving!"

Sam reluctantly complied, backing toward the wall.

"Now turn around and face the wall," Gil said.

"What are you going to do?" Brad asked.

"What I started to do yesterday," said Gil.

Frank giggled nervously, wondering what it was Gil had done the day before. "Yeah," he said. "We're gonna finish what we started!"

Sam studied Frank's face. "You in on this all the way, huh, Frank?"

Frank shrugged. "Gil's my friend. Whatever he says goes."

Frank's involvement surprised Sam. Frank was pompous and loud—and greedy. He was always with Gil, ever since they were kids, providing Gil with the emotional crutch he needed to bully and intimidate. Gil ordered him around like some hapless stooge. It never seemed to occur to Frank that he was the one being bullied as much as any of their victims.

As adults, Gil's hold on Frank continued. Sam wondered what hold Gil could have that would allow him so much control. They were not friends—at least not in the sense that most men count friends. There was no trust. There was no camaraderie or common interest. Gil simply told Frank what to do and Frank did it. But Sam never figured him for murder.

"How'd you get Frank to agree to killing, Gil?" asked Sam.

Gil was furious. "Shut up, Sam! Turn around!"

Sam reluctantly complied.

"What does he mean, Gil?" Frank asked.

"Just shut up and hold 'em here!"

"But —"

"Just do what I tell you, Frank!" Gil reached out and took Rebecca roughly by the arm. "Just hold 'em here!"

"But what does he mean, Gil?"

"What do you think he means?" Sam asked.

Gil raised his rifle to Sam's forehead. "You want yours now? I said shut up!"

Sam's jaw clenched.

Rebecca held her breath.

"Just hold 'em here," Gil said, turning toward the door. "The lady and I are going for a little walk."

Brad took a step forward, but Sam grabbed his arm. "Don't be stupid," he whispered.

"Yeah," said Gil, "don't be stupid." He led Rebecca toward the door.

There was very little hope in the room as Frank held an unsteady finger on the trigger of the gun in his hand.

There was no way out.

"Father God," Sam prayed silently, "Lord of heaven, I pray that You would not allow evil to triumph this day."

Rebecca bowed her head as Gil led her toward the door, unsure of the words that formed silently in her mind, even as her lips formed silent words. "Dear Lord, please help us. I know I can trust You. Please help us!"

Brad mouthed awkward, silent words that only a day before would have been unthinkable. Yet now he prayed to a God still unknown to him with sincere humility and hope. "God, help us!"

Over in the corner, unseen by mortal eyes, an evil presence trembled with fear as an old but familiar feeling of impending doom returned. Its promised fate appeared all too certain.

The Centurion acknowledged the commands of his sovereign commander, the Lamb who stood in the midst of the two who were gathered in His name. The Centurion, sword drawn and shield raised high, nodded to the two warriors who stood poised and ready at the top of Fletcher's Peak. And the battle was joined.

Gil reached for the door's wooden latch, but it stuck, refusing to yield. He adjusted his grip and tried again.

It still wouldn't open. He swore.

"You need a hand?" Frank offered over his shoulder.

"No!" Gil said as he fought with the lock. He leaned the rifle against the wall and grabbed the bar with both hands. It wouldn't budge. "This thing worked fine a few minutes ago!" he said.

He adjusted his grip again and heaved with all his might. The bar suddenly gave way in his hands, and he fell backward on the floor.

Frank turned.

Like an arrow poised for battle on the taut string of a bow, Sam had been waiting for an opportunity. As Gil fell backward, crashing to the floor, Sam sprang forward, catching the off-guard Frank squarely in the throat with a hard blow. Frank staggered back and fell, gasping for air and clutching his throat. The gun he was holding spun through the air and landed on the floor a few feet away. Sam lunged for it, but as Frank fell backward, he grabbed at Sam's leg as Sam leapt over him.

Gil sprang back to his feet and leveled his rifle at Sam, but Rebecca grabbed the barrel as the roar of the discharge shook the cabin. The bullet crashed harmlessly through the ceiling.

Brad lunged through the haze of his clouded vision toward his wife. Gil recovered, pushing Rebecca away as Brad reached him. He brought the rifle around, but Brad lowered his shoulder and tackled Gil, knocking them both against the door. Gil tried to bring the butt of the rifle down on the top of Brad's head, but Brad was too close, making the position awkward. The blow glanced off to the side.

Sam tripped and fell as Frank held his pants leg. Frank recovered enough that the surge of adrenalin and his great size gave him a slight edge in strength over Sam. Frank dragged him back along the floor as Sam kicked at Frank's hand. Frank held tight. The gun lay inches from Sam's outstretched fingers. Sam kicked again, this time loosing Frank's grip. Both men scrambled for the gun.

Gil raised the rifle again to bring down the butt on Brad's head, this time with better positioning and more presence of mind. Rebecca screamed.

When she did, Brad reacted instinctively. He released Gil from his grip, rising up with a sudden burst of strength and speed. His clenched fist sought out Gil's exposed jaw, but in the haze that still clouded his vision, he couldn't focus. He landed a glancing blow under Gil's chin with the side of his arm. Gil staggered back.

Frank gripped the handle of the gun as Sam held his wrist. Both men rolled on the floor, vying for control.

The barrel swung recklessly around as they struggled.

"Get her out of here!" Sam shouted from the floor.

Brad hesitated in a split-second of indecision, and then turned to the door and found the latch. It lifted easily in his hand.

The door opened. Brad grabbed his wife's arm and pushed her ahead of him through the door.

The gun in Frank's hand came to bear on the open doorway and the young couple. As he struggled with Sam for control of the gun, Frank's finger squeezed back on the trigger.

Brad stumbled onto the porch behind Rebecca's dim figure. In the darkness of his world he misjudged the distance between them and tripped on the back of her heel. They both fell forward as the peace of the mountains was assaulted by another deafening roar. The bullet from Frank's gun ripped through the air inches from both their heads and sailed harmlessly on its way as they fell forward.

Brad didn't hesitate. "C'mon!" he ordered as he lifted her by the arm. They ran toward the old panel truck and ducked behind it. Brad pushed Rebecca to the ground just as Gil appeared in the doorway of the cabin.

Gil looked around briefly. Then his eyes found the truck. Rebecca peered around the fender in time to see him start toward them, rifle menacingly at the ready.

"Can you see him?" Brad whispered.

"He's coming!" Rebecca exclaimed.

"Did he see us?"

"I don't know."

"Where's Sam?"

Rebecca leaned back, breathless, against the side of the truck. "I don't know," she said. "I didn't see him!"

Brad slumped. There was no way out. The open clearing made any hope for escape impossible. Gil would cut them down before they got ten feet, but they couldn't stay where they were. Gil would discover them in seconds.

The truck rested on four crude blocks. Jagged berry vines, thick as a man's finger, had taken over, surrounding the truck and twining their way through the missing back door and out through the glassless windows until they had all but filled the truck to capacity. On the side that faced the cabin, they cascaded over the truck so completely that only the front fender was visible. Because of the shade, they were less dense where Brad and Rebecca hunkered down.

Brad pushed Rebecca down into the moist grass. "Slide under!" he whispered. Ignoring the thorns, he pushed aside a handful of vines. Rebecca wriggled under the truck. Brad followed, motioning for her to slide under as far to the other side as she could. A wall of berry vines hid them from Gil's view as he approached.

Gil's feet appeared at the front of the truck. Rebecca held her breath. Gil stood for a moment, took another two steps, and waited near the fender of the truck. Rebecca could see his hands holding the rifle at his side. Gil's feet turned away for a moment as he searched the mountainside, but then he stepped to the side of the truck and stopped.

Rebecca felt her heart beating in her throat. Gil knew. She was sure of it. She could see the matted grass where they had crouched behind the truck. She was sure Gil would see it too, if he hadn't already.

She glanced over her shoulder at the wall of vines that covered the side of the truck between them and the cabin. No sunlight shone through them, and she wondered how thick they could be.

She stuck the toe of her shoe into them and began carefully working them aside, making a small hole in the wall of vines. She stopped when the rustling of the vines seemed sure to alert Gil.

"You can't hide," Gil said calmly. He chuckled as he started slowly around the side of the truck.

Rebecca began kicking a hole in the wall of vines, ignoring the wicked thorns that cut into the flesh of her ankles. Brad realized what she was doing and started kicking the vines until there was a hole big enough to crawl through.

Gil crouched down and peered into the meager cavity under the truck. Rebecca and Brad froze. Gil grinned.

"So here we are," he mocked. "Not much of an escape effort —"

He gave the situation a quick survey. Gil turned his attention to the block of wood that held the corner of the truck in the air, and then back to his captives.

"Too bad," he said to Rebecca. "It might have been fun." He turned to Brad. "You see, my sister is not the only one who appreciates a little forbidden fruit."

Brad felt his anger rising.

Gil turned a cruel eye back to Rebecca. "That's right, Sweetie—your husband and my sister—I just thought you should know."

The eerie stillness of the mountains shook with another blast from inside the cabin.

Gil shot a worried glance toward the cabin and then peered under the truck as he raised the butt of his rifle above his head. With unemotional purpose, he brought it down against the block of wood under the truck's axle. He struck it two more times before it gave way and rolled to one side. The truck creaked, settling slightly, but it hung suspended in midair by the thick vines.

Rebecca and Brad ignored the thorns that dug into their legs as they shimmied backwards through the small opening they had made with their feet. Gil instinctively, and without thinking, reached under the truck to grab them as Brad and Rebecca wriggled out the other side. But as he did, the vines that temporarily held the truck broke free. The truck crashed to the ground, pinning Gil at the chest. He gasped once, then clenched an agonized fist in the soft earth.

Rebecca heard a rush of air as Gil's last breath escaped his lungs. His body writhed under the weight of the truck, arms flailing wildly in search of relief—and hope. Then, he lay still.

Brad and Rebecca helped each other to their feet.

Brad held her close. "Are you all right?"

Rebecca nodded. "I'm fine," she said as she turned her face from the truck and held him close. A moment later she pushed away. "What about Sam?"

"Wait here," he said, turning toward the cabin.

She held his arm. "Don't go," she pleaded.

Brad gave her a look that said he had no choice.

"I'm going with you," she said.

Brad started to protest, but as he turned again toward the cabin, Frank Downs stepped through the door and slumped against the doorframe. He stared into space for a moment, empty-handed, glanced over his shoulder, and then shuffled from the porch into the clearing. A weary and wounded Sam Michaels followed him, holding Frank's gun loosely in his hand.

Brad and Rebecca ran to Sam. Brad caught him as he slumped to his knees in the dirt.

"You're hurt!" Rebecca said when she saw the blood running down Sam's arm.

"It's nothin', ma'am," he said. "Just a flesh wound."

"You're not OK," said Rebecca as she inspected the grazing wound in Sam's upper arm. "We'd better get you to a doctor."

Sam nodded weakly. "We'll need a ride," he said. He drew a deep breath to fight the wooziness in his head and stomach, and then nodded toward Gil's lifeless body. "Looks like you managed just fine."

He took another breath. "They had to drive to get here so fast. Must have been them we heard earlier," he said to Brad. Sam motioned to the sheer face of Fletcher's Peak. "The road leads up there from the other side. That must be where they parked, up at the top."

Sam drew another labored breath and started to get up. "Why don't we go see?"

"You're in no condition to walk," said Brad. "I'll go."

"And what makes you think you're in any better shape?" Rebecca said with her hands on her hips. "Besides that, who's going to drive—you?"

"I suppose that would be kind of silly, but you're not going without me," said Brad. "I'm not letting you go anywhere alone!"

Sam sat back against the porch post, nodding reluctantly. "All right. I'll stay here and hold Frank. You two go get us a ride." He turned to Frank and held out his hand. "Keys, Frank!"

"They're in the ignition," Frank said.

Rebecca took Brad's hand and led him along the road that circled the mountain. Brad felt helpless and awkward—helpless because he had to be led and awkward because he didn't know what to say now that his wife knew about Sara.

"I'm sorry," he said as they neared the top of Fletcher's Peak. "I'm sorry about everything."

Rebecca squeezed his hand. She felt like she should say something—something profound— but nothing seemed right. "I love you," she whispered.

Brad cringed. The gentleness she offered him in place of the rage and indignation he deserved made him ashamed.

He lowered his head as they walked. "I don't deserve you," he said.

She squeezed his hand. "We'll work it out," she reassured. "There's always hope. Remember?"

Brad nodded. Words failed him, but a tear fell as he followed his wife to the top of Fletcher's Peak.

From the clearing below, Fletcher's Peak appeared to be a sheer cliff. But as Brad and Rebecca neared the top, they could see that an unstable shale deposit sloped toward the edge of the cliff before it dropped away into space. Frank's four-wheel-drive sat a few feet away from the edge near where the shale deposit began.

Rebecca helped Brad into the passenger seat, closed the door, and hurried around the front of the car. As she opened the door to get in, movement from behind the car caught her eye. But before she could turn, her head wrenched back hard as someone grabbed a handful of her hair and pulled her backward. Hard steel pressed against her throat. She screamed.

Brad was out of the car in an instant, but before he could reach the back of the car, Rebecca had been dragged to the treacherous edge of the cliff. Behind her with a knife to her throat stood Sara Doucet.

"Stay back!" she demanded. "Just stay back!"

Rebecca could feel the blade digging into the flesh of her neck under Sara's firm hand as Sara jerked Rebecca's head back by the hair with her other hand. Unsteady feet tried to find solid ground among the shale.

From below in the clearing, Sam looked up.

Brad pleaded with Sara. "What are you doing? Just take it easy!"

"You think you've won!" Sara screamed. "You think you've won, but you're wrong!"

Sara gave the knife a quick jerk against Rebecca's neck to remind her captive of her advantage. With the knife held firm, she released her grip on the hank of hair. She raised her hand high, revealing a golden medallion dangling from a chain that intertwined her fingers.

"I have power you cannot comprehend!" she shrieked. "By my own blood I have it!"

"Sara!" Sam called out from below. "Sara! What are you doing?"

Sara jerked Rebecca around and looked down on Sam. "You know what I'm doing! You know!"

"Sara!" Sam shouted. "Let her go. This is crazy. Let her go!"

"No. Never!" She turned back to face Brad. "Do you know what this is?" she asked as she held out the medallion.

Brad gave her a cold stare, refusing to acknowledge her question.

"It is power, and it's mine. By the blood of my own two hands, it's mine!"

"Sara!" Sam called out again.

If Sara heard him, she gave no indication. "I dug it out of the ground with my own two hands, digging and scratching in the sand and rock under three feet of water! I nearly drowned, but I found it, and now it's mine!"

"Sara!" Sam called out again.

Brad took a step closer, but Sara inched nearer the edge, sliding unsteadily on the shale. "Stay back!" she threatened.

Brad held up his hands in surrender. "All right," he said, "all right."

"Look at me, Sara," Sam called out.

Sara turned.

Sam took a grim, deep breath. "Don't do this, Sara," he said as calmly as he knew how.

"No one can stop me," she said. "I have all the power I need. I can do anything!"

Sam shook his head. "No, Sara. It has no power. It never did."

"You're wrong." She clamped down on the medallion and swept her hand around her. "Look at what it's done. Look at all it's done!"

"There is no power, Sara. Only the power to kill and destroy."

"You don't call that power? It has always had power!"

Sam shook his head. "Only destruction, Sara. It even destroyed your own family."

"No! She had the power, and she's given it to me!"

"She died an unhappy and broken woman, Sara. It has no power. And even if there is power, it's not in the medallion, and you are not its master."

Sara's sultry and irresistible beauty was unchallenged in the little town of Creek Junction. Her dark eyes and soft lips had given many men a reason to risk all they had for fleeting pleasure. The gentle curves of her torso created a symphony of movement that rivaled the grandest work of art.

But at that moment, her lips curled into an unnatural grotesqueness and her eyes flashed with unrepentant hate. Even in the dim haze that clouded his vision, Brad could see it. For a moment he wasn't sure if she intended to jump, push Rebecca over the edge, or both. But something told him his time was now, and that whatever he planned to do, he'd better do quickly.

Sara focused all her rage toward Sam. "No! You —"

Brad lunged forward.

Sara turned. Brad's feet pounded the loose shale as he sprang forward. Sara whirled around to push Rebecca over the edge.

Had he been able to see clearly, Brad would have noticed the shift in Sara's eyes. He would have seen her bitter resolve and her lust for blood. He would have seen her twisted, pathetic lust for death. If he had seen, he might have hesitated. But he didn't see.

From the bottom of Fletcher's Peak, Sam called out one last urgent plea. "Sara! Don't let the past destroy you!"

As Sara struggled with Rebecca to bring her to the edge of the cliff, Rebecca planted her feet. But the loose shale gave no footing and she began to slip toward the edge.

Rebecca reeled, clawing at the air in desperation as she grappled with Sara.

Brad lunged.

Sam held his breath.

Sara, slipping on the loose shale, lost her grip on Rebecca. Then she regained her footing and raised the knife high above her head to bring it down into the chest of her victim.

Rebecca turned to defend herself, but she slipped again and fell to her knees as the knife cut the air, just missing her. Bits of shale rained down on the clearing below.

Brad reached Sara as she raised the knife for a second blow. As it came down, Brad caught the blade in his fist. Blood flowed as he wrenched it from Sara's hand in blind fury. He stumbled and fell toward the edge of the cliff. Sara screamed as she fell backward and tumbled headlong over the cliff.

Brad's weight pulled him along, slipping and sliding, in the loose shale toward the edge. His feet scrambled for footing. He managed to turn, grabbing at a solid outcropping as his body swung over the edge. His feet dangled. Desperate terror struck him hard as he felt the shale outcropping giving way under his weight.

Sara's lifeless body lay below him. He tried to find a foothold, but the shale crumbled each time he tried. The outcropping under his hand began to crumble. His hand slipped as the outcropping gave way.

Fear took over. He was afraid to die, but he feared the consequences of his actions more. He feared the long drop to the clearing below, but at the same time he feared leaving Rebecca to wonder and doubt. He feared dying, but more than that he feared his life had served no meaningful purpose. He realized how much he wanted to live.

In that moment, hanging in space, he suddenly knew all he had been and done in his twenty-eight years of life had counted for nothing. His only purpose had been selfish indulgence and self-promotion, and now all the things that mattered to him—nice cars, bigger houses, position, recognition—seemed in one hideous moment to turn to dust. He knew he had failed. As his hand slipped away from the outcropping, he knew and he was sorry. He looked down.

Rebecca never considered herself a brave woman. If the truth were known, she felt inadequate in the modern world. She didn't consider herself especially smart. She had no great ambitions beyond making a good home for her family. She marveled from a distance at the women she knew who had conquered a man's world and made it their own. She would have laughed quietly to herself if anyone had suggested that she could perform an act of bravery. Yet, when she saw her husband slipping toward certain death, something noble and strong swelled inside her—something she never knew was there.

Flesh on flesh. He felt it. A firm grip, precarious at first, but then shifting for a better hold. Rebecca gripped Brad's hand as she slid under his weight on her stomach toward the edge. "Hang on!" she said.

Brad latched onto her wrist and pulled. As she lay flat on the ground, Rebecca slipped toward the edge as the loose shale slid away underneath her.

Brad grimaced. Their eyes met.

"Hold on!" Rebecca said again.

Brad froze for a moment and then tried to pull himself up again, but Rebecca slipped closer to the edge.

"It's no good!" Brad shouted to her. "You'll fall!"

He tried to let go of her hand, but she held him tight.

"I'm not letting go! Hang on!"

Sam saw what was happening. He struggled to his feet and ran toward the road that led to the top of the cliff, digging deep inside him for the strength to take each step.

Shale and stone dug into Rebecca's chest and arms every time she slipped a little more, but she refused to let go.

Brad was afraid to move for fear of pulling her farther down the slope. For a moment, one that seemed to stretch into hours, neither of them moved. Brad looked up at her.

"I love you," he said. He let go.

"No!" she cried and tightened her own grip. "I'm not letting you go! Hang on!"

"Rebecca," he pleaded, "I can't do it. You'll fall. Please, just let go!"

"No!"

Rebecca slipped again, but this time she slid far enough that momentum caught her in a deadly, irreversible journey toward oblivion. She slid only a few inches, but more than inches they did not have. Her struggle to gain a footing only hastened her descent.

She could see the look of terror in Brad's eyes and she knew it was not fear of death, but fear for the one he loved. And she loved him for it. If it was to be that they should die together, then so be it. She felt at peace.

Sam pumped his legs hard as he raced toward the edge of the cliff. His arm was on fire from his wound and he felt weak, but he couldn't let it stop him. He dove headlong in the dirt, sliding along the jagged, sloping surface of the shale. His fingers wrapped around Rebecca's delicate ankle and locked firm.

All was still.

"Hang on!" he shouted as he shifted recklessly for a better grip.

No one moved.

"Now what?" Brad asked.

"I don't know," grunted Sam. "I can't get a foothold to pull!"

"Well, I can't either!" shouted Rebecca. "I'm facing the wrong way!"

Sam thought for a moment.

"What's going on up there?" Brad said.

"Can you pull?" Rebecca shouted over her shoulder.

"No," Sam said. "I can hold you, but there's nothing for me to grab onto."

"So what do we do?" Rebecca asked.

Good question, Sam thought. "Brad?" he shouted.

"Yeah?"

"Is there any chance you can find a foothold?"

There was a moment's pause and then Brad answered. "No."

Sam winced. His arm began to ache. He closed his eyes as he tried to think. At the same time, he tried not to let images of falling creep to the front of his mind. There had to be an answer, and he had to think of it soon.

Oh, God, help me! he prayed in desperation.

In the distance, he could hear gentle four-footed footsteps. It grew louder. Slowly and deliberately, the Lamb he had seen in the clearing was making its way along the edge of the cliff, dragging the rope that dangled behind it. It seemed to be in no hurry, as if time was of no concern, though it continued purposefully along the cliff toward them. Eyes straightforward, it never looked to either side or slowed its gait, nor did it stop to graze. Its eyes were clear and bright.

Sam blinked in disbelief.

The Lamb continued its methodical march along the cliff and then stopped inches away from Sam's grasp. Its eyes were deep and dark, as if something mysterious lay hidden behind them. Sam brushed aside the brief but real sense of inadequacy that flooded his heart for a single moment. Before he could consider why he felt it in the first place, it was replaced by an abiding sense of peace. Somehow, he knew, the hand of God was with him.

The Lamb took a step forward and then turned and walked toward Frank's car as though led by an invisible hand. The rope trailed along behind him. Sam started to reach for the rope as it snaked along the ground, still just out of reach, but something told him to wait. He pulled back his hand.

The Lamb stopped near the rear of Frank's car and looked around at Sam. Its eyes, Sam noticed again, were gentle and kind. It was as if they promised peace and hope. They seemed almost to smile.

The end of the rope rested on loose shale. The Lamb bucked playfully, causing the end of the rope to slide toward Sam.

Sam reached out and grabbed the end of the rope. The Lamb shook its head playfully again, and once more it bucked and reared, twisting in midair. As it came to earth, the rope snagged on the bumper of Frank's car and wedged tightly between the bumper and the frame. The Lamb shook its head again and pulled against the rope. Resisting briefly, the loop slipped from around its neck. The Lamb scampered off into the forest.

Sam blinked once more in disbelief before he wrapped the rope around his wrist and gave it a tug. It held. "OK," he shouted, "pull yourselves up!"

Brad hesitated for a second. "Are you sure?"

"It's OK," Sam shouted back. "I'm secure. Just pull yourselves up."

Brad grabbed Rebecca's free hand and pulled. A moment later, he climbed to safety with Rebecca and Sam close behind.

Sam staggered away from the cliff and fell to his knees in the dirt, letting his lungs fill with air and fighting the wooziness in his head.

Rebecca and Brad hugged one another.

Brad noticed the rope. "Where did you get that?" he asked, nodding toward it.

Sam didn't answer right away. He wasn't sure himself. Finally, he shook his head. "You wouldn't believe it if I told you."

Brad nodded as though he understood. Sam fixed disbelieving eyes on the place where the Lamb had disappeared into the trees, unsure of what to think. In his spirit he thanked God.

The mountains were still. No one spoke again for several minutes until Rebecca began to sob quietly to herself. Brad held her close and kissed the top of her head. He stood up and offered her his hand.

"C'mon," he said. "Let's go home."

CHAPTER THIRTY

GIANT FIR TREES cast long shadows across Interstate Five in the late afternoon as the sun sent its last rays peeking through the boughs of majestic timber along the western ridge. But Rebecca didn't notice as she drove. It had been three weeks since the ordeal with the Doucets. Brad's eyesight had returned, though the doctor had not released him yet to drive. The cut on his hand from the knife had healed nicely. So had the crease in his forehead from Gil's bullet, but the scar remained—a reminder to him of his failure.

Sam had offered to let them stay with him until Brad's wounds had healed enough to make the trip home. They gratefully accepted and it wasn't long before Brad and Sam had become close friends. Brad began chiding Sam about his story of the lamb with the rope. Sam took it good naturedly, though he insisted that it had happened just as he told them.

Though Brad registered his disbelief, he knew Sam believed it was true, and it was hard to dispute the very real presence of the rope dangling from the bumper of Frank's car. After a while, Brad's objections began to lose some of the forcefulness of his earlier appeals to reason. He even began to ask some very direct questions about religion and this Savior of Sam's and Rebecca's.

Brad and Rebecca had used the time at Sam's, wisely Rebecca felt, to mend their fragile relationship. It was funny, she thought, how fragile it really was. She had always considered hers a strong marriage, and yet it almost crumbled so easily.

Rebecca reached across the Toyota's console and stroked the back of Brad's hand. He responded with an upturned palm. Their fingers locked.

"I love you," she said.

Rebecca drove on in silence.

"I'm going to miss this place," she said a few minutes later.

"Mmm," he said.

She glanced over at him and then back to the road. It still hurt to think he could look at another woman. The pain of knowing how empty a promise can be had dulled only slightly in the last few weeks. But there was hope. God was on her side now—or she was on His. She knew in her heart that with God's help, she and the man she loved could overcome and endure anything. There was much she didn't know about her newfound faith. She was patient, though, and she was certain God would help her.

Brad shifted his weight in the seat. "I love you too."

Rebecca sighed.

She marveled at how she had changed in the last few weeks. Three weeks ago she never would have considered forgiving Brad. Now she looked to the future with a sense of expectancy. Somehow things that mattered most to her only a short time ago didn't matter as much anymore. It puzzled her. She still wanted a baby, but now she felt she could live a peaceful, happy life without children—if it came to that. Before, the thought of living her life without children was unbearable. It still mattered, but she had a peace she couldn't explain.

She didn't know if curses could be real. Brad had scoffed—still scoffed. She had to admit, it did seem silly. But at that moment she didn't care. God was in control. She would let Him deal with it. From now on, that would be her prayer.

"You know," Brad said, "I've been thinking. If we sold our house and sold your aunt's house, we could afford to rebuild on the old homestead. We'd have enough to live on it for a while until I found something."

"What could you do?" Rebecca asked, afraid to hope too much.

"I don't know. I'm sure I could find a job in town."

"But what about our friends? What about —?"

Brad squeezed her hand. "We don't have to, if you don't want to."

Rebecca smiled. "You know I want to."

She turned back to the road. Yes, things would work out. She was sure of it. God was in control. She would trust Him—no matter what.

High above the freeway and invisible to mortal men, the Centurion smiled down on the occupants of the Toyota as it rolled along Interstate Five headed south. His eyes flashed with benevolent purpose, and his shield offered sure protection on all sides to his new assignment, a single cell deep within Rebecca's womb, no bigger than the head of a pin and not yet endowed with the spark of life. The time had not yet come, but time mattered little to the Centurion. His directive was clear. The little speck of human flesh would enjoy his presence, and his faithful protection, for a lifetime.

Printed in the United States
133613LV00001B/172-174/P

9 781414 112060